THE FIRST CUT

ISBN: 978-0-578-40133-1

Cover Design:
Giovanni Auriemma
Developmental Edit/Line Edit and Manuscript Evaluation:
Ann Castro, AnnCastro Studio
Proof via Editorial Lens:
Emily Dings
Interior Formatting:
Mallory Rock

This book is a work of fiction. Places, events, and situations in this book are purely fictional, and any resemblance to actual persons, living or dead, events, or locales is entirely coincidental. *The First Cut* contains adult themes and is recommended for a mature audience.

For Gar
My partner in crime

I don't feel guilty for anything. I feel sorry for people who feel guilt.
—Ted Bundy

PROLOGUE

TUESDAY
FEBRUARY 14, 2018
MADDIE

MADDIE lies in bed, tapping her fingers on her tummy, just the way she'd practiced on Miss Ellie's piano.

The itsy bitsy spider climbed up the water spout.

Down came the rain and washed the spider out.

She doesn't like spiders, but that song is stuck in her head. An earworm, Mommy had called it, wriggling her finger behind Maddie's ear and making her giggle. Mommy is good at being a silly goose and making her feel better.

But sometimes Mommy is grumpy. Daddy too. Like tonight. And it makes her tummy hurt. So she pulls the covers up over her head and practices every song in the *I Can Play Piano* book Daddy bought her.

Snug under her blanket fort, Maddie can still hear them shouting in their outside voices. Louder than the rain beating its fists against her window. Daddy's yelling reminds her of thunder, even though she's never heard it in real life. And tonight, it's worse than ever. So loud she drags her blanket and Mister Bear into the closet where it's dark and cold and probably full of spiders. But at least she can't hear Daddy.

She wonders what she's done now. What she's done wrong.

Once, she'd heard Daddy say Mommy turned into a different person after Maddie was born. That Mommy didn't love him anymore. But Maddie knows that's not true. Mommy is the same Mommy as she ever was. And she loves Daddy a bajillion because she'd told Maddie so.

Just today, Maddie had asked, "Mommy, who is your Valentine?"

And Mommy said, "You."

"But what about Daddy?"

"Of course, Daddy. Daddy too. I love you both."

"A bajillion?"

Mommy giggled at that. "Yes, a bajillion."

Before Mommy got home from the doctor, Daddy had taken Maddie and Mister Bear on a special trip, and he'd let her eat all the Valentine's candy from school. Even the lollipops and those little hearts with words on them that tasted chalky and too sweet. Maybe that's why her tummy hurts. Maybe that's why they're fighting. Because Mommy found out about the candy or she's sad they went someplace special without her.

A door slams somewhere, and Maddie clings tight to Mister Bear, afraid the whole house is falling down. Or maybe it's an earthquake. "Earthquake, earth shake," she whispers, feeling clever.

"Madison? Where are you? I told you to get dressed."

She peeks out from the closet, and Mommy is there, standing by the dollhouse. And her tummy really hurts now, because Mommy looks scared and sad and furious all at the same time. Probably because Maddie didn't use her listening ears the first time.

"I don't want to leave Daddy."

"C'mon. It will be fun." But Mommy doesn't sound like she's having fun. She's not even very good at pretending. "We'll spend the night."

"Like a sleepover?"

Mommy nods. And then Daddy's in the doorway, yelling again. "The hell you are. You're not taking her anywhere. Do not get dressed, Madison."

Maddie starts to cry—she can't help it. She doesn't want to go with Mommy, not if Daddy can't come too. She holds her hands over her ears and puts her head down into Mister Bear's soft fur. She cries and cries and cries. Until she stops. And Mommy and Daddy are gone.

Then, Mister Bear has an idea, and Maddie thinks it's a good one. She pats him on the head as she searches for her princess backpack in the cave at the back of the closet, next to her rain boots. In the front pocket, she finds the two chocolate hearts she'd hidden there. The ones with the pretty seashells on the wrappers. She'd been saving them for tomorrow. But Mommy says chocolate makes everything better. Maybe it will fix Mommy and Daddy too. The way Mommy's kisses fix her ouchies. *All better.*

With the hearts buried in her fist like Jack's magic beans, she makes her way down the hall toward the bedroom, toward the shouting. Except now, it's quiet. Somebody's crying.

Mommy is crying. "Don't. Don't, Ian."

"Why not? You don't care if I die. You don't want me. You don't even love me anymore."

It's Daddy, but he sounds like the kind of monster Caleb told her about on the merry-go-round right before he jumped off and skinned his knees. The kind of monster that hides under the bed, just watching you. Watching and watching and waiting. That's the worst part, the waiting. The never knowing what's going to happen next.

"Stop it, Ian!" Mommy doesn't sound right either.

Maddie hurries down the stairs. Away. She won't be able to hear them in the kitchen, she's certain of that. She'd gone there the last time they had a fight. And Mommy found her asleep on the floor the next morning.

The light from the back porch makes a rectangle on the kitchen floor, and she feels smart knowing that. A rectangle has four sides.

Just like a square. The window by the door is a rectangle too. The rain is coming down hard on it. Washing that old spider away.

And only then, she realizes—her hands are empty. She'd been so scared, she dropped the chocolates. She lost her magic beans. And now she can't fix anything. She's just a stupid little girl. A fraidy cat, like Caleb said.

Mommy screams upstairs, and Maddie thinks of the bookcase in the foyer. The one with the shelves where Daddy stacks the books he and Mommy wrote together. That bookcase has a secret. It's not just a bookcase. It's for hiding too. Mommy showed her once.

But when she hears the front door creak open, she doesn't dare look into the foyer. *It's the monster*, she thinks. Creeping around on long monster legs.

Maddie starts to hum again, hiccupping through tears. She won't let that monster know she's afraid. She'll be a big girl. A good girl. So she sings out loud the whole "Itsy Bitsy Spider" song so many times she loses count. Until the last time. She doesn't finish. The sun never comes out and dries up the rain, and the spider stays all wet.

Because Daddy's friend is at the window, waving. Soaked with no umbrella. Just like that spider.

Somehow, Maddie feels certain everything will be better now, so she wipes her sad face on her hand. She walks to the door.

She opens it.

THE MONTEREY COUNTY COURIER

"SUSPICIOUS DEATHS OF 'LOVE DOCTORS' STUN SMALL, AFFLUENT PEBBLE BEACH COMMUNITY"

by Jackson Lamont

The Carmel Police Department confirmed the deaths of Dr. Ian Culpepper (48) and his wife, Dr. Kate Culpepper (30), after their bodies were discovered in the early morning hours of February 15 in their upscale home on Cortez Road. Police called the scene suspicious but have not disclosed the manner of the doctors' deaths, pending autopsy and further investigation. Their four-year-old daughter was discovered unharmed and has been placed in the care of Child Protective Services.

Otherwise known as the "Love Doctors," the Culpeppers rose to fame in 2014 when their reality television show, *Love Doctored*, made its cable debut on the BXA network. The show, which featured couples in crisis, drew ire from critics who claimed the pair exploited their guests' problems for ratings. The show was abruptly canceled in early 2016 after the death of a guest; the couple relocated to a multimillion dollar estate a few miles from the historic Pebble Beach Golf Course. The Culpeppers, fixtures on the Carmel social scene, also made the *New York Times* best-seller list with their self-help books, *Prescription for Love* and *Love CPR*.

"We are shocked and saddened to learn of the passing of Love Doctors Ian and Kate Culpepper," Marty Emerson, BXA president of programming, said in statement released on behalf of the network. "They were passionate about life, love, and most of all, each other. Through their unique combination of empathy and wisdom, countless couples rediscovered love. The Culpeppers will be sorely missed."

CHAPTER ONE

WEDNESDAY
FEBRUARY 15, 2018

I believe in karma. Because Ian's dead. Kate, too. But mostly because the news is delivered to me by the half-naked man in my bed.

"Are you okay?" Luke's voice is measured. Ninety-nine percent hotshot cop. Which he is. One percent boyfriend. Which he wants to be but isn't. Not officially anyway.

The faint furrow between his brows deepens. *How cute. His first wrinkle.* "Talk to me. *Please.*"

"Is Madison alright?" I ask, my own voice high and breathy as a child's. Ian's daughter is quite possibly the only good thing he ever did. And I swear I'm not a heartless bitch. Though Ian had branded me one more than once. Back in the days of old when I'd called him a poor excuse for a husband and an even poorer excuse for a man.

"She's fine. At least that's what Coop said. He was first on the scene." Luke gestures to his cell on the nightstand. The one that had buzzed us awake five minutes ago and exploded the world as I'd known it. "I'll know more when I get there."

Guilt, that slippery eel, writhes in my stomach, reminding me I've done something wrong. But I lop off its head. To hell with guilt. Whatever happened, Ian brought it on himself. He'd all but asked for it coming back here to my hometown. Invading my turf. With *her*. Besides, guilt is a useless emotion.

Ian had said it himself years ago, after I'd told him I didn't want any special treatment in his class. "The back-row girls will talk," I'd said. And he'd pushed me up against his desk and kissed me like a pathetic cliché. Dr. Culpepper always had his favorites. Easy come, easy go.

"Ava? Are you sure you're okay?"

Luke strips off the covers, hurries into his jeans, and tucks his badge into his back pocket. I can't look away from the lean muscle of him. Ian never had abs like that. Though to be fair, he'd been pushing forty when I met him.

"Ava?"

"Yes, I'm sure."

"Because I don't have to leave if—"

"You do. And I am. I promise."

When Luke leans down to kiss me, his lips impossibly warm, I run my hand across his taut stomach and stifle a grin. Then, a grimace. Karma may be as slow moving as a freight train, but boy does she pack a wallop.

CHAPTER TWO

I scurry to the window and peek through the blinds, watching until Luke's truck disappears in the early morning fog. I usually feel relieved, content in my solitude. Today, though, I wish I'd asked him to stay.

But Dr. Ava Lawson doesn't need anybody. And certainly not a gallant young man—sometimes, the eight years between us feels more like twenty—who says things like *Let me take care of you* and *You're so beautiful in the morning*, when you know good and well your mousy brown hair looks more like a rat's nest and the dark circles under your eyes could pass for bruises. Luke is the type who writes more than just his name at the bottom of a Valentine. And who needs that?

Me, apparently. Because without him, I'm left alone to fend off the eel of guilt I'd beheaded—which turns out to be more like a Hydra, the mythical nine-headed monster with poisonous breath.

I open the heart-shaped box of chocolate Luke gave me last night and scarf down two—okay, *five*—pieces, hoping in vain for the creamy caramel. When your ex-husband turns up dead, along with his mistress—okay, *wife*—you're allowed to bend the breakfast rules a little.

Still chomping on a mouthful, I clear last night's wine glasses and dump the cheap red in the sink. It washes over the steel, splashes up, and spots my T-shirt. Red as blood. *Ian's blood.* It might as well be. I stare at it like Lady Macbeth, knowing it's the sort of stain that won't wash out. It's ruined. Just like my marriage to Ian. Just like me.

The old-school phone on the wall starts its keening. That shrill, wailing ring. And the glass falls from my hand. Its fragile skull cracks against the counter. Shatters onto the floor.

I feel caught. No one ever calls the house.

I shouldn't answer, but I can't stop myself. What if it's Cleo?

"Hello?" I sound the way I used to. Pre-Ian. Curious and hopeful. And I stupidly wonder if his death broke some kind of curse, lifting the shroud of bitterness from my heart like a bride's veil.

"Hello?" I say again, into the void.

"Ava Lawson."

It's not a question. And it's not Cleo. Of course not. She wouldn't have this number. It's a man. A stranger. Worse, a stranger with the chilly calm of a reporter. I should hang up.

"Yes?" As if I'm not sure who I am. And after last night, how could I be?

"Your ex-husband is dead."

How could a reporter have found me so fast? Not that I've been hiding, but . . .

"What?"

"You already knew that, didn't you?"

I slam the phone into the cradle and stoop to gather the broken glass, breathing hard.

I don't realize I've been cut until I see the rivulet of blood trailing from my finger down my wrist. A drop falls to the floor, fat and perfect against the linoleum.

I strip off my T-shirt—it's done for anyway—and swathe my hand in it, holding both under the hot water until the bleeding stops. The cut is minor. Not what I expected. Just a thin slit in the flushed skin along the side of my index finger. It's a wonder that much blood can come from a wound so small.

****

The fog is still thick when I walk the five blocks through downtown Carmel to my office. It's wet and white and cold—magical, even. The closest thing to snow we'll ever get here. And I feel safe in it, hidden somehow. Or maybe it's the rest of the world that's hidden. Whited-out. As hazy as a half-forgotten dream.

But Ian's dead. There's no forgetting that. My heart thrums to the rhythm of it. It's in the sound of my heels clicking the stones on Ocean Avenue. It's in the scream of a seagull diving toward the beach. And the break-neck crash of foamy waves on the rocks. His death music is in my head, a knell.

I know what I need to do. Exactly what Ian would do. What he always did. What I'd done before too, if I'm being honest.

Pretend I'd done nothing wrong.

Besides, most of Monterey County—most of the world—has no clue I used to be Ava Culpepper. I hadn't even told Luke. He'd done the digging, figured it out on his own a few months after we'd started . . . well, whatever it is we were doing. I suppose that's what I get for inviting a cop into my bed.

But really, what *have* I done? The question looms like the edge of a sheer cliff. And I refuse to look down below at the grisly remains.

The splattered guts of my once decent self. The buzzard-picked bones of my morality.

I poke my head in the door at Seaside Sweets and wave at Marianne, same as I always do. It's too early for tourists, and the shop is quiet. She beckons me inside and shoves a heart-shaped doughnut in my direction. "Got a bunch of these left. Jack always says day-old doughnuts are the best."

On any other day, I'd make a silly cop joke, so I force a laugh. "He would know. I suppose thirty years of doughnut eating qualifies him as an expert."

Marianne chuckles, nudging the doughnut closer. I shake my head, but she insists, and I don't argue. Not because she's a cop's wife, tough as nails. And not because she's raised two more of them—Cooper and Luke. But because this morning of all mornings, I need the path of least resistance.

"Take a few for Luke too." She smiles at me the way Luke does, like she knows a secret. Possibly mine. Even so, it soothes me a little, seeing him in her. The rest of Luke's face belongs to his father, Jack. Eyes sturdy and brown as the trunks of the cypress that line the coast. Marianne's and Cooper's, the quiet blue lapping at the shore.

"I doubt I'll see him. He left early this morning."

She takes a bite from a powdered heart, the sugar dusting her lips. "I know. Cooper was the first one on the scene. And Jack got the call too. Can you believe it? The Love Doctors. On Valentine's Day. It's just too . . . what's the word? Ironic."

I focus on chewing, the sticky sweetness coating my tongue like thrush. When my hands shake a little, I press them against the counter. I'd lie to Marianne—sugar rush—if she noticed. I'd tell her about her son and his irresistible box of chocolates. But she keeps talking, oblivious it seems. And all I can think is how quickly I slip back to lying, how willing I am.

"You're a natural," Ian had teased me after the first time, the first small lie. Then, he'd asked, "Should I be worried?"

Marianne takes another bite and washes it down with a swig of coffee. "Did you watch that *Love Doctored* show? I never understood all the hubbub. Sure, that guy—Culpepper—was good-looking. A little too good-looking, if you ask me. And then there was that whole business with the—"

I wave my hand, swatting at an invisible ghost. "Never saw it."

"Well, you didn't miss much. It's sad though. The little girl and all. What was her name? Madeline?"

"Madison." The name lodges in my chest, a barbed arrow. Just after she was born I'd seen her cherub face plastered on the pages of a celebrity gossip magazine, a precise merger of Ian and Kate. I'd envied her that—how she'd gotten the best of both of them. However little that was. Me, I only see my father in the mirror. And the darkness in his eyes that only got darker near the end. I wonder about Madison. What she'll see, who she'll see, twenty years from now in her own reflection. The eyes of dead parents gone before she learned to tie her own shoelaces.

My throat closes, and I snatch the bag Marianne packed for Luke, intending to make a break for the door before my act is exposed and I lose it entirely. Or worse, I don't. I just go on pretending.

"Busy day?" Her gaze probes mine, asking the questions she withholds. No wonder Luke calls her the best detective in the family. Though his dad had won the Monterey County Excellence in Investigation Award five years running.

"I have a ten o'clock, but I'm not sure if she'll show." I smile through it. Easy-breezy. Like nothing. Just any old Wednesday *before*. Before karma came calling. Before I met Cleo. Before I did something unforgivable. Again.

CHAPTER THREE

CLEO is always late. But today is different—I'm different—and I expect her to be here, tapping her sneaker in the waiting room. Her face flushed after the five-mile bike ride from her campus apartment in Monterey and burning from the same combustible cocktail of guilt, fear, and exhilaration I've been nursing all morning.

But the two chairs in the waiting room are vacant. Above them, the photo of the lone cypress I'd taken with my first camera. My mother had it framed for me four years ago, when I'd come back here—tail between my legs—and rented this office. A lone cypress, myself. That was when she still remembered me. When she still remembered most things. Like the way to the house she could barely afford on the outskirts of Carmel, and how to make the perfect grilled cheese sandwich, and that my dad had left us in the worst way. She remembered Ian too, then. The *real* Ian. And what he'd done. Now, her moments of clarity are wasted, asking me about the oh-so-charming husband I no longer had.

It's exactly ten when I fit the key into the lock on my office door. At 10:01, I fluff the pillows on the couch where Cleo had sat cross-legged every Wednesday for the last four months. By 10:03, I'm in my chair, and it's my foot that's tapping. What if she doesn't come?

And just like that, I'm sure of it. She won't come back. Not ever. Why would she?

Now, it's 10:05, and there's a new horror working its way through my brain. Cleo is dead too. Sprawled next to Kate and Ian on the plush bedroom carpet, half her face gone—exploded—from a single bullet. One dead doe eye fixed on the ceiling. Just the one. The other, God knows where. I've seen it before—once—a bullet to the head. The memory clear and bright, enduring as a photograph. Someday, if I wind up like my mother, I hope it will be the first to go.

I lunge for the trash can in the corner, my no-rules breakfast burning my throat on its way back up. I heave until my stomach feels empty, except for the Hydra of course, its tentacled heads tying me in knots. And squeezing. Squeezing.

The knock on the door startles me, and for an agonizing second I think it's the man from the phone with ice in his veins. He's found me. And he knows. He knows everything. *Everything.*

"Doctor Lawson? It's me. Am I too late?"

I wipe my mouth with the back of my hand. Stash the wastebasket in the closet with a spritz of air freshener to hide the smell. Examine the bandage on my finger. Still intact. The clock above my desk reads 10:09. As close as Cleo has ever come to breaking the ten-minute rule. One minute more, and I'd have sent her home, billed her for a full session. Like a good little shrink maintaining the therapeutic frame. Too bad I'd blown the frame to bits myself months ago.

"Come in," I hear myself say. But I stare at the knob as it turns, suddenly afraid of her—this wisp of a girl with hair like flame licking down her back—and what she's done. What I might have pushed her to do.

"I'm so sorry." Slipping her leather messenger bag from her shoulder, she flops onto the sofa, sighing and laughing at the same time. Then she kicks off her sneakers and pulls her socked feet beneath her like a child. And at twenty, isn't she still in all the ways that count? "I overslept."

I nod and force the corners of my mouth upward in a pleasant smile. But behind it, I'm reeling, stumbling backward like I've been kicked in the teeth. She could have said anything—*I killed Ian. I killed your ex-husband and his uppity bitch wife.* Even that. And it wouldn't have stunned as completely as her casual dismissal.

I overslept. Seriously?

"And the fog is a real mess," she adds, pinching the hem of her T-shirt between her fingers. The fabric clings to her chest, heavy with moisture. I pretend to look out the window, when really I'm riding another swell of nausea. I breathe through the crest of it, and it subsides.

"It's surreal," I say, still avoiding her face. "Like another world." And I'm not sure if I'm talking about the fog or something else. The kind of world where old husbands and new wives turn up dead. Where young mistresses—murderesses?—oversleep.

"Totally. But it's sort of romantic, don't you think?"

And she's so easygoing, so relaxed, I wonder if she's mocking me. I examine her eyes then. Not the one bulging, dead eye of my imagination, of my memory. But two of them. Deep-set stones of amber. Not a shred of makeup, just a sheen of sweat, because she has nothing to hide. No red rims or dark circles under those lashes. She blinks, and I realize she's waiting for me to answer. To say something. To therapize.

"Speaking of romance, how did your Valentine's end up?" As far as questions go, it's a litmus test—cruel but necessary. Perhaps a bit more directive than my usual approach, but hell, I think the circumstances allow it. Call for it, even.

She flips her hand as if to say, *I've had better.* "It didn't go quite the way I planned." A pause that extends for an eternity. "I hope you're not disappointed in me."

I lose my breath a little. "Disappointed?" I croak.

"Well, we'd talked about me confronting him. Or her. Finally having the courage, you know? Making him own up to his promises. But, I couldn't do it. I spent the night binge-watching crazy chick flicks and eating my pain." She shrugs, smirks. "Who knew it tasted like Rocky Road?"

With her sarcasm comes a new horror. One I hadn't considered. *She doesn't know.* I swallow it, a bitter pill. "What would it mean to you if I was disappointed?"

"I don't know. That I failed somehow. I know I need to do it. Just lay down the law. Tell him I won't go on this way. It's her or me. But I've been afraid of the answer. Afraid of the end."

The end. I know exactly what she means. The hard stop, the last page, the void after. Because everything ends eventually. One way or another. Love. Marriage. My father. Even Ian.

"Would that feel like a failure too? The end of your love affair?"

I watch the tears in her eyes rise like floodwater. She swipes a knuckle across her cheek, then reaches for a tissue. And I sit still, unflinching. Empty as a box waiting to be filled. It's the one thing I've always been good at—holding a client's pain—even though I loathe the expression, the touchy-feely way it sounds. When the reality of it is cradling a deformed creature, soothing it as it claws and howls.

"I hate crying," she says finally. Her eyes bleary, the way I'd expected from the get-go. "And yes, Doctor Lawson, tears are the ultimate failure."

I know she's teasing me. But still. "Did someone teach you that? Your father?"

"Probably. Who else?"

"We always come back to this, Cleo. Success and failure. Winning and losing. Your dad and his demands. I wonder if that's why you're drawn to a man like The Professor. Married. Old enough to be your father and just as unavailable. One of your teachers, no less. I suppose it would mean winning the unwinnable. Getting the un-gettable. Wouldn't it?"

She pauses, considering. I like that about her. She thinks before she answers. "It's not about winning. Not with him. He's so happy when we're together. And so miserable with her. He certainly doesn't trust her."

"Did he say that?" I silently curse myself, snuff out a flicker of glee. What does it matter anymore?

"He doesn't have to say it. I *feel* it. He trembles when we kiss. How could he stop wanting that? How could anyone?" She's never sounded so breathy, so young. "Momentum. That's what I've got on my side. And it's a powerful force."

"Indeed." It aches to look at her. I see myself. I see Kate. What she's talking about is hope, and it's as fragile as a flower. As fickle as the wind. As dangerous as a blade. "But his wife has something too, don't you think? Something just as powerful."

Again, she puzzles for a moment, twisting her mouth. Wringing her hands. And I worry for her. Losing him will crush her, turn the petals of her heart to dust. I should know.

"What?" she whispers.

"Inertia."

My cynical quip doesn't hit her like I expect. Instead, she grins, raises one sly eyebrow. A neat trick. "I wasn't going to show you. Not until I knew it was real, but . . ." She unhooks her feet from beneath her, slides her phone from her pocket, and leans forward across the chasm between us, a green text bubble glowing bright. "It's from The Professor."

I'm going to confront her. Tonight after dinner. And I'll tell her everything.

"When?" I ask, almost to myself. But it's right there: Tuesday, February 14, 2018, 7:08 p.m.

She snorts. "I'd shut my phone off. Go figure. Somewhere in the middle of *Fatal Attraction*, I'd guess."

CHAPTER FOUR

ONE hour until my next client, and I do what I've done so many times. I follow Cleo. With two questions banging around in my brain like rocks in a tin can, smacking hard enough to throw sparks.

The first: *Ian, what did you do? What did you do?*

And the second: *Did you ever tremble when we kissed?*

I stroll the cobblestone. Pretend to window shop. All the while, obliterating the therapeutic frame as I trail Cleo and her bicycle the few blocks through the fog, toward the water.

"I texted him back this morning and asked him to meet me," she'd said, just before our fifty minutes were up. Typical Cleo, sneaking it in under the wire. "Down at the beach here."

My skin had prickled. "Did you tell him you were in therapy?" *With me?* The unspoken question. Because even Ian, self-absorbed as he is—was—might've figured that one out. Me and her. Ex-wife meets new mistress. And then what?

"No. I'm afraid he'll ask how it's going. What I talk about. I told him I was seeing a friend in Carmel for breakfast. That it would be a good place to meet. But, he didn't respond. Not yet anyway." I'd felt relieved. Then stupid.

Ian is dead.

And I did nothing wrong, I remind myself again. Nothing that can be proven anyway. But absence of evidence is not evidence of absence. Ian had said that on the first episode of *Love Doctored*, trying to make himself sound smart. As in, *don't despair, Mrs. Painfully Insecure. Of course, your husband still loves you even if he can't bear to say the words aloud.* Absence of evidence . . . what a crock.

And of course, I'd watched it. I'd ogled it. Like a car wreck. Or a house fire. Or an episode of that naked wilderness show with its stark white, soft bodies scrambling through the mud and the underbrush. I couldn't look away. There was something obscene about my ex-husband handing out love advice on national television, dispensing his special brand of hypocrisy the same way he doled out medication.

I stop short of the beach parking lot, inhaling the briny ocean air, and wait for Cleo to lock her bike on a rack. Messenger bag slung across her chest, she walks with purpose past the cars to the white sand. She pauses to strip off her sneakers and socks, then trudges down the hill and past the cypress where the sea is the same gray-blue as the sky, and the fog blurs the horizon—trees, cliffs, houses—like a charcoal drawing.

I open my own bag, take out my Nikon, and shadow her. The camera is the perfect excuse. The perfect cover. And with the superzoom lens that cost me four and a half sessions with Cleo, I can see her face as clearly as if she was still sitting on my sofa, without getting too close.

The beach is nearly empty. Just Cleo, two black labs, and a man with hair as white as the seafoam. He tosses a piece of driftwood toward the water, and the dogs splash in after it. Cleo throws her head back and laughs. Exposing her swan-like neck, pale and graceful. Ian kissed her there the first time I'd seen them together, the first time I'd watched them through the eye of my lens.

Now, she glances back over her shoulders in both directions. Looks at her phone. And I know what she's thinking. Part of me is holding my breath beside her, expecting to see him. Sauntering up, with his tousled hair and ice-blue eyes, designer jeans rolled up to his calves. And a chameleon smile that could be whatever you need it to be.

"Hey, Aves," he'd say. Aves. That's what he called me. *He*, meaning The Professor. Ian. Though Cleo had never said his name out loud. The Professor and his wife. Always that. Only that. It had been her idea. "Because they're sort of well-known," she'd said, with the kind of careful discretion The Professor valued in a mistress. And an ex-wife. Hence, the nondisclosure agreement I'd signed along with our divorce decree.

The dogs bound down the beach, barking at seagulls, and the man follows. Shrieking, the birds take to the air, scatter, and disappear in the fog.

Cleo is alone. And I wonder how long she'll wait.

She examines her phone once more, removes a book from her bag, and settles in against the sand for the long haul. Waiting, after all, is the task of a mistress. And an ex-wife. Who knew we had so much in common? I snap a single photo of her this way. Relaxed and in profile. I want to remember her *before*. Before she knows what I know.

Ian is dead.

Kate too.

The permanent kind of inertia.

A sudden ring cracks the stillness like a whip, and Cleo jerks her head toward the sound of it. Me. And my pocket.

I stumble backward, juggling the camera, and fumble for my phone, answering the unknown number with a curt *hello* as I duck behind the twisted limb of a cypress. And just like that I'm back in my kitchen, caught and bleeding and breathing hard. The cut on my finger throbs under the bandage like a heartbeat.

"Hey. It's me. You sound weird." Luke's voice, warm as it is, chills me like a spray of ocean water down my back. He never calls when he's working. It's a rule. Technically, one of mine, not Luke's. Rules I assemble around my heart like iron bars. Though a quickie on his lunch break is perfectly legal. "Are you at your office?"

"Uh . . ."

Cleo's gaze lingers on the spot where I'd stood. I want to hold the lens up, examine her face, but it's too risky. Instead, I start walking away. "I went out for a bit. Why?"

"We need to talk." Four little words. *Cursed words.* Where have I heard them before?

Honey, we need to talk. Daddy is sick. The kind of sick that makes him sad all the time. Be a good girl and don't bother him.

Aves, we need to talk. I'm in love with someone else. I want a divorce.

Doctor Lawson, we need to talk. Your mother is suffering from progressive dementia. She'll have good days and bad days. Until she has bad days and worse days.

"About what?" I ask, steeling myself for the blow. For the sucker punch to the gut that will drop me to my knees. "Where are you calling from?"

"The payphone at Bruno's Market. Can you meet me?"

"The payphone?" A burst of nervous laughter breaks free, escapes. I sound slightly crazed. *Hypomanic,* Ian might have said. He'd always been fond of diagnosing me. "I didn't know you knew how to use one of those things."

Luke lets out his breath like he's been holding it. And just as sudden as the laughter bubbled up, there's a lump in my throat I can't choke down.

"I have a client in twenty minutes," I manage.

"I think you should cancel."

"I can't just—"

"Ava, cancel your client. Meet me at our spot. Now."

"But—" The line goes dead. And the dial tone is my flat line. *We have to talk*. Doomed words, I already know. Because it's the first time—the only time—Luke has ever hung up on me.

****

The *Valentine* statue—our spot, as Luke called it—is roughly a ten-minute walk up Ocean Avenue. Luke is already there, in uniform, sitting on one side of the bronze sculpture of an elderly couple who have just exchanged a valentine.

I hold in another fit of hysterical laughter and take a seat on the other side of the couple, next to the sculpted woman. Her head rests on her lover's, a tender smile on her face. Forever. Only a love frozen in stone could sustain that long.

"When was the last time you saw Ian?" Luke whispers, each word weighted with worry. With accusation. And those words sink me like stones tied to my waist.

"What?"

"Just answer the goddamn question, Ava."

"Summer, I guess. I ran into him on the street." Luke doesn't know it yet, how well I lie. But he'll learn. "Why are you asking that?"

He stares straight ahead. His cop face.

"Please tell me what's going on." I grab for his hand, but he shrugs away, beyond the reach of my persuasion.

"What happened to your finger?" As if I've done something wrong. But I haven't. I didn't. *Keep telling yourself that, kiddo.* And the voice in my head is Ian's. Again.

"I dropped a wine glass this morning cleaning up. I cut it. That's all. You're freaking me out looking at me that way. Like I'm a criminal or something. Did you forget you were with me all night? Or did I imagine you in my bed?"

He shakes his head, rolls his eyes at me, and sighs. Like I'm the young one, the one who's still on the good side of thirty.

"I shouldn't be telling you this," he says. And suddenly I wish he wouldn't. But it's too late to stop him. "Ian and Kate were stabbed. It was bad. Really bad. The sort of bad that doesn't happen here. Not in Carmel."

I feel the air rush out of me, my lungs like deflated balloons. "So it wasn't . . . Ian didn't . . ."

"God, Ava. Spit it out."

"It's not a murder-suicide?"

"No. Why would you say that?" The cop face again. It cuts me to the bone. But I pretend to shrug it off.

"A hunch, I guess."

"A hunch? What are you not telling me?" It's a loaded gun, that question. A revolver with a bullet in every chamber. Round and round and round it goes, where it stops . . .

"You think I'm lying to you?" I try to find the answer in his eyes, but he won't even look at me.

"They haven't figured it out yet—about you and Ian—and I'm not gonna tell them." And by *they*, he means his father, Detective Jack Donovan. And his brother, Cooper. A chip off the old gumshoe block. "But, Ava, they will. And soon. So you better get your story straight."

"My story. Right. So you *do* think I'm lying."

"I didn't say that. I just don't know how else to explain it." His frown softens, and I realize I prefer anger over this. He pities me.

"Explain what?"

"Your name was at the scene." *The scene.* I get stuck on the words. Because that's how it feels. Unreal. Staged. I'm in a scene, and Luke is acting. He's the handsome, do-gooder cop who's fallen for the black widow. "Ian wrote it on the bathroom mirror before he died. Or at least that's what it looks like."

"He wrote my name?" *Why does my voice sound like that? Like I'm sinking underwater and Luke's up on the surface, nodding his head.*

"In his own blood."

CHAPTER FIVE

ARE you sure you don't want me to drop you off at home?"

Luke pulls his cruiser over to the curb in front of my office, tucks a strand of my hair behind my ear, and leaves his hand to rest on my shoulder. He's tender again. It might've been the dry heaving that did him in. Or the way my teeth wouldn't stop chattering. Still won't.

"No. It's okay. I only have two more clients, and they're both easy. Besides, it'll look suspicious if I leave now."

He squeezes my shoulder and returns his hand to the wheel. "Fair enough."

"But, Luke . . . will you come over later? After?" God, I sound pathetic, teetering on the edge of desperation. This is why I have rules. And I know I'm breaking one, asking him to stay over two nights in a row.

"I don't know if that's a good idea."

"Alright." I open the door and put one foot out in the world. That world—mine now—where old husbands and new wives turn up dead. Where ex-wives' names are scrawled in blood like the scene of a Manson murder.

"Hey, Ava." I turn to look at him even though it hurts. "I'll try."

And I know, right then, Luke's been telling the truth. He loves me.

****

I push through the door to my office, vowing not to think. To shut off my brain and its wailing panic button. I can do this. Two fifty-minute sessions.

But first I have to check. It would be careless not to. *Be good, and if you can't be good, be careful.* That little nugget came from my father. He and Ian are dueling it out in my head, taking turns mocking me. *On second thought, Ava, just be good.*

Sorry, Dad.

I open the drawer of the antique secretary desk Ian had bought me long ago and dislodge the false bottom. When I'd first discovered it, it thrilled me. I ran to get Ian, to show him the desk's quirky little secret. Back then, I delighted in the way it could show me one face while concealing another. So much like myself and my patients. So much like everyone really. But Ian especially.

I don't bother with the ring box. I used to look inside it all the time—at the perfect round diamond atop the white gold band—like pressing a bruise. But what's the point? The man who'd offered it once and then changed his mind is dead. And the girl who'd accepted it, her heart is as hardened as a walnut shell.

The envelope. That's what I've come for. It sits exactly the way I left it. Exactly as it had been since I'd first placed it there for safekeeping. Crisp, white, and unmarked. Almost virginal.

I pick it up, open it, and drop the tiny memory card into my hand. The are-you-fucking-kidding-me memory card, as I like to call it. That's what Ian said when I'd told him about the pictures I'd taken of him and Cleo. Making out like teenagers in the dark alleyway by the Flying Fish Grill. Half-dressed in the backseat of his AMG Mercedes. Sneaking kisses in the grove of pines near campus.

"No, I'm not fucking kidding," I'd told him, mocking his PhD-turned-frat-boy vocabulary. "I'm dead serious."

"Doctor Lawson?" The sound of my name on Cleo's lips is a lightning bolt. A clap of thunder. A single raindrop, cold on the back of my neck. She's standing in the open doorway—*didn't I close it?*—weeping.

"Cleo, are you alright?" It's the sort of question I use to buy time. Time to flip the switch from Ava Lawson, crazy ex-wife, to Ava Lawson, the professional. I slip the memory card back into the envelope and lay it on my desk.

"When he didn't come, I . . ." A sob gurgles in her throat, and she holds out her phone, open to the Monterey Community College website with its breaking news headline, gruesome in its starkness: "Professor Ian Culpepper and Wife Found Dead."

"It's my fault. It's all my fault," she says.

I try to remember who I'm supposed to be. Who she expects me to be. "This is him? The Professor?"

She answers with a choked cry.

"Oh, Cleo, I'm so sorry."

"It's my fault," she says again, even more certain this time.

She crosses the threshold into the office, her sneakers still sprinkled with beach sand. And I think how sad it is. How the beach will be spoiled for her forever. Ruined the way summer twilight is for me.

"What do you mean *your fault?*"

Her face tightens. She opens her mouth to speak. Closes it again. "I lied to you."

Another lightning bolt. Another cold drop of rain. And I hide my unease behind a mask of surprise. "Oh."

"I saw Ian yesterday afternoon. I went to his house to confront him just like we'd talked about. He was furious with me for showing up unexpected. And it was so strange being in their house, with their stuff. With her photo on the wall. I could barely breathe. But, I did it. I told him exactly how I felt. How fed up I was."

I side-eye the clock, listen for the sound of footfalls. My next client will be here any minute, but I can't stop now. I won't stop. "What did he say?"

She half-laughs, but it's joyless, tears clinging to its hard edge. "The usual empty promises. A whole lot of nothing. But I fell for it."

"And?" I want to shake it out of her, whatever happened.

"Well, we started making out in the upstairs bedroom, and we got carried away. And then—"

"His bedroom? I mean, theirs?" I sound like a lunatic, but I'm thinking of our bedroom—mine and Ian's—and how he'd probably taken Kate there. At least once. And how she'd probably let him undress her, tossing her clothing next to mine. Perhaps she'd even slipped my shoes on to see how it felt to be me. To be Ian's wife.

"No." She's whispering now, and I've stopped breathing altogether. "The little girl's. His daughter's."

I suck in a mouthful of air, a hungry gulp Cleo mistakes for disapproval. Judgment. As if I had the right.

"It's bad, I know. But it got worse, because Kate showed up early to drop off Madison. I guess Kate had a doctor's appointment Ian forgot about. So I had to sneak out the window of his study. I practically sprained my ankle running through the backyard. I should've known it was a sign."

I listen to her whimper as I watch out the window. My 2 p.m. parallel parks on the street in front of the office. Unfastens her seat belt, opens her door. I have to hurry.

"Cleo, you couldn't have known. Signs are just the brain's way to make sense of random chaos after the fact. How is any of this your fault? The murders, I mean."

Cleo swipes at her screen, scrolling through the article. She narrows her eyes. And there's something aggressive, something feral about the way she moves toward me. Toward me and the envelope, splayed on my desk, stark as a nude photograph. Toward the desk's false bottom and its secret, exposed. I almost cry out, tell her to stop.

"Because of this," she says, leaning over me. She still smells like the ocean, and I spot a fleck of sand on her face, glinting like a shard of glass in the overhead light. I read the words beside her finger, the statement from an unnamed source, careful not to gasp.

". . . The person or persons responsible may have gained access through an open window in the study."

The hardiest romances spring from common ground.
—Ian Culpepper, *Prescription for Love*

VALENTINE'S DAY
TEN YEARS EARLIER

AVA chewed on the cap of her ballpoint pen and watched the clock at the back of the lecture hall. It read 5:12 p.m. A full two minutes past the ten-minute rule, and her classmates had already run for the door like a herd of wild buffalo, leaving her stock-still at her desk. She listened to them stamping down the hallway, whooping with the exhilaration of unexpected freedom. It made her feel lonely. A girl set apart. But that was nothing new.

It was her father's watch that kept her there. Every morning, she wound the old Zenith and slipped it on her wrist. Not a bittersweet memento like her mother thought. More like the rubber band technique—a stinging lash to the heart each time she felt its weight against her skin—meant to remind her what could happen if her anger got loose again. If she was anything less than perfect. The Zenith was never wrong. She made sure of that. And according to the Zenith, Professor Culpepper had two more minutes.

She contemplated the watch's plain white face as their final scenes together—father and daughter—played like a bad movie. A reel that never faded, never erased, no matter how many years had passed. I hate you. I wish you'd just die. Those words born from some awful place inside her and set free at last, crushing him. She knew that now. Her throat raw as she'd slammed the door. Her body simmering with rage. And it felt so real. Even here in the pin-drop quiet of Tolman Hall.

An ironic laugh broke the stillness like a gunshot, and she flinched as the memories scattered, blackbirds taking to the sky. "The old ten-minute rule, huh?" Dr. Culpepper sounded different. Less like a professor and more like a man.

Her face flushed at the thought, and she didn't dare look at him. *Get a grip, Ava.* She refused to be like the girls who sat in the back row, giggling at their hunky professor. The girls who were more sorority sister than third-year graduate student. Doctor Love, they called him. Not to his face, of course. Which was, even she could admit it, devastatingly handsome. "That clock is ahead."

"So it is." She heard the door creak shut, the clack of his loafers against the tile floor. And she arranged her face into a polite smile and kept it there until he stood over her, smiling back. "But you stayed."

She nodded, feeling silly, and pointed to the Zenith, cinched tight around her wrist and clasped on the last buckle hole. The second hand *tick-tick-ticked* at her, making her wish she'd fled with all the others. Another buffalo in the herd, instead of the one left behind. "You still had two minutes."

"A rule follower then, I see."

Was that a bad thing? She couldn't tell. But, she remembered that first day when he'd winked at the shy, studious girl in the front row. Her. And the way he'd scrawled *solid analysis!* in long, cursive strokes at the bottom of her last essay. Suddenly, she felt brave. "I like your class, that's all."

He tossed his leather satchel onto the floor and sat backwards on the desk in front of her own, facing her. It was strange being this close to him, with no lectern between them. And she could see everything. The pinkish tone of his freshly shaved skin. The cool blue of his eyes, which warmed when he looked at her. And the single thread that had begun to unravel from the top button of his dress shirt. It was endearing, that thread. Evidence of imperfection.

"So tell me, Ms. Lawson, what do you like so much about my class?"

Ava shrugged, as if she really hadn't thought about it much. The truth couldn't be said aloud, but it writhed under her skin. "Psychopharmacology has always been an interest of mine. I'd like to understand why so many people believe all their problems can be solved with a pill. You can't medicate unhappiness."

"Tell that to the pharmaceutical companies." His laugh was both prod and salve to the anger that burned so close to the surface. Even now. Especially now.

"Oh, I intend to," she blurted, surprising herself. "I mean, I hope my dissertation will establish that pharmacological therapy is not a panacea. In fact, drugs can do more harm than good in some cases." *Like my father's.*

Her diatribe warranted a raise of the professorial eyebrows. *Shit.* "I'm sorry, Doctor Culpepper. I don't usually do this." *I never do this.*

"And by *this* you mean—?"

She sucked in a breath. "Ramble, proselytize, get up on my soapbox, so to speak."

"That's a shame," he said. "It suits you. You should do it more often. And please, call me Ian."

She cast her eyes to the Zenith, touched it with her fingers as if it was a grounding rod, and opened her mouth to speak. To tell him something. Maybe everything. For once, she didn't plan it. "Ian," she began, and her heart fluttered in her chest as if it had grown wings. She wondered when she'd turned into a back-row girl. "I need to—"

He held up his hand to stop her. "I apologize for keeping you. You must have somewhere to be. Someone to meet, now that you have a free evening. A valentine, perhaps?"

She imagined how her face must look to him. Blank as a chalkboard. Her stutter, the twitter of a nervous child caught in a lie. "No," she managed to say. "There's no one." *And there won't be unless you loosen up a little.* Hadn't her mom said exactly that?

"You forgot, didn't you? About Valentine's Day?"

She nodded without meeting his eyes.

"Well, Ms. Lawson . . . Ava . . ." His voice softened. "That just might be the saddest thing I've ever heard. And I'm a widowed couples' therapist."

Widowed. She winced at the word, and her mouth hung open a little. Gaping at him. She shut it fast. And tried to act normal. She'd never met anyone with a story worse than her own. "That's awful."

He stood up and slung his bag over his shoulder. "So, that settles it. We're both sad sacks. Want to drown your sorrow in a slice of pizza? We'll call it an anti-Valentine's."

****

"Extra large, extra garlic," the waitress announced, setting the pizza on the table between them.

Ian smirked at Ava as he served her the first slice. The blazer he'd lent her on the walk over hung on the chair behind her, and each time it brushed her bare skin, it felt like his arm around her shoulder. She leaned back, reveling in its secret caress.

"It doesn't get any more anti-Valentine's than extra garlic, right?" he asked.

She took a small, careful bite and smiled back at him. "You know, I would've guessed a couples' therapist might be a little more pro-valentine. After all, is it not the holiday of love?"

Ian scoffed, just as she figured he would. Ava knew cynical when she saw it. And she saw it every morning in the mirror, staring back at her through her own jaundiced gaze.

"It's the absolute worst. Too much pressure. Too many expectations. Do you know how many emergency sessions I've had to schedule over the years? All because some poor sap bought flowers from the grocery store. Or heaven forbid, only signed his name at the bottom of a card. I mean, how many chocolates does it take to say I love you?"

Ava laughed, hard. And the knot in her stomach—*how long had it been there?*—loosened a little. *Take that, Mom.*

"No, seriously," he said. "How many chocolates?"

"Seriously? Hmm . . . it depends. What sort of chocolate are we talking about? Hershey's or Godiva? It makes a difference. And a caramel center is worth more than coconut."

There was no misreading Ian's crooked smile—he liked her—and she realized she'd gone too far. Way too far. Flirting with her professor. Might as well head straight for the back row next time. But that's what happens when you let one string loose. The whole of you comes undone.

"I knew it," he said. "There is a number."

She flattened her smile, took another delicate bite, and changed the subject, stoking the coals of her disdain instead. "Do you typically prescribe medication for your patients?"

Her voice sounded cold, her question way out of left field. But Ian kept smiling. *Oh God*, she thought, *I've already started calling him Ian in my mind*. "Sometimes. But, I don't want you to get the wrong idea about me. I'm really not a pill pusher. Despite that stupid joke I made the first day of class."

"So what do you think of the CDC's black-box warning? Have you seen increased suicidal ideation with antidepressants?"

He studied her for a moment, then tapped the stem of his fork like a microphone. "Is this thing on?"

Stone-faced, she waited, thinking of her father. And the blue pills he'd washed down with a swig of orange juice every morning for one week. Until the coroner carted him away. "Well?"

"Okay, Barbara Walters. Are you sure you picked the right degree? You know, Berkeley has a great journalism program. And the law school is next door. It's not too late for a career change."

"No pressure. I'm just curious. And you are the expert on psychotropic medication, right?"

He cocked his head at her, his face grim. "It's obvious you're not here for casual conversation. What do you really want to know?" It happened so fast, the way his mood darkened. Like the rare LA thunderstorms that had sent her running for her father back when she still could. The cloudbursts and the lightning flashes changing the world within minutes. "Did Julie's family put you up to this?"

Ava nearly overturned her soda as she jerked away from the table as if she'd been slapped. And that's how it felt. Stinging humiliation. "What? Who's Julie?"

Ian dropped his face behind his hand, saying nothing. When he finally looked at her, her heartbeat quickened. His eyes were electric, fierce darts of pain fixed on her. "My wife."

"I thought your wife was . . ."

"She is." And Ava wondered if he couldn't say the word either. She had trouble with it herself. The simple finality of it. The questions that always came after. Why? And how? "But her parents blame me. They always have."

Ian raised his hand to signal the waitress. But he didn't wait. He stood up and tossed two twenty dollar bills on the table. "I'm so sorry," he said. "I was totally out of line."

"Why do they blame you?"

He shook his head at her, but she wouldn't let it go. Not now. Not after that sudden squall had left her reeling.

"Please. It's important to me," she said. "I won't say anything, if that's what you're worried about."

He reached for his jacket, pulling it roughly from behind her. Without it, she felt bare and ashamed. "Because I convinced her to participate in a research trial for a new antidepressant. She'd been up and down for a long time. And nothing worked. It was our last hope, but I couldn't save her."

Ava saw him teetering on the edge she knew so well, walking the line between pushing her away and letting her in. Between indignation and vulnerability. All he needed was a nudge. And she needed one too. So she reached for him, laying a hand on his forearm. He flinched at her touch but he didn't pull away.

Then, he said it. And said it again when she'd asked him to, not believing. Not trusting her own ears.

"She killed herself."

40

Ava had felt alone for so long that it might have been that moment—right then—when she fell in love with him. She marveled at it, their shared pain. That out of all the wrong people, he was the right kind of wrong. The same kind of wrong as her.

THE MONTEREY COUNTY COURIER

"BLOODY VALENTINE: LOVE DOCTORS' DEATHS RULED HOMICIDE"

by Jackson Lamont

Police are investigating the deaths of Ian and Kate Culpepper as a double homicide. The Culpeppers' housekeeper discovered the bodies early Wednesday morning inside the doctors' upscale home on Cortez Road, located near the famed Pebble Beach Golf Course. Police initially called the scene suspicious but were reluctant to disclose additional information pending further investigation.

Thursday morning, the Carmel Police Department (CPD) issued a statement confirming the manner of death as homicide by stabbing, noting that both victims suffered from numerous stab or slash-type wounds, any number of which could have been fatal. Toxicology and autopsy results are pending. According to police, they found no signs of forced entry at the Culpepper residence; however, various news outlets, citing an unnamed source close to the investigation, have reported that the person or persons responsible may have gained access through an open window in the study. The murder weapon has not been found. "At this point, we have more questions than answers," Police Chief Scott Morrow said.

CPD also confirmed they are investigating the possibility that the Culpeppers were targeted by someone they encountered in the course of their professional duties as marriage counselors. CPD has not yet publicly ruled out a connection to the 2016 death of *Love Doctored* guest Vanessa Sherman. While appearing on the show, Sherman was found dead in a dressing room from an accidental overdose. Sherman's widower, Ricky, unsuccessfully sued the Drs. Culpepper and the BXA network, claiming the show had led to his wife's untimely death. Chief Morrow added, "We're considering all leads at this time." Mr.

Sherman did not respond to *The Monterey County Courier's* request for comment.

Ned Gotleib, the academic dean of Monterey Community College (MCC), where Dr. Ian Culpepper taught advanced courses in psychopharmacology, issued a statement today, calling him a "natural-born teacher" who relished the opportunity to guide his students. Dr. Culpepper had previously taught psychopharmacology at the University of California Berkeley, where he began his storied career as a renowned psychiatrist and couples' therapist, and more recently, taught at the University of California Los Angeles. A memorial vigil is scheduled for Friday night at 7 p.m. at the MCC main campus.

CHAPTER SIX

THURSDAY
FEBRUARY 16, 2018

IT'S well after midnight and Luke is asleep, one arm draped across my stomach. I say his name out loud just to be certain. But the push and pull of his breath, the rise and fall of his bare chest, is as steady as a metronome marking time. I envy him that—the spell of slumber and the way he falls under it. The flutter of his eyelashes, the slackness of his jaw, render him younger than his twenty-seven years. The soundness of his sleep had come as a surprise to me from the beginning. So unlike Ian whose eyes darted open like a lizard's at the mere shift of my weight.

So unlike me too, eyes fixed on the ceiling, a death parade marching through my brain in a never-ending circle. Ian and Kate, stabbed. Cleo on the beach, waiting. Then sobbing in my office. My name in blood.

I can't fix it. Can't solve it. Can't make it stop. A sob wells up, not for Ian or Kate or Cleo. Not even for Maddie, poor orphaned girl. It's for myself. For the things I've done. The things I failed to do.

I choke it down and scoot out from under Luke. His hand seeks the tangle of sheets, the same way he always winds his fingers around the nape of my neck and up through my hair, drawing my mouth closer to his own. Strong and searching. I want to curl back beneath his arm, scoot into the warm wall of his chest, and pretend yesterday never happened. For once, I wish denial came as easily to me as it did to Ian. That I could box up whole parts of myself and leave them to gather dust like childhood mementos in an attic.

I step over Luke's boxers, discarded in a hurry at the foot of the bed, and risk a quick glance at his badge on the dresser. It winks at me like it knows me, glinting in the slash of moonlight that cuts through the blinds. And for one aching instant it's summer and I'm fourteen again—and the badge is my father's, and my father is dead on the floor, blood pooling around his head like melted ice cream.

I look away, and the memory retreats to the shadows. It hunkers down in the dark. Waits to be summoned again.

I pad across the hardwood into the bathroom and shut the door. The night light makes a small halo on the counter. And in the mirror. But I don't look there. I'm afraid I'll see Ian's face, or worse, his finger tracing my name in red with his last ragged breath.

I run the water in the sink until it's cold and scoop a handful into my mouth. Splash my face. Better.

Then, I slink out of the bedroom to the kitchen. My laptop sits on the counter, where I'd left it last night, the home screen lighting up with a gentle touch of the mouse. I pull up a stool and lean into its glow like a moth to a flame.

I should wait until the morning. Wait for Luke to leave. But I won't. It's as unavoidable as a head-on collision. And it reminds me of Verna, my 10 a.m. Friday, who spent half her retirement on the home shopping network. The urge to splurge, she'd called it. Just like

Verna, I can't *not* do it. Though in my case, it's been more of an urge to scourge.

My chest tightens as I open the browser, fast-type my password, and click the Sign In button.

The gates of hell unfurl before me. One new message in my inbox.

> To: Avenging Angel <avengingangel@pacbell.com>
> From: <rsherm13@quickmail.net>
> Date: February 16, 2018 12:03 AM PST
> Subject: WTF?
>
> Is it true? And how? I don't know what to think or maybe I'm just afraid to ask. Are you really that kind of avenging angel? And what happens now?

I stare at Ricky's questions, the marks at the end like crooked fingers pointing straight at me. He expects me to answer, to know what to do. Because he's only twenty-seven, Luke's age. But in the photo leaked to the press—a candid shot from his wedding day—he looks younger. He and his shiny new wife, Vanessa, surrounded by friends and family. The picture had been chosen with intention, I'm sure of that. Meant to convey a message of trouble brewing. Because Vanessa looks at Ricky like he's the puppy she's always wanted, with his linebacker shoulders and ruddy face and scruffy hair the color of a penny. Meanwhile, Ricky's gaze wanders to the perky blonde in the tight dress.

Of course, I'd dug up other photographs: Ricky and Vanessa kissing at midnight at a New Year's bash; Ricky and Vanessa splashing in the waves at the beach; Ricky and Vanessa, pressed and polished, at the annual Collins and Bloch Accounting Firm charity fundraiser. I'd squinted at the screen, coveting their clueless smiles. This is what I love about photographs. What I hate about them too. They're undeniable proof that once, even if just for a heartbeat, everything was perfect.

I type fast in case Luke wakes up. He may be a heavy sleeper, but he's still a cop. And cops have a sixth sense for secrets. My dad always knew when I'd kept him in the dark. Never mind that he had secrets of his own. "Spill it," he'd say, with that steely glower I couldn't sneak past. Luke's not so different.

> *To: Ricky Sherman <rsherm13@quickmail.net>*
> *From: Avenging Angel <avengingangel@pacbell.com>*
> *Date: February 16, 2018 12:35 AM PST*
> *Subject: Re:WTF?*
>
> *It's true. Don't talk to anyone. Lay low for a while, and I'll be in touch. Remember, I'm the kind of angel who gets shit done. And if anybody asks, you don't know me.*

I push Send before I can rethink it and close the browser. Delete my history. Like I do every single time. Not that it matters. Online footprints can't be erased. And mine lead to Ian. And Kate. The Shermans. Cleo too. And down a thousand other rabbit holes that make me look like a criminal. A murderer even.

Ricky thinks I killed them. And I'd let him think it. God knows I'd wished them dead, both of them, so many times. When I was fourteen, wishes like that had power. The last words I'd spoken to my father, for one. I hate you. I wish you'd just die. And then, he did.

I hear Luke before I see him shuffling down the hallway in my baby-blue bathrobe, eyes half-closed. "Ava? What the hell are you doing?"

"I couldn't sleep."

He runs a hand through his hair and frowns at me. "You should've woke me up."

"I tried."

"Oh. Sorry." He pulls a stool up next to mine and angles his head over my shoulder. I want to snap the laptop shut, but I don't. I'd only look guilty.

"What are you doing?" he asks, suddenly alert. And I wonder if it's all an act. Choir boy Luke with the mussed hair and the sleepy eyes.

"Looking at the news. It's everywhere, you know. Love Doctors is trending." I point to the headline on the screen—"Bloody Valentine"— and the picture of them, baring their matching perfect teeth at a BXA premiere. I'm drawn to Kate, like always. Her hair, blonde as a sunray, styled in a careful updo. Her glacier-blue eyes lined in black. Diamond chandeliers dangling from her ears. And the showpiece, the jewel in her crown: Ian's tuxedoed arm, tight around her shoulders. It's that arm I can't look away from.

"So, does this mean you want to talk now?" Or am I still only good for one thing? He doesn't say it, but I know he's thinking it. Resenting the way I'd dragged him straight to bed, ignoring all of his questions about Ian, about last night, tossing them aside with my clothing, his. Resenting the way he'd given in to me. It's there in the razor's edge in his voice. And I wonder, not for the first time, how I'd fallen for the one guy who wants his sex with strings attached.

"Not really." I spin on my stool to face him, pull at the tie of my robe cinched at his waist and tug it loose, half-smiling. "I can't take you seriously in this thing."

Stiff-jawed, he stands up and tightens the belt. The surest way to rock Luke's boat is to tease him. It's his little brother complex. And with a smug big brother like Cooper, he hadn't stood a chance. "I'm going back to bed."

Somehow, seeing him turn away from me is worse than talking. Worse than lying. "Wait."

"For what?"

"I'll talk. What do you want to know?"

He sighs, shakes his head. "The truth. I just want the truth."

"I already told you the truth. I haven't seen Ian since the summer. And you know where I was last night."

"Yeah, but I got here around 10:30. What about before? Before I came over." There it is. That look. My father's look. Spill it.

"The usual. I went for a run at Mission Trail. Stopped by Mom's on the way back. Showered. Read a little. Got Chinese delivered. And waited for you." Luckily, I'm not a little girl anymore.

"Are you sure that's all? It was your anniversary, right? Yours and Ian's? And the guy wrote your name in blood. I don't think I need to tell you what an officer of the law would call that."

"Do tell. What would you call it, officer?"

Luke cocks his head at me. Like he can spot my cover—fluent smart ass—a mile away. "Suspicious as hell. Maybe even a dying declaration. This is serious, Ava."

"I know that. Don't you think I know that? I can't explain what I don't understand myself. I answered your question. That's what I did last night, but you still—"

"Then why is there a receipt in the trash from a gas station in Monterey? With yesterday's date on it?"

Ian's words bubble up inside me. They spew out—"Are you fucking kidding me?"—just as foul as I remember them. "You went through my garbage?"

The phone rings. And for a moment, we're both paralyzed, Luke's face frozen in disappointment, mine in indignation. Like someone pressed the pause button. "Don't answer it," he says, three rings later. "It could be a reporter. It's only a matter of time before the media gets wind of you."

Too late. I've already lunged for it. Better me than him. Because who would be calling after midnight with something good to say?

"Hello?"

Above the static, someone breathes, and I watch Luke's face watching me. The worry there makes me sad, knowing I can only hurt him. That must be how Ian felt when he looked at me. His pitiful, stupid wife.

Luke grabs for the receiver, but I clutch it to my ear and step out of his reach. "Hang up," he says.

I want to, but the breathing holds me there, transfixed. Until a voice fills the void, the voice from yesterday morning. "I know what you did, Doctor Lawson. I know what you did."

"Who is this?"

Luke yanks the jack from the wall, and the phone goes dead.

"Wrong number," I say, shutting him up before he can ask.

CHAPTER SEVEN

IT makes you realize how precious life is, you know, Doc?"

I nod at David, my 9 a.m., but I feel half-asleep. Or half-awake in a never-ending bad dream. Not surprising since I'd tossed wide-eyed for hours listening to Luke snore, the ultimate not-so-silent treatment. After the telephone call, he'd retreated to the bedroom, too much of a choir boy to leave. Me, too proud to ask him to. But he's a choir boy who'd dug through my garbage. And I can't forget that.

It doesn't help that I can't get that caller out of my head. *I know what you did.* It could mean anything. A disgruntled patient. A prankster. A reporter just getting a rise. But to me, it can mean only one thing. *The* thing.

The thing Ian promised me no one would ever know. Another promise he couldn't keep.

David leans back against the sofa, resting his hands on his middle-aged belly. "One minute you're here. And the next—*bam!*" I flinch, his voice sharp as a starter's pistol. "You're lying in a pool of your own blood, deader than a goddamned doornail."

He's talking about his golf buddy, fifteen handicapper, and fellow member of the invitation-only Monterey Peninsula Country Club. Ian.

"So, how are you coping?" I ask. "I know you and Doctor . . . uh . . ." I pretend to forget the last name that had been mine for five years. After Ian proposed, I'd practiced writing it, exaggerating the half-moon of the *C*, relishing the bold loops of the *p*. All three of them. *My name.*

"Culpepper. Doctor Culpepper. You might've have seen him on that *Love Doctored* show. But he was just Pep to me." His shoulders droop. Mouth sags. "I don't know if it's normal. But I feel numb."

Better to be numb than raw. That's what I want to say. To not feel than to lose control entirely. But therapists aren't supposed to say things like that.

"Sudden tragedies like this are a shock to the system. It can be difficult for our brains to process. The way you feel is perfectly normal. But, your feelings may change over time. And that's normal too." Now *that* is therapist-speak. The perpetual reassurance of normality. "Did you see Ian recently?"

I ask the question as if I don't already know the answer. As if I hadn't watched him through the Nikon, arguing with Ian in a parking lot on Valentine's Day night. Truth, I'd been more interested in Kate. Ian had left her inside the restaurant, and I'd turned the lens to their window table, where she sat pecking away at her smartphone in an impeccable red dress. She'd lifted a finger to her cheek, wiped at something. A tear? An eyelash? I'll never know.

"Not since we played the course at Pebble last week." A smooth liar. I'll admit I'm impressed. Impressed and disturbed. But I can't see David wielding a knife. Underneath the cool guy get-up Tara lays out for him every morning—the Hugo Boss and Burberry and Panerai—he's still the geek who acquired his fortune selling SimuLife, a virtual reality video game company. Hardly a merciless assassin.

"Tara's totally lost it too. She just saw Kate a few nights ago at yoga. And get this—she thinks we should hire security. Crazy, right? Like I can afford that with Sophie's private school tuition and ballet lessons. As it is, I can barely swing the mortgage."

"Slow down, David. It sounds like you're feeling out of control, and I'm worried this kind of thinking could trigger a relapse."

He pulls a tissue from the obligatory box beside him—standard therapist issue—and wipes the sheen of sweat from his ever-expanding forehead. Give it a year, and he'll be nearly bald. Unless Tara has her way. "Hair plugs," he'd told me at our last session, rolling his eyes with contempt. "What's next, Doc—Viagra?"

"I can't afford a relapse. Literally. I'm broke."

"Any urges?"

He grunts. "Hell yes. I keep getting these text alerts with play vouchers from The Pearl. And I drove by Marina Club last Saturday. I told Tara I went to the gym. They've got that big poker tournament coming up with the one-hundred-thousand-dollar prize. It took everything in me to keep driving."

"Have you given any more thought to my suggestion about sharing your problems with your wife? I can help you do it. We can tell her here. Together."

"You know I can't do that."

"That sounds like a cognitive distortion. I think the word you're looking for is *won't*. I *won't* tell Tara, because . . ."

"I won't tell Tara, because she'd drop my ass faster than you can say jackpot. Look at me. I'm no prize. Before I met her, a big night out was Star Trek and Dungeons and Dragons. Hell, I wore Crocs to work. I can't even grow the balls to tell her—or anyone—that I'm seeing a shrink."

And thank God for that. He pays in cash. Two hundred dollars every week.

"It sounds as if you're afraid, David. You fear you're only worthy of your wife if you can maintain the illusion you've created—even if it kills you. But you refuse to give her a chance to prove otherwise. She might surprise you."

A short burst of something like laughter dies as soon as it leaves his mouth. "Trust me, Doc. If you saw my wife, you wouldn't say that." And he's right. Because I have seen her. Through the lens of the Nikon again, speed-walking with Kate down Cortez Road. Both of them swathed in Lululemon, their straight blonde ponytails ticking back and forth like the Newton's Cradle Ian had bought me for my first office.

"It must be hard to feel you have to be perfect to be loved."

He lowers his head, hangdog. "You have no idea."

I did, though. All those afternoons I'd snuck home after school, careful not to make a sound. *Your father's sleeping. Don't disturb him.* The smile I'd plastered on my face—big and toothy and fake as the Easter Bunny—thinking it might be contagious. That he'd actually be happy for once. To be that perfect required one thing. You had to swallow a shitload of rage.

"But is it sustainable?" I ask David, trying for the precise mix of provocation and empathy. "This life you've so carefully constructed." As tired as I am, I get it right. Because he takes a breath, looks up at me, and shakes his head.

"Of course not. It's a ticking time bomb."

****

Coffee—I need coffee. That's my first thought after David leaves. Because the way I'm slogging, I'll never figure it out. Someone knows. But who? And how? My mind is a complete blank, a hollow drum. But in my stomach, the Hydra is awake.

I trudge down the sidewalk, a light mist peppering my face, and duck into Seaside Sweets. Marianne emerges from the back, a tray of freshly iced cupcakes in her hand. She deposits them in the display case and smiles up at me.

"What a nice surprise. I wasn't sure if you'd be coming by this morning. Luke said you weren't feeling well yesterday." I search her face—*what else did he say?*—but come up empty.

"Probably too many of your doughnuts," I offer, returning her grin. "Your chocolates didn't help either. I've got your son to thank for that." And for the sleep deprivation. But I keep that to myself.

"So what can I get for you? No doughnuts, I presume."

Grimacing, I stick out my tongue at her, and she laughs. It's such a lovely sound I almost let down my guard, tell her everything. "Some of your strong coffee. ASAP. Unless you've got a caffeine drip I can hook up to."

"That bad, huh?" She pours a steaming cup and sets it on the counter in front of me. I wrap my hands around its warmth and imagine myself saying the words. *That too-good-looking Love Doctor was my ex-husband. He wrote my name in blood. We did something bad together, and now someone knows. But wait, there's more.* Instead, I put the cup to my lips and take a small, careful sip.

"Worse. I've got back-to-back retired CEOs till three."

"I don't know how you do it, Ava. All these rich folks griping and moaning would drive me straight up the wall. *Boohoo, my kids are so spoiled, and my conniving ex-wife got the beach house.* Cry me a river."

Marianne sounds like my mom. Back when my mom sounded coherent. Now she can't string a sentence together on her worst days, and those well-to-do clients she'd rolled her eyes at pay for her private room at the Cliffside Memory Care Facility.

"They're not all rich. I see a few clients on a sliding scale." Really just one. Cleo. And only because she seemed so desperate and familiar. So much like my younger self, I couldn't tell her no.

"I know. I'm just teasing." She gestures to the newspaper someone left behind. Another picture of Ian and Kate on the cover, folded in half so I only see Ian's Cheshire grin. "Rich folks have problems too. Problems that get them killed, apparently."

I take another sip of coffee. Swallow too fast, my throat burning. "Has Jack said anything?"

"Not much. He's been even more cagey than usual. But . . ." Her eyes flit to the door and back to me. The shop is empty, and the spitting rain threatens to keep it that way. Still, she lowers her voice. "He let something slip last night. Pillow talk, you know. Something about evidence of an affair."

I stare at my hands, still strangling the cup. "Really?"

"Isn't it scandalous?"

Ava. Ian had written it with his own hand. The way he'd penned me love letters in the beginning. *My darling Ava.* But this, a death note, inked in the life blood that ran out of him.

"Do they know who he was involved with?"

I wait for her to say it, for my name to drop from her lips like a bomb, exploding everything.

"That's just it. As far as they know, it wasn't him cheating. It was her."

I gape at Marianne, force down another scalding sip. Along with it, the questions I want to ask but shouldn't. She senses it though, mistakes my shock for morbid curiosity.

"I'm sure you can pick Jack's brain tonight at dinner. Maybe you'll get him talking. You're still coming, right?"

The prospect of sitting across the table from a decorated homicide detective isn't high on my list right now, but I've been doing the twice-monthly Donovan family dinners for a while—and if I back out now, Luke will only keep digging. And there are far worse things for him to unearth than a gas station receipt.

"I wouldn't miss it."

****

Ten minutes and counting till retired CEO number one, so I log in to my Avenging Angel account. Just to check. Because that's what you do when someone you blackmailed ends up dead. You check everything. Relentlessly.

One new message. I take another swig of coffee from the to-go cup Marianne insisted on. It soothes, but not entirely. Turns out Hydras can swim.

> *To: Avenging Angel <avengingangel@pacbell.com>*
> *From: Ricky Sherman <rsherm13@quickmail.net>*
> *Date: February 16, 2018 12:45 AM PST*
> *Subject: Re:WTF?*
>
> *What about the pics? I want to see them. I want the world to see them. There's nothing stopping us now.*

I picture the Ricky I know typing those words. But the truth is, I don't know him at all. He's a collection of pixels. A projection of the real Ricky. And for the first time, I feel afraid. Of what will happen. Of what's already happened. Of what I'd set in motion.

I compose a reply, hit Send.

> *To: Ricky Sherman <rsherm13@quickmail.net>*
> *From: Avenging Angel <avengingangel@pacbell.com>*
> *Date: February 16, 2018 2:53 AM PST*
> *Subject: Re:WTF?*
>
> *Think about what you're saying. Now is not the time.*

My cursor hovers over the little x in the corner, plotting my escape. Close your browser. Delete the account. But something keeps me holding on, holding my breath. And then, the pathetic little beep that zaps like a cattle prod. New mail. He's out there, right now, issuing his demands. Fueled by the insatiable hunger that is revenge.

To: Avenging Angel <avengingangel@pacbell.com>
From: Ricky Sherman <rsherm13@quickmail.net>
Date: February 16, 2018 2:54 AM PST
Subject: Re:WTF?

Now is the only time. We had a deal.

****

Luke is still mad at me. Because he doesn't kiss me at all. Not after I open my office door and let him inside. Not after he backs me up against the desk and undoes the buttons of my blouse. Drops his pants to his thighs. Not even when he moans my name against my neck, making me shiver.

And not after. When he rests his forehead on my shoulder, panting. "I have to get back to work."

Fine. Then I'm not over it either. He'd looked through my trash for God's sake, accused me of lying. Never mind that I had. "I know you do."

"Mom said you came by the shop this morning." I watch as he puts himself back together. Buttons done up again. Zippers zipped. Buckles re-buckled. It's the only part of Luke that's anything like Ian. The way he can compartmentalize, go from Romeo to no-nonsense cop in five seconds flat. I wonder how men do that. Flip themselves off and on like a switch.

"She told me Kate was having an affair. Is that true?"

Luke's eyes narrow. And I see fire there, hurt too. "Is that why you texted me to come over here?"

"You're the one who brought it up." He can't possibly understand what it's like to have a Kate. A younger, prettier version of yourself who'd detonated a bomb in the center of your life. Then floated above the rubble, a shimmering ghost, and took your place. Kate was supposed to be better than me. "I just didn't like how we left things. And we've got dinner tonight. I didn't want it to be weird."

"I know the last couple of days have been hard for you. But I don't like being lied to. Whatever it is, you can tell me. We can deal with it together."

If I could, I would spit out the truth like a bite from a poison apple. But it's too late for that. I'm too far gone. So I give him what I can. Who I can.

"I saw something," I whisper, disgusted at the sound of my barely there voice. The way it draws him in. "But I didn't want to say, because—"

The rest of it catches in my throat, and Luke is there in a heartbeat, pulling me to his chest. "Because?" He's so gentle it hurts.

"Because he's my patient. David Fairfax. I was on my way back from the trail. I'd just finished my run, like I told you. And I saw him arguing with Ian in the parking lot at La Noche. But you can't tell anybody I told you. It would—"

Luke holds a finger to my lips. "I won't."

And when he kisses me goodbye, he tastes sweet. Sweet and bitter.

****

"She's good today." That's what Head Nurse Patty Ellerby tells me as I head past the main desk and down the corridor to my mother's room at Cliffside. Meaning she may remember me. Honestly, it's easier when she doesn't.

I focus on the hollow click of my heels against the linoleum. *Don't make eye contact.* That's the trick to Wheelchair Row—the stretch of hallway where the worst patients sit, shuffling their feet, smacking their gums, reaching out their sticky hands like toddlers. One of them shrieks at me as I pass, the desperate keening of a banshee. I know what she's saying. She's cursing me for all the things I've done.

I deserve it. Because coming here gave me an excuse to drive by 151 Cortez Road, where the wrought-iron gate at the entrance had always drawn me in like a homing beacon. Ian thought cameras were too intrusive—we'd never had one at the rental in LA. So a few times I'd been bold enough to open their mailbox, stick my hand inside. Mostly, I'd just parked nearby, sunk low in my seat, and waited for Kate to return. By five o'clock, Madison would be finished with preschool and piano lessons, and Kate would cart her home, piloting the Land Rover like a battleship. I'd watch the gate open and wonder if she knew. That I'd been the reason Ian fell in love with Carmel. That I'd always told him I wanted a house here. That the life she'd claimed had been promised to me.

Today, I didn't stop. Didn't even slow down. But a part of me had relished the gaudy crime scene tape strung across the gate. My gate.

I keep walking, faster now, nearing the end of Wheelchair Row, and the woman howls again. See? That's what I mean. I deserve it.

Affixed on the wall outside my mother's door is the shadow box we created together during her first week here. Doctor's orders. *Choose pictures and mementos with emotional significance. Those that are easiest to recognize can aid in recall.* And so I had. Her and my father outside the Los Angeles Courthouse on their wedding day. Me, newly born and swaddled in a blanket on her chest. My father flanked by the mayor and the police chief, the LAPD Medal of Valor pinned to his chest. Who knew then that it was a death mark? There are other memories too, of course, the kind you don't photograph. The kind too ugly for a shadow box.

My mother sits on the bed, her back to the door. Though it's already dark outside, she's looking out the window. Her dull gray hair is braided and resting like a hanging rope between her thin shoulder blades.

"Hello?" Not *Mom.* Because despite the nurse's sunny forecast, I'm not completely sure yet how she'll be. And it's better not to assume. I'd made that mistake before—*I don't have a daughter!*—and I can't deal with the wounded animal inside her. Her confusion. Her anger. Her pitiful tears. Not today.

"Is that my girl?" The joy in her voice is childlike, and her muddy eyes light when they meet mine. "How was school today?"

I don't bother to correct her. "It was fine, Mom."

"C'mon, Ava Marie. You can do better than fine."

I sit on the bed next to her, and the mattress depresses slightly with my weight, my substance. Next to me, she's a shell. A hollow husk. An in-between person. And I feel a sudden sadness rise like bile in my throat. "Actually, I had a really bad day, Mom."

"Oh, honey." I lean into her, and she wraps an arm—brittle as a bird bone—around my shoulder. The way she tries to comfort me, even now, breaks my heart. Even when she's got nothing to give. I could never be that selfless. *Maybe you're not cut out to be a mom.* Hadn't Ian said that? Well, he'd been right. "Don't cry. You'll upset your father."

"Dad's not here right now," I say, stopping my tears anyway out of habit.

She turns to me, bright-eyed again, and points to the television. The muted picture hits me hard and deep like a knife to the gut. "Look. That show I like is on."

This she remembers.

I tap the button on the remote in her lap, and the music swells. Two figures walk hand in hand toward the camera, flashing their matching smiles. They wear starched white coats and an air of superiority. Even though they should know better. Neither is *that* kind of doctor.

"Welcome to *Love Doctored*," Ian says, in the voice I'd known so well. The voice that had promised to have and to hold, for better and for worse, as long as we both shall live. "Where love is always the best medicine."

I stare at the screen until their faces blur. "It's a rerun."

But she shushes me, transfixed.

****

Luke rubs my knee under the table and leaves his hand there, resting on my thigh. Like he knows it grounds me. And I need to be grounded, anchored to someone sturdy.

Because already I feel it. Even with Marianne's famous lasagna steaming on my plate, the cheese bubbling at the center, and the scent of garlic still wafting from the oven. Even with the warmth of this house that's become a comfort to me. Though I'd never admit to Luke how good it feels to belong, just for a while, to a family again. Even with Luke squeezing my leg, reminding me he's here, I can't shake it.

The death of the Love Doctors is spread like a pall, a shroud across the five of us. And despite the February gloom, there's a spotlight boring into me, bright as the sun. Sweat beads under my hair. And I glance toward the mantle in the living room, the wooden sign there: WE BLEED BLUE. I don't know why I thought I could do this.

Marianne and I exchange a tight smile. As if she's saying it's up to us. We're in this together. To lighten the mood. To be the normal ones. If she only knew.

"So, Ava," she begins, and my stomach flip-flops. "How were the retired CEOs? As dreadful as you feared?"

My laughter comes out tinny as a cymbal, prompting another squeeze from Luke. "They weren't so bad. Babes and boredom, the usual complaints." A laugh and a nod from Marianne, and I keep talking, afraid to stop now that I've started. Afraid of the silence and what will fill it. "You know Freud said love and work are the two things we all need to be happy. And having a lot of money, well, it can undermine both."

"Touché." Jack's voice catches me off guard, the steady baritone of it. The kind of voice that's accustomed to demanding answers. To getting them. "I'm no Freud, but thirty years in law enforcement, and the one thing I know for sure, money is the root of all evil."

"Actually, it's the *love* of money," I say, taking a sudden interest in my plate, stabbing the edge of the lasagna and forking off a bite. *Why am I correcting Jack?* "I mean, that's the line from the Bible. 'The love of money is the root of all kinds of evil.'"

I'm relieved when Luke chuckles. "Well, in that case, just give me the money. I promise not to love it."

"That sounds familiar," Cooper says, his dull voice hacking off the end of my laugh. It drops back in my throat, sticks there. "Isn't that what you said when you tried to convince Mom and Dad to put your ass through law school?" In the silence of his purposeful pause, I can almost hear Cooper's glee though his face looks ashen. "To work for the other side."

"Here we go," Luke mutters. And he's right. I've heard this act before. The one where Cooper reminds Jack he's the better son, because he'd never once considered any other fate—*God forbid!*—but cop-dom. And once Cooper gets rolling, he's a boulder down a hillside, impossible to stop.

But today is different. Marianne shakes her head at him, and he averts his eyes and cowers. Stuffs a hunk of garlic bread in his smart mouth.

I risk a sideways glance at Luke, but he's steady as ever. Though it must sting. Not Cooper's sarcasm—his skin is calloused against that—but Jack's tacit agreement. Luke had told me that back then his dad had said the only difference between a criminal defense attorney and a criminal was a suit. And as sick as I feel with my own sordid secrets, I can't keep my mouth shut.

"I'm sure Luke would have paid back every penny and then some," I say. "UC Berkeley Law is nothing to sniff at."

Jack snuffs anyway, a smug shot of air burst from his nostrils. Funny how a sound so small can resonate. "Luckily, he came to his senses."

At that, the room goes quiet, except for the occasional clink of silverware against Marianne's porcelain plates. The thud of a glass against the maplewood table Jack had carved himself. And the air grows so tense between us all it practically hums.

"You went to UC Berkeley—right, Ava?"

Innocent enough, but I know better than to trust Cooper's abrupt questions, the ones that come flying out of left field. Especially not now. Not today. Like the time he'd asked me why I moved back here. "Big city lost its charm?" Or the time he wondered how it felt to get paid to be someone's friend. Or just two weeks ago, when he laid me bare: "You ever tell Luke a patient's secret confessions? That'd be unethical, right?"

It's the first he's spoken to me since he took the seat directly across the table. Better him than Jack though. "Yes. That's where I earned my psychology degree."

"Summa cum laude," Luke adds, nudging me with his elbow.

"So you knew him then?"

"Who?" I stuff in another mountainous bite, gulp down a mouthful of wine. And the Hydra laps it up. All of it. Because I know *who*.

"Ian Culpepper. I read in the paper he taught there a while back. You have any classes with the guy?"

The only part of me that isn't numb is under Luke's gentle fingertips. "Oh. I think I might have. It was a long time ago."

Cooper doesn't answer, but he meets my eyes with his own, a dreary blue. Tired and red-rimmed. On any other night, I'd wonder if this was his payback for my defending Luke. Or if he knew even more. And how he planned to use it against me. But he looks—I try to find the word for it—the way I'd describe it in a patient. *Shell-shocked.*

"Are you okay?" I ask him, eager to deflect. Turn that spotlight onto somebody else. "Luke said you were first to arrive. That can't have been easy."

"I'll never forget my first one," Jack pipes up, shaking his head. "We found her down at Hidden Beach, laid out on the shore like a piece of trash. Turns out she'd had a fight with her boyfriend. She came out there for some peace and quiet, and she got herself raped and strangled by some drifter. You never forget your first one. No sir."

"Jack."

"Sorry, honey. But it's true. And if the boy's ever gonna make detective, he's got to get used to it."

The scrape of Cooper's chair on the hardwood makes a statement. It says what we both know. Already passed over three times, he'll never make detective. He stalks out of the dining room, and I hear the front door open and shut behind him.

Eyebrows raised, Marianne turns to her husband. "What are you thinking? Go after him."

"I'll go." And just like that, Luke pulls up his anchor and leaves me.

Abandoned, I resort to nervous chatter. "This isn't Cooper's first murder, right?" And immediately I wish for a take back. "What I mean is, he's been to other murder scenes before?"

"Of course," Jack says, with a sage nod. "We had that gas station robbery-gone-wrong a couple months ago. And the banker that offed his wife a few years back. But this was the first one that got to him. He doesn't usually get this worked up about a case. Though I don't blame him. The brutality of a stabbing, that'll shake anybody up. Takes a really rageful person to do something like that."

What can I say to that? What can anyone say?

Nothing, apparently. But the silence I'd feared is a welcome respite. I chew and swallow, chew and swallow. Until my glass is drained and my plate empty. Not because I'm hungry, but because it keeps my mouth busy. And shut.

"I shouldn't have used that canned tomato sauce." Marianne pushes her plate away. "It tastes a little funny. Don't you think? Like metal."

"It was delicious," I say. Because I'd scarfed it down so fast I barely noticed the taste at all. Just the red, red, red sauce, making me queasy. So I focus on the sound of Luke's voice, barely audible from the porch. I can't make out the words, only the tenor of it, calm as low tide.

"I usually make it myself, homemade. But I just didn't—"

"He was the one who found the little girl too." Jack stares ahead, talking to no one. And I'm glad he doesn't look at me, because I'm crawling out of my skin. "We'd searched everywhere. Called out for her. But Coop went right to that bookcase, that hidden closet. And there she was. Shivering like a lost puppy."

The door opens and shuts again, and I expel the breath I didn't know I'd been holding.

"Enough shop talk, Jack. Anybody save room for dessert? I made cobbler."

Cooper takes his seat across from me, pain wafting from him. As tangible as the cinnamon in Marianne's apple cobbler. And I hate myself for being such a coward. For postponing the inevitable. For lying to all of them. Maybe I should just blurt it out.

I married Ian Culpepper.

"Actually, I—"

But I feel Luke's hand from behind on my shoulder. Three solid squeezes. Our unspoken signal. I can't believe I almost said it.

"Actually, I have an early patient tomorrow. We should probably head out."

And I resist the urge to spring up from the table and run.

****

As soon as Luke pulls out of his parents' driveway, we both groan. I put my head in my hands. "I shouldn't have come. I'm so sorry. Now, I've outright lied to them."

"No, I'm sorry. I led you straight into the lion's den. Honestly, I didn't even think Dad would show. He never comes to dinner when he's working a case."

Another groan from me, more hopeless this time. "That makes me feel worse. He probably *was* working the case. A little unscripted interview with his prime suspect. Seriously, Luke, do you think he knows? I mean, my name *is* Ava. How many Avas could there possibly be in Carmel?"

Luke slows, guides the truck to the shoulder. Because that's the kind of man Luke is. Careful. "Don't freak out. I'm sure Culpepper knew a lot of Avas. And the thing is, the writing on the mirror, it's . . . messy." I try not to picture it. "I guess what I'm saying is, I only knew because I *know*. Really, it could say anything."

I am positive Luke is only saying the words he thinks will hold me together. But, still, I'm grateful.

"And you didn't lie. Dad will understand." *That's what you think.* "He's a private guy too."

"A lie of omission is still a lie. And what's with Cooper? Is he alright?"

Luke doesn't speak for so long, I touch his arm to make sure he's heard me.

"I don't know. It was pretty gruesome in that house. And he's like Dad. Keeps it all inside . . ." His voice fades, and he turns on the radio. Maybe he's done talking. "I told him he needs to see a shrink. That you could give him a referral."

I laugh in spite of the queasy churn in my stomach, guilt's many heads chattering about the lies I've told. To cover other lies. "I'm sure that went over well."

"Like a ton of bricks."

＊＊＊＊

The text comes before midnight. It's from Luke, and I delete it right away. Mostly because I can't stand to look at it. I'm not just Ava Lawson anymore. I'm the jaded ex-wife. The former Mrs. Culpepper. The one with her name inked in blood.

Dad got a message from Ian's attorney. He knows.

*Seducing a woman is a game of chess. You've got to think three moves
ahead.
You need a strategy. Or you'll lose every time.*
—Ian Culpepper, *Prescription for Love*

VALENTINE'S DAY
NINE YEARS EARLIER

IAN in her bed was still a marvel. Ian in her bathroom, shirtless and shaving over the sink. Ian in the kitchen, sipping coffee from her *Keep Talking, I'm Diagnosing You* mug. Ian pressed between her thighs, his hands guiding her hips. And most of all, Ian saying those words, the ones no man had said to her, not since her father.

"I love you, Aves." Now that was a marvel.

Ian pecked her forehead and slung the strap of his satchel over his shoulder. She knew he'd be late, but she latched onto his tie anyway, bringing his mouth to hers. Coffee and toothpaste and Frosted Flakes. He moaned a little and deepened the kiss. Nearly a year and he couldn't stop kissing her. For once, she'd done something right.

"Don't let him get away, Ava." That's what her mother had said after Ian charmed her at Christmas, making her forget Ian's age—a full twelve years older than her baby girl. *He's a keeper.* All Ava heard: "Don't screw this up."

"Are we still on for tonight?" she asked, checking her lipstick in the hallway mirror. Smoothing her blouse, ruffled by Ian's wandering hands.

"Pizza and beer? I wouldn't miss our anti-Valentine's for the world."

"And maybe . . ." She watched his face for signs of disapproval, but he turned toward the door, giving her the broad blankness of his back. "I can stay over at your place for a change."

He glanced back at her, and she felt relieved to see him smile. "You know I like it here. It makes me feel like a student again. My place is too big and stuffy."

She pushed out her lip in an exaggerated pout to hide her annoyance, her disappointment. With the way Ian could fill her up, then take a pin to her like nothing. Bursting her balloon.

"Maybe," he said, pausing for a moment. And just like that, she turned bright and buoyant and hopeful again. "And don't let that prick, Whitlock, get to you. Okay?"

She nodded, playing along as if she didn't notice he'd changed the subject. *Pop.*

****

Ava sat across from the prick himself, Dr. Chuck Whitlock, her clinical supervisor at New Beginnings Inc.

"So, Doctor Lawson, how are things?" He always began supervision with the same inane question. The same tug on his beard. The same infuriating smirk.

"Good. I think I'm making real progress with Ms. Williams. We've been discussing her history of sexual abuse and the way she masked her feelings of shame with methamphetamine. She read the Bradshaw book you recommended."

Dr. Whitlock looked impressed. With himself, no doubt. "I trust she found it useful. In my ten years of experience working with this population . . ."

Ava tuned out, letting her mind drift to the morning. To Ian. *Where else?* She'd driven by his house again on the way here, even though Claremont Avenue was ten minutes out of her way. A two-story, modern white stucco with a small patch of manicured grass in front. Ian had never told her his address, but she'd found it with ease. *Thank you, Google.*

"I'll give you a chance to look it over now, if you'd like." Dr. Whitlock waved a packet of papers in her face, oblivious to her mind-wandering.

"Uh, alright."

A quick look at the heading told her what she'd missed. And her stomach clenched. Six-Month Intern Performance Review. She flipped to the second page where Dr. Whitlock had rated her skills one to five and written a short appraisal of her work. Her eyes skimmed the ratings—all fives, all exemplary—and snagged on the lone three circled next to the word *professionalism.*

As she read on, Ava felt the flush creep up her neck until her cheeks burned. *Dr. Lawson left her internship early on a number of occasions without my permission and without notifying staff. An astute clinician with flashes of brilliance, her commitment to her coworkers and place of employment is simply average.*

She couldn't look at him, so she stared at his words instead. In her head, her father's hypocritical voice played like the soundtrack to a movie she wished she hadn't seen. *You can do better, Ava Marie. I didn't raise you to be mediocre. If you can't be the best, why bother?*

Dr. Whitlock cleared his throat. Still, she avoided his heavy brows, his owl-like eyes magnified behind his glasses. "Questions?"

"I only left because my work was done. I'd seen all my clients and finished my notes. I didn't think anyone would mind." Her voice broke at the end, and her father was right there. *Don't think those crocodile tears will get you out of this.*

"Overall, you've shown real promise as a therapist. The clients respond to you. That's half the battle. But, if I can be completely honest, you're not a team player. You're too insular. Too aloof. If you finish your work, there's plenty to be done around here. Plenty to learn. Remember that."

She forced her chin up, even though it trembled. And he regarded her the way she would a crying patient. Empathy from a distance.

What would it be like to say how she really felt? Not to fall on the grenade but to launch it instead. To watch somebody else burn.

But then, she remembered—*I hate you. I wish you'd just die*—she already had.

"I'm sorry, Doctor Whitlock. I'll do better."

****

"Fuck him." Ian took the last swig from his third bottle of Stella and signed the check. "Too aloof, my ass. That guy is threatened by you."

"Why would he be threatened by me? I'm an intern."

"Exactly. The best intern they've ever had. And smarter than he ever was or could hope to be." Ava followed when Ian stood, letting him slip his jacket over her shoulders. "Trust me. We were at Berkeley together. He was a prick then too."

She leaned into him, not drunk at all, but somehow tipsy with his words. The fierce way he defended her. It was intoxicating.

"And I can't stand that he made you cry."

"Not in front of him, but—"

"It doesn't matter. He's an asshole."

Outside the door of the Pepperoni Shack, he tugged her into the alley and pushed her against the wall. Before he kissed her, before she felt the press of his body against hers, the unyielding urgency of his desire. Before she realized that it was her, that *she* did that to him, he whispered, "I've got an idea."

****

Ian kept his hand on Ava's knee as she drove. Let it creep up her thigh, reminding her what he wanted. "Pull over here," he said, when they were close.

"He might not even be here. It's past nine."

"He will. That loser has no valentine, Valentine."

And Ian was right. Dr. Whitlock's gray Prius occupied its usual spot outside of the clinic. Ava had overheard him say that he'd planned to stay late, writing, to meet a last-minute deadline for a grant proposal.

"Are you sure about this? What if we get caught?" Ava's skin buzzed. Her body hummed. *My dad is watching*, she thought, as silly as it sounded.

"I won't let you get caught. Promise." He pulled a single key from the ring in his hand, keeping the rest for himself, and gave it to her. With a kiss that tasted like tomato sauce and garlic and beer and something faintly, deliciously Ian.

Hand in hand, they slunk down the sidewalk, giggling. Ducking behind bushes, skirting the shadows. Until finally, their keys were poised like weapons at the smooth side panel of the Prius.

"I can't do it," she admitted, slipping the key into the back pocket of her jeans. She couldn't decide what it meant. Coward or stalwart?

"It's okay. You be my lookout, and I'll be your avenging angel." Ian squeezed her hand and mouthed a question. "You with me?"

She didn't need to answer.

****

They made out in the backseat until they were breathless. "Where's the key I gave you?" Ian asked, his lips lingering on her collarbone.

"In my pocket."

"Good. Keep it. It's yours now."

She pulled away a little so she could look at him. Into his blue eyes that were more fire than ocean. "What does it open?"

"My front door."

And later, he led her up the stone walk, the one she'd studied from her car. Past the mailbox. To the stairs that wound around. To the door she'd longed to be on the other side of. He let her unlock it and go in ahead of him.

He flipped the light from behind her, and she caught her breath when she saw it spotlighted on the mantel. The massive, in-your-face wedding photo. Ian and Julie airbrushed to perfection, facing the camera, and lit from within by pure joy. Her tears came fast and hot—*why am I crying?*—and she felt like a child when he soothed her, hugged her from behind.

"That's why I didn't want you to come here." He breathed the words against her ear. "She's everywhere. I hope you don't think I'm a complete nutso. I've had a hard time moving on. Obviously."

Ava focused on Julie's face. She knew it by heart, of course. From the internet. From the *San Francisco Chronicle*'s obituary notice. From the photographs, exactly five of them, that she'd saved to her desktop. Still, seeing Julie here, in the place where she'd lived and loved and died, it overwhelmed her.

"But I want to, Ava. With you. Will you marry me?"

THE MONTEREY COUNTY COURIER

"NO NEW LEADS AS INVESTIGATION INTO BRUTAL SLAYING REACHES THIRD DAY"

by Jackson Lamont

The Carmel Police Department has reached out to the public for help in solving the Valentine's Day double homicide of Love Doctors Ian and Kate Culpepper. Police Chief Scott Morrow issued a statement Friday morning urging anyone with information regarding the crime to contact the Carmel Police Department. Information can be provided anonymously.

"We strongly believe someone saw something that night. Even a small detail could give us the break we need to find the person or persons responsible for the gruesome killing of this lovely couple." Kate Culpepper's family has also offered a $10,000 reward for information leading to the arrest and conviction of the perpetrator.

While investigators say they have not yet ruled out robbery as a motive for the murders, there were no obvious indications that anything of value was taken from the home. Still, some residents of the affluent community where the Culpeppers resided remain fearful the attack was financially motivated. "Kate was always so generous and kind," Tara Fairfax, a neighbor, said. "If someone showed up at the door asking for help, she wouldn't turn them away."

No suspects have been publicly identified, and police officials have been tight-lipped regarding the progress of their investigation. A vigil in memory of Ian Culpepper is scheduled for Friday night at 7 p.m. at the Monterey Community College's main campus, where he taught several classes.

CHAPTER EIGHT

FRIDAY
FEBRUARY 17, 2018

THE first time I met Detective Jack Donovan, I stole from him. My mother had just taken a job as a hostess at the Seventeenth Mile, an upscale restaurant located near the Pebble Beach Golf Course. We'd made the whole three-hundred-mile drive—LA to Carmel—in silence, with everything we owned stuffed into the back of our station wagon. Me, fuming. Her, resigned.

That's what happens when your husband offs himself with his service weapon. When your daughter finds the body. You accept whatever stones life throws at you—because what could be worse?—and the pissed-off glares of a surly teenager bounce off your armor like pebbles. You run like hell as far as you can.

Now, I understand my mother's desire to uproot. To flee. Hadn't I done the same after all, coming back here? The only trouble—I hadn't run far enough. But I was fifteen then. A sophomore at Carmel High. My mother was the enemy. And Detective Donovan and his badge were casualties in a war waged against her.

I'd seen its shiny pointed edges poking out of his jacket pocket in the coat room where I sat staring at the pages of my biology textbook and waiting for Mom's shift to end. I can't explain why I took it, only that it called to me. I needed to touch it. To feel its cold skin, smooth between my fingers. "My badge is a talisman," my dad had told me, before he fell apart. Before he had a reason to. "It can stop bad guys in their tracks. It can make wrong things right again."

So I'd slipped it into my pocket and waited to be caught. Which I was, of course. An hour or so later. I'd stood behind my mother, red-faced, while she'd done the one thing she'd sworn to me she never would. Told the detective—and his entire family—our whole sad story. I'd said nothing.

"Your daughter probably just wanted to feel close to her dad again," Jack had told my mother. "No harm in that."

Jack had patted my shoulder on the way out, absolving me, Marianne by his side. Only seven, Luke had hardly noticed, too busy mashing the buttons on his Game Boy. But Cooper was my age, and he had eyed me like a rattlesnake.

Still does. *Is.* Right now.

"Ava." And he says my name like he's scolding me. Like he knows I've done something bad again. Something far worse than pilfering that badge. Or wooing his baby brother. But at least he's got the fire back in his eyes. "Can I help you? Luke's not around."

"I know. I was hoping to talk to your dad. It's about the murders."

"So now you want to talk?" His nostrils flare as he sucks in a breath, grits his teeth. "Sounds like my brother's got a big goddamned mouth."

"What do you mean?" I'd planned for this. A lie without a plan is a rookie mistake. And Ian had taught me better than that. "Luke doesn't know I'm here. And hey, are you feeling better?"

"Save it, *Ava*." Now, it's a dirty word, a word I wrote in Ian's blood myself. "The detective will be out in a few minutes."

****

Cooper walks me to the interview room and leaves me there with nothing more than a curt nod. I take a seat at the table, choosing one of three nondescript chairs. I fold my hands in front of me and examine the cut on my finger. I'd removed the Band-Aid in the shower this morning, exposing the scab, brown as bread crust. *Nothing to hide here, Officer.*

I stare ahead at the blank white walls, the dull gray carpet. The whole room is a psychological exercise. Meant to suss out guilt. To draw it to the surface like the festering tip of a boil. I resist the pull of the two-way mirror, knowing Cooper's probably watching from the other side. Waiting for the boil to break, for guilt to seep onto my face and run down my neck in hot, red splotches. *Nothing to see here, Officer.*

Hours pass.

Well, not really, but it seems that way. Time, weighted like a corpse and sunk to the bottom of the ocean. I'm glad I wore my father's watch. Because I can look without being obvious. After twenty minutes, there's a *tap-tap* on the door—more pronouncement than permission—and a woman enters the room. Stocky, her face bare except for a shock of red lipstick and the obligatory worry lines that come standard with being a cop. She smiles at me as if we know each other. And I like her without wanting to, already knowing she'll use it against me.

"Good morning, Doctor Lawson. I'm Detective Lennox, but you can call me Doreen." She extends a strong hand with short, squat fingers. Her other hand—her left—sits atop her hip, ringless. Like mine. "Jack is finishing up some paperwork. He'll be joining us shortly."

Which means he's watching too. I casually side-eye the mirror so she knows I know. *Nothing gets past me, Officer.*

She selects the chair across from me and slides it alongside the table kitty-corner to my own. Closer. Better for sharing secrets. Especially the kind you have to whisper.

"You had something to tell us about the Culpepper murders?"

I nod, postponing the inevitable. Once I say it, once I tell them who I am, there's no taking it back. They already know and still the words are stuck. Lodged in my throat like a hunk of rancid meat. "I'm sorry I didn't come in sooner. I should have. But I needed to consult an attorney. Ian asked me to sign a nondisclosure agreement following our divorce, and I—"

"Your divorce? You and Doctor Culpepper were married?" She's good. Too good. I almost believe she didn't know.

"Unfortunately, yes. We were."

The door behind her opens, and the air shifts. I feel fifteen again, with that badge burning a hole in my pocket. "Hello, Ava."

"Hi, Jack. Detective Donovan, I mean." I shrug and smile up at him sweetly. "Sorry."

He drops a folder at the center of the table—bullseye—then drags the remaining chair into the corner, as far away as he can get. Leaning back, his long legs crossed at the ankles, he could be anywhere. As casual as a picnic. "It's alright. I've asked Doreen to take the lead this morning, given our preexisting personal relationship." Which is a nice way of saying I'm breaking bread with his family. Sleeping with his son.

"So your marriage was *unfortunate*?" Doreen doesn't miss a beat. But why would she? This whole dance between them is expertly choreographed. A real cha-cha-cha.

"It didn't start out that way. We were happy, once. After I finished my degree at Berkeley, we got married. We moved to LA, and I started a practice there. But when your husband knocks up a graduate student—his graduate student—happily ever after takes a real nosedive."

"Sounds like my ex. Chasing every skirt in a fifty-mile radius. They must've studied at the same school. You know, the one for shitty husbands." She laughs—a real laugh. That or she's even better than I thought. And I spot the lipstick, bright red, on her coffee-stained teeth. "You must've been real pissed about that. I tell ya, when I found out about Eddie, I wanted to put a bullet in the bastard myself."

I know where she's going, where she's leading me. And I play along. "Yeah, it was a difficult time. But we were divorced four years ago."

"And then you moved here? From LA?"

"I wanted to start over. And we'd always talked about coming back to Carmel. Ian loved it here. The small-town charm, the ocean, the golf. But I never imagined he'd follow me." *Hadn't I wanted him to? I'm not sure anymore.*

Jack makes a noise of disgust, mutters under his breath. "And with his pretty, young wife no less." It stings that I can't tell whether he's only pretending to be on my side. He's got those cop eyes—he's been at it longer than Luke—calm and all-knowing. They take me in, giving nothing back. Not so different than a therapist really.

"So why the nondisclosure thing?" Doreen asks, scrawling the letters *NDA* on her notepad. At the end, she adds a question mark, crooked as the road that got me here. "It's pretty uncommon, isn't it? He wasn't even a *Love Doctor* yet." There's an invisible eye roll there, a silent scoff. And I smile at her.

"Right. Well, Ian thought he was on the verge of making it big. When I found out about Kate, we were already in talks with BXA about the show. We'd filmed a pilot episode."

"We?"

This is the part I'd been waiting for. The part no one knows, not even Luke. And I realize I can't wait to say it. Finally. To hang it out in the air and let the stink off of it. "Ian and me. I was the original Mrs. Love Doctor. But as it turns out, the viewing public prefers to get their relationship advice from a blonde. With an ample chest."

It surprises me how much it hurts. Still. Some wounds never close because we refuse to let them. The hurt serves a purpose.

"You're kidding me."

"I wish I was. They had a focus group. I was out. And Kate was in. In the show. In my house. My bed. My whole life. Turns out Ian preferred blondes too. The NDA was a way to protect his image. How would it look if the Love Doctor himself couldn't keep it in his pants?"

Doreen reaches across the table and pats my hand, the way my mother would if she still remembered. "I certainly understand why you'd hate the guy." Meaning I've got motive.

"I don't hate him." It takes everything in me to say it. To force those words out. But it's true. I don't *just* hate him. It's more of a poison stew—envy, fear, bitterness, love, and loathing—and I drink it down even as it burns. "*Didn't*, I mean."

Jack sits up, squirms a little, and rests his elbows on his knees. "Sorry," he says. "I know I'm supposed to sit still and keep my trap shut, but I don't buy that. Hell, I hate the guy and I've never even met him." There's a quiet fierceness, a sheathed blade, behind his eyes, even as he chuckles. The same sort of subtlety he'd passed to Luke. But not to Cooper. Who's all razor-sharp edges right in your face.

I shrug at him. Give him the only answer I can. "In my line of work, love and hate are two sides of the same coin. And I'll be damned if I ever give him that much power again. So I'd say I've been mostly indifferent."

"You're a better person than I am, Ava, I'll tell ya that. If Marianne ever did me that way, I'd hate her with the fire of a thousand suns."

I laugh, but I don't relax. He's leading me too. Just like his partner. "Let's just say it took a lot of therapy to sound this blasé." And by therapy I mean vandalism, mischief, and blackmail. And karma. That too.

"Any violence in the marriage?" he asks.

Violence. A word that sounds like what it is—sharp and severing. It cut our marriage in two. But not the way they'd think. "Ian never hit me."

"What about his mental state? Did he ever threaten suicide? Or hurt himself?"

I can't tell them the truth. It would dangle like a loose thread, and they'd unravel it all. "Ian loved himself too much to do anything like that."

Their eyes meet for a moment, then flit back to me.

"Did Ian have any enemies?" Doreen asks, sliding the file folder toward her. It makes a delicate swish against the table, soft and sinister as a snake.

If not for that folder—menacing in its ordinariness—I'd laugh again. "You probably won't be surprised to hear Ian was a bit of a jackass. His students at Berkeley loved him. UCLA too. But his colleagues not so much. He could be abrasive. Demanding. Egotistical. But no one stands out. Not as a potential murderer."

"When was the last time you spoke to Ian?"

"Summer, I think. I ran into him outside my office. We said hello and went our separate ways. It was cordial."

"Really? In a small town like Carmel? I can't go to the post office without running into my ex. You sure you haven't seen him since then?"

"If I have, I don't remember." Best to hedge my bets.

"Lucky girl, then." Doreen says as she sets the folder on her lap. I eye it, nervous, already knowing it will bite. "Ever been to Ian's house?"

"I've driven past it a few times. It's quite a palace from what I remember." An answer that's not an answer. Not really.

"For a mansion like that, I'd reckon a girl could put up with almost anything." She winks at me, and I play along with an ironic smirk. "Now you know I have to ask where you were that night. The night of the fourteenth, Valentine's Day."

"Of course. I understand. I was at home. With Luke."

"All night?"

"Starting a little after ten, I think. Before that, I went for a run and stopped by Cliffside to see my mom. I ordered Chinese from Happy Dragon." Doreen scribbles Happy Dragon, then circles it, as if it's the smoking gun. "I kept the receipt."

A perfunctory nod from Doreen. Another step in the dance. She's just getting to the good part. The big finale. "I'd like you to take a look at something for me. We're having a hard time explaining it. Maybe you can help."

She sets the folder in front of me, the edge of a photograph peeking from its cover. It reminds me of a door. A door in a house. The house of my childhood. Left slightly ajar, dust motes dancing in a thin stream of summer twilight. And I'd called out to him—*Dad?*

"Open it," she says.

****

Two clients later and dead Ian is still all I see. He followed me on cold, stiff legs from the police station. But more than that, he's in the room with me. He's there with Verna, as she blathers on about the heart-shaped cake pans she ordered on sale from QVC. And with my eleven o'clock, Claus, who's mourning the loss of his beloved schnauzer.

I try not to look at him—dead Ian—but he's in the corner of my office, slumped over the side of a claw-footed tub. The old-fashioned kind I'd always told him I wanted. His skin is all wrong. Pale and waxy and starting to loosen. And the rug beneath him is saturated with blood. It's wet. You can tell just by looking.

"What does that say?" Detective Lennox had asked me, pointing me to the mirror in the photograph. Oversized, ornate, and completely unnecessary—just the sort of thing Ian would buy—it towers behind the tub, even now, even here, reflecting the top of his head. His chin drooping lifeless against his chest.

"It—it looks like . . . well, it could be my name. Ava."

Luke hadn't lied. The letters are rust-colored smears, dripping and streaky. Dead Ian's fingers are wet too. The rigid tips of them just visible in the mirror. *He wrote my name.* The last thing he did. And I worry what it says about me that I like that.

"We think so too. Any clue how it got there?" I could have sworn her voice echoed against the stone tile beneath Ian's bare feet. As if we'd been standing in the middle of the crime scene all along.

I hadn't trusted myself to speak so I shook my head, though it seemed not to belong to me, the way it wobbled on the stem of my neck like a cattail in the wind. I shook it at Jack too when he'd asked if I needed a ride to my office. And now, I shake my head at dead Ian. He's eyeing me in that ridiculous mirror. And he wants me to feel sorry for him.

"So we can't reschedule next week's session?" Claus asks, his face scrunched in a kind of wary confusion. I think how I must look to him. Unhinged. A therapist gone wild.

"I'm sorry. I must've misheard you. Of course we can. When would you like to come in?"

****

Dead Ian trails me home like a zombie. And I thank God I didn't walk to the office today. Pedal to the floorboard, I tear down Ocean Avenue like a bat out of hell. Too bad he's still there, staggering behind the car, tracking red footprints. And pointing that blood-stained finger right at me.

Better him than Kate, though. Because when I think of her—of the other photo Detective Lennox had shown me—it's more than I can bear. The Hydra feeds on my shame, and I can't get home fast enough. I rush inside and drop to my knees at the toilet. An altar of sorts, I offer up what remains of lunch and sit cross-legged on the cool tile, praying it's enough for absolution.

"Kate put up one heck of a fight," Detective Lennox had said, tapping the edge of the second photo with her bitten-down nails. She expected me to look, so I had. At Kate lying on her side on the floor near the bed, still wearing the red dress she'd had on at dinner. One arm stretched outward. The other pinned awkwardly beneath her. The arm I could see was crisscrossed with cuts, a deep gash in the palm. Defense wounds, Detective Lennox had called them. As if a delicate hand like Kate's could defend against anything, much less a knife. Broken near her feet, the remains of one of two matching bedside lamps. A wicked trail of blood, heavy at first, meandered between her body and the bathroom. And beyond, extending to the threshold of the door.

Looking at her too long had hurt, like staring into the sun. So I'd set my eyes adrift, scanning the bedroom that should've been mine while the detective went on sticking her pins at random, casting a particular kind of voodoo. The law enforcement kind.

"Were you having an affair with your ex-husband, Doctor Lawson?"

Before my incredulous no, a laugh had spurted out, sharp and sour, as I'd spotted an overnight bag crouching at the center of their bed—the marital bed—like a toad. It bore Kate's initials. *K.A.C.* And her clothes spewed from its mouth, littering the stark white comforter.

I'd noted the T-shirts, the designer jeans, the matching lingerie, all the while wondering why Detective Lennox would call it an affair when I'd had him first.

"We believe Kate was killed first, before Ian. He might've been drunk or . . ." On the corner of the oversized dresser, a bottle of Far Niente Cabernet—Ian's favorite—and a half-empty glass. Just one. Because Kate hadn't been drinking. But I'd kept that to myself. It would've come with a question I wasn't prepared to answer: *How do you know?*

"Did your ex-husband ever abuse illegal drugs or prescription medication?"

I shrugged and shook my head, noncommittal, ignoring the furious churning in my gut. Stamping out the sparks of memory that had threatened to catch like a wildfire.

"And the show? The suicide? The lawsuit against the network? Did Ian ever mention any of that to you?"

Another shake of my head. *Had I lost my voice entirely?*

"So, help us out then. If you had to venture a guess, what do you think happened here?" And she'd pointed at Kate again, at the blinding, white-hot center of the sun. An impossibly long gash that stretched across her neck and splayed open to the core of her. Unreal in its utter finality. Not so different than the bullet hole in my father's head.

When I'd finally found it, my voice sounded stronger than I felt. Forged in fire and all the years of pretending not to feel anything at all. "I want to help. I wish I knew something. But I don't. I'm sorry."

I pushed the photos back to her, desperate to be rid of them. Ian first, then Kate. But Detective Lennox had left them there—testing me, taunting me—until Jack returned with a camera and a cotton swab and a pitying half-smile. He photographed my hands, collected my DNA, took my prints. I walked out the door, measured and steady, like an innocent woman. Which I was once, I suppose. But I wanted to run.

I did nothing wrong. I stand up and find my reflection in the mirror. The doubt there. I flip open the medicine cabinet and find the bottle of Xanax Ian had prescribed to me just before our divorce. "To take the edge off," he'd said. Like it was my problem to fix. And a pill could fix it.

I shake the bottle, rattling the little white bars meant to dull the blade, to file the sharp teeth of agitation. *Fuck you, Ian.* That's what I think as I dump it, bombs away, into the toilet and flush. The pills and my vomit swirling down toward a quiet oblivion.

I couldn't tell Detective Lennox what I really thought had happened, so I say it now to myself. Like a mantra. Like a prayer. Like a curse. *You reap what you sow. You reap what you sow.*

CHAPTER NINE

I make my way to the center of the crowd, cupping my hand around the flame of a thin, white candle. It flickers, curls, stretches in the wind. Nearly snuffs out. Cold and vicious, the sudden gusts lash my hair across my face like a whip. *Punishment for coming here.* I'm sure of it. Because this is a crime against nature. Practically sacrilegious. Still, here I am, smack-dab in the middle of Ian's vigil, wedged between rows of weepy mourners. Most of them students clad in their MCC sweatshirts and flip-flops. There are cops too, at the periphery. But what have I got to hide?

I hold my candle like an acolyte. Paying homage to a photo—a headshot, enlarged to ghastly proportions—and a smattering of dying flowers, hand-scrawled cards, and stuffed things.

"Did you know him?" a young man asks me, leaning so close I see the raw scrape of his razor burn, the eruption of acne on his cheeks. I smell the oniony bite of his breath.

I resist the urge to recoil. To run, even. I don't belong here. "A little."

"Lucky. I tried to get into his weekend lecture for the spring semester. But, of course, it was full."

I shrug and say nothing. Pretend I hadn't scoured the online MCC course catalog, reciting the names of Ian's classes as if they were precious to me somehow. Like the names of our children, never to be born.

Introduction to Psychopharmacology—M/W/F 8–10 Gleeson Hall

The Science of Love: A Total Eclipse of the Brain—Sat/Sun 10–3 (April) Lawrence Research Center

Psychopharmacological Treatment of Major Mental Disorders—Tu/Th 11–1 Gleeson Hall

"Science of Love," he says, wistfully. "A total eclipse of the brain. That's what the class was called. Cool, huh?"

I stare straight ahead, worried he might read my eyes. See the contempt there. The bitterness. Though I suppose I'd won in a way. Ian had ended up teaching here—community college—after the *Love Doctored* scandal. And that must've galled him. To be relegated to this bastion of mediocrity. "Clever."

"Isn't it, though? I hear he was an amazing teacher. Funny and charismatic and . . . well, he obviously knows his stuff. *Knew* his stuff, I mean."

"Obviously." I shuffle to my right, searching for an escape route, but I bump against a solid shoulder, mumble an apology. A chain of backs in front of me, jack-o'-lantern faces behind, I'm boxed in now. By hundreds of thin, white candles, just like mine, casting half-moons of shadow and light.

"Not like these other MCC hacks. We were lucky to have him here." Onion Breath leans in again. "Did you ever get a chance to hear him lecture?" The thought of it, the memory—Ian with chalk on his fingers, my fingers, my face—is a touchstone. The vigorous rub of an old scar.

"A while ago." Mercifully, a man ascends the stage, walks to the podium, taps the mic. The throb of it beats in my chest, reverberating like a drum. "A lifetime really," I add. Though it feels like yesterday. The smells of Tolman Hall, Room 25. The coffee. Ian's sandalwood aftershave. "Good morning, future drug pushers," he'd teased that first day, grinning. "Welcome to Psychopharmacology." And I'd thought he was clever too then—so clever and so funny. So handsome when he winked at me. Even if his words had rankled me.

"What do you think happened to him?" Onion Breath's exaggerated whisper seems to rise above the din of the crowd. And in front of us, two heads turn to look. My face gets hot, even as the cold wind thrashes against it.

"Probably a murder-suicide. That would be typical." The voice comes from a girl with a long sheet of black hair and red-framed glasses. Quirky, I'd call her. "I'm sure he got caught screwing the babysitter or his assistant or—"

"But the cops said they'd both been stabbed," Onion Breath counters. "That's a tough way to off yourself. And surely, they'd be able to tell if it was self-inflicted. Have you ever watched *CSI?*"

"Whatever. The guy was brilliant, I'll give you that. But he's still a guy. A husband. And it's always the husband. Am I right?" The girl snickers. The question is mine to answer, but my mouth hangs open. Nothing comes out.

"Best not to speculate, I'd say. Leave the theorizing to the police." Rescued by the stranger on my right, the shoulder I'd bumped a moment ago. Kind eyes meet mine, and he puts a finger to his lips, points to the stage. Onion Breath and Quirky go silent, reverent, as MCC's Dean Gotleib addresses the crowd, extolling Ian's many virtues.

"I first met the Culpeppers two years ago when my wife and I had the privilege of attending one of their sold-out lectures on love. That day, I believe Ian and Kate saved my marriage. So when Ian asked to teach a few classes at MCC, I was floored and beyond thrilled. As many of you know, he was larger than life. He had a way of making you feel like you were in the presence of a . . ."

In another life, I yell out *fraud*. Or *narcissist*. *Asshole*. Any number of expletives really. But in this one, I simply grit my teeth and mouth a *thanks* to the man next to me before I implode. He smiles and extends his hand. The other grips the neck of the candle, holding firm, just below the small circle of paper meant to catch the melting wax. As if we'd be here all night, wide-eyed. Devout followers of the cult of Ian. "Dan Jarvis, Psychology Department."

"Jennifer Davis." The name slips from my tongue as effortlessly as my own. It's *his* name that sticks. I know it. And I can't resist. "I think my friend is doing an independent study with you. Cleo Campbell?" The lines in his forehead deepen, furrows etched in sun-spotted earth. And Gotleib drones on in the silence between us. Until I can't stand it. "Do you know her?"

"Cleo, you said?"

I nod, impatient.

"Are you sure it's *Cleo*?"

It's almost obscene, the wet click of his tongue as he invokes her name again and again. But it's me who feels spotlighted, called out, as if I'd been caught passing a dirty note in his class. "I'm sure. She's working on her thesis. The father–daughter dyad and its impact on..."

I stop talking. His face is a blank. "Nope. Not one of mine."

"Tall redhead. Bikes to class." *Screws her professors. Or just one really*. I feel desperate. Confused. Like I've wandered into a dream. But I'm not wrong. Cleo had said it herself, so many times. *Doctor Jarvis says it's smart to pick a topic from my own life. Doctor Jarvis says I write like a graduate student. Doctor Jarvis says I have potential.*

"Doesn't ring a bell. And truth be told, I took a leave of absence last semester." His eyes shift back to the podium, to the oversized Ian and his stark blue eyes, bearing down on us all. Jarvis sighs, so long and so deep, I watch his candle in fear it might burn out. And the therapist in me senses an opening, a soft spot to probe with careful precision. A scalpel rather than an axe.

"Did you know him well?"

"I'd been helping Kate with some edits on the new book. She was a talented writer. Ian was lucky to have her. I'm not sure he knew how lucky he was."

I'm embarrassed to admit how much it pains me to hear that. How I wish he'd said anything else. So I spit out the first question that comes to mind.

"Did she ever mention a Cleo?"

He blinks at me strangely and steps away. As if whatever I am is contagious. "I'm sorry. I already told you. I don't have any students by that name."

Panicked, I turn away from him and back to Gotleib. Towering above the podium, the cave of his mouth is open wide, words wheeling like bats from the dark heart of it. But I can't hear what he's saying. It's all static, white noise. All but this. *Cleo.*

****

I can't leave. Not yet. I stand at the edge of the dwindling crowd, still holding my candle and scanning what remains. The empty quad, the trampled grass, the litter. A sign discarded on the ground and marked by a muddy footprint. WE LOVE THE LOVE DOCTORS. RIP. The aftermath of a vigil, it turns out, isn't so different from a concert or a football game.

And my eyes keep playing tricks on me. It's Cleo, arm in arm with Onion Breath, whispering in his ear. Cleo, sword fighting with her candle. Cleo, scurrying away from me, vanishing into the woods like a fox with a rabbit in her mouth. Or worse, she's watching me. And laughing. I feel unsettled—a subtle shift in the earth beneath me, a fault line threatening to quake—so I wait.

I observe.

I analyze.

THE FIRST CUT

Dean Gotleib blows his nose into a handkerchief and pushes a thin wisp of hair over his bald spot. His pants are tight at his waist, straining to hold him. If he sat on my therapy couch, he would confess he's clinging to middle age. Afraid he's well past his prime. *I'm not the man I used to be*, he would say.

His wife is smiling at him, but I don't believe her. There's anger there, veiled beneath, in the toothless stretch of her lips. She would sneer when she'd tell me, *The Love Doctors didn't save our marriage. I just gave in. Gave up. Decided to stay.*

A few students gather at the base of the podium, the impromptu memorial. A girl places a teddy bear at the edge of the pile. Then she aims the lens of her smartphone at herself and fires. A vigil selfie.

I breathe in, breathe out.

And find the face I've been avoiding.

Sheila Pope. Kate's mother and her carbon copy with her dancer's body and golden hair. Orange County resident, widow, retired real estate agent, active member of the Turning Pages Book Club. *I know her.* Or at least that's how it feels when you look at someone long enough, when you type her name into Google, when you scroll through her Facebook photos, squinting your eyes so you don't miss it. *It.* Whatever it is that made her daughter good for Ian. Better than you.

Ian wrote my name, I want to tell her. Mine. *Not your precious Kate's.* But it doesn't matter, because I don't know why he did it. Or if he did. And because they're both dead now anyway. There's no prize left to win. If Ian could even be called that, there's no one to watch me win it.

Sheila moves like Kate. Graceful and reserved. Like she's holding something back. A delicate part of herself, a breakable part. She follows Dean Gotleib and his wife from the stage. They walk toward me and my candle, with its meager flame rounding to the shape of a teardrop.

Our eyes meet. Hers, flat and worn, like pebbles at the bottom of a dry creek bed. Mine, no less so. Grief wears you away. Not all at once. But eventually. Cruelly and completely. But to grieve a violent death is worse. It's an amputation. An axe to your soul.

91

I wait for her to speak. To tell me we're kindred spirits, both left behind. Or to curse me. To recognize me, at the very least. To have looked me up, studied me, the way I'd studied her. But I'm nobody to her. Nobody to Kate either. A stand-in wife. An extra on the set. Just filling in until the real talent showed up.

With a single puff, I blow out the candle and drop it into a waste bin.

Kate's mother strides past, oblivious, Gotleib and his wife right behind her.

I follow.

****

The parking lot is nearly empty. Just a few cars and even fewer people. Most are heads down and rushing away to their safe, warm homes. Where murder is spoken about in hushed tones, then forgotten. Where dead professors are dinner conversation but nothing more. There's an uneasy stillness in the air. Like the whole world, or at least the entire MCC campus, is holding its breath. And waiting. Waiting.

I watch nearby from my car, the window cracked, while Dean Gotleib folds his arms around Kate's mother, strangling her in an awkward embrace. Like a child with a cat.

Sheila purses her lips and smooths the black fabric of her dress. She's like Kate that way too. Dignified. "Thank you for honoring my daughter and son-in-law. It was lovely."

"Of course. My pleasure—uh, I mean I'm glad to do it. We were quite fond of them both. And Ian told me how close you all were. Well, with his parents being gone, he looked to you as a mother. His mother."

I imagine punching Gotleib in the throat. The satisfaction of listening to him gag while I force-feed him a mouthful of truth. Ian had said almost the same to me about my mother.

"How is Madison?"

Sheila tenses, and so do I, gripping the steering wheel till my knuckles whiten. She shakes her head at Gotleib's wife. "Not good.

She hasn't uttered a single word since the police found her. Not even to the child psychologist we saw yesterday."

Both Gotleibs gasp. Later, this might be pillow talk, a way to ease the tension between them. Other people's problems are the best therapy. My line, not Ian's.

Gotleib's wife speaks first. "I thought Maddie didn't see anything. That they found her downstairs, hiding."

"We don't know. We just don't know. The detectives scheduled us another appointment with the doctor on Monday. He said severe trauma can cause this sort of thing. That she won't talk until she feels safe. It's called selective mutism."

Selective mutism. I feel featherlight and cold. So cold. My throat closes like a flower in the darkness—the way it had the moment I'd found my father with his head halfway there, halfway gone. I'd heard the therapist tell my mother my silence was about control. What the hell did he know about all the ways the brain can betray you? The rush of cortisol, the shrinking hippocampus, the fierce little amygdala overriding protocol like a crazed pilot at the helm. In that three months of near silence, speaking to no one but my mother, I'd never felt more out of control.

And Maddie is just a girl. A talker, like her dad. She'd spoken to me before when I'd been a complete stranger, but I push the memory away before it takes hold. Before it makes me feel worse than I already do. "Kate put up one heck of a fight." That's what Detective Lennox had said. A death like that doesn't come quietly. Maddie must've heard something. Seen something.

The thought sickens me. I have to get out of here. I shut the window, start the car. The Gotleibs' mouths contort into predictable shapes—grimaces and downturned lines—as Sheila holds up her hand to say goodbye.

I swallow hard, my tongue thick and heavy and dead. Just a slab of meat. I say my name out loud to prove to myself I still can. The sound of my voice, shaky as it is, comes as a relief. And a reckoning. I'm not fourteen anymore.

CHAPTER TEN

I'M still thinking about Maddie when I pull into the drive. Where she's staying. Who's taking care of her. When she'll find her voice again like I did, and what she'll say when she does. The questions spring up like weeds, invasive and unwanted, trapping me in the tomb of the car. And the memory comes again, insistent.

"Why are you taking my picture?" Maddie had asked me, with the unguarded innocence only a child could pull off. I'd stared at her blank-faced, the unsayable truth corroding my insides. That I'd wanted to see her with Ian, to capture him laughing as he'd caught her at the bottom of the slide. That she should've been my daughter. *Our daughter.* Mine and Ian's. But she'd already darted from the fence, back to the playground, and I'd hurried away before Ian spotted me, feeling admonished. And creepy as hell.

"I am creepy," I mutter. That's what the cops will think if they ever find the photos. Any of them. That's the least of what they'll think.

I push the car door open, desperate to breathe in the cold night air, to free myself from the tangle of the past. But as I head up the path to the house, I realize I'll never be free. The past isn't a dream. It's a real thing, a solid thing, an unfixable thing. It's the ramshackle foundation I built my very self on. No wonder I'm such a mess.

And then I see him, standing in the glow of the porchlight.

I have to look again.

And once more to be sure. His face is darkened with stubble, and he's buzzed the scruffy copper hair from his head. He's gained weight too. Looking more ex-con than accountant. Not exactly the man from the photographs, but close enough. *Ricky Sherman.* And the certainty pinches my lungs shut. Because he doesn't belong here.

He hasn't spoken yet, but my cheeks already burn hot. I want to run from him. This man I've never met, not face-to-face, but feel I know somehow. At least the dark, vengeful heart of him. It's not so different than my own. And running would only make me look guilty.

"Can I help you?" I ask, gripping the house key like a blade in my hand.

He barks a bitter laugh from the hollow of his throat. And with the night sky cloaking the empty street, the sound is practically sinister. The cackle of a madman. "You're her, aren't you? The Avenging Angel?" The vowels of his words are soft and wet, soaked in alcohol. And he sways slightly as he speaks.

"I'm sorry. I don't know what you're talking about. My name is—"

"Ava Lawson. I know who you are." I wonder how long he's been waiting to say that, how long he's known. "We had an agreement, remember? You were supposed to get the money from Ian. You were supposed to give me half."

I shake my head at him. "A deal? I've never seen you before in my life."

"Fine. If that's how you want to play it." He leans back against my front door—a thick wall of a man—and fixes his bloodshot eyes on mine. I can't believe how stupid I've been. "But I doubt the police will buy your Little Miss Innocent routine. See there's this thing called an IP address. And this one traces back to you. So why don't we just cut the bullshit and talk about what we both want?"

"What I want is for you to leave. I told you I don't know who you are, and you're making me uncomfortable."

"Just give me my half of the money or release the goddamned pictures. I thought you hated the bastard as much as I do. I saw you at the vigil. You heard the way they talked about him. Like he was a goddamned saint. Meanwhile, it's my wife, me, and my family who get dragged through the mud. And now they're saying I had something to do with his murder. Hell, for all I know, you did it."

"Go," I tell him, with as much conviction as I can muster.

"I'm staying at the Bay View in town. When you change your mind."

"*Now.*"

He steps away from the door and stumbles toward me, bumping my shoulder with his. His breath is warm and sour. "You said you'd make it right. That you'd make him pay."

"He's dead." Ricky is halfway down the walk, when I hiss the words through clenched teeth. Silently, I add, *What more do you want?*

"Yes, he is." He spins, levels me with bloodshot eyes. "And thank God for that."

****

I hurry inside and lock the door behind me, collapsing against it. My chest aches, and my legs are heavy. Like I've run a hundred miles to get here. I leave the lights off and watch through the blinds as Ricky shuffles down the street. I see him go—where to I can't tell—but the smell of beer and sweat lingers, an acrid perfume.

He looks back once. I can't see his eyes, but I feel them. The intensity of his stare, the vicious undertow of his wants. Because the things he wants are things I've wanted too. And I feel sorry for him.

It's not a far walk to here from town. He'll be back. And I know what I have to do. It's what I should've done from the start. Or in the middle. Or even at the end, when Ian and Kate turned up dead. Better late than never.

I need to destroy the photos. But first . . .

Heart beating fast, I head for the bedroom. There's no denying I'm my father's daughter when I drop to my knees at the bedside and slide out the lockbox where I keep the gun. My gun. I don't like to look at it—its cold body, its long black neck, its single, disinterested eye—but I've learned to do it anyway. To do what must be done. To wall off some soft, vital part of me when I hold it in my hand. This thing that's taken so much from me. And in that too, I'm a cop's kid. After all, my Dad had taught me to shoot. To aim for the center mass of a paper bad guy.

After we'd moved here, I forced Mom—under the threat of mutiny—to take me to the local range every Saturday. Until I got so good, I blew away the X. So good, I made Cooper jealous. So good, the range master asked me to help him teach the other kids. But what would I tell them? That I pictured my father's face? Because he'd decided something for me, something irrevocable. And I couldn't forgive him that.

I slip the gun into the front of the concealed-carry leather handbag Luke gave me for Christmas. I'm a cop's girlfriend too, then, I suppose. *There, Luke. I admit it.*

For a moment, I want to call him just to hear his steady voice. But I know he wouldn't leave it at that. He's already texted four times since this morning. Four texts I've ignored. There's no summoning Luke without getting Officer Donovan too. And him I can do without. Because Officer Donovan would not approve of what I'm about to do.

****

There are no other cars on Ocean Avenue. It stretches, gray and lonely, as far as I can see in the glow of my headlights. I park around the corner from my office, in case Ricky followed me here. Before I force myself out into the cold, I scan the tree-lined street. But even the shadows are still.

Be quick, Ava. Quick but careful. My father's coaching me, so I jog up the stairs two at a time and fit the key into the lock. Smooth as an officer of the law. Or a cat burglar. Both. The door creaks open, and a chill goes through me.

"Bad guys like the quiet," Dad always said. And I couldn't be sure if that had been before or after he'd become one. "So good guys have to learn to like it too."

Then, it had seemed so clear, that hard, dark line between good and bad. If only I knew which I was now. Which my dad had been.

I crouch at my desk, open the drawer, and take out the false bottom. I reach inside for the envelope and hold it in my hand, feeling a sudden wave of relief. I can still make this right. I can still be a good guy. Or at least not as bad as I have been.

But then, my neck prickles. The envelope is featherlight.

I pull back the flap.

Turn it upside down.

Shake it. Claw at it, with a visceral kind of fear. The kind of fear that speaks to me like an old friend. *Hello again*, it says, hissing into my ear, whispering through my veins. *It's been a while.* And I bite my cheek to keep from screaming.

The envelope is empty.

Panicked, I turn on the study lamp and lean over the drawer, feeling sick.

The memory card is gone. But there's something else here. Something new. Set beside the ring box.

A brown paper bag, the dreary kind you'd get from the mini-mart or the liquor store. The kind a dutiful mother would pack for a school lunch. Ordinary. But remarkable too, this bag. Because it has a smell that takes me somewhere. Back to that summer evening. To my father dead on the hardwood, his Glock indifferent at his side. To the horror of my own silent scream. To the smell of his blood—raw and sweet and festering.

And without thinking, I reach for the bag and look inside.

I make no sound as it falls from my shaking hands.

****

Footsteps.

How long have I been here? The soft thuds blare like a siren through the white noise in my head.

It's Ricky. It must be. He found me at home. Surely, he could find me here. But the measured steps don't sound like those of a drunk man. Or even an angry one. The pace is too calculated, too expert. Too sly.

Then, I think of the voice on the phone, the steady timbre of those veiled threats. I know what you did, Doctor Lawson. I know what you did. But it's not him—whoever he is—I picture climbing the stairs, steady as a ticking clock. It's another man, from a lifetime ago, long dead now. A man who'd reminded me of my father, which made what we'd done even worse. Unforgivable. And now, he's a ghost come to collect the debt I owe. With Ian gone, it's mine alone to pay.

I push the drawer shut—*quiet!*—and reach for my gun. There's nowhere to hide, so I scurry behind the open door and wait.

The footfalls grow louder. Until whoever it is—man or ghost or something in between—is standing in my doorway.

I hear his breath like a stirring of the wind off the ocean. In my hand, the gun trembles.

"Carmel Police. Show yourself."

"Luke?" I slip the gun under my sweater and step out into the dimly lit room feeling like a criminal. But worse. Because it's Luke I have to lie to. Again.

"Jesus Christ, Ava. What the hell are you doing here?"

My eyes flit to the desk drawer and down to my feet. I half-expect it to be open again, gaping like the star-shaped hole in my father's head, the gash in Kate's neck. But it's closed. Watchful.

I rush to gather my bag, straighten the papers on my desk. Shut the lamp. Anything not to look at him.

"I forgot to lock up," I say, with a laugh that clunks from my throat. "I didn't want to take a chance with my client files, so I drove back the moment I realized."

As soon as I get it out, I feel better. It sounds believable enough. But when I finally meet Luke's eyes, there's doubt there. In the subtle tilt of his head, the tension in his jaw. His gaze that fixes me in place. I may as well be handcuffed.

"With a gun?"

I start to deny it. *How could he know?* The gun is solid and cold against my back. Hidden.

"I'm a cop. Did you forget? And anyway, I saw it when you reached for your purse. The concealed-carry purse I gave you, by the way." My heart thumps in the silence of Luke's deliberate pause. "The Christmas gift you've never used. Until tonight."

I sigh and let my shoulders droop. "With what happened to Ian and Kate, I just . . . I don't know. I guess I'm a little rattled. I was scared to come up here alone. I should've called you."

It's true enough. And I add the last bit to really sell it. Because all I want—*all I need*—is for Luke to wrap his arm around me and walk with me through the door. Walk away.

"Coop told me you went by the station this morning. But I didn't hear from you all day. I was worried about you. I went by the house, but you weren't there."

I shrug and take a casual step forward, wishing I could grab him by the hand and pull him behind me. "I got your texts, but I didn't know what to say. I don't want you to feel caught in the middle."

He frowns. "That's why I told you to go in. Answer their questions. Cooperate. If you've got nothing to hide, then neither do I."

100

The Hydra twitches and writhes. And I take another step. "Let's talk about it at home," I say, knowing he'll warm to that. Me calling my home his. Isn't that all he wants?

Luke goes first. Through the door. Down the steps. And I follow, each step a relief. When we're outside, he turns to me, his face as unreadable as his father's. "You can talk to me, Ava. You know that, right?"

And I nod at him. I let him hold me for a moment in the middle of the empty street, the fog rolling in around us, before he crosses to his truck on the other side. But I can't even enjoy how good it feels when he pulls me flush against him. Because I'm still waiting for him to walk away.

Away from the office. Away from the desk drawer. Away from that ordinary paper bag. And most of all, away from the bloody knife inside it.

Marriage is not for sissies. But then, neither is divorce.
—Ian Culpepper, *Love CPR*

VALENTINE'S DAY
EIGHT YEARS EARLIER

ARE you sure you're okay with this?" Ava asked, studying her mother's face for the answer. *The eyes always tell it truer than the lips.* Something Prick Whitlock, as Ian had started calling him, got right. She'd seen it in her patients. And now, in her mother too. Because when she smiled at Ava, the corners of her eyes were weighted with worry.

"Honey, it's your special day. If you're okay, I'm okay."

Ava didn't know if she was okay or not. She wanted somebody to tell her how to be. Somebody other than Ian. Which seemed wrong to think on her wedding day. "You know I never wanted a big wedding."

"I know."

"And I don't care about frilly dresses or flower arrangements or registries."

"I know that too." Her mother patted her hand with such tenderness she wanted to cry. Of course, she wouldn't, though. "I sense a *but* coming."

"Well, I guess I never pictured myself getting married in a dress I bought at The Limited." She looked over her shoulder at the grand old building behind them. It was stately. Regal for sure, but so formal. "In the same building where I could record a property deed."

Saturday, 9:00 a.m. The anti-Valentine's wedding they'd been fortunate to book with City Hall officially closed for business. The result of a last-minute favor Ian called in to Judge Clemmons, who he'd counseled through a messy divorce. That seemed to Ava a bad omen and to Ian a lucky break. She'd insisted on one tradition at least, that they'd spend the night apart.

"Did you tell your fiancé how you feel? I'm sure he wants to make you happy."

"Yes. But I think he already feels bad enough. I didn't want to make a big deal out of it. He's right. For him, it's hugely anticlimactic. He's been through the whole fancy-schmancy wedding deal before."

And Ava should know. She'd seen all the photos. Sometimes, after Ian left for work, she pulled out the album he'd stashed at the back of his underwear drawer. He and Julie, married in the spring. A traditional ceremony at Shakespeare's Garden in Golden Gate Park. Reception to follow at the Julia Morgan Ballroom. The iconic San Francisco wedding.

"Plus, he got invited to speak at that conference in Paris this weekend, and we thought it would make the perfect honeymoon."

"It sounds logical," her mother said, winking at her. Prick Whitlock would've said her heart wasn't in it. But what did he know? He'd been fired for stealing office supplies a week after Ian keyed his car. And Ava was a licensed psychologist now. *So there.* "Weddings are overrated anyway. Your father and I always wished we'd eloped."

That settled it. Her mom was only trying to make her feel better. Because she never mentioned Dad unprovoked. And in a flash, Ava went back there. To the bedroom. To the suicide note she'd stuffed in her sock before the cops got there. The things her father had confessed. Ian would never leave her like that. To clean up his mess. Or live with it. To be forced to make that kind of decision alone.

She said what was expected of her. "I wish Dad could've been here."

"He would've said you're the most beautiful bride there ever was. Even in a dress from The Limited."

Ava didn't argue, though she couldn't remember a single compliment from her father. And when she'd asked him once if she looked pretty, he'd told her not to be so vain. She understood it now, how unhappy he must've been, but it still throbbed like a toothache when she thought of it.

"I do have this going for me," she said, waving her left hand with its perfectly round diamond. Two and a half—*holy cow!*—carats she couldn't stop staring at. Mainly because they proved something: she belonged to someone—already she felt better—but not just anyone.

Him.

Ian charged up the sidewalk. Right on time. Electric blue eyes and a megawatt smile. All meant for her.

Her mother whistled, and Ava laughed. *My husband*, she thought, anxious to earn the right to say it out loud. Three syllables of total validation.

"And him," her mother added. "Don't you let him get away. He's a keeper."

"I know, Mom. You've already mentioned that."

****

Mrs. Culpepper could barely zip her suitcase. Mrs. Culpepper had packed too much. That's how Ava thought of herself now. A *Mrs.* Even though she was actually a doctor, and the name change wasn't exactly official yet.

Ian, fresh from a shower, brushed his teeth at the sink, and she caught his eye in the mirror. "I can't quite believe it. We're married."

He half-laughed, his mouth foaming with toothpaste. "Indeed. You're stuck with me, Lawson."

"You mean Culpepper."

"Only if you want to change it. You can still keep your name, you know. I wouldn't be offended."

She stood behind him, pulling his damp body close to her own. His bare back warmed her cheek, and she closed her eyes. For the briefest moment, she felt inexplicably sad.

"I wish your parents could've been there," she whispered against his skin, hopeful he'd finally open up about them, now that they were bound by a sacred promise and a legal contract. All she knew, she'd learned from Google. Marty Culpepper had been an investment banker at Goldman Sachs. His third wife, Carrie, his secretary. They'd gone over a bridge in the back of a taxi cab straight into the freezing Hudson the year Ian started at Princeton.

"That makes one of us. I already told you. My parents were . . ."

"Were what? And no, you didn't tell me."

His heavy sigh meant she'd push no further. "They weren't like Frances Lawson. You're so lucky, Ava. She's the mom I wish I'd had."

Ava traipsed back to her overflowing suitcase, feeling like a scolded child.

"Hey, will this fit in your bag?" Ian offered up his toiletry kit with an oblivious grin, momentarily disappearing her melancholy.

"As long as you promise to carry it."

She knelt beside her bag, rummaging to make space. The suede high heels would have to go.

"This too," he said, tossing her a small bottle with a bright blue label. *Take one tablet by mouth once daily.* The pills rattled around, tiny bones, unnerving her.

"Adderall? What's this for?"

"Shouldn't you know that, *Doctor*?"

A flare of anger sparked inside her. She hoped Ian didn't see it. Not today. Their first day as husband and wife. "I know what it's prescribed for. But why do *you* have it?"

"The same reason half of America has it. I need to focus for the conference. There's going to be some real heavy hitters there and my speech has got to be sharp if I ever want to sell my book to an agent. Plus, I'll be staving off a major case of jet lag."

Ava rolled her eyes, playful and jokey. But inside, she regarded him like a stranger. With suspicion. Like he'd changed the rules of the game without her knowing. "I thought we felt the same about that kind of thing."

"We do. But I am a psychiatrist, Ava. I prescribe medication. I can't be a total hypocrite."

"You don't have Attention Deficit—"

"Look. If it's such a big deal, I'll flush it right now. Give it to me."

He snatched at her bag just as she clutched it to her, the towel around his waist loosening. Falling to the carpet in a heap. Shocked, she gaped up at him.

"Now look what you've done, Mrs. Culpepper."

So, she did.

THE DOWNTOWN STAR

"SECRETS EXPOSED: MURDERED LOVE DOCTOR CAUGHT RED-HANDED WITH MISTRESS!"

See the exclusive photos from a fairytale marriage gone bad.

Ian and Kate Culpepper appeared to have it all. A loving marriage. A beautiful daughter. Two advanced degrees between them. And a household name they created—The Love Doctors—which spawned a television show and several best-selling self-help books.

Sadly, the Love Doctors' fairytale ending turned to a nightmare this Valentine's Day, when the couple was discovered brutally stabbed to death in their posh Pebble Beach home. Now, shocking new evidence has revealed trouble was already brewing behind the scenes of their picture-perfect union.

In stunning photos obtained exclusively by *The Downtown Star*, Ian Culpepper can be seen cavorting with an unnamed and much younger female. In one photo (seen below), the dashingly handsome Culpepper pulls the red-haired beauty in for a sultry kiss in the shadowy alley behind a restaurant. Another photo (also seen below) appears to show Culpepper and his mistress in a compromising position in the backseat of his car.

Culpepper was no stranger to controversy. When interviewed on *The View* last year, he skirted around long-standing rumors of a second marriage he kept secret from fans, telling the hosts, "Honestly, I don't remember anybody before Kate. It's a timeless love. As if we've been together all our lives." Culpepper has always been tight-lipped about his first marriage to Julie Avery, which ended with her death in 2006.

But Ian Culpepper wasn't the only Love Doctor who had fallen out of love. An inside source tells *The Downtown Star* that police discovered a secret love note stashed in Kate's belongings, penned by the blonde bombshell herself, that spoke of her plan to leave Culpepper in the days leading up to the slaying.

A source close to the couple adds, "Even the most ordinary marriage has its secrets. And Ian and Kate, as extraordinary as they were, had more than their fair share."

CHAPTER ELEVEN

SATURDAY
FEBRUARY 18, 2018

I keep my eyes shut and pretend to be asleep. Maybe if I lay here long enough, the world will right itself again. The bloody knife will disappear. In its place, the memory card reincarnated. Maddie will speak. Ricky Sherman will vanish. And Ian and Kate will bolt upright, healed, alongside my father. It comes to me, then, that my three months of purposeful silence was exactly like this. A suspended state. A protest. A vicious, vicious hope.

Luke slipped out of bed an hour ago. I'd felt the tug of the sheets, the brush of his lips across my forehead. But he didn't leave. He'd never do that. Especially not on a Saturday, when he has the day off. I hear him in the kitchen, cooking me breakfast. The smell of eggs and strong coffee lures me back to this world, however wrong it may be.

ELLERY KANE

I know Luke is making his case. He's always making his case. Even after we'd come back here last night, in the middle of his stern lecture about my recklessness. Going to the office, alone and so late, with a gun and a killer on the loose. He'd still managed to work it in. Of course, he had. "You might feel safer if we lived together."

I dress quickly, quietly, in my running clothes, already forming the story I'll tell him. An excuse to get out of here and back to the office. To do something about the knife. The knife with blood on it. Blood that surely belongs to the man I used to love and the woman who took my place. The knife that someone planted in my office. Someone who wants me to look as guilty as I already feel.

"Fuck." Choir boy Luke doesn't use that word. Not unless he means it. And the hush after he says it is worse. He's been shocked.

I crack the door and peer down the hallway and into the kitchen, where Luke is stanchioned behind the counter, gawking at his phone. He tosses it aside and runs a nervous hand through his hair. Then, he catches me looking. Offers my name up as softly as a prayer.

"Is everything alright?" But in the pit of my stomach, the Hydra answers for him, shakes its many heads.

My feet carry me toward Luke, even as the rest of me wills myself away. Back to the bed. Under the covers. To the in-between world, where I can pretend to be okay.

"Just some pictures of Ian and a woman on one of those gossip sites. I don't think you should look."

"Why?" What I really mean is how—and who?

"It'll only upset you, bring back memories. They're probably photoshopped anyway. Not even real." He reaches for his phone just as I do and holds it away from me, gripping it with two hands. As if I'd wrestle him for it.

"Fine." I turn around and storm back to the bedroom, snatching my own phone off the table in the hallway.

Luke calls to me. "Ava, don't." A half-hearted objection. But I slam the door behind me, knowing he won't follow.

110

The photos—*my* photos—are the lead story on all the internet news sites. Smack-dab between a Kardashian breakup and the Academy Awards buzz. "Murdered Love Doctor Caught Cheating." I've gone viral—in the worst way—against my will.

No matter what I'd promised Ricky, I'd never intended to release the pictures. To expose the link between Cleo and me, the choke chain that binds us. Soon enough the cops will catch the scent and follow it straight to my doorstep. And what will I say then, with all my lies laid bare? I used to be ethical. Once upon a time. Before I broke the one rule that really mattered: First, do no harm.

I scroll past the banner-sized photograph at the top of my screen, the one they've all latched on to. The one I'm ~~most~~ least proud of. Captured at dusk through the back window of Ian's Mercedes, his cheek, tan and peppered with stubble, melds into Cleo's. Their mouths joined like strange creatures intent on devouring each other. I'd huddled in my own back seat for an hour to get it, with a baseball cap shadowing my face. But I would've waited for days. A revenant intent on revenge.

I cringe when I spot Ian's line, half-buried at the bottom of the first article I open. "Honestly, I don't remember anybody before Kate." His casual dismissal of me. Of us. I'd heard it before, of course. Spoken in his public voice, words as bright and shiny as a newly minted penny. And worth about as much. Hell, I'd taken off work to watch that piece on *The View*. But to see it in print is something else entirely. A bloodletting. Each word is a cut. Each cut deeper than the last.

"Is it safe to come in now?" Luke asks, knocking softly. He cracks the door and puts his hand out, tempting me with a cup of coffee. Like I'm a caged animal who still requires taming. "A peace offering."

"Fine," I groan. "If you have to. But only because you brought coffee."

The door swings wide, and I steel myself. Prepare to face the rest of him, his cop stare. But it's just Luke, with his kind eyes and bare feet. "I warned you not to look."

"You were right. But it's worse than I thought. I know this woman." I take the mug between my hands and scald my tongue with a bitter sip.

"What do you mean you *know* her?" Luke sits on the edge of the bed, but he leaves a space between us. Because my need for closeness is unpredictable. Because I'm unpredictable. Because I want him to hold me. But I need him to leave. "You've seen her before?"

I have no choice but to say it. Whatever this is, I have to get ahead of it. "She's a patient of mine."

"A therapy patient? Seriously, Ava. Is that even allowed?"

I remember the first day when Cleo had arrived at the office, lugging her bike up the stairs, her face flushed with the effort. The muscles in her forearms taut as rope. "I had no idea she was involved with him."

"So you didn't know about the affair?"

The first ten minutes, Cleo had worked up to it. The big reveal. Then: "I'm sleeping with a married man." And I'd wondered if God was punishing me again. Reminding me of all I'd done wrong with Ian. Of all the wrong we'd both done. I'd deserved Kate, hadn't I?

"Not exactly. She called him The Professor. I knew he was married, but she never mentioned him by name. She was careful about it." Until she'd slipped three sessions in and uttered *Kate*, and I'd thought God had given me a gift. A reward for my suffering. A tool. A weapon. If only I could figure how to use it.

Luke dips his chin, readies a rebuttal. "About as careful as O.J. Simpson." He gestures to my phone in my lap. To the headline. To the pictures I'd taken, meant only to spur Ian into action. Because he owed. We owed.

"Fine. But, is this whole thing really a surprise to you, Kato?" I pause for Luke's obligatory eye roll. "Surely, you saw the texts between them, the phone calls. I assume his cell phone was at the scene."

"We couldn't find it. Kate's either. Now I guess we know why."

"What do you mean?"

"I mean *her*. Your patient. She certainly had motive. And it would explain Ian's missing phone." Luke pauses, his frown deepening. "Christ. Did she say anything to you? Never mind, don't tell me. But when Dad gets wind of this, he's going to want to see your notes."

"You know he can't. My notes are privileged."

"He'll try to get a warrant."

"Good luck with that. Besides, Cleo couldn't stab two people. Not by herself." My coffee is still too hot, but I gulp it down anyway so I'll stop talking. "I need to clear my head. I'm going for a run."

"I made you eggs," Luke calls after me. "Scrambled with milk the way you like them."

I'm not hungry—how could I be?—but guilt demands to be fed. So I stalk toward the plate he's kept warm for me in the oven like it's my last meal.

****

I never liked to run until after Ian and I imploded. Before that, it was just something I did. Something I had to do. A chore, no different than brushing my teeth or dusting the baseboards. But after—post-Ian—I laced up my sneakers with a visceral need, the road beneath them as dull and flat as life without him. And I ran like hell. Like I could still catch up with my old self and reclaim her if only my legs were fast enough.

But now, it's just habit. I've got no use for the old me. And if I caught her, I'd leave her limping behind me, choking on my dust. She'd call me hard-hearted, callous. And I'd call her a spineless worm.

I take big breaths of the morning air, letting the cold burn my lungs. It feels right to suffer. Because I've told Luke another half-truth. Another half-lie. That I'm running to the beach and back, four miles round trip. And he'd believed me. He'd kissed the corner of my mouth and cleared my plate, and all I could think of was the knife. How I had to get rid of it.

When I reach Ocean Avenue, I hit my stride. And even though I know there's no one behind me, fear snuffs at the back of my neck, bares its sharp yellow teeth. Prepares to bite. So, I run until my quads prickle with the effort, until the wind stings my face. Until my office looms at the finish line. The knife, my trophy. A hollow victory.

Who? I've asked myself the question a thousand ways, a thousand times. Who wants the world to see me as a killer? The names whip and toss around in my head—*Cleo? Ricky? David?*—like lawn chairs in a tornado. So fast, each one is lethal. At the eye of the storm, just one name, the name I try to never think of: Wallace Bergman. The things we did to him. This is my punishment. And his ghost holds the whip.

I slow my pace. But I keep jogging, head down, past Seaside Sweets. I can't be too careful. Marianne would out me to Luke without meaning to—"Guess who I saw this morning?"—and I'm already on shaky ground.

I let myself in and take the stairs two at a time. The office is warm, the ancient heater grumbling at me, and I shed my long-sleeve layer and tie it around my waist, above my running pouch. Usually, it holds my cell phone, pepper spray, and a tube of energy gel. Today, it's empty. A body bag waiting to be filled.

Just get it over with, Ava.

I'm still breathing hard when I reach the desk. When I open the drawer. When I touch the bag and pick it up and shove it inside the pouch without looking. And when I zip the pouch tight, my breath is the sound of the ocean in my head. Obliterating everything. And each rise and fall of my chest brings a wave of relief.

It's half done. The hard part is over. I replace the false bottom, push the drawer shut with my foot, and head for the door. I lock it fast and slip my office key inside the pouch without looking. Legs twitching and ready to run.

But then, the screech of sirens. Faint at first. Though it's meant for me. I'm sure of it. Like music only I can hear. I know it in my bones, the same way I'd known that summer so long ago. I'd stood there listening—like now—frozen and waiting. For the police, the ambulance, the professionals. Waiting to be told what I already knew. My father was dead. My father had killed himself. And I was to blame.

Well, me and DeAndre Mack, the armed drug dealer he'd shot dead inside a warehouse two years prior. The biggest cocaine bust in LA County since 1989. "People shouldn't get medals for that shit," I'd heard Dad tell Mom on the way home from the commendation ceremony when they thought I was asleep in the back seat. "It's bad karma."

Now, the siren is loud and wailing. And right outside. I see two squad cars through the window. They're coming. For me.

I pull the long-sleeve shirt back over my head and tug it down over the pouch.

I start down the staircase—there's no time to toss the knife, nowhere to toss it to—and try to remember how to look innocent. When I'm anything but.

****

"So you were in your office for about ten minutes?"

Before I can answer, Cooper speaks into the radio at his collar, calling off the dogs. Now that we've established there is no masked intruder breaking into my office. No burglary in progress. No laws being broken—well . . .

He regards me the way he always does. Like I'm a coffee stain on his best dress shirt. A scuff, a black streak, on brand-new white sneakers. And I remember the look. Junior year, Carmel High. At the end of the football game, I'd spied Cooper under the bleachers making out with a cheerleader. Not his girlfriend, Jenny, who played the flute and worshipped the holy ground he walked on. He'd seen me too, flashing that same glare over her delicate shoulder. I swear I didn't say a word to Jenny. But if someone happened to drop an anonymous note in her locker, it would've been more than deserved. Right?

"Right," I say. "Ten minutes. I just wanted to be sure I'd shut off my desk lamp when I left last night. I figured I'd swing by on my run down to the beach."

"And you didn't call the station?"

"No."

"Well, someone did." *The same someone who put a bloody knife in my drawer.* That's what I want to say. But I shrug instead.

"Do you mind if we have a look inside the office? To be sure."

I fight the urge to refuse. To return the smug tilt of his head with one of my own. *I closed the drawer. I have the knife. There's nothing to worry about.* "It's fine. Go ahead."

Cooper nods to the other officer, Donnelly, and she brushes past me toward the door. Her hand meets the knob. And that's when I realize.

"We'll need the key, Doctor Lawson," she says, giving the knob a jiggle that rattles my bones.

Can a laugh sound guilty? Mine does. At least to me. "Of course." *The key.* The one that's tucked in the pouch at my waist. Nuzzling against the paper bag that holds my secret.

Somehow, I keep my hand steady as I unzip the corner. My fingers root for the smooth metal. *Don't look at him. Don't look up.* But I do both, meeting Cooper's eyes as I find it. Glacial. And beneath the ice, more ice. Layer upon layer of frosty judgment.

He knows. Again, I think it, squinting in the glare of a perpetual spotlight. Because that's how it feels when you've got a secret. *More than one.* When you've told a lie. *Many.*

I hold the key out to him, the distance between us vast. A deep crevice in the ice.

"I suppose you've seen the pictures of your ex-husband," he says, mid-reach. "Or was your marriage so long ago you forgot what he looked like too?"

The key falls from my hand. Bounces and skitters to rest at his feet.

"Uh, sorry."

He bends to pick it up, and I zip the pouch. Careful not to be too hurried. Or too slow.

"Yes. I've seen them." The key passes to Donnelly. She unlocks the door and wanders inside. "They're probably not even real."

Cooper grunts. "These days it's hard to tell what's real and what isn't. Or who. Don't you think?"

I shift my weight from one sneaker to the other, the way I did as a girl. As if the weight of all of it—of all of me—is too much to bear.

You, Cooper, are an asshole. Now, that's what's real. "I had a patient once who thought he was an alien. Who am I to say it wasn't real?"

Cooper blinks at me, perplexed. And I savor it, his confusion and the way he tries to hide it. It feels good to throw him off balance, to watch him stumble for once.

Over his shoulder, Donnelly stands at my desk, staring. And I look too long at her, because he turns, curious. "See anything, Donnelly? Or should I let you pose that question, Doc?"

I realize, then, why he's asking, why he's chuckling at her. Sneering at me. The framed Rorschach inkblot—card IV—propped atop the latest diagnostic manual. I don't tell him what we're taught to ask: "What might this be?" Or that IV is known as the father card. Or that I've always only seen a monster looming over me from a great height. Or that I remember showing him that inkblot and the other nine a few years back after he'd been referred to me for a psych eval following a few too many citizen complaints.

Silent, I will Officer Donnelly away from the desk. But she doesn't move, and Cooper leaves me to join her.

"I remember that test," he says. "Waste of time, in my opinion."

"Well, you'll be happy to know I don't administer it anymore. At least not for those types of evaluations."

Cooper's jaw tightens and Donnelly clears her throat. She steps aside, pretends to gaze out the window, then at my bookshelf. But the look on her face is twitchy, like she's stumbled into an ants' nest.

"Finally realized it's a bunch of BS, huh?"

"Actually, I realized a lot of cops look up the test online and just tell me what they think I want to hear."

He runs his hand along the polished oak, casually opening the top drawer. "You should probably check these," he says to me. "Just in case there's something missing."

"I'm sure it's fine."

He opens another, and I shiver at the sound of the scraping wood.

"I said, it's fine."

"Suit yourself." He lingers for a moment, shrugs. "Still looks like a run-over cat to me. *Splat*."

I nod, in that therapist way that can mean anything—good or bad. *Officer Donovan relates to the world in a conventional way, meaning he's likely to adhere to the rules. However, he harbors strong aggressive impulses that push against his need for order.* That's what I'd written in my report, which was generous if you ask me. *Fifty-two weeks of anger management recommended before consideration for promotion.*

Donnelly shuts the office door and returns the key to me with a nod. It rests in my palm for a moment, cold and all-seeing, before I bury it in my fist.

****

I'd planned to take the knife home with me, stash it under the mattress, and drive it to Pescadero Point after dark. Fling it like a madwoman from the rocks into the deep, churning water below. But I'm spooked, and I want to be rid of it. Now.

I wait until Cooper's car disappears down Juniper Street. Then I run—faster than before, wilder—down Ocean Avenue toward the beach. I don't look over my shoulder. Not once. Even though someone followed me this morning. I'm certain of that. Certain someone is playing with me. The way a cat bats at its prey until it's tired and dazed and a fatal bite to the neck comes as a relief.

That's how I feel. Worn out by something with bigger teeth than me.

When I hit the soft sand just past the parking lot, I walk. Let my feet sink in surrender.

I turn around.

Nothing. No one. What did I expect? Who?

The parking lot is mostly empty. It's still early. And February. Gloomy and cold. The tourists are nestled snug in their B&Bs, wishing they'd gone south instead. To LA or San Diego, where sunbathing in the winter is practical.

A hoarse laugh scrapes from my throat when I spot it. An orange tabby, all fur and bones, trotting toward me. A long, flesh-colored tail twitches from the side of its mouth. A mouse. A soon-to-be dead one. And I wonder if this is how it starts. Losing one's mind. Seeing connections where there are none. Thoughts blurring the edges of reality until there's no line between them at all. No way to tell one from the other. Soon enough I'll be no different than my alien patient. There's even a word for it, one Ian taught me.

Apophenia. The tendency to perceive connections where none exist.

"Drop it," I say to the cat, clapping my hands at it. "Go on."

It glances in my direction, with a look of judgment—*crazy lady*—then saunters away. Mouse still firmly in its mouth, of course. Both of us doomed.

I take one more nervous look around, before I start down the beach. When I reach the packed wet sand near the water, I start to jog again. The ocean—the smell of it, the sound—salves my wounds a bit. The vastness of it. The indifference. The serene brutality. It knows which secrets to swallow and which to spit back out again.

The day after my dad's funeral, I'd taken the city bus to the Santa Monica pier. Walked past the games and the souvenir shops and the Ferris wheel to the end, where a few fishermen stood behind their poles basking in the June gloom. I reached into my pocket and removed the lined paper I'd folded into a small square, the shape of a headstone. My father's suicide note. Leaning out over the water, I watched it fall from my hand. As if the words could be unwritten—and what was done could be undone.

I'm still thinking of my father—of those poison words he wrote—when I reach the natural jetty at the far end of the beach. Low tide is coming, and the water laps at the mossy rock faces, slick beneath my sneakers. I walk to the end, measuring my steps. Because with my luck, I'd fall and crack my head. The paramedics would be summoned. The police too. And then they'd unzip the pack at my waist, searching for my ID.

When I reach the last section of stone, I look up toward the horizon. Where the ocean goes on and on forever, as if all the world is water. I think of my father's note when I open the pouch, then the paper bag, and peer in at the knife.

I won't touch it. Because fingerprints don't just wash away. Not according to chapter three in my dad's old *Practical Guide to Homicide Investigation*.

It looks expensive, this knife. The sort Ian would've picked out from some snobby kitchen store in Beverly Hills. The handle is black resin, the blade stainless steel. The markings on the blade tell me it's a Wusthof. And that can't be a coincidence. No apophenia here.

I hold up the bag like an offering. Turn it upside down. And the knife falls out, sinking beneath the waves. I blink my eyes at it. Because for a moment, blood swirls in the water. Or is it ink?

****

If today had a to-do list, it would read like a jailbird's diary.

Lie to the cops, Luke included.

Get rid of the bloody knife.

Figure out what to do about partner in crime.

Now that I've put a hard black line through one and two, Ricky is on my mind. He might've stolen the pictures himself, sold them to the tabloid. He might've killed Ian and Kate and left the murder weapon for me as a gruesome *screw you*. But if he didn't—*how would he have known where to find the pictures?*—then he'll be livid, thinking I've sold the photos out from under him. Whichever it is, there's only one thing that can set it right. One thing that will send him packing.

When I reach home, Luke's truck is gone, so I let myself in with the spare I keep hidden in the birdhouse. The dishes are washed and put away, and there's a note on the counter. *Went to see Mom and Dad. Be back soon,* signed with Luke's usual well-ordered script. Even if it is easier this way, I'd expected him to be here, and the house feels strange. Abandoned.

I run the shower as hot as I can stand. Strip down and let the water pound against my forehead. *Don't think about the knife.* But it's my father's note that won't let me go. It's funny how a memory can stay buried for so long you think it's dead and gone forever. Until it claws its way to the surface, desperate and gasping. And very much alive.

I keep my head under. Squeeze my eyes shut. Hold my breath. Try not to see his last words, the handwritten lines I'd committed to memory. *To Franny and Ava, my darling girls: I'm no hero. I'm not who you think I am—*

My cell phone trills from the kitchen, its happy little ring lopping off the rest of the words. I suck in a breath. And a mouthful of water. I choke on it, and it burns through my nose. My wet feet smack against the floor as I step out, dripping, and reach for a towel.

The ringing starts again. And water pools beneath me as I stare at the screen.

Ian is calling. It's his number. The same number he had since we met. Dread creeps in like the cold, and I pull the towel tighter against me.

I pick up the phone with damp fingers. Speak, though my throat hurts.

"Ian?"

I listen hard. I fill in the silence.

Hey Aves. How's your day?

And I'd answer, with a smile: *Crazy as usual. And then there are my patients.*

But it's not Ian. Because Ian is dead.

It's the breathing man.

"I saw you today. At the beach." His voice is all one note, wooden and clunking like a dead piano key.

"Who are you?"

"Consider me a debt collector."

"What do you want from me?"

Like the tip of a finger, a drip of water zigzags down my back. I shiver as it joins the small puddle at my feet. I wait for the answer. For my sentence to be handed down. My fate sealed.

"Only what's owed to me," he says. "Only what you took."

He means: Everything.

****

My hair is still damp. It clings against my T-shirt, leaving wet spots on my shoulders. I twist it into a bun at my neck, hoping my mother won't notice. Or ask questions. Not that she'd remember the answers. It's the asking, the disapproval that sticks between my ribs, keen as a blade. With any luck, she'll be asleep and I won't wake her.

Keeping my head down, I sign the log, wave to the nurse at the desk, and rush down the corridor. If I focus, I can be in and out in ten minutes.

She's in bed. Awake. *Shit.*

I give her the phony smile that comes so easily to me. The one I'd used to greet Dad when I'd find him in bed in the middle of the day. The same one I'd offered Ian at the end, when we were both still pretending we weren't irrevocably broken. And it feels exactly the same. At thirteen. At thirty-five. *I am a fraud.*

I step into the room, and she's up in an instant, clutching at my arm.

"Help me," she whispers. "I don't belong here."

Some days, her eyes are pools of stagnant water. But right now, they're wild and bright. And I panic looking into them. "This is where you live," I say. "This is your room."

"No, no, no." She shakes her head back and forth, her braid whipping from one shoulder to the other. "I live at 774 Evergreen Circle in Los Angeles. With my husband. He's a police officer, so you better get me out of here."

"Okay. Let's sit down and talk about it." So much for in and out in ten. I offer her my hand and wait for her to take it. I've been cautious ever since she clocked me in the jaw last summer, terrified I'd been sent to bring her to jail.

I lead her to the vinyl sofa near the window. "What's your husband's name?"

"Jerry." She says his name with a kind of familiar tenderness. Like slipping on a well-worn pair of blue jeans. And my eyes well.

"Tell me about him."

"We met at the Eagles concert. In the middle of that song 'Hotel California.' He spilled his beer on me." She laughs then, and the girl she was flickers behind her eyes, glinting like pennies at the bottom of a fountain, too far down to reach. "He was so handsome I could barely speak. And he wasn't even in uniform. We were married last year."

I nod at her, knowing better than to disagree. *Thou shalt not argue.* The first commandment of dementia, the first thing you learn. That and patience. Radical patience. Neither of which comes naturally. Not to me anyway. "Sounds like you're a lucky lady."

"The luckiest." She sighs, giddy as a teenager. "You know, we're trying for a baby. We want a big family. At least four little ones. That way nobody's left out."

"Four, huh?" It's not the first time she's surprised me with something she must have kept locked up tight in her brain. Until her brain turned to Swiss cheese and some things were lost and some things remained. And she couldn't remember which of those things were secrets anymore. I can't be sure it's true, but it rests heavy on my chest. The crushing weight of the past. Of questions I can't ask, because there's no one to answer them. It's a brutal kind of melancholy. This I know: Dad made Detective in the LAPD

Narcotics Division one year after I was born, and there were no more after me.

"At least four," she says, winking at me the way she used to do.

I peek at the clock behind her bed. It's already been ten minutes. "Would you like to wear your wedding ring?"

It's cruel, but what choice do I have? In an instant, her face clouds, and she stares at her left hand, at her ringless finger. "I thought . . . I . . . where's my ring? What have you done with it?"

I shush her, patting her arm, as she starts to cry. "It's okay. You put it somewhere for safekeeping."

"I did? I don't remember."

"I know. But I do." I leave her sniffling on the sofa and head to the small closet where I'd hung the clothes she never wears anymore. It's all sweatpants and gray gripper socks now. I reach beneath her lipstick-red peacoat and pull the safe toward me, out into the light.

"I have a—?" My mother points at the perlite box, straining. "Oh, what is that called?"

"A safe. It's fireproof, and it holds all your important papers and belongings, including your wedding ring. Do you remember the combination?"

I'm a horrible daughter. "I'm not sure," she says.

"It's your birthday. One. Four. Fifty-six."

A horrible person. My fingers turn the dial to another date. One I know she'd never guess. Because it fell through the holes in her brain a long time ago. 6/5/96. The day my father killed himself.

Appeased by my effort, by my guilt, the lock clicks, and I open the door. "Here you go," I tell her, handing her the best engagement ring my father could afford on a cop's salary. A simple gold band with a half-carat diamond.

"Thank you, dear." As my mother admires the ring, loose on her finger, I find what I came for and stuff it into my purse, closing the safe with a satisfying thud. "You look so familiar," she says. "Do I know you?"

I'm going straight to hell. "I don't think so. I just have one of those faces."

****

I follow routine—it would be suspicious not to—and stop at the nurse's station to exchange pleasantries with Nurse Ellerby before I book it back to the car. Later, I'll call Cliffside and tell them I forgot to return my mother's ring to the safe. I'll ask them to keep it for me at the desk. For now, I put on the usual mask.

"Mom is pretty out of it today," I say, shrugging. "She thinks it's 1981."

Nurse Ellerby grins. "Leg-warmers and parachute pants. My favorite decade."

"Don't forget shoulder pads. And cheesy John Hughes movies."

"Like I said, my favorite decade." She glances over her shoulder, then motions me to the log book at the corner of the desk. "Is everything alright, Doctor Lawson?"

"As alright as can be expected. Why do you ask?" I keep my face solid, but my insides are mush. Hydra food.

"A guy came by here asking to see the log book. He wanted to know who visited your mom last week."

"That's strange. What did he look like?"

"He was young. A stern, good-looking fella. Said he was a cop."

"Did he leave his name? Or sign in?" She shakes her head. "He said he'd be back though. After I told him he'd need a warrant."

"Is that true?"

"Probably not, but it sounded good. And I had fun saying it. Anyway, I thought you might like to know."

"Thanks, Patty." I pretend to turn to go. Then stop short and look back at her, hopeful. "Hey, would you mind if I took a look at the log? Without a warrant."

"You know I can't let you do that." Her eyes flit down the hall and back to me. "And I'm about to go on my break, so make sure you don't sneak a peek."

"I'd never."

"Didn't think so."

I wait until the sound of her footfalls grow faint and disappear. I flip the pages of the spiral-bound book and slide my finger down, down, down, until I find it. Tuesday, February 14. The afternoon before the murder. My name is there. At 6:30 p.m. As shaky as I'd been, the signature is neat. Legible.

I scan the lines below it, not sure what I'm looking for. But it comes anyway. Certain as the tide.

Wednesday, February 15, 1:15 p.m. Luke Donovan.

I stare at it, still unsure. Trying to make sense of it. Luke has never come here alone. Hell, he's never come here at all, not for lack of trying. And Luke doesn't lie. I nearly laugh out loud at the absurdity of my faith in him. When will I learn my lesson? Lies attract liars, and I tell lies.

I snap a picture of the log with my phone and head for the door, nerves buzzing. I drive a few blocks before I pull to the shoulder and open the bag from the safe. The blue canvas is stamped "Monterey County Bank and Trust."

"It's all I can give you for now. I'll have the rest next month." That's what Ian had said when he'd tossed the bag at me, disgusted. Like he couldn't stand to look at me. "This isn't you, Ava. You're not like this."

"Like what?" I'd asked.

"Spiteful."

"Really, Ian? That's *all* I am. That's what you made me. And you're no different. Spite is the glue that held us together." His lack of protest had leveled me. But at least his silence proved it. I was right.

I count the money again, same as I'd done the night he'd given it to me. Ten stacks of one hundred crisp hundred-dollar bills. I sit back and breathe it in for a moment, thinking of Ian. Inhaling the sharp smell of ink and cotton. If spite has an odor, this is it.

If the first year of marriage is the hardest, then you picked the wrong person.
—Ian Culpepper, *Prescription for Love*

VALENTINE'S DAY
SEVEN YEARS EARLIER

AVA leaned into the mirror and studied her face. The swollen spot above her left eyebrow ached, tender to the touch but not bruised. Luckily. Because she'd never been that sort of girl. Skilled with concealer. Handy with a makeup brush. She would only end up looking spackled and obvious.

"Do people actually run into doors?" Ian asked her, pressing his lips to her neck. She tilted her head, giving him access, but kept her eyes on his reflection. His dark head of hair, speckled with gray. His hands looping around her waist. She never tired of looking at him and thinking—*mine.* "Because my patients are always saying that. And it's usually . . ."

"The husband?" she teased, turning to face him. "It was sort of your fault. I told you we need a night-light." She didn't mention that she'd been crying. That bleary eyes can't see bathroom doors.

"Yes, dear."

She swatted at him as he darted out, laughing. But her smile died when she saw his suitcase open on the bed, half-packed.

"So, I guess you decided then."

"Don't give me a hard time, Ava. It's just one night. A quick flight to LA. I thought we talked about this."

Talked, meaning Ian had sulked, and she'd caved, nodding along to all his decrees. Yes, it was his first invitation to a major network talk show. Yes, it could be his big break. Yes, he'd been waiting for the chance to build his brand as a relationship expert, to show he's heads and tails above all those other yahoos. Yes, on all counts.

Then, she'd given her back to him and feigned sleep—tears trailing in silence toward her pillow—until she'd heard his light snoring, escaped to the bathroom, and walked into the door. No good deed goes unpunished.

"It's not just any night though. Have you ever heard the saying about New Year's Eve? That how you spend it is the way you spend the rest of the year?"

"It's not New Year's."

"Exactly. It's Valentine's Day and our first anniversary. And you're leaving me alone. It's worse."

"I'm here with you now. Valentine's morning."

"It doesn't count."

"Fine." He took a few pointed steps toward the door, glanced over his shoulder, the corners of his mouth drooping. "I guess I'll just go spend the morning with someone else then. If you don't want me anymore."

Ava knew this trick—loathed it—and she swallowed hard to quell the fire in the pit of her belly. "Of course I do. And come to think of it, it's perfect you'll be gone. What could be more anti-Valentine's than being without you?"

She took a breath and reached for him like he wanted, but he pulled away.

"Please don't be grumpy," she said.

One year of marriage and already Ian could remind her of him. Maybe she had married her father after all.

****

Murphy's Law of therapy: The last client of the day always had the crisis. And this time Ava was genuinely worried. Hannah, her 5 p.m.

angsty teenager with a penchant for cutting, had shown up with fresh marks on her arms. The handiwork of a safety pin during sixth period. And then she'd said the magic words: "Some days I just don't want to be around anymore."

"I know it's hard, Hannah, but I think we should tell your mom how you've been feeling. It's my job to keep you safe."

Hannah glared at her beneath jet-black bangs, and Ava steeled herself for an unfair fight. Because that's what happens when you poke a bear. Or an adolescent female. "I thought it was your job to listen to me. Not to go blab everything I tell you. What's the point of this shit anyway? You're not even a real doctor, are you?"

"If it's easier, we'll tell her together. Or I can sit with you while you tell her. It's your choice."

"Whatever." Which meant she'd chosen option three. Indignant silence.

Hannah didn't speak another word until she and her mom were on their way out, her cheeks striped with tears and mascara. And even then, it was more of a mutter. "Thanks a lot, Doctor Lawson."

Then, with a pointed glance, she reached into her jacket pocket and tossed a tiny envelope into Ava's trash can. Ava knew instantly what was inside. She remembered slipping them into red and pink tissue papered boxes as a girl. A valentine. With Dr. Culpepper printed in block letters on the front.

As soon as they left, Ava fished it out and crashed into the sofa where her patients usually sat. She ripped open the envelope and read Hannah's loopy cursive.

Roses are red

Violets are blue

You're the first shrink I like talking to

She sighed and tucked the card into her pocket. She wanted to call Ian, but he'd scheduled drinks with some bigwig television producer after the show taping, and he'd be annoyed if she interrupted for no good reason.

A soft knock on the door made her sit up. *What now?* she wondered, stifling a groan.

"Yeah?"

"Can I come in?"

Ava stood up and opened the door herself. Former back-row girl Brandy leaned her head in, grinning. They'd been working together at New Beginnings for two years now, but that didn't stop Brandy from checking out Ian every time he came to meet her for lunch. It gave Ava a sick little buzz every time.

"So I heard your hubbie's out of town. Want to grab drinks with us single gals tonight?"

She could think of only one worse thing. Going back to the empty house alone and spending her first anniversary with Julie's ghost. Who was more like a shadow person.

There, in the rug she'd picked out at an antique shop. There, in the dusty crime novels at the bottom of the bookshelf with her name written inside. There, in the strand of long blonde hair Ava had found clinging to the inside of one of Ian's old sweaters. There and everywhere but always just out of her view.

"Count me in."

****

Ava wished she hadn't come, and she rubbed the diamond on her finger like a genie's lamp. Sadly, still there. At the Uptown, a club near the UC Berkeley campus.

She tossed back the last of the cherry vodka sour, paid her tab, and spun around on her barstool to face the dance floor. Brandy and the other girls were out there somewhere with all the other losers. Sweaty, drunk, and valentine-less. Grinding against each other beneath an artificial sky of starry hearts. Here because they had to be.

But she didn't. Not that this sort of place had ever been her scene.

Brandy pushed her way through a tangle of bodies and grabbed Ava's arm, yanking her forward.

"C'mon, Mrs. Culpepper. When the cat's away . . ."

The mouse misses him? "I should be getting back. Ian and I made plans to talk at midnight, so . . ." She backpedaled from Brandy, waving at her with exaggerated cheerfulness. As if they were friends now. The moment she reached the crowd by the door, she hurled herself forward through an imaginary finish line. Although it was stale with smoke and cologne, she gulped the outside air greedily. Because it meant she was free.

Free to be bumped, it seemed, because an unforgiving arm shoved past her. A voice trailed behind, mumbling an apology.

"Watch where you're going," she said, eyeing the man's drooped shoulders, his sad bald spot, with sudden familiarity.

"Pri—Chuck?" She'd have a laugh with Ian about this later, she thought. Because she'd nearly called him Prick.

"Ava Lawson. Wow. What's it been, two years?"

"It's Culpepper now." She tried not to gloat. "Time flies, huh? So where did you end up?" *After you got canned.*

His owl eyes showed her his surprise, his embarrassment—or was it pity she saw there?—and she fought off a flash of hatred she couldn't explain. "I thought Ian would've told you. I took an adjunct professorship at Berkeley. We work together now."

She shrugged it off like nothing. Like it didn't knock her back. "He probably forgot to mention it. He's been so busy lately. He's actually in LA tonight meeting with a—"

"I'm glad to hear it. It seems that you've done him some good. He was pretty wrecked after Julie left him." The name sits between them, not a shadow person at all, but a bottomless black hole. A tear in the fabric of the night.

"I didn't realize you knew her."

"Oh yes. Quite well. She was also one of Ian's students, and she interned at New Beginnings. A lot like you, actually. Smart. Ambitious. Young."

Flustered, she couldn't quite think what to say. So Prick kept right on going, picking the bones of her life apart with surgical precision. "But I guess we all have a type, right?"

Her mouth hung slightly open, and she shut it fast. The click of her teeth startled her like the chambering of a gun. And she realized what he'd said. "Uh, Julie *left* him?"

Immediately, she regretted asking, letting him in. Giving him that power. But still, she had to know what Ian hadn't told her. Even if it meant kowtowing to Prick. "Oh. Well, yes. They separated a few weeks before she died. He took it very hard. You know how he is about . . . losing. I don't want to overstep here, but you weren't aware?"

Ava felt not good enough. The way she had that day in his office. Like he'd circled the three—mediocre or worse—in grading her marriage.

"I should probably go," she said, rubbing her ring again. A nervous habit.

"I didn't mean to upset you, Ava." He put his stubby fingers on her arm, and she flinched.

"But I would like you to know I didn't steal anything from work. A few days before I was fired, Ian came by to talk to me about changing your performance review. He thought I was being too hard on you. But I refused."

"Are you accusing him of—?" She stepped away from Prick and nearly stumbled off the curb. Words spun in her head, a million words, and she could have said any of them. But she chose the four that were untrue. "I don't believe you."

****

The hum of vodka in Ava's blood had long worn off. She sat in her car, seat belt on, heat blasting. Going nowhere.

She thought of her father. Then, Ian. Then, her father again. And the note she knew by heart.

To Franny and Ava, my darling girls: I'm no hero. I'm not who you think I am. I'm a bad cop, a crooked one. I have been for a long time.

And at the end of it—an entire page worth of her dad's confessions—one last request, a request she'd denied him:

Tell my story to the LA Times. Help me make it right, even if I won't be there to see it.

When her cell phone buzzed in her hand, she barely felt it. But the name on the screen brought her back to life. Her life. With Ian.

"So, are you the next Dr. Phil yet?" She sounded so normal, even she believed it, laughing at her own joke. But Ian didn't laugh, and she felt her face get hot.

"Where are you?" he asked.

"At home."

"No, you're not."

****

"Marriage is like an onion," Ian had told her once. "Every day you peel back another layer. You see more and more."

"And sometimes it makes you cry," she'd added, teasing him.

But it made sense now. Layers stripped away, ripped off and discarded. Until there was only this.

Ian pacing beside their bed, his eyes welling. "I'll do it, Ava. If you leave me. I will. I'll blow my goddamned brains out just like your father."

He knew the combination to the lockbox where she kept the gun—0214—and Ava watched as he moved toward it, where it gathered dust in the back of the closet. "You'll have another one on your conscience. Is that what you want? You want me gone?"

How did we get here?

Her brain felt slow and stupid, clumsily retracing her steps like a drunk bum. Brandy and the bar. Cherry vodka splashed on her tongue. Prick Whitlock. Julie. Julie. Julie. Ian's unexpected call. "Surprise, I'm home early! Surprise, you're not here. Surprise, why the fuck did you lie to me, Ava? Are you screwing around on me?" And then, she'd let loose and told him everything. Not told exactly but raged. Raged was more like it. Because she hadn't lied about anything important. Not the way he had. And maybe she didn't know him at all. And maybe this marriage was a mistake.

Of course, she didn't mean it.

And he didn't either. She saw that when he collapsed onto the edge of the bed, defeated. But still. "I'll blow my goddamned brains out." What kind of person would choose those words? The very ones meant to destroy, to detonate inside her like a dirty bomb.

She sat next to him, mute, her hands shaking. The rage went bone deep. And she imagined herself shaking his shoulders, rattling his perfect teeth. *If you ever say that again, I'll kill you myself.* Those were the words she imagined speaking. The layer of herself—raw and stinging and vile—she kept carefully hidden. She wanted to shove it in his face, watch him recoil from it.

Instead, she heard herself plead with him. She spoke the words a dutiful wife should speak. "I love you, Ian. I could never want you gone. Never."

They lingered there, side by side, for a while. Ava felt strange when she finally got up and went to the window, looked out at the street and found it the same. Somehow, she'd expected to see a wasteland. The houses around them leveled. The ground flat and lifeless. And herself floating above it all, distant as a dream.

"I got you something," he said finally, nodding toward the bathroom. His voice was steady and soft, the Ian she knew best. She felt reassured by that. That he could still sound like the person she loved.

She walked past him, her leg brushing his knees, and he reached for her hand, pulling her onto his lap. She surrendered to him but couldn't quite look into his eyes.

"It's a night-light," he whispered against her mouth.

And sure enough, she caught the glow of it as he kissed her, the shimmering halo in the mirror. The dark shadows it cast.

CHAPTER TWELVE

SUNDAY
FEBRUARY 19, 2018

I picked a fight with Luke yesterday afternoon. He gave me no choice. I needed time alone. To count the money one more time just to be sure. To email Ricky. But mainly to get a freaking grip. Without a cop—albeit a ruggedly good-looking one—breathing down my neck. Plus, he'd started asking way too many questions about the false alarm break-in at my office, the one Cooper had filled him in on. Gleefully, no doubt.

"What were you doing there—again?"

"Did you notice anything suspicious?"

"Is someone following you?"

"What aren't you telling me, Ava?"

And he didn't bite—not one nibble—when I'd fished around about his visit to Cliffside. Somehow, the fishing only made *me* feel guilty. Because Luke had been asking to come along on a visit there since . . . well, since he started saying the L-word.

After I'd slammed the bedroom door and Luke had sulked out as expected, I'd logged into the Avenging Angel account and sent Ricky a message. To which there had been no reply.

> *To: Ricky Sherman <rsherm13@quickmail.net>*
> *From: Avenging Angel <avengingangel@pacbell.com>*
> *Date: February 18, 2018 4:53 PM PST*
> *Subject: Let's make a deal*
>
> *I need to talk to you. Sunday at noon. Your room at the Bay View.*

And that's how I ended up here. Outside the seediest motel in Carmel that's still ten times more upscale than my undergrad dorm room at UC Berkeley. I push through the glass doors and into the lobby, where the baby-faced clerk barely looks up from his cell phone.

"Excuse me," I say, approaching the desk. He grunts—an acknowledgment?—but his eyes stay fixed on the screen where a half-naked model poses on the hood of a sports car. So predictable. "Could you—"

"I'm on break."

I spot his name tag. Alex. And consider letting down my ponytail and flirting a little, but my sweats are as baggy as my tired eyes, and I doubt Alex would be convinced. Or interested.

"Is there someone else who could help me? I need to get in touch with one of your guests."

"Nah. The other guy called in sick. You'll have to wait."

"Can't you just—"

"Look, it's the law, lady. California Labor Code. Have a seat, and I'll be with you at exactly twelve-thirty."

Lady. The word makes me sound anything but. As he hones in on the model's bare breasts, smirking to himself, a flash of memory slips through like quicksilver. I clutch at it greedily the way a toddler snatches at a toy. The time Ian had called the Department of Housing Preservation to report bedbugs at a ritzy hotel in New York City after they'd screwed up our reservation. That was before we met Wallace. Before I knew how far Ian would go. And how far I would follow him.

"Alex, I would really hate to have to tell your boss you were looking at hard-core pornography on your break. In front of me and my children." I return the lopsided, smart-ass grin he'd given me and wait for him to cry uncle. To acquiesce to me and my imaginary offspring.

Which he does. Such an amateur. "What can I help with you, ma'am?"

"I need a room number for a guest. Ricky Sherman."

"I can't give out room numbers. It's not—"

A well-timed raise of my eyebrows. "You were saying?"

"Let me check on that for you." A few clicks on the keyboard, and he's got it. "Room 51. Just go out the way you came in and take a right. It's on the lower level."

"Thank you, Alex. Enjoy your porn—I mean break."

It feels so good I don't even blink when I hear him mutter crazy fucking bitch under his breath. He has no idea.

****

Ricky is drunk. No surprise there. He's emptied the minibar and moved on to the fifth of Jack Daniels. A half-eaten rotisserie chicken rests on a greasy paper bag, a sad sack of soggy fries beside it.

He belches once, swaying in the doorway, before he lets me in and closes the door behind him. The sound is so definitive, so final. I'm relieved when he doesn't latch it. "About damn time. You said noon."

"Yeah. Well, you didn't exactly make it easy not responding to my email. You never told me your room number."

"I came back and left a note on your door Friday night. What were you waiting on? A gold-plated invitation?"

A note? It unnerves me. Because Ricky strikes me as the kind of guy who lies about the big things, not the little ones. And if he'd been creeping around, someone else might have been creeping behind him. "What did it say?"

"That I'm only asking for what you promised me. What I'm owed." And it's not lost on me that he sounds like the breathing man. "And my room number. That too."

"Well, I'm here now. So—"

"So talk. But don't go breaking your promises."

"I never made you any promises."

"Bullshit. Do you want me to read the first email you sent? You practically begged me to help you stick it to this guy. I kept up my end of the bargain. And now, it's your turn. I'll bet they paid you a pretty penny for those pictures."

"I didn't sell the pictures." Even I don't believe me. And the truth is only as good as what you can convince somebody else to believe. "But I do have something for you."

"I'm listening."

In my stomach, the Hydra awakens, whipping its many heads. Once I give him the money, it's official. Someone else will know I'd gone through with it. I'd extorted Ian. Another belch from Ricky, and the smell of booze and fried meat makes me queasy. "Would you mind if I used your bathroom first?"

"Knock yourself out."

I turn the flimsy lock and lean against the sink, peering into the mirror. My skin is gray, the color of that festering chicken meat. But it's probably just the grim lighting. I wonder if Ian did the same before he died and what he saw there. If he'd made peace with the man looking back at him.

On the counter, there's a razor, a toothbrush, and a familiar bottle. Inside it, the same little white bars Ian had prescribed for me. One or two in Ricky's drink, and he'd be three sheets to the wind. A few more, and he'd be hallucinating. Or unconscious. The whole bottle, and . . .

I smack the sides of my head with my hands, like I can shake loose the memory of what I've done. And get rid of it. But it's stuck. Forever, I'm afraid. It's a barbed spear, lodged deep. Pull it out, and it all unwinds.

Just one to take the edge off. Isn't that what Ian had said?

So I take two. Wash them down with a swig of tap water.

"You okay in there?" Each strike of Ricky's fist on the door echoes in my chest, and I fling it open, desperate to stop the pounding.

"Fine." I expel the word with a forceful breath and push past him, taking the bank bag from my purse. "This is what I got from Ian. All I got. I don't want it anymore. It's yours."

He reaches for it as I step back, holding it close to me like a child or a lover. "On one condition. You have to promise you'll leave here today and forget all of this ever happened."

"How much is it?"

"A hundred thousand dollars."

He waves a hand at me, dismissively. "You said we could get at least half a mil."

"That was before Ian got himself stabbed. Your cash cow is dead."

"Well, you need to resurrect him, Avenging Angel. Because one hundred thousand is a fucking insult. I lost my wife because of that asshole. Along with my job. My reputation. And I don't care what they say, Culpepper's to blame."

He stalks to the table, takes a long swig from the bottle of Jack, and wipes the dregs from his mouth on his hand.

Uncertain what to say, what to do now, I sit on the bed, facing the electric fireplace. This is what passes for a cheap motel in Carmel. The picture on the mantel reminds me of something from another lifetime ago. Another memory I can't forget.

What I mean to say: I need to think.

But it comes out wrong.

"I need a drink."

"Now you're talkin'."

****

Dust motes dancing in a thin stream of fading sunlight. And dread thick as cotton in my mouth.

Where am I?

It comes back in a rush and I shut my eyes again. The last thing I remember: the bite of bourbon at the back of my throat.

I lie there, still and groaning. Everything hurts. My head especially. And I rub my temple with my hand. The other feels heavy and wet and sticky.

I sit up fast. Too fast. And the picture on the mantel is a wedding photograph. It's Ian and Julie, and they're laughing at me. It's my mother and father, a bullet hole where Dad's right eye should be. It's Ian and Kate, their throats cut into bright red smiles.

I look down at my hand. And I scream. Or I want to, but no sound comes out.

I'm holding a knife. It's the knife. The one I'd tossed into the ocean. I'd watched it sink.

Still, here it is. Black handled and sharp and slick with blood that catches the light from the window.

Beyond it, the room—and my place in it—takes shape.

I'm on the bed. The money too. The stacks split apart, bills strewn around me like confetti. The clock on the nightstand reads 5:00. Nearly five hours I can't account for.

And there's a hand. Oh God. Clawing at the floral comforter. A single hundred bunched inside the frozen fist.

What have I done?

I lean over the edge. It's a steep cliff, and there's a body down below. Ricky's body.

His chest blooms red as a rose. And I can't tell if he's breathing.

I lay back and shut my eyes tight, ignoring the insistent throbbing behind them. It's not the first time I'd tried this trick. When you open your eyes, he'll be gone. That's what I tell myself.

My head lolls to the side, toward the window. And I force my eyes open. On the table, I spot the chicken carcass. The bones picked clean. The fries devoured. I lick my lips and taste salt and grease.

That's how I know I'm not dreaming.

****

Like a zombie, I lumber. Legs stiff, head fuzzy. Every step comes with effort. But I have to move.

Avoiding the claw hand on the bed, I stagger to the other side, scooping the money and the knife into the bedspread. I give the quilt a tug, freeing it from beneath the hand that makes a sickening thud as it falls against the floor.

"Okay," I say aloud. What else?

The bathroom glass I drank from. The empty bottle of Jack. The pills. Ricky's phone sitting idle near the television. All of it into the bedspread. I'll have to burn it.

"Every criminal makes at least one mistake." That's what Dad used to say. "If you look hard enough, you'll find it."

And my mistakes are everywhere.

I'm not ready to contend with the chicken and its trimmings. Or with Ricky. God no. So I head for the bathroom, scrubbing at the counters, the nightstand, the television remote with a soapy, wet washcloth.

I know it's not enough. But it's all I can do.

Slowly. Slowly. I walk around the bed. And it's like walking to my father. To where I'd knelt beside him, eyes on his chest, his hands, his shiny black shoes. He'd actually put on his uniform. Anywhere but there.

I steel myself.

And I look.

Ricky is slumped on his side, his blood stained T-shirt sticking to his chest and riding up. Ample stomach exposed beneath it.

No. No. No. What have I done?

I spin away, not ready after all.

Instead, I toss the chicken carcass into the bag, the bones picked clean. The crumpled napkins. A plastic fork. And a lard-spotted receipt for Joe's Chicken Shack.

The sick feeling swells like a wave. It knocks me to the bed. To the bathroom. To my knees. I vomit twice into the toilet, trying not to touch anything. Flush, with my hand wrapped in the washcloth.

Legs shaking, I make my way back to the body.

I touch the meaty shoulder with the tip of my finger. Warmer than I expected. I lift his bloody shirt to see the damage. To see what I've done.

What have I done? That question again. Always that question.

Beneath the shirt, a smooth white chest, wiry black hair.

I check again, running my hand along his clammy skin. And that's when I spot it.

An empty packet of ketchup squashed against the carpet. Another on the nightstand.

I dip my finger into the red stain at the center of Ricky. Touch it to my tongue. Sweet.

When I look down at him, his eyes are open, wide and skittering. "What the hell?" he asks.

This time when I scream, I wake the dead.

****

"So you actually thought I was dead?" Ricky's laugh is derisive. But his eyes tell me more when they flick across the room, landing on the bundle of bedding I'd intended to burn. They tell me I'm a spider. A spider that might bite. "Sorry to disappoint, but you can't take me out with a few shots of Jack and a squirt of Heinz."

"And the knife?" I point to the table, where it sits, mocking me. With its straight blade and walnut handle. Not *the* knife after all. But Ricky's, apparently. "It was in my hand when I woke up. What was I supposed to think?"

"You asked to use my pocketknife. You said you wanted chicken. I guess you got chicken."

He laughs again, heartily this time, and my stomach roils at the thought. Me chewing that oily, gray flesh before it slid down my throat. "Well, I thought there was blood on it. I must have been hallucinating. A trick of the light, you know." Sure enough, the blood, nothing but ketchup smears. Ricky had licked it himself to prove it.

"And the booze. Don't forget the booze," he adds, popping the top of a Miller Lite from his mini-fridge. "I'm guessing you don't usually drink that much."

"Actually, I don't ever drink that much. Do you remember anything?"

He takes a swig from the can, his throat constricting like a snake's belly, and points to a stray hundred-dollar bill that's gotten free of the sheets. "Money. That's the only thing worth remembering. You promised me more."

"I said I'll try." I don't know what I'd said. Only that a part of me wishes he'd stayed dead. Not that I'd stabbed him, but that he'd just stop. Speaking. Breathing. Existing. "I'm not rich."

"You're the asshole's ex-wife. You'll figure something out."

"And if I can't? I—" What I'm about to say disappears in a gust of panic. *How does he know Ian and I were married?*

Ricky senses it. My utter blankness. "Yep. Turns out money isn't the only thing I remember. You get real chatty when you're drunk."

I don't bother to deny it. It seems the least of my worries. The most of them: What else did I say?

He kicks at the bedding with a satisfied grin. "What were you planning to do with this?"

I shrug as if I'm clueless. "I've never seen a dead man before. It came as a bit of a shock." It sounds like the truth. Even though it's not. "I freaked. How did that ketchup get on your shirt anyway?"

"Hell if I know." He fishes his phone from the pile of money, wipes it on his jeans. "So what did Culpepper do to you? What sins are you avenging?" He pauses, daring me to answer. Daring me to not. "Let me guess. Kate."

The one syllable that shoots an arrow through my chest every time. I try not to let it show.

"If a man cheats with you, he'll cheat on you. Am I right?"

Let him think that it's that simple. That I'm that simple. As simple as him. "Something like that," I say.

****

I won't stay at your place. The first rule I made for Luke. The rule I'd never broken. Because staying meant he'd start to picture me there. That I'd start to picture me there.

But tonight, I drive straight from the Bay View to his house at the edge of Carmel Woods. As if I'd been living there all along. Knowing he's close quiets my mind, even if I can't see him. Soothes the suspicions that flare like a hot rash beneath my skin.

Someone is following me. Watching me. Trying to make me feel crazy. Or guilty. Or both.

Luke is a grounding rod, so I dial his cell and wait.

"Hey," he says, his voice more gentle than I deserve. "I was wondering when I'd hear from you. Sorry I gave you the third degree last night."

"No. I'm the one who should apologize. I'm just—it's been hard."

"You don't need to explain. I get it. Just don't shut me out."

"That's why I'm calling. I need to ask you something."

"Anything." I can tell he means it, and it makes me jealous. The way his heart opens to me again and again. A flower in the morning sunlight, perfect and unscarred.

144

"Did you visit my mom last Wednesday?"

"What? Is that why you were asking me all those questions about Cliffside? I've never been there. I seem to recall you saying we weren't ready for that yet."

"Are you sure? Because I saw your name written in the log book at one-fifteen the day after Valentine's."

I wish he'd say something, put an end to this quiet. An end to my doubt. But not the way he does it, with a tired sigh.

"I was at the crime scene most of that morning. Then we met up at our spot. What is this really about? Have I ever given you a reason not to trust me?"

"No," I concede, though I don't need a reason. Long before Ian, my father had made sure of that, murdering my trust and faith and soft place to fall with one clean shot.

"Do you want me to come over? I've got to be at work at ten, but I—"

"Stop by when you get off in the morning, okay?"

After we hang up, I sit outside in my car, watching the warm glow of the lights through his window. I imagine myself inside, curled next to him on a sofa I've never seen. Sipping wine from a glass I've never touched.

Maybe I am crazy. God knows, I'm guilty for sure.

When the house goes dark and the garage door cranks to life, then, only then, I drive away.

THE MONTEREY COUNTY COURIER

NEW INFORMATION IN BRUTAL "LOVE DOCTOR" SLAYING

by Jackson Lamont

Five days after the discovery of the bodies of Dr. Ian Culpepper (48) and his wife, Dr. Kate Culpepper (30), in their upscale home on Cortez Road in Carmel, sources close to the investigation have revealed that prescription drugs may have played a role in the brutal slaying. Speaking under the condition of anonymity, a law enforcement official informed *The Monterey County Courier* of a wine bottle at the scene which tested presumptive positive for benzodiazepines, a class of drugs that includes those commonly prescribed for anxiety, such as Xanax, Klonopin, and Valium. Toxicology results from the deceased are still pending. A photograph on Kate's Facebook page confirmed she and her husband dined at La Noche, a popular spot for celebrity sightings, on Valentine's Day. It is unclear if the bottle of wine was purchased at the restaurant or brought from the couple's private collection. The manager of La Noche could not be reached for comment.

On Sunday, the parents of Vanessa Sherman (Laramie), Helen and James Laramie, released a statement through their attorney, expressing their sympathies to the Culpepper and Pope families. "We wish to extend our deepest condolences to the families of Drs. Ian and Kate Culpepper. We are sickened by those in the media who would insinuate our involvement in this tragedy, and we pray for speedy justice for those responsible." Mr. and Mrs. Laramie's daughter, Vanessa, died of an overdose of prescription medication and alcohol that caused multisystem organ failure. Drugs in Sherman's system included opioids and benzodiazepines, none of which had been prescribed to her by the Culpeppers, who were cleared of any wrongdoing in her death.

CHAPTER THIRTEEN

MONDAY
FEBRUARY 20, 2018

I should have canceled my Monday clients. That's what a reasonable psychologist would have done. An ethical one. But me, I show up at the office at 9 a.m. with frayed nerves and a fierce headache. Overnight, the clouds rolled in—this morning, intermittent downpours—and my feet are soaked by the time I start the slog up the stairs, holding my dripping umbrella. Cleo's red bicycle is there, propped inside the door and slick with rainwater.

She'd left five messages over the weekend, each more desperate than the last. Until finally I called her back, told her to come in today. That I'd be here early. Then Ricky happened. And the pills, the knife, the goddamned ketchup. The things I'd said—who knows what?—but can't remember.

Cleo needs me. She'd said as much. But I'm not here just for Cleo. It's for me too. To drive my brain to distraction. That place where someone else's voice, worry, pain drowns out my own. And if I'm honest, I'm curious. Because she'd lied about Dr. Jarvis and I don't know why.

On the top step, Cleo sits, shivering, with her backpack between her knees. "I got caught in the rain."

I nod and offer a sad smile, wondering if she means it as a metaphor. Ian is—*was*—not unlike the rain. Capable of destruction, but vital somehow.

"Come inside. I'll turn up the heat."

I open the door, and she follows through the waiting room and into the office, folding herself into her usual position on the sofa, arms hugging her chest. The tears are already there, waiting. "I assume you've seen the pictures."

So many times, I was practically there. Oh wait—. "I did."

"You and the rest of the free world. I just don't understand. We were so careful."

"Remember, we talked about this. The risks you take having an affair. I don't want to sound harsh, but . . ." I can't help myself. It's like talking to Kate. "Exposure. There's always that chance. And this is exposure on a grand scale."

"The grandest. Guess who else has seen them?"

"Your father?"

"Yep. I honestly don't know which is worse. Him calling me a whore or Ian being dead. Murdered." She lowers her head, damp ringlets falling over her shoulders. "That sounds bad. Of course Ian being dead is worse. But my Dad didn't even ask how I am. If I'm okay. All he cares about is his precious reputation."

"Are you? Okay?"

She breathes deep, and her eyes overflow. "Not really. One minute I am, and the next I'm a wreck. I have a million different feelings. But the worst is I have no right to any of them. He didn't belong to me. He belonged to her."

That last bit gets me. We're soul sisters, Cleo and I, even if she doesn't know it. Both left out in the cold. "Your feelings are legitimate. Even if your relationship was unorthodox."

"I won't even be able to go to the funeral. It's tomorrow, you know. Can you imagine the scandal if I turn up? The tabloids would have a field day. And what if they find out who I am? Then what?"

I let the room fill with silence before I answer. "Then what? Let's play it out. What's the worst that could happen? Will the people who matter think any less of you? Will the world end? Will they kick you out of MCC? Will Doctor Jarvis refuse to chair your thesis?"

Testing her when she's at her weakest is completely unprofessional. And still I watch her face for signs. Study her as if through the lens of my camera. She blinks, then looks up at me, stone-faced. And the brazen set of her jaw reminds me of Ian and all his denials: "Kate is my student. I would never."

"I know the world wouldn't end, but I'd want it to. I'm skipping class today. I haven't been to campus at all since the vigil on Friday."

"How was the vigil?"

"Weren't you there? I thought I saw you."

For one frenetic heartbeat, I feel outmatched. Outwitted. *What is she hiding? What does she know?* But there's something to be said for experience. "It's best if we stay focused on you, Cleo."

****

My tone must've been perfect—the exact right blend of admonishment and pity—because Cleo spends the next forty-three minutes focused solely on herself. Her grief. Her shame. Her completely *fucked-up* life. Her words too.

And by the end of it—"Our time's up for today"—there's only doubt. The way it always was with Ian. It's the worst part of lying. Of being lied to. You learn to mistrust yourself.

"Can I still come on Wednesday?"

"Of course. And Cleo, this session is on me." That's guilt talking, all nine heads of the Hydra in chorus. Because I've been full-on paranoid thinking she knew anything about me. She's a college student, for God's sake. So what if she'd lied about Jarvis? I've done far worse. Taking her picture in secret too many times to count. Pictures that had spread like an incurable virus. Whatever happens to her, I've done it. I'm patient zero.

"At least it stopped raining," she says, slinging her bag over her shoulder. She seems lighter, better. Put back together. And I feel competent. I've done my job. Even if I had a hand in the breaking.

I open the door for her. But she freezes at the threshold of the waiting room, ensnared. As if she's stumbled into a trap.

My 10 a.m.—Joan McCorkle—is reading a magazine in the corner. She lifts her eyes and nods at me. But Cleo doesn't notice her at all. She's focused straight ahead.

Leaning against the wall, red-eyed and ragged, is David Fairfax. He flinches when he sees her, then looks away too fast.

Silent, Cleo scurries past him. A red flush stains the back of her neck.

With her gone, David straightens. Shoulders back. Head up. As if I hadn't noticed the drama that played out between them. "Doctor Lawson, I know you have another patient, but I need ten minutes."

****

"This is a one-time thing," I say, watching David's loafered foot tap against the carpet. "I understand you're feeling overwhelmed, but you can't just show up here, expecting to be the first priority. That's not how it works."

He nods, rapid-fire, his whole body chattering. Like a junkie desperate for a hit. "I know. I know. I know. But I'm freaking out."

"Okay. You look nervous and you sound agitated. Just take a deep breath, and—"

"The police called my house. They asked me to come into the station. They said they had witnesses. People who saw me and Ian arguing."

"What did you tell them?"

"I told them I didn't fucking kill him!" The words charge from his throat, raw and incensed, as if he'd been saving them for me. For this moment. A rickety breath clatters out behind them. "I'm so sorry. I'm losing it. Pep loaned me some money. Alright, a shit-ton of money. This is confidential, right?"

He's rambling now, gaining momentum like a rolling stone, and he doesn't wait for an answer.

"I had to pay off a debt at The Pearl. And yeah, he wanted it back. He said something came up and he needed it."

Something like extortion. Blackmail. Revenge.

"The cops told me I wasn't a suspect. Yet. That they'd check out my alibi. But it doesn't matter what they said. It's what they didn't say. That one guy, Donovan, he looked at me like I was goddamned Robert Durst."

"You felt accused." *Join the club, buster.*

"Exactly. And it's the same with Tara ever since those pictures came out. All of a sudden, she thinks I'm having an affair. If Pep could do it, could lie like that, then I must be too."

"Well, you have been lying to Tara about your gambling. Perhaps she's sensing that deception."

"And then, I show up here. And *she's* in your office. Jesus Christ."

I hear Ian in my head. *Sometimes, you just have to let them keep talking. Dig their own graves.* Along with another one of his little gems: *Empathy is overrated.*

"Did she tell you about me?" David asks.

"You know I can't discuss—"

"I know you can't answer that. *Fuck me.* What was she doing here? Is she going to tell Tara?"

As much as I hate to admit it, Ian had been right. David is digging and digging and digging. Faster than I could have unearthed whatever he's got buried. "I'm not sure I follow you, David."

"Fine. You want me to say it? I'll fucking say it. I slept with her. Ever since Sophie was born, Tara's got a constant headache. We barely do it anymore. And it was one time. One time!"

"Okay. I understand. You only did it once." I stay in the moment. Trying not to spook him.

"Right. And I didn't even know what she was. I didn't pay her. One of the guys at the bar told me a month or so later when I saw her again. But that's not what I was there for. I just came to play poker."

"You met her gambling? You relapsed?"

He's slowing down a little, now that the worst is out. "At the Pearl Casino in Monterey. Last June. I tried to tell Pep, but he refused to believe it."

"Believe what? That you had sex with his mistress?"

He gulps and swallows hard, looks up at me with wild eyes that haven't slept. Probably won't tonight either. "That she's Cleopatra James. That she's an escort."

****

If I could make Mrs. McCorkle disappear, I would've followed David. But, she's still here—real as her fake double Ds—even if I'm not. Mentally, anyway.

"For the life of me, Doctor Lawson, I can't understand why Jacqueline wants to get married in a church when I've offered her the country club. It's just so pedestrian."

If I could shake Mrs. McCorkle, I'd grab her by the shoulders and rattle her bones until her veneers cracked. If I could scream at her, I'd wail until her bleached-blonde hair blew back. But I only have one weapon available to me, so I wield it like an axe. Swift and without mercy.

"Perhaps your daughter is more traditional than you. After all, you are on your third marriage."

She scowls at me, as much as the Botox will allow, and I go back to clock watching. Enjoying my small victory with a nod to Ian. *Empathy really is overrated.*

After I send Mrs. McCorkle back to husband number three's Pebble Beach mansion, I flee the office with my Nikon. I need to think. And sometimes my lens helps to order the chaos. Or create it, depending.

I fast-walk, dodging puddles and listening to the thwack of my flats against the rain-soaked cobblestone. Before I pass by Seaside Sweets, I cross to the other side. My nerves too frayed, thoughts too jumbled, to face Marianne and her questions. By now, I'm sure she knows I'm the ex-wife of the too-good-looking and very dead Love Doctor.

When I spot the sand at the end of Ocean Avenue, my breath quickens. An unmarked police car, like the one my father drove, is double-parked, empty. I skirt into the cover of the windswept cypress and remove the lens cap. Aim my lens down the beach, where a lone figure is bent over the sand. I see sturdy shoulders and gloved hands. A bad knee that hitches when he hoists himself up and brushes sand from his trousers, a clear plastic bag in tow.

He turns toward the camera—Jack Donovan—and I nearly lose my balance, though he's at least a hundred yards from me. Nearby, the white-haired beach comber I've seen before stands guard, his two black Labs leashed and stanchioned beside him.

As the two men talk, beginning the slow trek back up the beach, I lower my focus to the bag in Jack's hand and snap a photo. And another. And another. I'm sure of what it is even if I don't want to be. That black handle—that long, glinting blade—the same slate gray as the sky. It must've been the storm that dredged it up from the bowels of the ocean, spit it back to shore like I feared.

I sit on one of the low cypress limbs blown smooth by the wind, thinking of Wallace Bergman, and I worry. Because secrets float to the surface, wash up like shells on the beach. Secrets come unearthed, rising like bones from a shallow grave.

CHAPTER FOURTEEN

JUST before 3 p.m., I lock my office and drive up Ocean Avenue in the direction I rarely go, away from the beach. Past the bookstores, bakeries, and art galleries, the curlicue rooftops of the charming cottages that belong in a fairytale. I leave it all behind. But I carry my secrets—old and new—and my shoulders droop under the weight of them. Guiding the wheel takes effort. Like turning a stuck rudder. And I wonder if I'll ever feel light again.

The place I'm heading to is just off Ocean, a converted house with a swing set out front. Just looking at the place—the wood planters with pink geraniums, the friendly welcome mat, the unwashed Volvo in the drive—you'd think a family lives there. But if you watch long enough, you'll see them. The broken children with their broken parents filing in and out every fifty minutes like clockwork. In a pilgrimage to see him. Dr. Maury Littleton, renowned child psychologist.

I don't know him personally, but I know of him. I'd even referred him a patient or two. He'd retired from practice at the Kennedy Krieger Trauma Center in Boston a few years back—*The Monterey County Courier* had done a story about him—and set up shop here among the cobblestone streets and storybook homes. It seemed fitting. Especially when I'd seen his picture. His smile took up most of his face, his wiry gray eyebrows the rest. And set beneath them, teddy-bear brown eyes. The perfect mixture of grandfather and wizard. Where else would the cops send Maddie?

I'd telephoned the police station this morning, pretending to be Dr. Littleton's secretary, confirming his 10 a.m. appointment with Madison Culpepper. And I'd feigned just the right amount of surprise and concern. "Oh. Let me check. You're absolutely right. It is at 3. No. That won't be a problem." I'd hung up the phone, exuberant. Relieved.

But now that I'm here, parked on the street and lingering on a sidewalk bench a block away, I don't know why I'm here.

Well, that's not entirely true.

I need to talk to Maddie.

Even if it sounds completely certifiable, in my professional opinion.

Sheila is right on time, looking as put together as when I saw her last at MCC. Dark jeans, a black sweater. Black pointy-toed boots. And oversized sunglasses that make her look mysterious and elegant. Just the sort of woman who'd give birth to someone like Kate.

She opens the car's back door and Maddie emerges, clutching a stuffed bear in one hand. With the other, she reaches for her grandma, latches onto her sweater, and follows her up the walk.

If I didn't know, I'd never guess about the ghosts walking beside them. The kind of searing pain that must be festering beneath it all. Only the dead silence between them gives it away.

I expect them to disappear inside where the wizard does his work. But they stop at the swing set and Maddie hoists herself into the seat, bear on her lap. Sheila gives her a push, and the old chains creak to life. I watch Maddie go higher and higher without a smile or a giggle. Until I hear Sheila say, "How about we sing a song?" And then she begins, hopefully. "The itsy-bitsy spider . . ."

Halfway through, Sheila is still the only one singing when the whir of an approaching engine interrupts. I catch a glimpse of the driver.

Shit. I should've known they'd be here. They'll probably watch the whole thing go down behind a one-way mirror.

I duck my head and scurry off the bench toward my car, crouching beside it. I feel like a criminal. The way my breath is heavy with guilt. The way sweat pools on my low back, slickens my armpits. It's all too familiar.

I peer up over the hood as Detectives Donovan and Lennox make their way from the unmarked car to the swing set. "Hi, Maddie," Jack says, with a wide, overeager wave. "Hi, Mister Bear."

The only answer is the squeak of the chains until they grind to a halt.

****

After the four of them go inside—a macabre little family—I sit in my car and think. About how I should get the hell out of here before someone sees me. About how my life became such a colossal mess. About how I need to get Maddie alone. And so I don't leave. Not yet.

Instead, I wait, hunkered down. Window cracked.

Fifteen minutes later, the detectives emerge first, stone-faced. Sheila trails behind, lugging Maddie on her hip and Mister Bear in her purse. Maybe mutism is contagious, because none of them are speaking. Four mouths, four tight lines devoid of expression.

Finally, Jack turns to Sheila, and Maddie buries her face in her grandma's shoulder. "We'll try again after the funeral. Hang in there, Maddie."

He pats her shoulder, and her little body trembles. I remember the way it felt to hold my words inside me like lightning in a bottle. To know that to set them free, to wield them, would make it real. And once it became real, my whole world would end.

While Sheila situates Maddie in her car seat, the detectives drive away. And I turn my key, ready.

Clueless, she pulls out of the drive. And I do what I do. I follow.

****

Sheila speeds right past the house on Cortez Road. The crime scene tape is gone now, and it guts me how normal it looks. As if Ian and Kate might still turn up, alive, to reclaim it. I slow down without thinking and watch the windows the way I'd sometimes done in the evenings, looking for signs of them. Holding my breath, afraid to blink. Gasping a little when I'd caught them—Kate's silhouette in the upstairs bedroom, Ian at his desk, Maddie's face pressed to the glass—as if I'd been given a gift. Spotted a rare bird.

Sheila turns into the gate of a rental house a half mile up the road, and I stop. This is the end of the line. But at least I know where they're staying.

I plan to drive home. Really, I do. But somehow I end up parking down the street, getting out of my car. Scaling the back fence and standing at the kitchen door of the Culpeppers' house.

Because I have an itch I need to scratch. A hunch. A feeling.

I stare in at the stainless steel Viking refrigerator. It looms at the back of the kitchen like a hulking beast. And I wonder what's inside. Ice cream for Maddie. Greek yogurt for Kate. And for Ian, Diet Coke or Evian.

A monogrammed dishtowel—THE CULPEPPERS' KITCHEN—hangs on the stove, slightly crooked.

A stack of unopened mail waits in a letter box.

Otherwise, the counters are bare.

So I'm right. It's gone.

I suppose the police might've taken it. But the story in *The Monterey County Courier* made it clear. No murder weapon found. And the Culpeppers owned a set of knives, an expensive set. Wusthof. I know, because I saved for months to buy it, paid cash at Sur La Table, and mailed it to them as a wedding gift. Anonymously, of course. With a note only Ian would understand.

And when I'd seen it here last Tuesday night, Valentine's Day, placed carefully by the sink in a position of honor, it had felt like a victory. A hollow one, empty as a sun-bleached skull washed up on the beach. But a victory nonetheless.

There are always secrets between husband and wife. But not all secrets are created equal. What's essential to determine is whether your secrets are the kind that corrode love or preserve it.
—Ian Culpepper, *Love CPR*

VALENTINE'S DAY
SIX YEARS EARLIER

AVA loathed LA no matter how hard she tried for Ian's sake. Every morning, the city rose up through the smog exactly as she'd remembered. The palm trees. The relentless heat. The ocean air that smelled briny and alive. Nothing had changed, which was exactly why she'd never planned on coming back. Most of all, because her dead father still lived there, his presence as oppressive and oversized as the sun that blared at her through their cheap mini-blinds.

She rolled over and squeezed her eyes shut against it, wishing it would go away. It woke her up every morning, cruelly, ten minutes before the alarm.

"The place is cozy, and it gets lots of light. Perfect for a young newlywed couple. And there's room to grow. The office would do nicely as a nursery." That's what the real estate agent had told them when they'd rented the guesthouse in Ocean Park sight unseen last March. The pitch, an unintentional, overly cheery litany of everything that felt wrong between them. Everything she couldn't fix.

Ava had wanted to tell the realtor: "But we're not that young. And we're not growing." And after last year's valen-pocalypse, as she'd taken to calling it in her mind, even the word *newlywed* clunked in her brain with a dissonant thud. We're not newlyweds anymore.

Because she still couldn't get past Ian's lie. Not the one about Julie— that she understood somehow—but Prick Whitlock and the missing office supplies. As if she couldn't have handled him herself. That, above all else, nettled.

But today could be different. A fresh start. Today she could put things right again. Prove to Ian how capable she was. Make the best of it, just like her mother told her to do when she'd cried to her about moving back here.

With a renewed sense of purpose, she intercepted the alarm— that chipper melody she'd come to despise—and headed for the bathroom. Ian had driven off hours ago to sit in bumper-to-bumper traffic on the way to UCLA for his 8 a.m. Tuesday/Thursday Intro to Pharma class. But he'd left a Post-it note for her stuck to the mirror.

Happy anti-versary! Good luck with Wally and call me after.

She crumpled the note in her hand, feeling disappointed, mostly in herself. *This is the sort of romance I inspire*, she thought.

Tossing the note aside, she splashed her face with cold water, then let the tap run, rinsing the ring of shaving cream and a haphazard line of Ian's whiskers from the sink. Since his agent told him he had a young face, he'd started shaving every day, coating his skin with some exotic product they couldn't afford. But he'd finally started booking news talk shows, making the rounds as an expert on couples or psych meds—or both—and that made him happy. So Ava sucked it up and said nothing.

She opened the towel cabinet and reached behind the fluffy stack to the makeup bag she'd hidden there. She zipped it open and popped the pill that would guarantee their office would remain an office. There would be no blue or pink paint. No zoo animal appliques. No bottles or diapers or 3 a.m. wakeups. No new little person with insatiable demands to widen the wedge between them.

Of course her mother had something to say about that too. "You're nearly thirty, Ava. Don't waste time." But Ava knew she had to right the marital ship before they added more cargo. Otherwise, they'd sink. And fast.

She stripped down and stepped into the steaming hot shower, feeling hopeful. Because her best shot to steer the *SS Culpepper* to safety—Wallace Bergman—would be making his way to her office for his one o'clock Tuesday session.

****

Nearly every weekday for the last ten months, Ava had taken the Line 18 Big Blue Bus from their house in Santa Monica to her office in upscale Brentwood.

LA had no shortage of psychologists. But Brentwood had no shortage of would-be patients. "Deep pockets and empty souls," Ian had told her, when he'd gone with her to rent the shiny modern space on San Vincente. And again when they'd printed her fancy business cards on heavy stock, branding her Ava Lawson, PhD, Psychotherapist.

It had been Ian's idea to use her maiden name. That way they could refer patients to each other. His idea to bend the ethics code. "Just until you make a name for yourself," he'd said. And she'd gone along with all of it, sending him desperate housewives seeking SSRIs, burned-out execs demanding Adderall, and wannabe starlets with bad nerves who needed a little something to make it through the next audition.

In return, he'd sent her no one.

Until two weeks ago.

Wallace Bergman, President of Programming for BXA.

The bright ding of the bell told Ava someone waited outside. And she jumped to attention. Wallace didn't like to wait and neither did she. They had a lot of ground to cover. Never mind if they were plowing in different directions.

"I'm ready for you, Mr. Bergman," she said, beckoning him into the office that felt nothing like her. The cold white leather sofa. The glass table with fresh flowers and magazines she'd never read. The austere clock that watched them both. Only the antique secretary desk Ian had found at a yard sale gave her comfort. It felt like a kindred spirit with its eyes of knotted wood, its secret compartment for a heart.

Wallace removed his hat—a pale pink fedora—and shuffled to the sofa. He offered her a blank face framed with thinning gray hair and a cashmere scarf, his eyes hidden behind dark sunglasses that probably cost her monthly rent. *Eccentric,* she'd written in her notes during their first meeting, underlining it twice.

"Would you like to pick up where we left off last week?" She pretended to consult her notes, but she needed no reminding. She'd discussed all of their sessions ad nauseam with Ian, relishing the way he hung on her words when she talked about Wallace. "You were telling me about a documentary you'd watched on the Stonewall Riots. And coming out to your parents in your thirties."

He threw back his head and laughed wildly. "Ah yes, the worst-kept secret of my life. Things were different back then, but I always say everybody knew I was gay. Everybody but me. Even my wife."

"You were in denial?"

"The deepest. It wasn't until I fell in love with Richard that I realized." His shoulders stiffened, bearing an unseen weight as he held his sunglasses from his eyes, blotting beneath them with a handkerchief. Ava caught a glimpse of watery, red-rimmed blue. Elusive as a strange and distant planet you could only spot once a year and only then if the conditions were right. "We were both married to other people at the time. *Other women.* When I met Richard, that's when my real life began."

"Have you told him what he means to you?"

"Words fall short, but yes, I've tried. The thing about Richard is he's a bit in denial himself. He'd been in remission for so long, he thought—we *both* thought—he'd beaten the damn thing. Turns out it was there all along, lying in wait. Building an army. Planning a fucking coup."

"I'm sorry. It sounds as if you've both been blindsided." Ava knew exactly what he meant. Cancer. Depression. All evidence of the body's betrayal, its desire to destroy itself. But she tried to stay focused. "You told Doctor Culpepper you've been feeling pressured at work as well. Is that right?"

Of course, she was right. She'd heard it straight from the horse's mouth, after Wallace had shown up at Ian's office a few months ago needing something to help him sleep. "Get him talking, Aves. Feel him out. And if he asks how we know each other, I'm just your highly respected colleague," Ian had said.

"Are you from LA?" Wallace's question startled her. Back in Berkeley, she'd learned to deflect when her clients got personal. But here in LA, nobody asked, and she'd begun to feel as invisible as the chic wallpaper Ian had insisted she purchase.

"What would it mean to you if I was?"

"That you'd understand what Jack Kerouac meant when he said this city is a jungle. Lonely and brutal."

"Is that how it feels to you?"

"Worse." The bitterness in his laugh felt familiar to her, as familiar as her own. "Ever heard of The Suicide Forest?"

That stopped Ava cold. "The one in Japan?"

"Aokigahara Forest, it's called. They say you'll see bodies hanging from the trees there. Bones clinking around like wind chimes. It's not so different in Hollywood, you know. You have to step over the dead to get to the top."

Ava thought of her father. Of DeAndre Mack. And she shivered. "That's a powerful image of despair. Have you ever thought of doing something else? Leaving your job?"

As soon as she said it, Ian started gnawing in her head. *What the hell are you doing, Ava?* Wallace Bergman leaving BXA was definitely not part of the plan.

"A million times. A million and one now. Especially with Richard sick. But I'm not ready yet. My past couple of pitches have been real flops, and I want to go out on a high. With a big winner. Emmys, ratings, the whole nine."

"It sounds like you're busy navigating a route through the forest. To get you to the other side."

One corner of his mouth barely turned up. It was the saddest smile she'd ever seen. It made her think of her father. "I like you, Doctor Lawson. But I'd guess you're not from LA."

"What makes you say that?"

"Anybody from here will tell you, there's no way through the forest. Nobody makes it out alive."

****

After Wallace left, Ava didn't call Ian like she'd promised. Because she couldn't help but feel she'd let him down. She slogged through her afternoon clients and took the bus home, dodging the shiny-red heart balloon someone had left tied to the seat in front of her. It bounced eagerly toward her head every time the bus lurched forward. Like it wanted something from her. When she got off, she loosened the Mylar string and carried it outside where she released it into the gray sky. She walked the rest of the way to the Santa Monica Pier, glancing up every few minutes until the red dot had faded from view. As if it had never existed at all.

Once, in college, Ava had looked for DeAndre Mack's family. She'd spent a Saturday in the library, scrolling through microfilm from the 1994 *LA Times* until she spotted the headlines.

"LA Detective Makes Record Drug Bust"

"Agents Seize Five Tons of Cocaine from Artist District Warehouse"

"Shootout Leaves One Dead, Cop Hailed as Hero"

One dead. DeAndre reduced to a number, a brief mention at the end of an article. A non-person. Just another balloon disappeared into the sky. But Ava dug until she'd uncovered an obituary and his mother's name. By the time she'd worked up the nerve to dial the number she'd found, the man who'd answered told her Carlotta Mack had died that spring. Heart attack. "But what can I do for you, young lady?"

Ava could still hear the curious lilt in his gravelly voice. Or was it judgment? She wasn't sure. Not then. Not even now. Here. Waiting for Ian on a bench near the boardwalk, where the whole world seemed as simple and predictable as the rolling waves, the spinning Ferris wheel.

She'd replied—"Nothing"—the silence tightening like a rope between them until the man hung up, leaving her alone with the flat dial tone, as lifeless as Carlotta's heart. She'd been too late.

"Hey, Aves." Ian's hands squeezed her shoulders, and she turned to look at him. His shoes were off, dark jeans cuffed, and he sank his toes into the sand. "You didn't call me."

"I had a client right after, and we ran late." Ava wondered when she'd gotten so good at lying to him. And when it had started to feel necessary.

"Late, huh? That's my girl. I knew you'd get him talking." He joined her on the bench, leaning in to kiss her like she'd earned it.

"He asked," she said. Two words that distilled everything between them.

"And what did you tell him?"

"That you were a highly respected colleague."

He kissed her again, and she hated herself. Not for betraying Wallace. But for being so pliable, so dutiful, so eager to please. She'd become her mother.

"You're a natural, babe. Should I be worried?"

His adoration, his teasing—it warmed her, no sun in sight—and she gave him a playful shove. "You were right. He's definitely looking for ideas. But whatever you pitch him, it's got to be better than good. He wants his next show to be his swan song."

He jumped up, blue eyes dancing, and pulled her to her feet with an urgency that made her giddy, though she suspected it was Adderall-induced. His bright-idea pill, he called it. "Let's brainstorm over pizza."

"A working dinner? How anti-Valentine's of you."

****

Ian slumped off of Ava and onto the bed, sweaty and unsatisfied. "I'm sorry," he said.

"It's okay." She left him there, stepping over the lingerie she'd discarded an hour ago, and retreated to the bathroom, embarrassed. Like it was her fault. And not the Adderall he'd been popping at least once a week, staying up all night to work on the book he wouldn't show her. "You'll kill the muse," he'd said. Which always seemed ironic with him on top of her, struggling to get it up.

She stood naked in the mirror, looking hard at her reflection, trying to imagine how Ian saw her. Maybe it was her fault. She'd gotten too skinny, running every day. Her curves had flattened, hardened to sinew and bone. Like LA had sucked the meat right off her. And she didn't try the way she used to. The lipstick at the back of the drawer had sat untouched for months. Boring black flats and a ponytail—her standard uniform.

"Ava? Are you mad?"

She caught her half smile in the glow of the night-light as he groveled. This part, only this part, made the Adderall worth it.

"Of course not." She slipped back in bed and curled against his chest. "Let's try again in the morning."

When Ian finally fell asleep, Ava rolled away from him and reached for her phone. She typed *suicide forest* into the search bar and scrolled through the images, page after page, with quiet desperation. She wondered if Wallace had ever done the same. And why she kept expecting to see her father's face.

THE DOWNTOWN STAR

"MURDERED LOVE DOCTOR'S MISTRESS IDENTIFIED AS HIGH-PRICED SAN FRANCISCO ESCORT!"

The mysterious red-haired beauty at the center of the *Love Doctored* cheating scandal has been unmasked as Cleopatra James, an employee of Spellbound Services International, a San Francisco-based escort service. According to Cleopatra's profile, she is a university student with an irresistible combination of girl-next-door innocence and the sensuality of a temptress. Her profile describes her preferred client and gives a glimpse of what she may have seen in Ian Culpepper, the now-deceased doctor of love: intelligent, witty, spontaneous, romantic, and mature. Though it remains unclear as to whether Dr. Culpepper knew of his mistress's double life or perhaps even paid for her services, one thing is certain: the entire world is watching her now. A spokesperson from Spellbound Services International declined to comment on the story, citing the privacy of their employees and clients.

CHAPTER FIFTEEN

TUESDAY
FEBRUARY 21, 2018

TODAY, they will bury my ex-husband. What a strange thought, a morbid one. But there it is, front and center, the instant I jar awake at the turn-click of Luke's keys in the door. From my bed, I see the rain cry tears down the window. It's dark out—well past midnight—but the drops catch the streetlights as they fall.

Luke kicks off his shoes, drops his duffel bag on the chair, and slides in next to me, still dressed. His body is cool against mine, his hair damp from the rain. But I let him wrap me in his arms anyway. His heart drums against my back, and I turn to face him.

"Hi," I whisper, finding his lips with mine and tugging him closer. The first time Luke kissed me, he wasn't Ian. And the simple fact of it wedged between us like the sharp end of an axe. But now, it's what draws me in, what holds me there, magnetized. *He is not Ian.* It could be my favorite thing about him. "How was work?"

Luke lays back, sighs. I wonder if he's parceling out which parts to tell me. And which to leave out. "A knife washed up on Carmel Beach. Some old guy's dog found it."

"The murder weapon?"

"Don't know. Dad took it to the lab for testing. I doubt it though. I mean, what're the odds?"

I let my head loll back to the window, where the rain looks black, slick as oil. The Hydra lashes in my gut, and I almost wince. "Slim to none, I'd say. How did the old guy even figure to call the cops?"

"Gumshoe detective. You know the type. He says he saw someone toss something from the jetty on Saturday. He thought it was suspicious."

"He sounds like a busybody."

Moving back toward Luke, I slip my hand beneath his T-shirt to distract us both. Myself with the swells and dips of his chest. Him with my teasing fingertips. But instead, he lays his hand over mine, stilling it. "Dad said the guy might've planted the knife there himself. For attention or something."

"That seems like a stretch."

"That's what I said. But, I guess we'll wait and see. Now . . ." He sets my hand free again and finishes the thought on my neck. No words, just his mouth, hot and insistent. And I lose myself there. I picture myself on the beach, with the white-haired man and his dogs at my side, all of us squinting at the jetty. At some other person— someone *not me*—and the object in her hand that reflects the sunlight as it's swallowed by the ocean below.

****

Ian and Kate will be buried side by side in twin mahogany coffins at Whispering Cypress Memorial. Of course, they will. Husband and wife for eternity. *What did you expect, Ava? A plot for yourself in between them?*

But it's Julie I'm thinking of most. Her lonely grave at the top of the hill in Piedmont Cemetery, where on a clear day you can see as far as the Golden Gate Bridge. Ian had taken me there once, and I'd laid a sunflower on the sparse grass that was only beginning to fill in. I'd felt like an impostor. And a thief. Especially when he dropped to his knee to uproot a small cluster of weeds from beside the smooth granite. Later, I'd gone on my own too, mostly to remind myself Ian belonged to me. Possession is nine-tenths of the law, right? But that was then.

And that's the ugly truth of a marriage. Whoever gets him last, gets him forever.

I watch the funeral through the lens of the Nikon, hunkered down in the front seat of my car. And I'm not the only one. A half-dozen reporters circle the road near the burial plot like vultures coveting a carcass. Occasionally, a lone bird, brave with greed, makes an approach, only to be shooed away by private security.

They're here for one reason. Cleopatra James. Not my fresh-faced Cleo, pedaling her bicycle down Ocean Avenue. But the other. I'd visited the Spellbound Services website that morning and found her profile. Face blurred, body clad in racy lingerie, she'd posed on her knees in white sheets. Listed beneath her photo, her "specialties": Discrete relationships. Mature clients. Looking at her, the blatant curves of her hips, her breasts, I'd felt betrayed all over again. By Ian. By her.

When the eulogy begins, I concede Cleo is a no-show. But David is there. Tara too. Ned Gotleib and his wife. And Dan Jarvis, the professor I'd outright lied to at the vigil. Though really I only watch Maddie. She clings to Sheila like a monkey. Little arms, little legs, wrapped around her grandmother. Little feet in black patent Mary Janes, dug in to Sheila's hips, little chin mashed into Sheila's shoulder. One little hand latched to her stuffed bear as it dangles against Sheila's back.

And the eyes Ian gave her—two little blue marbles—fixed on me. Or so it seems. The psychologist in me calls it dissociation. The criminal, indictment. And the girl in me knows that look as a bottomless well of grief.

But Maddie's blank stare, no matter how I label it, is to blame for my carelessness. Because I don't see Ricky until he's stumbling up the manicured lawn, red-faced and raving, in the middle of Ian's eulogy.

I crack the window, mid-tirade.

"Great doctor, my ass!" He careens toward the edge of the crowd and pushes his way toward the hole in the ground where Ian and Kate will lie together. "My wife listened to that sorry sack. And guess where she is now?"

Sheila tightens her grip on Maddie, looping a protective arm around her head. She side-steps away from Ricky as he reaches the raised coffins, covered in cascades of hydrangea, white as ocean foam.

"Rotting in the ground just like him, that's where."

I briefly redirect my lens to the stock-still minister as he waves to a security guard stanchioned at the periphery. Then, I return again to Madison, her eyes of marble unblinking, unfazed.

She's seen worse. What else *has* she seen? What does she remember?

Back to Ricky, cornered like a wild animal, snarling at the lip of the grave. He withdraws his pocketknife, wielding it like a sword, and the mourners gasp along with me. The vultures and their flashbulbs move in a wake.

The whole scene is so garish I instantly conjure Ian's voice—*A show about couples on the brink. It's a good start, Ava. But, the producers want more, something that will make us stand out from the rest. Think bigger. Louder. A bit more . . . what's the word? Garish.*

"I have every right to be here. I'm a goddamned truth-teller. And these people need to know the truth about this scumbag. The self-proclaimed Love Doctor."

He tosses his head back and lets a bitter laugh fly as security closes in around him. "You're Kate's mom, right? Poor, pitiful Kate. Hot little number though, wasn't she?"

Sheila flinches but not Madison. And I start to feel queasy, to wonder why I came here. Ricky takes another clumsy step backward, bumping up against Ian's coffin. Later, they'll lower it into the dark soil below and cover it with dirt. Roots will wind among flesh. In a year or so, he'll be mostly teeth and bones. And in another fifty, his Zegna suit and Ferragamo dress shoes will have outlasted everything else.

"Your precious Love Doctor couldn't keep it in his pants. Not in this marriage or the last one. Maybe that's why he was so quick on the trigger, accusing everybody else. Accusing me. When really it was him who needed the famous Fidelity Five. Yep, that's right. Before Doctor Kate was his wife, she was his mistress."

My heart seizes, and the camera falls to my lap. I stare at my hands, afraid to look up. Afraid Maddie won't be the only one gawking at me.

"I know his ex-wife. We had a deal to expose the lying bastard but—"

I reposition the camera just in time to watch Ricky lose his balance and tumble down, wind-milling his arms in desperation. Almost as if I'd pushed him myself. The knife falls from his hand, as he grabs at the metal contraption where the coffins rest. They sway a bit, and for a moment, I imagine the irony of Ricky crushed beneath the box where dead Ian rests.

But instead he's covered by uniformed security officers, his legs writhing under them, like an insect on an ant mound. And the vultures move in, taking an endless stream of photographs.

As soon as I hear the sirens approaching, panic flames in my chest, licking up my throat and searing it raw. I glance down the road to the first squad car. *Is that Cooper?*

I duck, filling the car with the sound of my own ragged breathing, weighting it beneath worries heavy as millstones.

Ricky will be arrested.

Ricky will be questioned.

Ricky will talk. About me.

The urge to escape presses on my chest until it's unbearable. I start the car.

When I raise my head and look through my lens, Ricky's right there up the road, between Cooper and Donnelly, the other officer from my alleged Saturday break-in. There's a nasty bruise forming on Ricky's temple, and his face is spotted with dirt and grass. He spits more of the same from his mouth, and I can't look away, even though I should.

Our eyes are drawn to each other like a cord, cinching tight. Strangling both of us. "That's her! Ava! Tell them!"

I mash the accelerator, harder than I intend, tires squealing against the concrete, spitting out gravel.

I've done nothing wrong.

I've done nothing wrong.

I've done—

A blur of movement across the road startles me. Time tricks me—it's too fast and I'm too slow—and I slam the brakes. The wheels spin out, and the car comes to a stop. Then, I hear Sheila's throaty panic. See her awkward run in heels, each step stabbing the earth and sinking in deep.

"Maddie! Get off the road!"

Maddie stands there in front of the car, rigid as a small tree trunk. She's dropped her bear into a nearby puddle, his head half-submerged in muddy water that's splattered her tights.

I'm not sure what to do, so I do nothing. I wait till Sheila scoops her up, glaring at me, as if to say it's all my fault. Which it is. Till my breathing sounds less like a woman underwater.

I know I need to leave. And now. The cops are in my rearview, pushing Ricky's belly up against the squad car, his feet spread-eagle.

As I ease my car forward and check the mirror once more, Maddie's head swivels back to the road. To me. Her cheeks are pink from the cold. The rest of her, ghost white. I shiver, as if she really is a ghost sent to haunt me.

She raises her hand, her little skeleton fingers, and waves.

CHAPTER SIXTEEN

NERVES jangling, I drive back to the office and head up the stairs. I've canceled my afternoon clients, but it feels wrong to go home now. I'm too keyed up, too exposed, and the house is too empty. And I'd only sit there and wonder about Ricky. What he's saying and not saying and how long until they come for me, the jilted ex-wife with an axe to grind.

So I fall into my desk chair instead, open my laptop, and try to distract myself with yesterday's session notes. But with each tap of the keys, I only imagine Jack Donovan combing through them for evidence. His eagle eyes reading between the lines.

Name: Cleo Campbell
Session Date: 2/20/18

Client presented on time, oriented in all spheres. Mood was distraught, tearful, but client denied suicidal ideation. Discussed issues of grief and loss. Client continues to be hyperfocused on others' judgments of her, possibly due to complicated relationship with father. Challenged client's cognitive distortions (i.e., catastrophizing). Recommended book on grief, *The Year of Magical Thinking*. Next session scheduled for 2/22.

Jack would notice the session dates, that I'd seen Cleo outside of our regular schedule, that she'd been distraught. He'd ask how much I knew about her and when and how. And why. "Why did you provide therapy to a client involved in an intimate relationship with your ex-husband?"

And I'd have to answer: "Because I'm a vengeful bitch." That or "I dunno."

I mash the Delete key until every word is gone. The blank page makes me feel better, like I can still be redeemed. Like I'm not beyond saving. But I'll have to terminate with Cleo, refer her to someone else. Not right away. I can't abandon her. But soon. Very soon.

I stare at the screen until it starts to blur, the funeral replaying inside my brain, every miserable word. But these especially: *the Fidelity Five.* That had been my idea. A five-minute test of faithfulness. Tasteless and tawdry and bite-sized. Not to mention pure nonsense masquerading as pseudoscience. If it hadn't been so vulgar, it would've been brilliant—like naked daters or B-list celebrities duking it out in a boxing ring. The perfect, sordid combination for reality TV.

I have a sudden, desperate itch to see the video. As if it will be different this time. I open my browser and type in the search bar: *Love Doctored Ricky Sherman Fidelity Five.* That easily, I bring it to life.

BXA never aired Ricky Sherman's appearance on *Love Doctored*, but like all things dark and insidious, it had found a way. Posted anonymously on YouTube a week after Vanessa's death, it now lived forever.

The video starts with Kate. Her serious face. She's mid-interview with Vanessa Sherman, Ricky's wife of one year. They couldn't look more unalike, and I'm sure it's intentional. They'd positioned the dumpy wife—doughy and pale and exasperated—right next to Kate's undeniable beauty.

"We always know, don't we? Call it women's intuition." She makes eyes at the camera, and as always, I rankle. Every single time. "So when did you start to feel things weren't right at home?"

"I got a little worried when Ricky started staying late at the office. But I tried to be supportive. I know how important his career is to him. And it's hard to make partner at an accounting firm if you don't put in those extra hours. It's expected."

Kate murmurs, as if she understands. As if she ever could. "You didn't trust your gut, Vanessa. And now you're here on *Love Doctored* . . ." Pause, for the obligatory cheers from the studio audience. "So it must've gotten worse."

Vanessa sniffles, hides her eyes, whispers the next part. "It did. He started coming home drunk. And we stopped having sex altogether. It's been a long time."

"How long?"

"Six months at least."

Cue audience gasp. Kate pats her arm, gives her shoulder a squeeze. "Is that why you contacted us? You need to know for sure, don't you?"

Cut to Ian on a separate stage. He speaks as the music swells. "Ricky and Vanessa are about to embark on a journey to rediscover love. But a relationship is like a house. It must be built on a rock-solid foundation. And what is that foundation?"

He waits for the audience to answer in unison. "Trust!"

"Exactly. Without trust, the foundation is weak, and the house will fall. Before we can help Ricky and Vanessa, we have to test their foundation. And how do we do that?"

"The Fidelity Five!"

"That's right! When Vanessa contacted us and told us her suspicions, we set up a five-minute experiment using our lovely confederate, Lacey, to test Ricky's commitment. What you all are about to see, along with Vanessa, is the raw, uncut footage from that night. Vanessa, are you ready for the results of the Fidelity Five?"

Vanessa's eyes dart like a cornered animal. She's definitely not ready. But the video rolls on like a runaway train. It's the most explosive—garish, if you will—Fidelity Five in *Love Doctored* history. Ian and Kate tell us so afterward. Lacey approaches an inebriated Ricky in their local bar after work, tells him she's an accountant too. That she needs to unwind. That she thinks he's hot. Within five minutes, Ricky's pickled tongue is down her throat, and he's leading her to a dark corner when she offers an excuse and slips away into the night.

"We're all reeling from that," Ian says, in a voice so contrived I wonder how I ever loved him. "And I think Vanessa needs answers. We all need answers. Ricky's been watching backstage. He's only just learned he failed the Fidelity Five. Let's bring him out."

The video cuts out after Ricky takes the stage. But I can't watch that part. It's like watching myself, the exact moment Ian told me about Kate. The bottom drops out, and there's only the feeling of falling, falling, falling to a soul-crushing and inevitable end.

I scroll through the new comments, then the old, until I find it. Valentine's Day, 2016.

Avenging Angel—two years ago

Fucking hypocrite. How can you live with yourself? You should end your pathetic excuse for a life before you hurt anybody else.

Not my finest moment or my soberest, but I'm up to 9,503 likes. Apparently, I'm not the only sicko hiding behind a screen name. My cursor hovers over the X, not for the first time, but I can't bring myself to delete it. It feels like admitting I was wrong about him.

It's just as well, because my phone beeps. A text from Luke.

Just talked to Coop. You should go to the station.

****

Detective Lennox—Doreen—greets me with the same disarming smile, taking the seat next to me. "Thanks for coming in, Doctor Lawson. We appreciate your cooperation."

Jack follows behind her, silent and brooding. He says my name, greeting me with a nod, and leans against the wall like he has better things to do.

"This won't take long," she says. "We just have a few more questions. Is that alright?"

"Of course." As if there's any other acceptable response. "I want to help."

"Good. I'm glad to hear that. Your ex-husband's funeral was today, right? Did you attend?"

"Not exactly. I didn't think it would be in good taste to show up in person. But I watched from my car."

"You *watched* from your *car*?"

"It sounds weird when you say it like that. I just wanted to pay my respects. To get some closure."

"I see." That's therapist speak for *WTF*, and I imagine cop speak isn't so different.

"It's a lot to process, as I'm sure you can understand. Ian and Kate murdered. And now this business with the escort. I thought it might help me get a grip on my feelings about it all."

"And?"

I shrug. "It's all still pretty surreal."

"Indeed. Do you know Ricky Sherman?"

"The drunk funeral crasher?"

Doreen nods and chuckles, but I wonder if she's acting. Taking her directions from the good detective script.

"He approached me a few months ago online. I'm not sure how he found me. We wrote a few times about his wife. And then he asked if I would help him blackmail Ian. Of course, I said no."

I realize I have Ian to thank for the smooth timbre of my voice when I lie. The years of practice. It's a risk, lying, but Ricky isn't stupid. He wants the money I gave him. And he can't have it both ways. Besides, he's probably still too drunk to question right now, so I get first crack at the story.

"You didn't think to mention it when we last talked? When we asked about Ian's enemies?"

"Honestly, I forgot. The guy seemed like a drunk buffoon. I just figured he was broken up about his wife, and he'd get over it. I can't believe he showed up here."

"How did he know Ian had an affair with Kate?"

I lower my head, sigh. "I told him. I know it was stupid, but I felt like he understood. I actually thought he was too drunk to remember. He was usually drunk when we chatted online."

"How could you tell?"

"Well, there were the typos. And he wasn't shy about it."

"I don't suppose you saved any of those chats?"

I shake my head. Non-existent chats can't be saved, unlucky for me. "Sorry."

Doreen looks at a stoic Jack and scribbles something in her notepad. Probably about how she doesn't believe me.

Then, Jack clears his throat. He addresses the air, not me. "Fair enough. One more thing," he says, as if it—whatever *it* is—is merely an afterthought and not *the* most important thing. The thing they've been saving.

"I heard Coop got called out to your office on Saturday. A suspected break-in, was it?"

"More like a misunderstanding. I thought I'd left the desk lamp on, so I stopped in on my run to check. Maybe someone saw me and got suspicious."

Jack reaches into his jacket pocket, pulls out a photograph, and ambles over like we've got all the time in the world. He lays it on the table in front of me and returns to his spot, seemingly holding up the wall with the girth of his shoulders and sheer determination. "Have you ever seen this before?"

Too many times. "It looks like a kitchen knife. Not one I recognize, but it seems fairly ordinary."

"Where did you go on Saturday after you saw Cooper at the office?"

"I finished my run down to the beach and back to the house. Then I went to Cliffside to see Mom."

"How is your mother?" he asks, and I hate that he's doing this, that he's *good* at doing this. He's making it personal when he promised he wouldn't. And I can't tell if he's asking because he cares or because he wants to throw me off balance.

"As good as can be expected, I suppose. She has good days and bad days. That day was a bad one."

"So you ran to Ocean Beach?"

"Yes. It's one of my usual routes."

"Would it surprise you if someone saw you out on the jetty throwing something into the water?"

Fear rushes into my head, whooshing through it, like I've pressed my ear to an empty conch shell. "I walk out onto the jetty sometimes, but I've never thrown anything into the water." I'd only dropped it.

"Would it surprise you if your fingerprints were on this knife?"

"That's impossible."

My certainty warrants an eyebrow raise. "You sound fairly sure about that."

"I am. I don't own any knives like it. I've never touched it. And fingerprints aren't as easily planted as they are in the movies."

"I guess I forgot who I'm talking to. Your father taught you well. What about in Ian's house? Any reason your prints would be there?"

He's probably bluffing, but my hands tingle with guilt. The one thing I'd touched. So panicked I hadn't even thought to care. Somehow, I manage a demure smile before I stand up.

"My dad also taught me that unless I'm under arrest, I'm free to leave at any time. So am I? Under arrest?"

"Of course not." Jack opens the door and waits for me to dart past like a scolded dog. I try to saunter instead—or at least to manage a half-hearted stroll—but I'll admit he scares me in the same way Luke does. He's too steady, too solid. And I feel flimsy as a reed next to him.

From behind me, I hear Doreen fire one last shot, and it stings, because part of me thought she was on my side, that they both were. "Don't leave town, Doctor Lawson."

CHAPTER SEVENTEEN

LUKE'S truck is parked in my driveway. He taps the horn when I get out and motions me over to his open window. There's a sinking feeling in my stomach. A gaping pit. The Hydra's there too, circling the drain.

"Do you want to come in?" I ask.

He shakes his head. "You said you weren't going to the funeral."

"I didn't go. I just—"

"Enough, Ava. Enough."

"If you don't want to hear my explanation, why'd you show up here?"

His laugh is scathing. "Explanation? Is that what you call it? I came to tell you I went to Cliffside this afternoon, while you were sitting in your car stalking your dead ex-husband. I saw the log book.

And that's not my signature. I have no idea how it got there. But I needed you to know, because I wanted you to trust me."

"Wanted?"

"I can't do this anymore."

My mind goes blank—swept clean by those five words—and I stare at his hands on the wheel until I hear myself speak. "What does that mean?"

"It means I need a break. At least until this whole investigation blows over. And then, I don't know . . . we'll see."

"*We'll see?* Thanks for the consideration. I thought you wanted to make every day my favorite. Or was that just a line you wrote in a card?"

Luke sighs and sets his eyes on mine. I can't breathe. It's not supposed to happen this way. *Him* breaking up with *me*. Technically, I've never even called him my boyfriend.

"From the day you stole Dad's badge, I always had a crush on you. You were a badass, showing up with your mom at the gun range every weekend, going target-hunting like a pro. You didn't take any of Coop's shit, and you didn't follow him around all lovestruck like the other girls. And then, you showed up here again—beautiful and smart and a doctor—and I thought, for once, I could have something Cooper wanted. I really thought we had a chance. Now, I'm not so sure I want one."

"Cooper hates me." But even as I say it, I remember my first weekend back in Carmel. I'd run into Cooper at a local bar, and he'd bought me a beer without asking. "Look what the cat dragged in," he'd said, which hardly seemed like flirting.

"Yeah. He hates everything he can't have."

"So that's what you've been doing with me? One-upping your idiot brother?"

"Only at first. Until I totally fell for you. Now who's the idiot?"

I reach through the window to touch Luke's shoulder. His skin is fever hot even through his T-shirt. "I know I messed up. I told you I've got issues. Major issues. I have to take it slow."

"It's not about that. It's the lies, the half-truths. About the hang-up calls and Ian and Cleo and that jerk from the funeral. Between you and me, you need a lawyer, Ava. I just don't trust you anymore. And you, of all people, should know that's a deal breaker."

A surge of anger comes on quick, and my breath stutters, the way the lights flicker before they go out. I want to scream at full blast. Not at Luke, per se. But at my life in general. Which feels over somehow. *Who's catastrophizing now, Doctor Lawson?*

But I don't need Luke. I don't fucking need anyone.

"I love you." It comes out of my mouth without warning, and it feels true when I say it but wrong at the same time. A last-ditch manipulation. It's something Ian would do. And I haven't said those words to anybody but Ian.

Luke doesn't melt as expected. He's so calm, so unaffected. I realize then he's actually leaving.

"I know that. I've known for a long time. And yes, it's nice to hear you *finally* say it, but not like this. Not when you're just trying to keep me here. For a shrink, you're pretty clueless."

I shrug and try to smile, but it falters. I stop myself from crying. Because that would be conniving too. But more out of force of habit. "And for a cop, you're pretty enlightened."

When Luke drives away, when he makes the turn without waving, my heart throbs in my hands like an open wound, and the wind cuts right through my empty rib cage.

That's how it feels to be left.

****

I can't go inside. It would be admitting something to myself. So I get back in my car and drive. And think. And drive.

Twenty-one years later, I still don't remember exactly when my mom got there or how. I only recall the feel of my father's note in my sock, pressed against my ankle as I stood on the porch. The hard edges of it, digging in, felt real. Nothing else did. People rushed past in a blur. Some of them touched me, spoke to me. They must have. And then my mother appeared with two grocery bags, lumbering up the sidewalk. I remember the instant she saw me and her hands let go. The way her mouth opened like a sinkhole in the earth. The crack of my father's favorite vodka hitting the sidewalk. An orange rolling to the street. I thought, *Nothing counts anymore.*

That's also how it feels to be left.

I know where I'm going, but I take my time getting there. When I finally stop the car outside of Whispering Cypress Memorial, the sky is purple, a darkening bruise. And the sliver of yellow moon watches me like a jaundiced eye.

The wrought-iron gates are mostly decorative, and I slip through with ease, heading up the main road to the gravesite. From here, I already see two mounds of fresh dirt among the headstones, two mounds that will smell like grass and rain. I walk toward them, feeling more alive than I have all week. Skin, like frayed wire—exposed and buzzing in the cold. Breath, coming in wet, white puffs. Heart, hardened again, steely as the pavement beneath my feet.

The too-sweet scent of roses reaches me first. A bouquet of yellow ones lays at the foot of the granite headstone. I run my fingers across the stone, the names etched in it, the wedding date at the center, the birth and death dates. It's all ice cold and slick from the fog. And real as that note in my sock.

A sob rises up in my throat, and I don't try to stuff it down or swallow it. I let it come in like a wave and knock me to my knees. The tears follow, and I taste the salt of my own fathomless ocean.

"I'm sorry," I say, after a while, after I'm emptied. Because I am sorry. Mostly. "I'm sorry it happened this way."

And then, it hits me, and I chuckle. "I guess you one-upped me with the ultimate anti-Valentine's."

It gives me a sick and irrational satisfaction to stomp across Kate's grave and shove my hands in the dirt on Ian's side, digging down as far as I can go. The soil blackens my arms and roots under my nails. I'll have to scrub a long time to get them clean again. When

I'm satisfied with the burrow I'd made, I reach into my pocket and pull out the white gold band with its winking round diamond and drop it in.

"Goodbye, Ian."

I smooth the soil over it until there's no sign it ever existed at all. The death of a marriage should be like this. A ceremony. A burial. A stone set in the ground. Something to mark the end.

I stand and gather myself, putting the pieces back together. I'll go home and take a long hot shower, wash it all away. Tomorrow, I'll take Luke's advice and find a lawyer. But first, I'll head back to the car and check my phone. Maybe Luke has called by now. Or more likely texted since that's how millennials make up these days. He'll say he made a mistake. An unforgivable one. I'll forgive him, though. And I'll tell him everything. From the beginning.

I wipe my eyes with the back of my hand—*shit!*—and squeeze them shut against the burning. I'd forgotten they were covered in dirt, in grass, in the decomposing cells of Ian. And Kate. And all the others.

The sharp snap of a twig forces them open again.

Eyes stinging, I spin to the sound of it. But through the brine of my tears, all I see is a blur of night and grass and graveyard. Maddie's weepy face fixed on mine. And Wallace Bergman's sun-spotted hands reaching for me.

I run.

With the hounds of the past pounding the pavement behind me.

With footsteps thumping in time to the beat of my heart.

I risk a clouded glance over my shoulder, and I see hair like fire. Flames alive and licking the sky.

And then I fall.

****

"Oh my God. Doctor Lawson! Are you okay?"

Cleo looks down at me. Her fire-red hair is calm now, doused at her shoulders. Still, it's a striking contrast to her pale skin, almost translucent in the moonlight. In her hand, she holds a single red rose. One of the petals has loosed and fallen to the ground at her feet.

"I think so." I sit up and she offers me a hand. But I wave it away and scramble to my feet, too proud to accept help. Not from Ian's mistress. Even the one I like.

"You tripped," she says, as I brush the grass from the mud-caked knees of my jeans.

My toe throbs in agreement, stubbed at the edge of a small slab of granite. I read the inscription: OUR LITTLE ANGEL.

"I thought . . ." What can I say? I thought you were the man I killed. *We* killed. As crazy as I sound, in my mind, it's Wallace that's been calling. Wallace that's been following me. I'd even pulled up the obituary online to be certain. Still dead.

"That I was chasing you?"

"Something like that. It's so dark out here, and I got dirt in my eyes. I couldn't see who was there."

She laughs a little—high pitched and nervous—the sound as foreign at night as a robin's song. "You scared me too. I didn't expect to find anybody else in a graveyard this late. Not anybody living anyway."

Ian in the silence between us. Right in the middle of two women, where he always liked it best. She glances at my hands, my filthy hands. The dirt smeared on my shirt. My face too, I'm guessing. And I wait for the question—*What are you doing here, Doctor Lawson?*—but it never comes.

"Cleo, we have to talk. And I suppose now is as good a time as any."

She lets out a long breath and gestures to the gravesite. The rose dangles awkwardly. As if she can't wait to be rid of it. "Can we—?"

"Of course." I let her go ahead. And the long stem of her body tenses at the sight of it. "It feels real when you see it in stone," I say, thinking of Ian. But also of my father.

She drops the rose at the center of the dirt mound and whispers under her breath. Even on a night as still as this one, I can't make it out. But her sniffling is undeniable.

"Ian told me about you," she says, finally. And I feel a sudden jolt to my heart. "That you'd been a student of his. That you were a therapist in Carmel. I was curious."

I stare at her flummoxed. My thoughts are muddled, and I feel one step behind. As if I'd smacked my head on that stone when I fell and sent all the puzzles pieces flying. "Wait. You knew? The whole time?"

"Didn't you?" Her lips part in a coy grin, flashing the chalk white of her teeth, and the jolt comes again.

"No. Not the whole time."

"Not until I let Kate's name slip, right?"

"I don't understand. Why would you? Did Ian know?"

She sits on the headstone, shaking her head. More in defeat than disagreement. "He didn't have a clue. But I thought maybe you could help me. He was way out of my league, you know."

My laugh sounds like a cackle, a bird of a different kind. A crow, perhaps. "So you came to the woman he cheated on for tips on how to steal him from the woman he cheated with?"

"When you put it that way . . ."

"What about Cleopatra James? Doesn't she know how to seduce a married man?"

"Seduction is one thing. Commitment is something else."

I nearly laugh again, thinking of Ian, six feet under and listening. Gloating.

"Anyway, I'm sorry I lied. I dropped out of junior college two years ago, but I spent so much time at MCC with Ian, I started to feel like a student again. We'd even talked about thesis topics, and I really was planning on applying for next fall. Ian was going to write me a letter of recommendation."

"And Doctor Jarvis?"

She dismisses the name like an unwanted arm around her shoulders. "I thought it would make my story seem legit. I knew Jarvis was a professor at MCC, because Ian talked about him a lot.

And not in a good way. He thought there was something going on between him and Kate. He wanted him fired."

Another jolt, and I'm scrambling to catch up. To sift through the dregs of memory. The night of the vigil with its melting candles and jack-o'-lantern faces. And Jarvis's smile, kind but wary. His deep, deep sigh. No wonder he'd taken a leave of absence. He'd probably been forced out. Or desperate for an escape from the brutality of Ian's revenge.

Cleo shifts atop the gravestone, and her heel clunks against it with a hollow thud. She laughs nervously, then winces, as if the noises could offend the sleeping corpses under her feet.

"So Ian knew about your other life?"

"Not from the beginning. Sometimes I'd try to find clients at this upscale casino in Monterey. One night, he was there with that asshole from your office. David Fairfax."

"*David?*" Still a step behind.

"Yeah, David. He was wasted that night and getting buried in a poker game. I accidentally bumped his drink, and it spilled all over his watch. He totally lost it. He kept ranting about how expensive it was, how his wife would be pissed at him. And then . . ." Her voice trails off like an old dog hunting the scent of a rabbit in the underbrush. Her fingers whiten as she grips the stone.

"And then?"

"Then, Ian defended me, and things just took off from there. He made me feel like I could be so much more. It sounds stupid, I know. But I guess I had a Julia Roberts moment."

I think of my first date with Ian—pizza and beer and his unexpected confession. I'd felt saved somehow, seen. I can conjure the memory but not the magic. Not anymore.

"It happens to the best of us. And I understand why you lied." *Hadn't I done the same? Worse, really.* "Did David know you were an escort?"

She shrugs and wipes at her eyes, hiding them from me. And what I know makes me shiver. One of them is lying.

"I guess you can't be my therapist anymore," she says.

"I shouldn't have been in the first place."

We start to walk back toward the gate, and I spot the silhouette of her bicycle leaning against a tree trunk. The playful red of the frame and the ladybug bell I'd seen affixed to the handlebars seem ominous now, cast against the harshness of this place.

And when Cleo's cell phone rings, we both startle. With a nervous twitter, she slips it from her pocket, and I gape at the little screen glowing like a watchful eye. The number on it is Ian's.

"Uh, sorry," Cleo says, silencing the ring with a click of her finger. "I'll call back."

"Who was that?"

She trudges ahead of me, pulling her jacket tighter around her. Concealing or protecting, I'm not sure which. And I have the urge to tackle her, to grapple with her for the phone the way I'd done with Luke.

"Cleo! Answer me."

When she spins around, fear is cast like a shadow on her face. Even darker than our own silhouettes. "I don't know, okay? Someone's been calling me from Ian's number and saying some pretty messed-up shit."

"Like what?"

The breeze picks up as we near the entrance, and Cleo's hair is dancing again. The wind whips through the pines, whistles. Like an old man with wrinkled hands calling that old dog home.

"I don't want to talk about it."

"Have you told the police?"

She scoffs as she crouches and slips beneath the gate's lock. "I'm supposed to meet with the detectives tomorrow, but . . . I don't know. Ian didn't trust the cops."

"Why?"

There's a rustling behind me, and Cleo gasps. I spin around, certain someone is there. But there's only the sky and the road—and a sheet of muddy paper blown against my foot.

"You might've been right about seeing signs," I tell her, surrendering my question like a leaf taken by the wind. For now.

I hold the paper out to her through the wrought-iron bars, and she shakes her head as she reads the printed words on the cover of the pamphlet.

In Memory of Ian and Kate Culpepper
Above all, love each other deeply, because love covers a multitude of sins.
—1 Peter 4:8

I skirt out behind her as she tosses the sheet to the ground and swings one leg over her bike.

"Not all sins, apparently," she says.

And I have to bite the side of my cheek to stop myself from answering: *Amen.*

****

The whole ride home I think of Cleo, replaying every session, every tear and revelation, trying to sort out reality from the rest. Cleo from Cleopatra. Jarvis, the dutiful professor, or the cad. Her David from the one I know. And that inexplicable phone call so much like my own. But of all the questions I want answered, there's this: Did Ian say anything else about me? Pathetic, I realize.

Luke doesn't cross my mind until I pull into the empty driveway and check my phone.

Okay, that's not true. Luke is the backdrop of it all. The cause of the hollow cavity in my chest where Ian takes root again. Like a weed, he can grow anywhere as long as he has enough space. And with not a single message from Luke, there's plenty of it.

I let myself in and head for the kitchen in search of something to ease the sting. But Luke and I drank the last bottle of red on Valentine's—one week seems years ago now—and there's only an old bottle of beer hiding behind the ketchup. Luke's leftovers. I can't bring myself to drink it.

Instead, I open the heart-shaped box on the counter and work my way through the rest of the first layer and into the second, methodically discarding the red seashell wrappers in the trash beneath the sink. I'll regret this in the morning, but I can't stop. Piece after piece, I shove them in, not bothering to finish chewing before I swallow the sticky sweet lump.

I reach for a glass—cold milk makes the medicine go down—and my throat closes up when I see it. The eighteen-piece knife set and cherrywood block, a wedding gift from my work colleagues. They'd attached a funny note that had made me laugh and Ian groan and roll his eyes: *May your love never be severed.*

I'd been practical in keeping it. Every kitchen needs a good knife set. But now, I wished I'd taken it to the landfill, dumped it with the other remnants of my marriage. Saved up for my own Wusthof.

The chef's knife is missing.

Heart beating like a caged bird in my chest, I lean back against the counter and retrace my steps. I'd used the knife last weekend to chop tomatoes for my mom's spaghetti Bolognese, the one dish I can cook, then washed it by hand and slid it back into its place. I'm sure of it.

Had Luke used it? Probably. He'd made breakfast on Saturday.

I open the dishwasher. Empty.

The utensil drawer. Not there.

My breath is high and tight in my chest, pushing its way out with a wheeze. I open every drawer in the kitchen, cabinets too. Until my lungs feel ready to burst, and the taste of chocolate burns in my throat like poison.

Luke. I have to call Luke.

I reach for my cell, fingers finding the numbers by heart. Until it rings in my hand. And dread grips me with its cold fingers on the back of my neck.

Ian's number again.

I slide the green button to answer and wait for the voice that's become familiar to me now.

"You really should keep better track of your knives, Doctor Lawson. Or they may end up in your back."

****

I stand alongside the kitchen windows, careful not to be seen, and peer past my reflection out into the darkness, scanning my backyard for signs of life, the slightest movement stilling my breath and moving my eyes like a planchette across a Ouija board.

There. To the picket fence Luke helped me paint last spring.

There. To the broken cobblestone path still slick from the rain.

There. To the shadows that pool at the base of my own towering pine tree. To the little blue birdhouse Jack had carved for me and mounted to the trunk. With its secret hollow meant precisely for the spare key I'd hidden there. The only way the breathing man could have opened my door and come inside and slipped back out with my knife pressed against his flesh.

I shudder as I open the back door and step into the night, flashlight in tow. The wind swirls and whispers still, kicking up the smaller of the fallen pine branches, as if moved too by a spirit, an unseen hand.

It's less than ten steps to the birdhouse, but each one tests my resolve. Each one requires nothing less of me than indifference to the sharp stick of fear between my ribs. The cruel certainty someone is watching.

I reach it, finally, and open the bottom, shining the thin beam of light on the hook inside. The key hangs there, swaying a bit, as if it's chiding me for my foolishness. But I chase my relief with a shot of panic when I realize the small piece of black runner's tape I'd stretched across the key's teeth to hold it in place is missing.

I comb the ground with my flashlight, frantically at first, and then methodically, dropping to my knees on the wet ground.

And when I spot it, cast off and camouflaged against the soil and debris, I leave it there, making those ten steps to the house in two.

A dissatisfying sex life is like an unsightly rash. You don't want to talk about it, and every night you pray it will get better on its own. But it won't. Because it's not the problem. It's a symptom of the problem.
—Ian Culpepper, *Love CPR*

VALENTINE'S DAY
FIVE YEARS EARLIER
9:30 P.M. MULHOLLAND DRIVE

WHAT *have I done?* Ava stood at the edge of the embankment, gaping at the starless sky, the sparse cliffside. The small fire that had begun to burn there. She felt Ian beside her, but she didn't look at him. She couldn't. Instead, she started down the steep hill, measuring her steps. Surely, she could fix this. At least she had to try. But he stopped her, his hand around her arm like a noose.

"Leave him," he said.

****

ONE WEEK EARLIER . . .

IAN was angry. Ian was always angry.

And this time Ava knew for certain. It was absolutely all her fault. It started Monday morning when he woke her from a dead sleep, screaming bloody murder. She'd thought the house was on fire. For a split second, she was grateful, hoping the whole thing would burn down. Maybe then, they'd leave here for good. Start over. In a place that wasn't haunted. But then, she broke through the fog of sleep—too fast, like a diver jetting to the surface—and realized there was no fire. Only Ian's hot breath in her face.

"How long have you been taking these fucking things?" he yelled, tossing the packet of birth control pills onto the bed. Like a note from a secret lover. She stared at it, humiliated. "You know what? I'm glad. Maybe you're not cut out to be a mom. Maybe you're just too selfish."

She'd lain there shell-shocked long after he left, his wrath hanging in the air, thick as smoke. In the gray haze, she stared up at the cracks in the ceiling and wondered how far she would go to make Ian happy. If she even could anymore.

Please let Wally like it. She whispered that prayer against her pillow. Because if Wallace Bergman liked the idea Ian pitched for a show about couples in crisis—her idea, she called it *Love Doctored*—that would certainly make Ian happy. More than anything. Even more than a baby.

But when Ian didn't come home Monday night, she knew right then. She'd blown it. Another flop. Another failure. A whole year's worth of them.

She walked to the end of the pier that evening, where she'd always be fourteen and desperate, and stared into the water, wishing for a sign. Ian might have been right. Maybe a baby could fix the mess between them. Put it all right again. She'd throw out the pills tomorrow, give it the old college try, but first she'd see Wallace. She'd try to change his mind.

Tuesday's session started like all the others lately. Wallace unable to fight back tears. They streamed from beneath his sunglasses down his alabaster cheeks and pooled in his beard, which he hadn't shaved in months.

"They say it gets easier. Well, screw them. Whoever they are. Because it hurts just as bad today as the day we laid Richard in the ground."

"It's only been three months," Ava told him. "Be patient with yourself." Meanwhile, she was anything but. She'd needed to get him talking about BXA. To find out why he'd passed on *Love Doctored*.

"Sometimes, it can be healthy to distract yourself. With a hobby. A pet. Work."

He sniffled and nodded at her. "Richard always said we should get a dog. But I'm allergic. Besides, it would only be one more love to lose."

She fought off an eye roll. And then a wave of guilt. When had this happened to her? This absence of empathy. The *how* she knew. Ian had infected her. With his schemes of vengeance. Starting with the first—Prick Whitlock's keyed car. And the condition was terminal. Best not to fight it. "So, no pets. What about work? You told me last week your psychiatrist had been pitching some ideas to you."

If he was surprised by her direct approach, he didn't show it. She was the one taken aback. He took off his sunglasses, revealing those eyes she'd come to be a little frightened of. That clear unspoiled blue. "How do you do it?"

"Do what?" And already, she began preparing her silver bullet. Her get-out-of-jail-free card, Ian had called it. In case Bergman ever figured them out. *Remember everything we've got on him*—Ian's directive—*all the dirt he's dished.*

"Read my mind like that. It's like you're my goddamned conscience or something."

"You see me as someone to keep you on track. To help you do right." *What a crock.*

"You're about forty years too late for that." His laugh was throaty from all that crying.

"You're never so far down the wrong path, you can't do right." And neither was she then. Not yet.

"Okay, Doc. I'll bite. So, this guy, my shrink. Culpepper. He's a real asshole. You know the type. A hanger on. Thinks I'm gonna be his meal ticket. His big break into showbiz. Most of his ideas are real stinkers. But then . . ."

He leaned forward, and Ava was rapt. Not so much by what would come next but by the whole of it. She'd forgotten the way life could pivot in an instant.

"Bam!" Wallace clapped his hands together, grinning. "Yesterday, he pulls a rabbit out of his hat. So bad that it's actually freakin' good. We get married couples on the brink of ending it. The worse off, the better. Put them through a fidelity test. On air, of course. Do some counseling sessions. Yada, yada, yada. Sequester them. Then, they both make a decision. Divorce or stay together. We reveal it live. Sign the divorce papers right there. He calls it *Love Doctored*."

"That's . . . great!" Her brainchild, parroted back to her, had churned her stomach.

"Yeah. But here's the thing. He wants to be the star. And I can tell you right now—I mean, you know him a little—he'll tank the show with his massive ego."

"So you told him no?"

He'd nodded.

"And you're having second thoughts?" *Please God. Please.*

"Not exactly."

"So what then?"

Wallace returned the sunglasses to his eyes and leaned back in his chair. A better therapist would have noticed aloud—*you're hiding again.* But Ava had only cared about the answer. What it would mean for Ian. Therefore, her.

"Remember Aokigahara?" And she felt sick at the sound of the word in his mouth. "Well, I guess you could say I stepped over Culpepper's body. I took his idea to BXA this morning, and they went nuts for it. They want that hotshot shrink from the last season of *The Bachelor* to host. And you know the first thing I thought? You were right."

Her lungs felt flattened, like deflated balloons. Sliced tires. She barely could squeeze out an *oh?*

"I think I might find my way through the forest."

After he'd left, Ava wasted no time. She knew exactly what to do. Later, she'd tell Ian but not until she'd done it. It would mean more to him that way—if she took the initiative. Maybe it could even bring them together again. Not unlike a baby, a devil's spawn.

She flipped through her phone to the number Ian had given her months ago, when they'd come up with their bailout plan. Because surely, Wallace would catch on one day. And they had to be ready.

Her mouth dry as a bone, she dialed Ian's patient, Liza Munroe. The forty-something—*who could tell in LA anyway?*—columnist for the *LA Times* to whom he'd prescribed sixty milligrams of Prozac daily for the past year.

"*LA Times.* This is Liza."

Ava didn't hesitate. Not even for a second. Later, she'd replay it in her mind and wonder what that meant. What it said about her. Who she really was. And who was to blame for what came next.

"I have a story for you," she said. "A big story."

****

12:15 P.M., BEVERLY HILLS

HAPPY anti-versary, baby." Ian made their silly joke seductive, the way he put his lips right up against her ear. Pressed his body to hers, his skin warm with desire. "I want you. *Now.*"

And it thrilled Ava, his need. Never mind that they were at lunch at Spago in Beverly Hills. Or that Ava had a patient—*the patient*—in forty-five minutes. His need for her, the urgency of it, was a hard-won victory.

Ian pulled her into the men's lavatory. Locked the door behind them. And slammed his mouth onto hers until she felt dizzy. Like he couldn't get enough. And when somebody wants you like that, it drops you to your knees in the Spago bathroom, hikes up your skirt, bites your neck. Want like that, it hurts.

Ten minutes later, they emerged together, breathless, and faced a line of scowling men, unashamed. When Ava spotted her lipstick mark on Ian's collar, she felt proud. Smug, even. It seemed irrefutable proof of something important, something essential. Though she couldn't say what exactly. Only that her heart skipped like a side-armed pebble, light across the water, when she saw it.

"No matter what he says or how hangdog he looks, don't you dare feel sorry for him." Ian's last words to her before he put her in a taxi and made a left at the corner, to the office where he saw patients in Beverly Hills Tuesday and Thursday afternoons.

"I won't," she said. But only so he would kiss her again like that. Like his life depended on it.

The taxi ride took twenty minutes, during most of which the driver blathered into his cell phone, but Ava barely noticed. His chatter dissolved like elevator music as she rested her head against the half-opened window and thought only of Ian.

When she burst through her office door at 12:55 p.m., she expected to see a distraught Wallace sitting in the waiting room under the abstract print Ian had bought for her, his pink fedora clashing with the primary colors above him. He'd already rescheduled once this week. His assistant had called on Tuesday morning—"Mr. Bergman isn't feeling well." *No kidding*, she'd thought.

But the worst of the story had hit the news yesterday, and she'd imagined he'd be crushed. Desperate to talk to somebody who'd understand. Even if that somebody had put him here, cracked him herself as carelessly as a dropped vase.

The phone rang at her desk. "Hello?"

"Doctor Lawson, it's Wallace." He sounded worse than she'd predicted. His voice faraway and hollow. Like he'd fallen to the bottom of a well. "I can't come in today. The place is surrounded by paparazzi. I'm afraid to leave the house."

"We could speak on the phone," she suggested, suddenly needing to know what she'd set in motion. A pang of guilt gripped her, but she remembered Ian's admonition. Easy for him to say.

"Yes. Please. That would be wonderful."

"Where would you like to begin?" she asked, cruelly.

And he laughed. A laugh unlike any she'd ever heard. Sharp-edged as an axe, bitter as a lemon. "Well, have you seen the papers? Television? Internet?"

200

"Yes." And she had seen it all. *Entertainment Tonight. TMZ.* She'd even paged through the *LA Times* on Sunday morning, naked in bed with Ian. Eating the pancakes he'd cooked for her and giggling over the headlines that weren't funny at all.

"Jonah Vaughn, Teen Star of BXA's Top-Rated Sitcom, Admits Programming Exec Asked for Sexual Favors"

"BXA Exec Fired amid Sex Scandal"

"Up-and-Coming Star Alleges Misconduct against Bawdy Bergman"

And then Wallace's phone call. "I'm a joke, a cliché. I'm Bawdy Bergman. My whole life is over."

Sucker punched, she caught her breath, wishing she could hang up. But she knew exactly what he meant. She'd tried to save her father from a similar fate—the crooked cop cliché—by tossing his note into the ocean. But this was different. This, she'd summoned upon Wallace like the wrath of a vengeful god.

She gripped the receiver tight to steady her hand, listening to the sound of Ian's voice in her head. *You didn't lie. You did nothing wrong.* Ian believed that. Why couldn't she? *Everyone's got to live with the consequences of their behavior.*

"Doctor Lawson? Are you still there?"

"I'm sorry. I was just thinking this must be overwhelming for you. But you are far more than your job, Wallace. You must know that."

Another scornful laugh. "In this town, all a man has is his reputation. No network will touch me now. Hell, I wouldn't touch me. I'm a PR nightmare. They're making it sound like he was a goddamned kid. He was eighteen. Perfectly legal. And Richard was dying. Besides, Jonah was totally into it. He came on to me."

She flipped through her notes, the ones she'd read and reread again with Ian. The ones that had sat on her lap, silent partners, when she'd made that call to Liza. She felt certain he'd never said that.

"When we discussed Jonah in our sessions, you said he made you feel as if you were alive again. That you used him to cope with losing

Richard. Powerful emotions like grief and loss can be confusing for anybody. Might you have misunderstood his intentions?"

"I didn't misunderstand his hand on my dick."

Ava recoiled from the vulgarity of his words. The viciousness. Even though she deserved it, no matter the truth.

"I'm sorry," he said. "I didn't mean to be so crass. But I didn't tell you everything about Jonah. He confided in me. It's not easy being a gay teen. Not to mention a gay teen heartthrob on a show like his. I mean, it doesn't get more heterosexual than *Ocean Nights*. So I invited him to a few gay clubs in LA and things happened."

"Why didn't you tell me the whole story?" But the real question that burned in her throat: Would it have mattered?

"I didn't want to out him to anybody. Even to you. And of course, he won't admit it now. *Ocean Nights'* ratings have never been higher since the network started the rumor about him and Heidi Hudson, that bimbo costar of his. And this whole scandal will probably be a ratings boon. No good deed goes unpunished, they say."

"Do you know how the media got wind of it?"

She heard him sigh. Like the last bit of life left his body. "Who else but Jonah?"

"Right. Who else?" And she hated herself completely. Because he didn't even suspect. "But why?"

"Since Richard died, he'd been avoiding me, giving me the brush-off. Maybe he thought I was about to spill the beans. He wanted control of the story. He wanted the spin. In Hollywood, it's all about how you spin it."

"How will you spin it then?" she asked, trying to be a good therapist. Though it was too late for that. Much too late. "What can you do to turn this around?"

"That's what I'm paying you for. You and Doctor Culpepper. I've been trying to reach him all week. I need something stronger than Prozac. I can't even get out of bed. But his secretary said he couldn't get me in till Monday. And don't think I don't see the irony in it. Me needing help from the guy I left behind in Aokigahara. Now it's just me in the forest, Doc. Deep in."

Secretary, schmecretary. She knew it was all Ian, withholding. Punishing. But she heard the threat between Wallace's words. Conjured her father on that last day, his mouth contorted in anger. In disapproval. At her. When really, it was himself he hated. What would he think of her now? "Let me call him. I'll see what I can do."

****

8:45 P.M. BEVERLY HILLS

AVA sat in the downstairs garage of Ian's Beverly Hills office as he'd asked her to. Even though it felt like a waiting tomb—cold and gray and empty. Their used BMW and Wallace Bergman's Jaguar the only two cars left. Unnerved, Ava had locked the doors. As if any threat could be greater than her shadow self. Her own black heart.

She held her phone in her hand like a weapon, scrolling through the latest breaking news on Bergmangate and seething.

"Two More BXA Stars Allege Groping by Bergman"

"Vaughn Says BXA Knew Bergman Had Infamous Casting Couch"

Wallace had lied. Right to her face. Of course, other patients had deceived her. There'd been alcoholic Joe who claimed he hadn't touched a drop in a year. And clueless Pamela who insisted she had no idea why her check had bounced. Everybody lies to their therapist at least once. Hadn't Prick Whitlock told her that? But *this*. This rose to the next level. Because she wasn't in training anymore. Because she should have known. And worst of all, because she'd actually felt sorry for him.

Ian had agreed to see Wallace at eight o'clock, well after his last scheduled patient. "Tell him I have to see him in person to write the scrip. He can park in the secured garage downstairs. There's a private entrance." And when he whispered the words into the receiver—*let's play chase*—she'd known why.

They'd done it twice before but only once with a patient. A middle-aged banker who'd put his hand on Ava's knee during their first session and called her a bitch when she'd asked him to leave. They'd followed him from work, waited for him outside Patina, and tailgated him down the 101, forcing him to the shoulder. Speeding past, Ian laughing, she'd gritted her teeth, held her breath. Then they'd had frantic sex in a mall parking lot like reckless teenagers. The whole episode had scared her. Mostly because she'd done it.

And with that came the question—what else might she do?

Ava gasped when she saw Wallace emerge from the stairwell, red-faced and running. *Fast for an old man*, she thought. His eyes darted wildly, and she ducked down, afraid he might see her.

When she peered up over the steering wheel, he cried out, and she thought for certain she'd been spotted. But she followed his gaze and found Ian, jogging a few steps behind. A scream caught in her throat, stuck there.

Ian looked like an animal, frothy blood dripping from his mouth. He flung open the car door, breathing hard, and wiped his lip with the back of his hand. "That SOB hit me!"

Wallace had already fired up the Jag. He backed out, tires squealing.

And Ian did as they had planned. *But was this the plan?* He gave chase.

"What happened?" Ava asked, her tinny voice inconsequential against the drums of Ian's rage. She could see his pulse bounding in the spot beneath his chin. It looked like a tiny fist beating its way out of him.

"Fuck." He spit blood onto the steering wheel as he drove up Wilshire, tracking Wallace's bumper in the stop-and-go traffic. "I told him I knew what he did. With *Love Doctored*."

"You *what*?"

"I needed to hear the bastard say it, okay?"

"No, it's not okay. He'll know it was me who told you."

Ian said nothing. The car lurched forward, then screeched to a stop. Lurched, screeched, lurched. And screeched again. He pounded the dashboard. "This goddamned traffic."

"What did he say?" she asked, finally. Carefully. The way one might handle a grenade. "Ian?"

"Can't you just let me drive?" One car ahead of them, Wallace inched forward. Ava watched his frightened eyes check the rearview.

"But—"

"Shut the fuck up." Ian let out an exasperated breath, turned to her, softer. But she flinched when he touched her hand. "I'm sorry, Aves. This guy is an asshole. He's a sexual predator. And he stole from us. From you. Your brilliant idea. I won't let him get away with that. Are you with me? I need you to be with me on this. Be *my* avenging angel."

She felt her head nodding along, but she'd gone somewhere else. To their second Valentine's Day together, the parking lot. Prick Whitlock's Prius. When it all went wrong. Because she'd held back and let Ian do the dirty work. And he needed to know she was on his side. What did it matter anyway what Wallace knew? Surely he'd seen her by now, white-knuckling it in the passenger seat.

"Go. I'm with you," she heard herself say. And like that, the road opened up before them. First, the 405, a desolate stretch of ribbon all the way to the horizon. Then, Mulholland Drive, curving like a snake in black water.

Ian gunned it, with only Wallace's taillights to guide them straight to hell.

****

9:31 P.M. MULHOLLAND DRIVE

AVA couldn't stop seeing it. The way the Jag had taken flight, disappeared over the edge of the cliff. Gone. Like it had driven straight through the portal to another world.

And the fire transfixed her. She closed her eyes, opened them again, hoping it would all disappear.

"We can't just leave him, Ian. *I* can't."

Ian released Ava's arm, and she toddled down the embankment toward the Jaguar, her feet slipping on the loose dirt and gravel. As she got closer, the heat from the fire warmed her face, and she began to sweat. Or were those tears?

The car lay on its back—upturned like a dying beetle—smoke pouring from the cracked windows. The driver's side door was slightly ajar. Wallace's arm stuck out of it, ghastly white against the backdrop of flames and embers.

"Wallace!" The whipping wind carried her voice away, so she yelled again. His fingers moved, reached for her. He moaned. *Yes, she could fix this.*

Like all horrible things, it happened at once. And she'd never be able to remember what came first. Her hand on Wallace's. Ian yanking her back from the car so she collapsed against him on the cliffside. Or the ball of flame that exploded before them, lighting up the sky. From a distant planet, it would look like a shooting star. One that burned so bright you'd run out of wishes.

****

11:55 P.M. SANTA MONICA

SHE slept in fits. In stops and starts. The briefest moments of reprieve before she'd jolt awake again. And now, it neared midnight. The dawn of another day.

When they'd arrived home, Ava headed straight for her computer, hitting refresh on the internet news page until the story had broken.

"Former BXA Executive Dies in Fiery Crash on Mulholland Drive"

It hadn't felt real—still didn't—even looking at it right there in bold typeface. *Derealization*, Ian would've said if he'd been speaking. But his eyes had seemed as far away as her own. She hadn't bothered with a shower. Just fallen into bed, heavy, like her limbs couldn't hold her any longer.

Ian lay awake too. Though he said nothing, it comforted her to know he couldn't simply drift off to dream after what he'd done. What they'd done. Together.

In the glow of the sickled moon, she studied the singed hair on her right arm. It would grow back. *Strange*, she thought. How unmarked she appeared. How the body recovered while the soul only got sicker.

Ian reached for her then, called her name. To know he wasn't alone. Or to tell her all the things he'd kept secret, an entire world it seemed. Or to ask for a sip of water from the bottle she kept on the nightstand. But Ava would never know. Because she lay still as death. Mouth shut, eyes closed. A different kind of dead than Wallace but dead all the same.

CHAPTER EIGHTEEN

WEDNESDAY
FEBRUARY 22, 2018

DAN Jarvis has his very own set of back-row girls. I should know because I'm sitting among them in his 10 a.m. Monday/Wednesday/Friday Intro to Cognitive Psych class, listening to their whispers and giggles as he prints next week's reading assignment on the whiteboard. Here, in his element, Dr. Jarvis only vaguely resembles the slightly broken man from the vigil. But I'm exactly the same. A nervous wreck.

I'd spent the morning pondering the mystery of the spare key. Only four suspects, all of them Donovans. And searching for the missing knife. Emptied the silverware drawer, dug through the pantry. Even muscled the refrigerator back from the wall, thinking it might have slipped behind somehow. But the slot in the cherrywood block remained open, regarding me like an unblinking eye. Until I had to flee from its constant gaze.

I feel the gentle nudge of an elbow at my side and lean in to the oddly pleasant aroma of scented lotion and Doritos, the bright-red bag gaping open on the desk next to mine. "I heard that once a semester he does a class on the beach and teaches us all how to surf. You know, learning about learning by . . . *learning*." She giggles at her own cleverness. "Can you imagine him in a wet suit?"

Stumped, I offer a conspiratorial smile, hoping that will appease her.

"Smokin' hot." She pops another chip into her mouth as she makes her pronouncement, and I laugh against my better judgment.

Watching Dr. Jarvis's broad surfer shoulders stretch the fabric of his button-down, I understand her enthusiasm. And apparently so do most of the student body. He'd ranked just behind Ian on the MCC "Hot Prof" website I'd visited last night. Their two photographs side by side, captioned: *We'd lie on their couches anytime.* Both had received five eye-roll-worthy chili peppers. Meaning her assessment was entirely accurate.

Dr. Jarvis releases the class with a wave and a *see ya later*, and the herd begins to stir. To file toward the exits. As the room empties, my anxiety grows to fill it. What questions I'll dare to ask. And what answers I can possibly expect to receive from a man I've already lied to.

Next to me, Doritos girl stands and empties the crumbs into her waiting mouth, orange powder dusting her lips. Embarrassed for her, I look away until her crunching subsides.

"I haven't seen you before," she says, washing it all down with a swig of Diet Coke and securing her backpack over one shoulder. "Did Jarvis let you add the class late? I heard he's a real stickler about that."

I shrug. Because sometimes less is more. And sometimes less is easier. "Do you know why he was on leave last semester?" I ask.

She glances over her shoulder to the front of the classroom where Dr. Jarvis is fielding questions from a few eager beavers. When she

209

turns back to me, her eyes are alight with devilish glee. "Rumor one is Dirty Dan had a sex addiction. Apparently, he got caught looking at porn during office hours or something . . ."

Sounds like Ian's handiwork. "And two?"

"Prostate cancer."

I grimace at her. The MCC rumor mill must be brutal. "I need to ask him a question about the syllabus," I say as we part ways at the stairs.

"*Syllabus.* Sure. That's what they all say."

****

The empty lecture hall unnerves me. The way my voice echoes even when I whisper. And I do whisper it: "I'm not Jennifer Davis. I'm Ian Culpepper's ex-wife. Ava Lawson." I feel small but spotlighted—center stage in front of the whiteboard, with Dr. Jarvis staring at me as if I'm the strangest, most pathetic creature he's ever seen.

My father's watch ticks off an eternity's worth of seconds, each one as hard-earned as a mark on the wall of a prison cell. Until he speaks, finally.

"How may I help you?"

"I'm not sure if you can. Or if you'll want to. But I'm trying to figure out what happened. With Ian and Kate. Closure, you know?" I try to sound sincere. Like closure is something I actually believe in. Not a myth as fantastical as a unicorn. As elusive as the Loch Ness Monster. "And at the vigil you said you'd worked with Kate a bit, and I . . ."

"I wasn't sleeping with her, if that's what you heard. Is that what Ian told you?"

I blink back at him, stunned. "No. I didn't really talk to Ian much. Our divorce was—" My mind tosses out words—*contentious, bitter, ugly*—and I reject them all. "Brutal."

"Knowing Ian, that's not a surprise. He treated Kate poorly. Honestly, I think he was jealous of her. She really was a gifted writer, and we were working on a chapter together for Ian's next book. After we'd finished the first draft, he went off the deep end, accusing me of seducing her. I swore to him nothing happened. Kate did too. But he took me off the project and axed the chapter. He made life quite difficult for me here."

My stomach flip-flops, and I feel a little light-headed, regretting my meager coffee and half-a-bagel breakfast. Now the Hydra's gnawing on my insides. "How so?"

"Well, let's just say someone made it look like I subscribed to two hundred hard-core porn websites in one evening—from my work email. And that I forwarded some explicit pictures to my teaching assistant. I had to beg to keep my job. I had to promise to go to therapy. And I'm still on probation with the dean."

"Nobody did revenge like Ian," I say, hanging my head, almost begrudgingly. "Nobody."

Dr. Jarvis sighs as he packs his satchel with papers to be graded, notes to be read, lessons to be planned. And I nearly laugh out loud at the small tin of surfboard wax tucked into the side pocket. Sex Wax, it's called. Of course it is.

"I guess you found your Cleo," he says. "I saw her in the paper." I nod as my cheeks warm, grateful that he avoids my eyes. "It's always the guilty doing the accusing, isn't it? I only wish Ian was still alive to take the fall."

I watch his hands, palms cracked from too much sun and saltwater, squeeze the leather strap at his shoulder without mercy. He's not sorry Ian's dead. And I add his name to the list, right below my own.

"So what was your chapter about?" I ask.

With an ironic twist of his mouth, he leafs through his bag and shows me a stack of typewritten pages marked with red ink in a scratchy scrawl I recognize as Ian's. "Cognitive distortion in romantic relationships. The idea that our drive for closeness and our need for being loved by another are so strong, they can actually alter our thinking. We see what we want to see. Hear what we want to hear. Believe what we want to believe."

A shadow passes across my heart, graying everything. "Sounds fascinating."

"Take it," he says. "I've been carrying it around way too long." And I know exactly what he means.

****

Do you take the blame when your partner is angry, abusive, unfaithful, or neglectful? Do you ask yourself what you've done wrong? What you've failed to do right? You may be using cognitive distortion as a means of coping with the ugly truth: Your partner is angry. He is abusive. He just doesn't care.

I wonder if Kate wrote those words—the paragraph I read again and again—as I surveil the rental house on Cortez Road, where Maddie is tucked away under Sheila's watchful eye. I'd seen them pull in an hour ago, Maddie silent as a war-weary soldier, dragging a princess backpack behind her like a tiny pink body. Sheila chatting enough for the both of them. Smiling too. As if it was just any other day. And not this day. The day after Maddie had seen her dead-eyed parents packed into boxes and lowered into the cold, dark ground.

When Maddie emerges from the house, I catch my breath and hunker down in my seat. She pushes a powder-blue tricycle, silver foil streamers fluttering from the handlebars.

Through the crack in my window, I hear Sheila call to her from the front door. "Don't go past the mailbox!"

Maddie gives no sign of acknowledgment. She doesn't even look back. After the door closes, she mounts the tricycle and pedals down the sidewalk, the spitting image of Ian. Focused, determined, and stubborn as a mule. And when she blows by the mailbox and then the neighbor's house, there's no doubt whose blood runs thickest through her veins. However teensy they may be.

"Are you ready to try for a baby?" I remember the first time Ian had asked me, sitting on a bench at the boardwalk eating funnel cake. And I'd suddenly felt the urge to run. "A little Ian?" he'd teased. That didn't scare me. Him, I could manage. But the alternative carved out a pit of dread inside me. Because whatever had been wrong with my father was in me—one dark, corrupted cell, biding its time. Growing. And surely, a little Ava would be infected too. Her rosy-red heart would turn sick and blackened as a poison apple.

Maddie zips past two more houses, her spindly knees working like typewriter keys, and I think I know where she's going.

Sheila will look out the window, open the door. Any moment now. And come screaming down the sidewalk like a three-alarm fire. The way she had at the funeral.

Even so, I crack the car door and run after those three spinning wheels.

"Maddie!" I hiss her name like the snake I am. And she freezes, a baby bird tumbled from the nest, hoping not to be eaten.

The tricycle rolls to a stop, and I crouch to her level, shocked again by the pure blue sky in her eyes. "Do you remember me?"

She nods blankly and points up ahead. I see it too, just over the hill. The rooftop of 151 Cortez Road. Maddie's used-to-be home.

Questions form on my tongue and wait to be given life. Impossible questions. Did she even once peek out from the safe burrow of the downstairs closet? And who did she see there prowling the halls like a wolf? Did she tiptoe upstairs?

God, I hope not.

Mostly, I want to tell her I'm sorry. So, so sorry.

"Is that where you're going?"

Another nod. And both our heads spin backward to the sound of Sheila's voice calling for her, the edge of panic growing sharper each time. Maddie's eyes widen.

"Did you leave something there?"

I come closer, hoping for a word whispered. Just one, expelled with her breath. A word that will smell like apple juice and graham crackers. A word I will covet and decipher like a code. But when it comes, it's a shock of blood on white sheets. A shotgun blast in an empty field at daybreak. It's clear and bright as a church bell. And reverent too, as if the word itself has the power to make everything right again.

"Chocolates."

And then she pedals away from me. Until she's nothing but Kate's golden hair whipping in the wind.

When you leave a marriage, you may think you'll have a brand-new life.
The only problem: you're still in it.
—Ian Culpepper, *Love CPR*

VALENTINE'S DAY
FOUR YEARS EARLIER

DON'T be so histrionic," Ian scolded Ava the moment the door shut behind Marty Emerson, the new Director of Programming at BXA and Wallace Bergman's flip side. Young and slick and very heterosexual. Which explained why he'd just told them buxom-blonde Kate Pope would replace Ava in the pilot. "He's just trying to make the show a success. Isn't that what you want?"

"What about our marriage, Ian?"

"*What about it?* This has nothing to do with you and me."

"Oh really? So your suggesting your hot twenty-something graduate student as your co-host means nothing?"

Ava watched Ian's face for signs. Signs of what she already knew to be true. "Kate's got spunk, Aves."

"Don't call me that."

"But seriously. She reminds me of you way back when."

Back before you. Ava didn't say it though. There are some lines she still wouldn't cross. Unlike Ian, who'd crossed a football field's worth in one night. Taking Kate to dinner after class last week, laughing with her on the sidewalk out front. Ava had seen it all from the park across the street. Watched it teary-eyed through the lens of the brand-new Nikon her mom had given her at Christmas.

Ian gathered his notes from the meeting with Marty, tucked them into his satchel. "Besides, I don't make the decisions. Marty's in charge."

"Of course he is." More of Ian's rhetoric. Because Ava had been there when Ian threatened Marty last spring—"*Love Doctored* is my show. My idea. Hasn't BXA had enough bad publicity? You don't want to be known as the network who let Bawdy Bergman get away with copyright infringement, do you"?

Never mind that the show had been Ava's idea.

"You'll still be involved behind the scenes. The concept. The guests. Hell, even the music. Whatever you want. But we can't ignore the results of the focus group. And they decided Kate is more relatable."

Ava sneered at the thought of her. Fake blonde hair, fake tan, fake boobs. And an ego to rival Ian's. "Inflatable, you mean? Plastic and full of hot air."

Ian shook his head like she disgusted him. A look that said there was no coming back from this. Not from Kate or the show but from what they'd done. Because she'd seen him at his worst—the rotten core of the onion—and he would never forgive her for that. "Don't be mean, Aves. It doesn't suit you."

Tears stung her eyes, but she fought them off. "I have a few patients this afternoon. I guess I'll see you tonight."

Ian fumbled with his phone, didn't glance up. "Kate and I are having dinner with Marty at The Chateau at eight, so I might be—"

"On Valentine's Day?"

He shrugged. "I thought we always agreed it's just a stupid manufactured holiday. And this is important. We have a lot to discuss. Production starts in a couple of weeks."

It's our stupid manufactured holiday. "Sure. Whatever you need to do."

****

Kate and I. Ava couldn't get that out of her head. Especially when she realized Kate must have already known. About the dinner. About the show. Which meant Ava's agreement with it all was either assumed or irrelevant. Neither boded well, but one boded the worst—her marriage, flatlining on the table. Too far gone, too long dead to resuscitate.

After her last patient of the day, Ava booked it home to change into the highest heels and the slinkiest dress she owned. The kind of camouflage she'd need tonight. She slipped her secret weapon—her A-bomb—into a clutch and hailed a taxi to West Hollywood.

The forty-five minute cab ride dragged as she scrolled through Kate's Facebook page—*who has 1,125 friends?*—taking long, deep breaths to fight off waves of motion sickness. Or the inevitable nausea that comes when you register how stunning your replacement will look on your husband's arm.

Solemn, she stepped out of the cab and in front of The Chateau Marmont, the castle on the hill where everybody comes to see and be seen. Where everybody dons a mask and plays a part.

Fitting it would happen here, she thought. Like the end of a bad B movie. Slumber Party Massacre. Or Redneck Zombies. They'd call it Showdown at the Marmont, starring Kate Pope and Ava Culpepper. At least she could still claim his name. For now.

Ava stood blinking at the entrance to the bar, disoriented. Bathed in blood. That's how the place struck her. Red tassel lamps. Red lights. Red accent paint. The stench of smoke and vodka and regret. And on the ceiling, hundreds of silk butterflies, wings awash in red. She shivered.

With his back to her, a man in a pink Fedora, angry flames rising from his arms. When she blinked again, the man vanished. In his spot, a curvy Lady Gaga lookalike with magenta hair and a tattoo sleeve.

Not this again. Not tonight.

Wallace had been showing up uninvited all year. In the self-checkout line at the grocery store. At the movies, shoveling popcorn with those desperate hands. On a bench at the pier, feeding the seagulls. And in her office waiting room, baring teeth blackened by ash when he'd smiled. That one had done it. She'd fled the office and called Ian. "Meds might do you some good, Aves. Something to take the edge off."

That enraged her. Because she didn't want to file the edge. She wanted to know he felt it too. Remorse. The vicious cut of it. The way it slipped into the flesh between your ribs, angled up for the heart. And, when you least expected it, twisted.

Well after eight, Ava downed the rest of her martini, ducked into the bathroom, and checked her face in the mirror. She blotted the shine on her forehead. Reapplied a *come hither* shade of lipstick. Not that it really mattered. But Ian had given her a part—the vengeful bitch—and she wanted to look it. To act it too. If it came to that. So she concealed the A-bomb in her palm, ready for deployment.

Ava slunk through the lobby and peered into the corner of the restaurant to Marty's usual table. The table where Ian had issued his ultimatum and closed the deal with BXA months ago. Where he'd squeezed her knee and she'd felt hopeful. Where the three of them had toasted—*clink*—to *Love Doctored.* "It's sure to be a smashing success!"

But Marty wasn't there tonight. And even though Ava had expected it, the sight of Ian and Kate side by side, sipping champagne, crippled her. The appalling single rose that lay on the table. Kate's stunning ice-blue dress that matched Ian's eyes. Ava's body numb, all she could do was lean back against the wall, and still she couldn't look away.

The narrow space between them sucked her in like a vortex. She stared at it, watched it grow smaller. Until Ian's hand rested on Kate's exposed back, the golden canvas of skin Ava imagined would feel smooth and warm beneath his fingers.

Kate turned to him then, and he leaned in, the space dissolving completely.

When his lips pressed to Kate's cheek, Ava felt it. But it didn't break her. That came next.

Ian brushed a strand of hair from Kate's face—a gesture so small, yet so intimate—and Ava wondered how she could endure this. How anyone could.

218

Then, Kate stood and sashayed toward the bathroom, leaving Ian watching longingly after her, and Ava understood her father's need to put a bullet to his own soul. Because what else would end this?

Only one thing.

Ava's legs, numb as a dead man's, carried her to the maître d' stand.

"Good evening," she said, putting all her effort behind a jack-o'-lantern smile. "Could you tell Mr. Culpepper a friend would like to see him outside?"

She pointed at Ian's back, the dark head of hair Kate had probably run her fingers through. Had tugged at while he slammed against her naked flesh.

"Certainly. Who shall I say is waiting?"

"Wallace Bergman, please."

The man raised his brows and cocked his head at her. Gave her a worried look. Surely, he knew the name. Or he'd known it once. Before it had gone the way of all other Hollywood scandals. Replaced by the next shiny, tragic, titillating thing. "Of course, Madam."

She wanted to watch, to see the moment that name, spoken aloud, reached Ian. But that would ruin everything. So she scurried away, planting herself behind a pillar, and waited for him.

Predictable as her father's watch, he burst out of the restaurant, pale-faced. He scanned the lobby in a panic and headed outside.

Ava made her move—strutting toward Ian's table like she belonged there—the A-bomb tucked in her hand. She didn't flinch as she dropped two crushed Adderall into Ian's champagne glass and watched the pale yellow liquid bubble like a witch's brew. Then, she ducked through the kitchen and into the street, sucking in the night air like she'd been holding her breath.

Just that easy. Easier than she'd thought.

Try getting it up tonight, asshole.

She wanted to be there when Kate returned to the table and found him vexed. When she asked him what was wrong and he lied and said, "Nothing." When he downed that glass, and the Adderall kicked in. When the dopamine and norepinephrine started to fire.

But she couldn't, of course. It had to be enough to know the bomb she'd planted would detonate in time. That Ian would know the unpleasant sting of shame. The savagery of remorse.

Boom.

****

Ava lay on the sofa, not sleeping. She'd been waiting hours for this. The turn-click of Ian's key in the lock. The gentle creak of the door as it yawned open. The thud of his loafers, determined and hollow against the floor. But when the moment came, it twisted her stomach.

Backlit, he stood in the entry, looming like her father on his worst day.

"What did you do?" he hissed.

And she heard the awe underneath. Outrage too, of course. Indignation. But the awe made it worth it. The awe made her sit up, bright-eyed.

"You failed the Fidelity Five."

"What are you talking about?" He scowled at her, and it left her sad and empty. She'd hoped he could at least laugh at the irony. But he glared, sour. She'd expected too much.

"I saw you with Kate. I know what's going on."

"So you admit it then?"

"Admit what?"

"Apparently Wallace Bergman's ghost showed up at The Chateau to have a chat."

"Did he? Well, that must have been interesting for Kate. I'm sure you told her all about our friend, Wally. The unethical referral. The snooping on my session notes. The crash. The ketamine you gave him."

She'd read the articles like the rest of the world—"Autopsy Reveals Bergman Used Dangerous Drug." But she'd never said it out loud. Never given life to the suspicions that grew in the back of her brain like weeds. The kind that choke out all other life. And now that she had, she knew. They were done.

If Ian felt it too, she couldn't tell. He stood at the end of the sofa, working his jaw. Clenching and unclenching his fists. Part Adderall, part outrage. "Whatever I did, you did. Remember that."

"How can you live with yourself? Do you really think fucking Kate is going to make it better?"

A raised eyebrow. The faintest hint of a smirk. And she drew back from his smugness, repulsed.

"I'm not just fucking her, Ava. I'm in love with her. And I want a divorce."

THE DOWNTOWN STAR

"A DRAMATIC SHOWDOWN AT SLAIN LOVE DOCTORS FUNERAL! SCANDAL IN A SLEEPY TOWN!"

The memorial service for Love Doctors Ian and Kate Culpepper took a startling turn Tuesday when an intoxicated Ricky Sherman wielded a knife and confronted guests, awakening the dead at Whispering Cypress Memorial. Witnesses recounted Sherman's drunken tirade, which included his references to Ian Culpepper being a "lying bastard" and "scumbag." Sherman appeared to be upset about his 2016 appearance on *Love Doctored*, during which he was exposed as a philanderer in the now-infamous Fidelity Five. Later that same day, Sherman's wife, Vanessa, was found unresponsive in their dressing room at BXA studios.

Police arrested Sherman and booked him on charges of public intoxication, drunk and disorderly conduct, and brandishing a weapon.

Among the shocking allegations by Sherman, Ian Culpepper was still married to his second wife when he became involved with his third wife, Kate. *The Downtown Star* has exclusively learned that Culpepper's second wife, Ava Lawson, works as a psychologist in Carmel, just miles from where the lovestruck couple was found stabbed to death, and that she, like her predecessor, met the dashing Culpepper while his student. Another former student of Culpepper told *The Downtown Star* that Lawson was quiet and studious—"a bit of a wallflower"—and that it came as a shock when Culpepper announced their engagement.

Friends of Lawson say she was devastated by the breakup and disappeared from Los Angeles shortly after the *Love Doctored* premiere. With Culpepper's unexpected return to Carmel, some friends had worried Lawson might be swayed to rekindle their love affair. "Ava couldn't resist him," one friend told *The Downtown Star*, describing the young doctor's fixation on her ex. "I'd say it bordered on obsession."

222

CHAPTER NINETEEN

WHAT friends?" I say aloud to no one, which only proves my point. I close the article and shut my laptop, pushing it away from me like it's cursed. Even though my nonexistent friends are right. I had been devastated. And maybe a little fixated too. But that's what happens to love with nowhere to go. No one to give it to. It swells and rises like floodwater until nothing can contain it. It's poison. And sometimes people get hurt.

I pace from the sofa to the kitchen window and back again, not bothering to peek through the blinds. I already know I'm surrounded by a small army. Reporters outfitted with cameras and microphones and freshly pressed suits as body armor. TV trucks like tanks with their satellites aimed with machine-gun precision. I've been ambushed. Flanked. Outmaneuvered. Ava Lawson, second wife of Ian Culpepper, snuffed out of her hole and laid bare before the firing squad.

This morning, I canceled my clients for the rest of the week, hopeful none of them would answer my call. Only Verna did, prattling on about a relapse—a state-of-the-art back massager she'd bought on QVC—seemingly unaware of my newfound infamy. After I'd done a sufficient amount of reassuring and she'd repeated the ask-why-before-you-buy mantra she'd come up with last session, I unplugged the rotary phone. Set my cell to silent, the voice mailbox already full.

Now I wait in a stubborn standoff. I won't give them what they want: a look at my haggard face, drawn and gray from not sleeping. A confirmation of who I am: spurned ex-lover, fool, suspect, sucker. And they're not leaving. My resistance only serves as confirmation I'm worth waiting for.

Luke texted hours ago, three words:

Are you okay?

I knew he'd read *The Downtown Star*, along with the rest of Carmel. And I wanted to answer him, but what would I say? What could I say?

No.

Do you think I'm a wallflower?

Obsession is a bit of an exaggeration.

And by the way, one of my knives is missing.

I finally settle on humor, forced though it may be, staring back at the wood block as my fingers type:

I'd be better with doughnuts. Or your mom's red velvet cake.

****

"You don't deserve him. Which is why you don't have him. Not anymore." I'm talking to myself again, muttering really. Because Luke is striding up the driveway in plainclothes holding a pink box from Seaside Sweets, which only proves my point yet again.

A few reporters call out to him—"Hey! Is she in there?"—angling for a shot. But they know their limits, stopping at the sidewalk and gazing hungrily like starved animals desperate for scraps.

I open the door just wide enough for Luke to slip inside, careful to stay out of sight. Then I stick my hands in my pockets so I won't reach for him. Take a step back to maintain my distance.

"I can't stay long." Which is probably his way of doing the same. "But Mom insisted." He lifts the lid, and we both laugh at the words—*Happy 50th Birthday, Susan!*—swirled in what I'm hoping is cream cheese icing. "She said you needed it more."

"My deepest apologies, Susan. But she's right."

"How are you holding up?" Luke asks as he deposits the cake on the kitchen counter. "Did you talk to that attorney yet?"

"Yes." Because I *did* look online, researched a few. I even wrote down some numbers. But actually calling would mean something more. That I *am* in trouble. That I *have* done something wrong. "And I'm okay. They'll leave eventually, right?"

Luke's smile is sad. Like he can see inside me to the broken parts. I spin away from him, toward the cabinets before I tear up. But I hear him shuffling behind me, the clink of plates against the granite.

"Should I cut you a slice?"

When I turn, he's already there. At the knife block. And all I can do is nod my head and wait for him to notice. But he doesn't. He just selects the slicer—with its delicate blade, thin as a playing card—adjacent to the empty slot.

"I'm glad you're having one too," I say. "At least I can be sure your mom didn't poison it. She must really hate me. Especially now."

Luke rolls his eyes and groans at me. "She doesn't hate you. But she is disappointed you weren't honest with her. With us." I watch the way he holds the knife, careful and steady. It glides through the icing, then through the cake's flesh, with ease. "Hey, she's mad at me too, if it helps."

He plops the blood-red cake at the center of the plate and slides it to me. Maybe red velvet wasn't the best choice.

"Great. So what you're saying is she poisoned both of us?" Mid-bite into his own piece, Luke catches a sudden burst of laughter with his hand. And it makes my heart ache. "At least Cooper will be happy. Has he said it yet? I told you so?"

"He's been heads down in this case chasing leads for Dad. I feel bad for him. He wants it so badly."

"To make detective?"

"To get Dad's approval. After that last citizen complaint, Dad's been riding him hard."

I cut off a small sliver of cake and move it across the plate and back again, leaving a trail of white frosting. And a mouthful of words, thought but unspoken.

"I know what you're thinking," Luke says, preparing a mountainous bite. "But Coop's not a bad guy. He just forgets that sometimes."

More like permanent amnesia, I think. But I stuff in a forkful of red velvet instead. Best to leave it alone. "So, did Cleo give a statement yesterday?"

"She never showed," he says, between mouthfuls. "Have you talked to her?"

"Not recently." Two words, vague and deliberately chosen, and his face falls. *I'm doing it again.* "Look, I can see you don't trust me. And I can't blame you for that. You know, if I was your therapist, I'd say you made a mature decision."

"Aren't you supposed to be the mature one?" he teases.

I ball up my napkin and toss it at him, trying to be playful, but the ache in my chest only grows. "Gee, thanks. You really know how to kick a girl when she's down."

I'm not hungry anymore, but I match his bite with one of my own because it's expected of me. This is Susan's cake—whoever she is—and I'd demanded it. Practically stolen it from her. I damn well better eat it. And enjoy it too. That's the guilt talking. The squirming Hydra that wants to be fed.

We chew in silence until Luke finishes. He clears his plate and stands at the sink, fidgeting. "So . . . what was Ian like—as a husband? You never really told me."

I try to find the right way to say it. That Ian was exactly what I'd always expected a man to be. His dark moods, his tantrums, his threats. His insatiable needs and his desperate fear of being left. The only kind of man I'd ever known. Until Luke.

"Have you ever heard the line that the things you like most about someone in the beginning will become the things you hate?"

"Sure. Like the way you try to fix everything with sex? Great, at first." I smirk at him, shake my head. "Okay," he admits. "Still great."

"Anyway . . . that's how it was with Ian. When we met, he was passionate and confident. Driven and fiercely loyal. But on the flip side, he could be arrogant, vindictive, and relentless."

"Was he ever depressed?"

"Not in the conventional sense. But he'd get dark when things didn't go his way. And looking back, I'm not sure he was happy." *Two unhappy people make one unhappy marriage.* Ian had doled out that piece of wisdom on the second episode of *Love Doctored*, Kate simpering by his side. I'd wanted to throttle them both.

"Last week, you said you had a hunch Ian did it. Like a murder-suicide." There's an unspoken question, and I take another bite of cake, fearful of what he might suspect. About Ian. About me. About the things unhappy people do together. "Did he ever try to kill himself?"

"No. Not that he told me about anyway." Luke's eyes leave mine, and I feel his doubt. I hear my old self say *valen-pocalypse*, the silly word I'd made up for the first time, thinking it would be the last. Thinking that would be the worst of our Valentine's. "He'd make threats, and it would scare me. But I never really believed he'd do it. I thought he was just using what happened with my dad against me. Ian could be very manipulative."

Luke raises his eyebrows. As if to say *so can you.* I push the plate away from me, trying not to think about how right he is.

"Are you done?"

I nod at him, still burning from the heat of his words, unsaid. He takes my plate. Rinses it. Dries it. Returns it to the shelf. And sits on the stool next to mine.

"Do you want to know why I'm asking?"

"I don't want to get you in any trouble."

"Dad talked to Julie Avery's parents."

My mouth hangs open, and I imagine how it must look to Luke. Like a dark, dark cave. So deep the air is different there. The kind that makes you light-headed, the way I'd felt each time Ian said her name. *How can you be jealous of a dead girl?* And the question hadn't stunned as much as the way Ian had asked it. Like she didn't belong to him.

"Ian's first wife," Luke says, thinking I'm confused. Or I've forgotten. As if I ever could.

"I know who she is."

"They told him that every time Julie tried to leave, Ian would threaten to kill himself, and she'd go back. They said she'd left him for good a week or so before she died."

The Averys had told me as much and more when I'd called them a few years back. Still, hearing Luke say it out loud steals the air from the room again.

"Ian had eight stab wounds on his body. And four shallow incise wounds on his wrists, not enough to do any damage. All done with the same weapon. According to the coroner, the cuts on his wrists were self-inflicted."

****

Luke stays longer than he promised. He sits close to me on the sofa, lets me sink into his warm body. Puts his arm around my shoulder. Kisses my head. I let him. And it makes me wonder—*just how manipulative am I?*

I'm half-asleep when his cell phone rings. And I wish he wouldn't answer. The shrillness of it gnaws at my brain—it reminds me of a patient I had once with misophonia who couldn't stand the sound of her husband's chewing—and I want to destroy it. I want to stay in this world. The kind where somebody like Luke could forgive somebody like me.

"Hey, Dad."

Luke stands up and leaves me, fast-walking to the bedroom and talking in his cop voice. His dutiful son voice. My body stiffens in his absence. I hold my breath and listen.

"Yep. We're on the way." And seconds later, "She will. She's fine."

His serious tone starts my heart pounding, and I feel sick. I regard the pink Seaside Sweets box for what it really is. My requested last meal as a free woman.

When Luke returns, he looks right at me, earnestly, the way a choir boy does, and says my name. "I have to take you into the station."

"Am I under arrest?"

He nods. "I asked Dad if we could do it this way. And he trusts me. He trusts *you*. If you agree to cooperate, I won't cuff you. We can walk out together."

"And if I don't?"

"Then Dad sends in the cavalry."

Resigned, I get up and go to him. "Can you tell me why?"

"All I know is they found money in Ricky Sherman's hotel room he said was from you. That it was your idea to blackmail Ian with some photos you took and that you'd gotten the money on Valentine's Day. That's extortion, Ava."

"I didn't kill him or Kate though. I had nothing to do with—"

"It's probably better if you don't say anything, okay?"

I walk to the hall closet with a lump in my throat. Reach in for my jacket. And freeze.

There it is.

A knife.

But not my missing chef's knife. This knife matches the others. From Ian and Kate's set. Its black handle protrudes from an old sweater pocket.

Doubt, sly and insidious, seeps into the cracks in my mind, widening them.

Did I do it? Am I crazy?

I feel Luke behind me, his eyes on my back. I have to do something, say something. Get rid of it somehow. I slip my jacket from the hanger, trying to reach for it. But Luke takes me by the arm and guides me toward the door. And the space between me and the knife widens until there's nothing I can do but leave it.

All I can think of is the suicide forest. How I'd stepped over Wallace Bergman's body and now I had to pay. "Do you believe me?" I ask, searching for reassurance.

His touch is tender but firm. A lot like his answer. "I want to. I really want to."

CHAPTER TWENTY

IT'S like the worst sort of dream. Where you want to scream—you *need* to scream—but your body makes no sound. I know that feeling. I've worn it like a second skin. And now too, with the voices making their demands through the windows of Luke's truck, the knife I'd left behind for the cops to find, I want to wail with every bit of breath in my body. But I can't.

"Ava!"

"Over here!"

"Were you sleeping with Ian?"

"Did you kill him?"

Luke has one hand on the wheel and the other on the seat, my fingers clenched tight to his wrist. As we lurch forward, a camera lens bangs the window, and I jump back like I've been shot. I squeeze my eyes shut.

"Just tell me when it's over. When they're gone."

I finally feel the road rumble beneath us, faster and faster, and he whispers, "It's okay. They're gone now."

In the rearview mirror, I see them swarming, lenses trained on the truck. But Luke floors it until they're only shadow people. And then nothing at all but a bad memory.

"Do you think I'll get bail?"

"Possibly. Depending on the full extent of the charges."

I'm afraid to ask what he means by that, so I keep quiet. Until the questions in my head unspool like thread, and worries pour from an unstitched wound. I have to say something just to stop the bleeding.

"Luke?"

"Yes?" *Oh God, he already knows.* Not what I'll ask, but that I'll ask. I'll demand something of him. Something that's too much to give.

"If the judge doesn't grant bail, I could be in jail for a while. And I won't be able to see my mom or explain to her . . ." It sounds ridiculous. Like I'm grasping at straws. Which I am. "Cliffside is on the way to the station. Do you think we could—?"

"Are you seriously asking me that?"

I shrug, sheepish. Embarrassed at my own audaciousness. But I'm not willing to take it back. So I push further. Too far. "You can come in with me. I'm sorry I never invited—"

He smacks his hand against the dash. "*Don't.* Don't make this about me."

I sink back against the seat and turn toward the window, let my head rest against the cool glass. Ian once told me working with couples taught him one thing. In every relationship, one person inevitably loves the other more—*the success of the relationship lies in the magnitude of the difference.* Watching Luke take the turn to Cliffside, my heart breaks with the thought of it.

****

Nurse Ellerby pales when she sees me, but she's good at pretending normalcy. She'd have to be in a place like this. Where people wake up in different cities, different decades. In bodies that haven't aged. "Ava. It's been a while."

I nod at her, sadly. "This is my friend, Luke."

"Nice to see you again, Officer Donovan," she says, giving him a once over, waggling her eyebrows at me. "Luke stopped by on Tuesday to take a look at the log book. It wasn't him who signed it. I'd never forget a face like that." Her conspiratorial wink is further confirmation someone is screwing with me. And that Luke never lies. Which only makes me feel worse for having doubted him.

"We're just stopping in for a quick visit. How is she?"

"You picked a good day. Her first lucid one in a while."

"I'm glad. Because . . ." I glance at Luke, and he sighs. "I may not be back here for a while."

Nurse Ellerby pats the hand I've placed on the counter. "Alright. Well, we'll remind her you'll be back soon." *Soon.* What a soul-crushing word, with its promises, its hopeful little sound.

Luke follows me down the hall, past Wheelchair Row and the wailing woman. Today, she's quiet. Like she knows something I don't. We stop at the shadow box. "Should I give you some time alone?" he asks.

"Come in with me." I tug on his arm when he hangs back. "I want you to."

My mother sits on the sofa, flipping through the channels with the remote. She's wearing real pants today and one of her old favorite shirts. Her eyes catch the light from the window and shine when she smiles at me. "Hi, sweetie. I've missed you. And who's this?"

"Luke Donovan. You've seen him before. A while back. He's a police officer like his dad, Jack." Luke waves shyly. Like the seven-year-old boy he'd been when they'd first met.

"Oh. I suppose he does look familiar." She reaches for his hand, squeezes it. "A kind face. And one of the brave men in blue. Just like my Jerry. God rest his soul. I'm sure Ava told you he took his own life."

I stagger back. Like it's all brand new. She never remembers *that.*

"The job can be hard on all of us," Luke says, and I feel his palm on my back, steadying me. "I'm sorry for your loss."

I join my mother on the sofa, the vinyl warm from the sun. "Luke and I can't stay long. But I wanted to tell you—"

"Oh! *Him.*" She points to the television. Breaking News scrolls at the bottom in police light colors—blue and red—and Chief Morrow stands at a podium, flanked by officers. In the corner of the screen, a picture of Ian and Kate on their wedding day. And I struggle to keep my breathing even. What else does my mother remember? And how will I explain the things she doesn't?

I wait for her to say it. *Isn't that your asshole ex-husband? The one who ripped your heart from your chest and spit on it. Crushed it beneath his boot like a cockroach.*

"Who, Mom? Who?"

Luke's eyes widen, and I shrug at him. Let's just get this over with.

Or . . . *Isn't that the handsome and amazing Love Doctor? The one with that show I remember to watch even when I forget your name.*

Instead, she stands up and walks to the set, squinting her eyes. Lays her hand on the screen and points to one of the men flanking Chief Morrow. I only realize then it's Cooper.

"This young man here. What a sweetheart. I told him I had a beautiful daughter he should date. What was his name? Cory? Connor, maybe."

"Cooper?" Luke asks, and she nods so fast I worry she'll get whiplash. "What was he doing here?"

The question is meant for me, but my mother giggles and scurries to her bedside drawer, eager to show us. She reaches inside and holds up a handful of hearts, wrapped in red foil, embossed with seashells. "He brought me chocolate."

Some experts might say a divorce is like a death. But I say it's more like a murder. The thing you created together is dead. And nobody's hands are clean.
—Ian Culpepper, *Love CPR*

VALENTINE'S DAY
THREE YEARS EARLIER

AVA ran ten miles that Saturday morning, fueled by coffee and contempt. Her mother called her cell twice before she hoofed it back to the house, to ask her if she'd seen it. If she was okay.

Yes, Mom. I'm fine. And she was. *Fine.* More worried about her mother's forgetfulness than Ian and Kate's vomit-worthy spread in *People* magazine—"Love Doctors' Lessons: How to Make Love Last."

Lesson one. Don't screw a back-row girl right under your wife's nose. And two, don't get her knocked up before the ink dries on your divorce papers. Three, don't ask her to sign an NDA like you're the goddamned King of England. Like she'd sell your secrets to the highest bidder, like she'd stoop that low.

Ava had studied every page of the article without reading a single word of Ian's sanctimonious BS. Instead, she'd zeroed in on the photos. On Kate. Her eyes, the delicate blue of a robin's egg. She'd been certain she would find it there. A harbinger of trouble. Sadness behind the smile. But Kate radiated pure light. And Ian gloated, smug as ever, with one-year-old Madison swaddled between them like a tiny trophy.

She'd brought the magazine to work yesterday and shredded every page of it, satisfied as the cut ribbons spooled into the trash can. But she'd bought another on her way home, sure she'd missed something. And that nagging feeling hadn't gone away. Ten miles and three hills later.

Still breathless, she pulled up a stool to her kitchen counter and opened the magazine again. Page fifty. Right between Taylor Swift and an ad for diet pills. A drop of her sweat landed smack on the first line.

"I haven't always been lucky in love," Culpepper said. "But Kate's my four-leaf clover."

She couldn't take anymore. Her stomach knotted; her chest ached. Still, she kept reading. Self-flagellation, her mom had called it. Like when Ava had insisted they watch the first episode of *Love Doctored*. Ava had wanted to remind her mother of all the times she'd done the same—bended under her husband's will, kowtowed to his moods, suffered in silence. And gone back for more. *Where do you think I got it from?* twitched on the tip of her tongue, but she'd left it there.

"We've both had our share of heartache like everybody else. That's love lesson number one. Don't give up on your happily ever after."

Sweat stung Ava's eyes, blurring Ian's drivel. Even so, the absence was undeniable. No mention of her. A failed marriage. Of Julie. A dead wife. And inside Ava, a sudden fire erupted, shooting sparks. She flung the magazine across the room. It struck the wall hard and landed with an unceremonious swish.

She scrolled through the saved contacts in her phone until she found it. The number she'd looked up years ago, post-valen-pocalypse. The number she'd never dialed.

Until now.

Each ring thrummed through her body, winding her up tight as a chain, until she could hardly bear it.

"Hello?" The man sounded nice enough. Tired. But friendly. Not at all how she'd imagined his voice from his picture—Headmaster Avery—on the Eastmont Prep School website.

"Is this Marcus Avery? Julie's dad?"

She squirmed in the silence, afraid he might hang up.

"Yes. But Julie's been—"

"I know." She couldn't bear to make him say it. *Julie's been dead for years now.* "This may sound strange. But, I was married to Ian Culpepper. And I was hoping you could tell me about Julie. About what happened to her."

More silence. And she shouted down into the well of it, "I'm not a reporter," practically expecting an echo. "I wanted to call the first time I had doubts about him. When Chuck Whitlock told me Julie had left Ian right before she—"

"Chuck?"

"Yes. He told me he knew her from New Beginnings."

"Julie liked Chuck. He was a good friend to her."

Ava heard the scratch of Ian's key down the side of that Prius. She spoke fast to drown it out. "He told me Ian was pretty distraught about Julie leaving."

"Ian was distraught about being *left*. And Julie had her own issues. She'd battled depression since her teens. We were thrilled when she met Ian. He was older, and he seemed stable, charming. I'm sure you know. But it's all an act. Underneath, he's a mixed-up person. Or he was anyway."

"Still is," Ava said, feeling a strange sense of comfort in this twisted kinship.

"Two mixed-up people make a real mess of a marriage. Julie would threaten to leave. Ian would threaten to kill himself. Or her. Or the both of them. And when Julie started to get really sick, Ian got possessive of her. He wanted us out of her treatment so he could make all the decisions. And he'd started to prescribe her meds. As wrong as that was, we allowed it, because that's what Julie wanted."

Marcus sighed the sigh of a man scooped hollow. So emptied the wind could blow right through him.

"Then there was the research trial. Ian was insistent on it. Even though Julie never responded well to SSRIs. The first few days she got so agitated, she scratched her arms till they bled. But he told her to tough it out. That it would get better. She stopped cold turkey and left him. We still don't know what happened that night."

"Was there an investigation?"

"They ruled it a suicide. She accelerated into a brick wall in a parking garage. She wasn't wearing her seat belt. But I know Ian's at fault, as surely as if he'd had his goddamned foot on the gas."

****

"Is it me or does she look a little constipated?"

Ava frowned at her mother, feigning disapproval, as the closing credits rolled on: *Love Doctored*, at a special night and time. "Mom. Seriously. Have a little sympathy. Kate has a giant stick up her ass. And Ian for a husband. You'd probably look constipated too."

Chuckling, Ava shut off the TV and unwrapped another chocolate heart her mother had brought for her. Not one to let her self-flagellate alone, she'd come bearing gifts. Two expensive bottles of wine from The Seventeenth Mile and a pink box from Seaside Sweets. They'd already downed one bottle and uncorked the next. And the pink box was half empty, wrappers littering Ava's coffee table. Evidence of their gluttony.

"They're good, aren't they?" her mother asked, popping a whole piece in her mouth. "And with those darling little shells on the wrappers. I can't believe you've never been there. Marianne's shop is just a few steps from your office."

"I stole her husband's badge, Mom. I doubt I'm high on her list."

"Oh honey. You were what, fifteen? I'm sure she's forgiven you by now. Besides, she's got a cute son. That cop."

Ava's mother wiggled her eyebrows while she chewed.

"First of all, I'm not interested. Second, I'd need to start running two-a-days to burn off those calories. And third, I'm not interested. Cooper is off limits. Even if he wasn't a total jerk, I did that eval on him last month, remember?"

As if that mattered. As if her ethical standards were above reproach. She shouldn't have taken the case at all. Given that they'd gone to school together. And he'd bought her that beer at Mickey's. And she was most definitely biased. But she'd needed the work. After she'd used Ian's money—his payoff, she called it—to buy a fixer-upper near the beach and pay one year's rent upfront on her office, there wasn't much left. And in truth, she'd been curious to look under the hood of Cooper Donovan.

"Not Cooper. Her other son . . . oh, what's his name?"

"Luke? Are you kidding? He's practically a baby."

Her mom flopped back against the couch, laughing. "He looked pretty grown up when I ran into him at the shop yesterday. You know it's just a few steps from your office."

Ava doused a pang of worry with another sip of wine. "You just said that."

"Oh. Well, I didn't think you heard me."

One of her usual excuses. "You've been a little forgetful lately, don't you think?"

"When you get to be my age, a *little* forgetful is allowed. Some would say it's an accomplishment. Now, stop worrying and have some more chocolate. You could stand to gain a few pounds."

Ava rolled her eyes, but she didn't argue. She leaned over to her mom, put her head on her shoulder. "Thanks for being my valentine."

She saw her mother's chest rise sharply and then fall, and her own started to ache again. "I'm sorry about Ian," her mother said. "I hope it wasn't my fault."

"What do you mean, *your fault?*"

Her mother touched the watch on Ava's wrist, the one that belonged to the ghost of man who sat between them. "That you married someone like your father. You didn't have the best model of a marriage. I should've stood up to your dad more. I knew those pills were no good for him. Maybe if I had, he wouldn't . . ."

Her mother whimpered, then wailed. And Ava stared straight ahead at the television screen, a single, unblinking black eye. The portal to another world, no darker than this one.

It had been years since her mother had cried. And now, it was the second time in as many days. Ava gritted her teeth against the sound and said nothing.

But she knew right then. The same way she'd always known when her father's mood had shifted. Or when Ian was upset with her. The air changed frequency.

She held herself as still as stone, walled off the soft animal of her heart the way she would with her patients. Careful not to break it again—her world that seemed as fragile as an eggshell. But already the thought was growing, a poisonous weed pushing up through the cracks.

Something is wrong with Mom.

****

Ava couldn't sleep. And every time she nodded off, she had the same dream. Her arm on fire.

At 2 a.m., sheets soaked through, she slogged through the dark to find her cell phone.

Compose new text message:

Did you see Julie the night she died?

Delete.

Two deaths on your conscience must be a lot to bear. Oh wait. You don't have one.

Delete.

Happy anti-Valentine's.

Before she could rethink it, regret it, erase it, she hit Send.

THE MONTEREY COUNTY COURIER

"MURDER WEAPON IDENTIFIED IN CULPEPPER SLAYING"

by Jackson Lamont

On Thursday morning, just two days after the bodies of Drs. Ian Culpepper (48) and Kate Culpepper (30) were laid to rest, Police Chief Scott Morrow of the Carmel Police Department confirmed at a 7 a.m. press conference that a knife that washed ashore at Ocean Beach on Monday contained DNA belonging to both husband and wife. "We believe this is our murder weapon," Chief Morrow said. He declined to answer questions about the presence of third-party or suspect DNA on the knife, citing the sensitive nature of the ongoing investigation. He also declined to comment on the arrest of Ricky Sherman on Tuesday, after an incident at Whispering Cypress Memorial. Sherman was released on Wednesday on $20,000 bail.

CHAPTER TWENTY-ONE

FRIDAY
FEBRUARY 24, 2018

I sit on the top bunk in my holding cell, relegated here by the strapping young woman below me. She calls herself Marbles—*because I lost 'em all, Doc*—and she enjoys tattoos, marijuana, and long walks on the beach. But I shouldn't complain because she also likes to fight, and the girls next door are afraid of her.

I am too, of course, but she said she'd have my back as long as I need it, which Ivy Mercer from Mercer and Mercer assured me would be no more than twenty-four hours. *But protection ain't free*, so Marbles commands a small, non-negotiable fee.

Just gimme all your chow—'cept the green beans. You can keep those, Doc.

So it's been nothing but green beans for me since yesterday. A small price to pay for peace of mind.

Officer Kellogg (aka Frosted Flakes) knocks his baton against the bars. "Hey, Lawson. Somebody wants to see you."

"Don't tell 'em nothin', Doc. Snitches get stitches." These are Marbles' words of encouragement. And I flash her a weak smile.

Truthfully, I haven't stopped holding my breath since Luke walked me into the Monterey County Jail yesterday afternoon, where they booked me on one count of PC 518, extortion. According to Ivy, it's a felony that carries a two- to four-year term in this high-class joint or a ten-thousand-dollar fine.

Last night, I'd lain awake, wide-eyed, on my rock of a bed and listened to Marbles snoring beneath me. I couldn't shake the dreadful feeling of inevitability. That I'd somehow been headed here on a long and broken road since the day Wallace Bergman walked into my office. And now that I've arrived at my destination, concrete and barbed wire, the universe won't let me go.

From the corner of the interview room, Jack Donovan nods at me like he knows it too. This is where I'm meant to be. And next to him, Doreen Lennox is no better, burying her nose in a thick file folder. Of damning evidence. That's probably why she can't even look at me.

Ivy's there too, every bit the hard-nosed attorney I'm paying her to be. She'd told me she'd worked for the DA, before she came over to the dark side. When I'd frowned at that, she chuckled. "It's just an expression," she'd said. But it seemed like the truth. Did she see it too? That I belonged here. That I'd done things darker than dark.

"Sit down, Ava," Jack says, pointing to a chair opposite all of them. And I fall in line before the firing squad. "We have a few more questions for you."

"I told you yesterday. I don't have anything more to say about the extortion charge. I'm innocent."

I glance, helpless, at Ivy, and she bares her perfect teeth. "This is ridiculous, Detective. Ms. Lawson has been nothing but cooperative. Overly so, in my opinion. What more could you possibly want to know?"

"This is not about extortion. This is about murder."

I know he means Ian and Kate, but all I see is a charred hillside and the burned-out frame of a Jaguar.

"My client invokes her Fifth Amendment right to remain silent, and—"

Doreen smiles at Ivy, the same way she'd smiled at me that first day. Charming. "She doesn't have to say anything, ma'am, but we'd like to show her a few things, if that's alright."

Her hands rest on the folder, guarding it like a treasure trove. And I need to know what's inside. "It's okay," I say. "I'll hear them out."

"Good." Before Ivy can protest, Doreen slips her fingers inside and withdraws a familiar photograph from the top of the stack. "Let's start with something you've already seen."

The black-handled knife with a blade that measures eight inches, according to the sad gray ruler that lies alongside.

"Look familiar?"

I nod. "You showed it to me last Tuesday."

"Right." *Good girl.* As if there will be a grade at the end of all this. "Now what about this one?" She produces a second photo, prodding the Hydra sloshing about in my stomach. And I feel sick.

"That's my house. I didn't give you permission to—"

Jack raises his hand, and I stop speaking, ashamed of myself for cooperating in my own demise. I'm not shocked. How could I be? But the speed of it all has me spinning.

"We didn't need permission. Based on the circumstances of your recent arrest and the connection to one of our deceased victims, we obtained a search warrant. Care to comment on what we found?"

"She absolutely does not," Ivy says. And I manage to pry my eyes from the handle protruding from my sweater pocket long enough to shake my head *no*.

"Well, suffice to say, it's a match. The two knives are from the same set. And this knife . . ."—Doreen taps the edge of the first photo—"is our murder weapon."

Jack clears his throat. Like whatever is about to come out of his mouth needs its own introduction. "I like you, Ava. I always have. And there was a time when I thought you might be part of our family one day. But you've lied to me. You sat at my dinner table and lied. And then, you told me you'd never thrown anything into the water at Ocean Beach. That old man who saw you, he picked you out of a photo lineup. Said he was ninety-nine percent certain. That's good enough for me."

"We're done here," Ivy says, smacking the table with her palm.

"Were my fingerprints on it?"

"Ava. I said we're done. That means stop talking."

"One more thing," Jack says, undeterred. "We got a call from a nurse at Cliffside this morning. They found a cell phone hidden in your mom's room. And it looked like it had blood on it. Now, who do you think that phone belonged to, Avenging Angel?"

He whips another photo from the file as I fight the urge to scream my throat raw. Ian, from the front this time. An angle I hadn't seen. Plaster-white face marred by angry red scratches on his cheek. Eyes closed but not like he's sleeping.

"Ian, I guess." I look away when Jack produces another shot. An autopsy photo of Ian's chest, eight numbered wounds. "Someone called me from Ian's phone . . . from his number. Why would I do that? Why would I hide it in my mom's room?"

"You tell me."

"Cooper was there the day after the murder." My voice trembles as it rises. "You should ask him."

Jack doesn't react like I'd hoped. With righteous indignation. Curiosity. Anything really. He just signals to Officer Kellogg—the take-her-away nod—and lands a final blow. A knockout. "The DA amended your charges to reflect one count of first-degree murder."

Marbles would probably spit in his face or maybe she'd say nothing, shrug it off like any other Friday. But me, I do what I always do lately. I make it worse.

"One?"

****

I watch Judge Pardee's mouth move below his mustache, his lips hidden by wiry gray, but all I hear is Marbles. *Damn girl, you got a body on you?* That's jail speak for murder, apparently. And word travels fast.

"Ms. Lawson, do you understand the charges against you as I've read them?"

Ivy eyes me with concerned annoyance, prompts me with a whispered, "Go ahead. Answer the question." I wonder if she's ever fired a client.

"Uh, could you repeat the last one? I'm just a little rattled right now." The sounds of guilt reverberate around me. The hushed whispers from the gallery. The frantic scribbles of reporters' pens meeting paper. Above it all, my own shaky voice.

"Your Honor," Ivy adds through gritted teeth. A few purposeful head-nods toward the judge, and I finally get it.

"I'm sorry, Your Honor."

"Certainly understandable given the nature of the offenses for which you've been accused. In addition to one count of felony extortion, it is alleged that on or about February 14, 2018, you did willfully, unlawfully, and with malice aforethought, murder Ian Culpepper, a human being, as defined by section 187 of the California Penal Code. It is a felony."

A human being. What an odd thing to say. And I see Ian on our wedding day, slipping a ring on my finger. Ian asleep on the sofa, a book half-open on his chest. Ian in bed, poised above me, eyes fiery with lust. Ian, half-dragging me back to the car as Wallace burned. He'd said we didn't do anything wrong. And I'd railed against it and wanted to believe it, all at once.

A nudge from Ivy, and I startle. The courtroom suddenly seems too bright, too open. And I squint up at Judge Pardee. "How do you plead, Ms. Lawson?"

"Not guilty. I didn't kill Ian. Or Kate."

"Let the record reflect that the defendant has entered a plea of not guilty."

I only half-listen as the attorneys argue about what happens to me next. As Ivy parses me out in lawyer-speak. *Not a flight risk, no criminal history, valued member of the community, an ailing mother.* As they agree to set bail at two million dollars. And Judge Pardee tells me I'll need to relinquish my passport and my firearm.

But my mind is stuck somewhere else.

On my own words. And the hair's breadth between innocent and not guilty.

CHAPTER TWENTY-TWO

THIS is what my life has come to. I say goodbye to Marbles, return my jail uniform—the red-and-white jumpsuit that made me look like a deranged candy striper—and collect my belongings. My cell phone comes back in its own body bag, a clear plastic one, with the SIM and SD cards taped to the back. I give it a proper burial in the trash can right outside the station. A dead-end for bloodhound Jack, just in case he tries to track me. I try not to think of what he's already sniffed out on it. Some good, like the calls from Ian's number. What murderer would do that? Some decidedly not good, like the text Ian sent me on Valentine's Day night.

Ivy had warned me not to go home. To hole up for a few days in a hotel instead. "Let it all blow over," she'd said. As if it would be that kind of storm. A quick downpour. But I refuse to act guilty.

So I take a taxi back to my house instead. The same house I'd bought with my dead husband's hush money and put up as collateral for bail. The one I'd be damned if anybody could keep me from. Especially not *them*. The reporters who swarm the sidewalk out front like ants at a picnic, moving faster now as they sense my approach. I'm what's for dinner. The main course.

"Do you want me to walk you to the door?" Even the taxi driver feels bad for me. Or maybe he's seen me on the news and would rather keep on my good side.

I shake my head and climb out, too exhausted to cover my face.

All I want is to lie in my bed and sleep until it's over. But *it* feels impossibly large, a mammoth cloud darkening my whole sky. The sort of storm you build an ark for. And it only gets bigger when I open the door and take in what's gone. My laptop. My sneakers. The infamous sweater. And the cherrywood knife block with its one empty slot.

I sit on the sofa, reeling. All my secrets laid bare.

Well, not all of them. With Ricky arrested, I'd seen the writing on the wall. Writ just as conspicuous as a blood-red *Ava* on an ornate mirror. On Wednesday, before all hell broke loose, I'd wiped my hard drive. Deleted the Pacbell email account along with all my text messages. And dropped the Nikon's memory card down the garbage disposal, relishing the delicate crunch of its bones.

Still. I can't help but feel exposed. Because a hundred cameras are trained on my front door. Because Jack had called me Avenging Angel. But mostly because someone had been to my mother's with Ian's bloody cell phone. Someone had been in my house before the police, planting that knife and taking another. Someone had wanted me to look like a murderer. To feel like one. And now I do.

I shower fast with the door open and the curtain half-pulled. Tug my damp hair into a ponytail and leave a trail of wet footprints to the bedroom. I'm half-dressed when the doorbell rings. Each insistent push of the buzzer hits a nerve at the base of my spine, and a chill zips through me.

I pull on my robe and pick up the vase from the edge of my dresser, creeping toward the door. Through the peephole, I see a man in a blue uniform. And I gulp. *What now?*

But he's not a policeman.

"What do you want?" I shout the words with my mouth flush against the door.

"Registered mail for Ava Lawson."

"Can't you just leave it?"

"You have to sign for it, ma'am. And I'll need to see your ID. I can come back later if, uh—" He glances over his shoulder at the ants, excited and circling the perimeter. "If it isn't a good time."

"Who's it from?" I ask.

He smacks the oversized envelope against the window, and I lean in close.

My address is neatly typed at the center. In the left corner, a printed logo: G&M for Goldstein and Myers, Attorneys at Law, 1615 Wilshire Boulevard, Los Angeles.

The same G&M who'd crafted our divorce decree and bullied me into Ian's nondisclosure agreement. Ruthless and efficient.

"One minute," I say, scrambling for my purse. Certain that whatever is in that envelope has to do with Ian. And just like our broken vows—for better or worse—I've never been able to resist that.

****

The office had been cold. That's why I'd been shaking. With Goldstein perched on the conference table between Ian and me, the pen had quivered in my hand.

Irreconcilable differences. A nondescript phrase, so void of emotion it could have read *tin can* or *sliced bread*. It didn't sum what had gone on between us, layer upon rotten layer of wrong.

"You should've taken a Xanax," Ian had whispered. "It would've helped." And I'd steeled myself then, a giant *fuck you*, signing my name at the bottom as neatly, as purposefully, as I ever had.

But the papers on my coffee table take me right back there. The same look. The same feel. That same thick, expensive stock. And the words? Just as revelatory.

I regard Mr. Goldstein's letter with awe and suspicion before I pick it up and read it again.

Dear Ms. Lawson:

I am writing to you at the instruction of my client, your ex-husband, Ian Culpepper. As I am sure you are aware, Mr. Culpepper passed away on February 14, 2018, under suspicious circumstances. Please accept my sincere condolences for your loss. Enclosed you will find a sealed communication from Mr. Culpepper, as well as the prenuptial agreement I executed on his behalf with Kate Pope. Mr. Culpepper directed me to provide these documents to you in the event of his death. If I can be of further assistance, please do not hesitate to contact me at the number below.

Sincerely,

Ira Goldstein, Attorney at Law

Inside the larger envelope is another. Sealed, just as Goldstein promised, with Ian's signature scrawled across the flap, dated January 1, 2018. Over one month ago. And well before the are-you-fucking-kidding-me conversation.

I hold it in my hands, afraid of it. Like that other note, twenty-one years ago. But there's no backing out. I slide my finger under the glued edge, rip it open, and unfold the letter inside.

Dear Ava,

I know what you're thinking right now in that twisted mind of yours. I can picture you with that little furrow between your eyebrows. You're wondering why the hell you should care about anything I have to say, but you're curious too. And I'm obviously dead, so you feel a bit sorry for me. Or maybe you don't.

Perhaps this won't matter at all, but I feel I owe it to you anyway. A warning of sorts. When I married Kate, I thought she was different, and I tried to be honest with her. I told her everything. And that's the irony of my life. I picked the wrong girl to get it right with.

After Kate and I lost the show, she said I'd pushed too hard for ratings. She accused me of planting alcohol in the Shermans' dressing room and encouraging them to unwind between segments. She called me a hypocrite and a murderer. I tried to help her get past her doubts, but then she started cheating on me.

First, I heard rumors about her and Dan Jarvis, a professor at MCC. The pervert denied it, and so did she. So, I let it go. What's good for the goose is good for the gander. And if that's all it had been, then maybe Kate and I could've gotten past it. But it didn't stop there. She met this sorry sucker.

And Aves, I think she told him about W.B.

My eyes keep reading, two pages worth, but my heart seizes there. Stops. On that line.

I'd signed a nondisclosure agreement. I'd kept my mouth zipped shut. Locked that secret inside me and tossed the key down the well. And let it grow big and vicious as a monster, feeding on all the good things it found.

And Ian? What had he done?

He'd told *her*.

My fists clench so tight, my knuckles whiten. And I understand the knife's blade line between love and murder. How easy it is to step over. If Ian wasn't already dead, I would have no choice but to kill him myself.

****

The rain is my undoing. Because it begins the same as it did Valentine's night. With a single fat drop on the window, trailing like a tear. Then another and another and another. Until the whole pane is marked with tear tracks, and the world outside blurs behind them.

I'm right back there, fleeing from the mansion on Cortez Road. Driving way too fast, borderline reckless on the slick streets. Wipers whipping across the windshield with a quiet fury. And a scream stuck in my throat like a shard of bone. Then, bursting through my own door, soaking wet and shivering. So cold it had taken Luke to warm me.

Suddenly this house is the last place I want to be. But I'm trapped here and frantic as a netted bird. I pace from window to window as the rain picks up. Harder now. And my undoing becomes my saving grace. Because the ants don't like rain, naturally. Some run for cover inside the warmth of their stations' vans. Others give up and head for home. A few of the hardy little buggers prop up their golf umbrellas, determined to wait it out. But when the wind starts tugging at their canopies, pulling them downside up, they admit defeat.

While the rain pounds against the now-empty sidewalk, I open a duffel bag and prepare my getaway, full speed ahead to anywhere but here. I scoop up a handful of underwear and socks. Toss in a few T-shirts and my toothbrush. Tuck Ian's letter beneath it all like a precious jewel or a sordid secret. Because the truth always is. Precious *and* sordid.

Breathless, I lug the bag into the hallway and grab my keys, mentally tucking myself into a nondescript hotel bed. Locking myself behind a deadbolt and a security latch. Safe inside a room with very few hiding places. And only one way in and one way out.

The wind gusts outside the door like a warning whistle. And with my hand on the knob, I freeze. *Is that . . . ?* I lean in, look closer.

A small brown spider scuttles up the frame toward the beginnings of its web in the corner. It stops, and we regard each other with suspicion. The rain patters like a child's stamping feet against the roof, but all I hear is Maddie's little voice. *The itsy bitsy spider crawled up the water spout . . .*

I try to slow my breathing, but the Hydra's in control now. And my chest tightens as it bears down, one vicious head after another.

Down came the rain and washed the spider out . . .

It's not real.

It's *not* real.

But it sounds as if she's right behind me—her throat raw from crying, her voice cracked with fear.

I should know what to do. **How to Outsmart Panic**—I've got the damn pamphlet in my office. And yet, here I am, the room spinning around a spider and a little girl's nursery rhyme. I focus on a small spot on the floor, a discoloration in the wood, trying to ground myself. But it only turns to a spot of blood I'll never wash out.

Jesus. I wish I'd saved those Xanax.

I head for the bathroom anyway, thinking a cold shot of water might stop the neurons in my brain from rapid-firing. Slow the adrenaline rush. Get my power-hungry amygdala to surrender the reins.

Out came the sun . . .

One splash.

And dried up all the rain . . .

Two.

And the itsy bitsy spider . . .

Three splashes. And Maddie's singing is gone.

All I see is my reflection in the stillness of the mirror. My eyes, two shimmering stones in a lake of unfathomable depths.

All I hear is a fierce pounding, too methodical to mistake for my own wild heartbeat. It's the sound of someone insistent, intent on coming inside.

I peer around the corner into my bedroom where the pane of the window frames Ricky's face. The rain smudges his features, softens them. But there's no denying the brutal smack of his palm on the glass.

His dark eyes lock onto mine, and there's nothing left to do.

My legs as useless as leaves in the wind, I lumber toward the window, pulled by the gravity of his desperation.

I open it, and the rain comes blowing in.

****

"How did you get here?" It seems the safest question. The simplest. Where a therapist should start. With an easy one. A barometer.

Ricky wrings out the T-shirt clinging to his belly, adding to the growing puddle at his feet. He rubs his buzzed head with the towel I've given him, growling at me from beneath it. "I dropped in from a helicopter. How do think I got here? I fucking walked."

"Hey, I didn't have to let you in. You scared the hell out of me. I could've called the cops."

Truth is, he still scares me. The way his fists clench, strangling that towel. The unpredictable darting of his eyes. And the strong musk of misery that clings to him, as pungent as the beer on his breath. He's a drunk man with nothing to lose. And he's standing in my bedroom, his shivering flesh as real as my own.

"Go right ahead. I'm sure Daphne and Scooby Doo will be happy to hear I've agreed to be a cooperating witness."

"You already told them everything."

"Not everything," he says. "Not by a long shot."

I half-smirk at him, but he's right. I've got no leverage. "I know. You want more money."

"So there *is* more."

"I didn't say that."

He tosses the towel onto my bed, and I finally get a good look at him. The whole sad enchilada. But I only see myself. "Money won't give you what you're looking for, Ricky."

"Well, what am I looking for, Doc? Enlighten me."

"Absolution." When I say it, he flinches a little. Just enough to know I've hit a nerve.

"Alright. I'll bite. Sure, I cheated on my wife. And yeah, I got called out on national television."

I don't bother to correct him, to remind him the show never aired. Because it had found eternal life on the internet. Which was definitely worse.

"And if you must know, I brought the vodka to our dressing room, because I wanted to get fucking hammered after that prick ripped our marriage in half. And apparently so did she."

"You told me the show supplied the alcohol. That Ian knew you were both drinking."

"Either way," he says, like the truth is malleable. "Let's not kid ourselves. Nobody's innocent here."

It's sickening. The way I feign shock. "What are you talking about?" As if I can still claim to be innocent.

"Really? You want me to say it out loud?"

I don't. "Go ahead. Let's hear it."

His jaw juts out, sure of himself. "At least I didn't go full-on Betty Broderick and murder my ex-husband and his new wife. I mean, you said it, 'I'm the kind of angel who gets shit done.'"

Panic had already drained me empty, leaving only a numb dread. And a stark realization. I'm not so different from the infamous Betty. *A woman scorned.* "If this is about that email I sent to you, I wasn't serious. I just let you think I was behind it all. It was a stupid mis—"

"I saw you."

"You what?"

"I saw you that night. Valentine's Day."

"You were *here*? In Carmel?"

He shrugs, casually, knowing he's got me backed into a corner. "I got tired of waiting for you. I'd planned to confront him myself. After he and Kate got back from dinner. But then you showed up and . . . well, I'm not sorry you did. The world is better off without him."

"You actually think I stabbed Ian and Kate to death? By myself?" I try to look as harmless as a mouse. But I'm no mouse. "If I was going to kill them, I certainly wouldn't have done it that way. What is it that you think you saw exactly?"

"Well, I didn't see you go in—I must've gotten there too late— but I watched you come out. Fly out is more like it, a bat out of hell. I hightailed it out of there myself. Next thing I know, they're both dead and you're telling me to forget I know you." A smirk twists the corner of his mouth. "And I will. If the price is right . . . total amnesia."

"You don't know what you're talking about. You've got it all mixed up."

"*Do I?* You all but admitted it when you got plastered in my motel room. What do they say about loose lips?"

I turn away from him and walk to the window, where the sky is as black as a bruise. As black as the spot on my soul. Where the thought grows like a cancer.

I could get rid of him.

My eyes land on the glass vase I'd returned to the corner of my dresser. The set of dumbbells peeking from beneath the bed.

I could say he attacked me first.

One hard smack to the head. Maybe two.

The rain hisses down the roof. And I remember who I am.

No. Who I *used* to be.

"How much?" I ask.

****

I draw the cheap motel curtains and the shade beneath them. Triple-check the deadbolt and deploy the security latch. Ensure all potential hiding places are vacant. And put the hammer I'd packed on the table next to the nondescript bed at The Sandcastle Motel.

I exhale, finally, and shudder with relief, laying back against the bed. I want to call Luke. To tell him everything that's happened. To tell him about Ricky. And about Ian's letter and what I suspect. But I need to be sure because I've already hurt him enough.

I turn on the television.

Then turn it off again, when I see myself on the news, emerging from the taxi, my face blank and stark white.

And when I think of Ricky and what he knows and the promises I made him, the fluttering in my chest starts up again, so I use the peaceful-place trick from the second page of the pamphlet. *Visualization is the act of imagining yourself in the most peaceful place, free of anxiety, totally relaxed. Use all your senses to travel there in your mind, and you'll find your panic subsiding.*

Here goes nothing.

I close my eyes and remember the last time I saw Luke. After we'd left Cliffside and my mother, he'd taken the long way to the county jail. Seventeen Mile Drive to Highway One, stopping at a spot near the lighthouse. We'd sat there, silent, with the windows open, listening to the waves crest, the whitecaps roll in. The air smelled of the sea and the cypress. Until finally he'd said my name, urgent as a plea. Soft as a sweet nothing whispered in a lover's ear. And then the words I'd needed but didn't deserve: "I believe you."

Closure is a myth, so don't bother looking for it. The only things that heal a broken heart are time and distance and forgetting.
—Ian Culpepper, *Love CPR*

VALENTINE'S DAY
TWO YEARS EARLIER

AVA sat in her car outside The Seventeenth Mile, the restaurant where her mother had worked for the last eighteen years. As a hostess, then assistant manager. And for the last five, manager with a capital *M*. It rose up on the cliffside, the crags of rock visible through the panoramic windows.

She didn't want to go in. Not again. But what choice did she have? This was happening.

At the door, she took a breath and considered running. Somewhere. Anywhere but here. The world where her mother had simply forgotten. And Ava had been left alone to sort it out.

But the door decided for her, swinging open. A group of golfers walked through it, laughing and dressed in pastels. Her mother sat on the bench near the hostess stand, her face wet from crying. She wore the black pencil skirt and starched white button-down that had become her uniform, but a strand of hair had gone askew, pulled free from the tight bun she wound at the base of her neck every morning.

Antoine, the new capital *M*, waved limply at Ava.

"I'm so sorry to bother you, Doctor Lawson. She showed up about thirty minutes ago ready for her shift. And when we told her, well—" He glanced sideways at her mother, her face frightened and confused. A deer pinned by the headlights and waiting for impact. "She got upset."

Ava followed his eyes to the hostess stand, where a vase of hydrangeas lay toppled and broken. The pink and red petals formed a blood trail under the yellow WET FLOOR sign erected like crime scene tape.

"Okay. I'll take her home."

He nodded, then hesitated. "It's probably not my place to say this. But is it safe for her to be alone? To be driving?"

"I'm working on it." Ava bit the inside of her cheek to keep from crying herself. "This won't happen again."

Ava approached her mother cautiously and took her by the arm. "Time to go home now, Mom. We'll come back for your car later."

Her mother shrugged off her arm and let out an exasperated breath. "I'm not an invalid. Or a child. Let me walk out with some dignity."

Outside, her mother marched stubbornly in the opposite direction, heading straight for her black Mini Cooper. "You can't drive right now. You're not thinking straight. You don't work here anymore. Remember?"

Remember. Ava cursed herself for using the number one phrase on the doctor's not-to-say list. Of course she didn't remember. Or she wouldn't have driven here, pressed and polished. That was the whole point.

"The restaurant had to let you go a few months back because of the problems with your memory."

Her mother didn't look entirely convinced.

"What happened in there, Mom? With the flowers?"

"They don't go on that side of the stand. They'll get in the way of the reservation book."

Never mind that the restaurant hadn't used a reservation book in five years or that Ava's mother had been the one to push for a new computerized system. "You're right, Mom. That was a bad place for them. But you can't break things. And you can't drive home by yourself. Not today."

Ava watched her mother's forehead scrunch and wrinkle. It seemed she could almost see behind it, to the rusted wheels turning again, slowly and with effort.

"Come on. I got you those chocolate hearts you like from Marianne's."

Ava felt awful, coaxing her own mother, bribing her like a frightened cat beneath the bed. But this was what it had come to. The roles had flipped suddenly and without her permission, tricking her like the reflection in a fun-house mirror. And now, the time she thought she had to tell her mother everything—about Dad's note and what she'd done with it—had slipped through her fingers, as irretrievable as a single grain of sand on the beach.

"Is it Valentine's Day?" her mother asked, eyeing the chocolates through the car window.

Ava nodded.

"Shouldn't you be spending it with your husband?"

****

After her mother dozed off on the sofa, Ava poured her fourth glass of wine and opened her email to send the message she'd been dreading. The one she'd been putting off since she and her mother visited Cliffside Memory Care in December. Since the doctor had looked past them both and issued his judgment: "Your mother is suffering from early-onset progressive dementia."

Cliffside's Director had patted her arm and told Ava to take her time, to think about what would be best for her mother. Ava had wanted to laugh at her. *Best?*

But she found herself using that cursed word in the email—*My mom is getting worse, and I think it would be best if we schedule a move-in date*—and wincing as she clicked Send.

With her betrayal hurdling through miles of cable fiber, Ava downed another sip of wine—the perfect nightcap—and curled beneath the covers, letting the television keep her company.

Another stellar Valentine's Day. Next year she'd skip it entirely. Declare herself Valentine-agnostic. At least she hadn't embarrassed herself like last year. The crazy ex-wife text she'd sent Ian to which she'd received no reply. Just as well, because he'd gotten his due.

Three weeks ago, a *Love Doctored* guest had turned up dead in the dressing room. And Ava had stared open-mouthed at the television screen, convinced she'd been hallucinating until she'd seen Ian's face, a pack of reporters hot on his heels. He'd hidden behind his hand and ducked inside BXA Studios. Then, as wrong as it had been, she'd laughed.

With visions of Ian's pallor dancing in her head and a rerun droning in the background, she let the slow tug of the wine pull her under.

The dream she'd had before. But it felt different somehow. She sat at her desk, the antique she wouldn't part with even if it did remind her of Ian. And a patient was lying on her couch, obscured by a large pillow that didn't exist—not in real life.

Because that's how dreams work, she thought.

"Why are you here?" she asked the mystery patient, as she did each time. "Why are you in my dream?"

Ava heard the moaning. The desperate throaty gasps.

"Dad?" she whispered, as she did each time.

"Wallace?"

Then, the sounds stopped. All of them. Time held its breath.

Until she opened her mouth and—

No. Not this time. She didn't scream. Didn't wake up.

She stood and walked to the sofa, the way you'd walk to your own death. Your steps slow but inevitable.

And her eyes looked where she didn't want them to.

"Kate."

It wasn't a question but a statement as declarative as the bullet hole in Kate's otherwise perfect forehead. The shock of blood that ran onto the sofa, soaking it through.

"Who did this to you?"

But the question had already been answered by the gun in Ava's wet hands.

****

Ava saw blood when she opened her eyes. Blood on the bedspread. Blood on the carpet. Little spatters of it everywhere. She rubbed her face, sucked in a gulp of air, then looked again.

Not blood. Not blood. Not blood.

But wine—she'd knocked over the glass from the nightstand.

Her mind blown clear by relief, Ian's voice filled the empty space. She whipped her head to the television, where he stood between Marty and Kate.

"Vanessa Sherman was a troubled woman with a history of mental illness she concealed from us and our producers. No one affiliated with *Love Doctored* prescribed medication for Ms. Sherman, nor was anyone aware she was under the care of a psychiatrist. We do not provide alcoholic beverages to any guests on the show. Her death was an unfortunate accident for which the show assumes no responsibility."

At the bottom of the screen, three words. As glorious as the three little ones, the first time she'd heard Ian say them.

LOVE DOCTORED CANCELED.

Then and nearly as good:

VIDEO OF SHERMAN EPISODE LEAKED ONLINE

Ava ignored the overturned wine glass, the stains on the carpet. *Who cares?* She'd never been one to overdo it, and she already felt drunk. But she took another drink straight from the bottle.

Her laptop open, her clumsy fingers flew across the keyboard, taking her straight to YouTube and playing the video at max volume. No matter if it woke her mother.

The screen lit up her eyes, and she felt more alive than she had in years. Because finally, *finally*, Ian would have to pay for something he'd done.

The next morning, she saw it. Through a hungover haze. The comment she'd left.

Avenging Angel 11:58 PM

Fucking hypocrite. How can you live with yourself? You should end your pathetic excuse for a life before you hurt anybody else.

And she'd studied herself in the mirror—looking like some sick creature washed up on the beach—and wondered, *Who am I?*

THE MONTEREY COUNTY COURIER

"SHOCKING DEVELOPMENTS IN LOVE DOCTORS' SLAYING"

by Jackson Lamont

In a series of press conferences, Carmel Police announced several stunning new developments in the Valentine's Day slaying of Love Doctors Ian and Kate Culpepper, starting with the arrest of Culpepper's ex-wife, Ava Lawson. According to District Attorney Jett Mayfield, Lawson has been charged with felony extortion and first-degree murder. It is believed she stabbed to death Ian Culpepper inside his Pebble Beach mansion sometime during the evening of February 14. At her arraignment on Friday morning, Lawson entered a plea of not guilty. Lawson, a Los Angeles native who has been providing psychotherapy to local residents for several years, has established an unimpugnable reputation in the community. Speaking under the condition of anonymity, a former patient praised her as "insightful" and "caring." Though Mayfield has been tight-lipped about the evidence against Dr. Lawson, he suggested financial gain and revenge lay at the heart of this brutal crime. Lawson's preliminary hearing is set for Monday, March 19.

On Friday afternoon, in response to intense speculation regarding the nature of Kate Culpepper's death, Police Chief Scott Morrow issued the following statement: "Based upon the results of our investigation—including the time of death, the nature and location of the victim's wounds, DNA evidence found on the victim's body and the murder weapon, as well as other evidence found at the scene—it has been determined that Ian Culpepper likely murdered his wife shortly before he inflicted superficial wounds to himself. The coroner has also determined Kate was approximately eight weeks pregnant at the time of her death." Chief Morrow declined to answer questions, citing the sensitive nature of ongoing criminal proceedings.

"LOVE DOCTOR'S SECRET LOVE CHILD—AND THE REVENGE OF A WOMAN SCORNED"

When Kate Culpepper was brutally stabbed to death by her husband, Ian, inside their Pebble Beach mansion, no one knew she had a shocking secret. A secret so dark it may have led to her demise: she was pregnant with another man's child.

A source close to the investigation confirmed to *The Downtown Star* that DNA testing excluded Culpepper as the father of Kate's eight-week-old fetus. Did Culpepper learn of his wife's affair and stab her in a jealous rage? Insiders say the blonde-haired beauty had a wandering eye much like her husband and had hopped into bed with one of his colleagues shortly after their arrival in sleepy Carmel. But no one, not even those closest to the couple, suspected the truth about the Love Doctors' ill-fated marriage.

In another bombshell revelation, Ian's ex-wife, Ava Lawson, was indicted for his murder, after mounting evidence pointed to her involvement in the attack. Reminiscent of the infamous "scorned woman" Betty Broderick, the suburban housewife who shot to death her ex-husband and his second wife, it is believed that Lawson sought her revenge against her ex-husband in a vicious Valentine's Day slaughter. Pictured below, arriving back at her Carmel cottage, Lawson looks remorseless, apparently unperturbed by the allegations against her, leading some to dub her the "Valentine Vixen."

CHAPTER TWENTY-THREE

SATURDAY MORNING
FEBRUARY 25, 2018

SLEEP is a luxury I can't afford. And I can't sleep anyway. Even with the deadbolt turned and the safety latch in place. Because some monsters live in your head—they know their way around up there— and you can't lock them out. They've scoped out all the best hiding places, sinking their sharp claws in when you least expect it. Like at 4 a.m., when you're half-asleep and you swear to God you see your dead father standing at the foot of the bed, half of his face missing. Or Wallace Bergman grinning with his eyes of fire. You blink and it's your ex-husband, bleeding onto the cheap bedspread.

Though it's still dark out, there's the promise of the sun—a soft glow—at the edge of the horizon. I follow it as I drive to my office, with a quick stop to buy a burner phone. I park just off Ocean Avenue and fire up the screen. I shouldn't look, but I can't resist. The same way I'd been drawn to *Love Doctored* every Monday in prime time. The carnage, even my own, is magnetic.

Valentine Vixen. That's what they're calling me, apparently. It's the headline on the home page, right above that picture of me from yesterday, trudging up the sidewalk like a zombie. I scroll through the article the same way I'd watch a horror film, grimacing and peeking through my fingers. Waiting for the damning words to jump out at me.

Revenge.
Betty Broderick.
Remorseless.
A scorned woman.
And then I see it.

I rest the phone on my lap, drawing a shaky breath before I pick it up again.

My eyes scan the page, but my mind is back there, a million years ago, with Ian pacing beside our bed. His tear-soaked voice suddenly hardened. "I'll blow my goddamned brains out just like your father." All the times he'd made that threat, he'd never threatened me. But then, I hadn't been pregnant with another man's child. And Kate had been, apparently. Which only confirmed the suspicions in Ian's letter.

I sink back in my seat and turn up the radio, trying to blast out the thoughts, the memories. And the question that keeps turning over and over in my mind, like the undead in a shallow grave: Was Ian capable of that kind of murder?

Not the impersonal kind. A medicated Wallace, an airborne car, and a fire he could simply walk away from, hands clean. But an act of ancient warfare? The thrust of a blade into the soft flesh of the woman he'd loved. A deep slice across the neck he'd once kissed. Stabbing required physical effort. Intention. The kind of personal cruelty that not only sullied your hands but stained them, working its way beneath your fingernails.

"Kate put up one heck of a fight"—that's what Detective Lennox had said. And I thrust open the door, feeling sick at the memory of that gash, the one that had likely ended her. And the realization that the man I had once slept beside had wielded the fatal strike.

I lock the car behind me and do a slow spin, surveying the empty sidewalk. The road deserted. The businesses still shuttered. Seeing no one, I head up Ocean Avenue. Still wet from last night's storm, the gutters are clogged with sludge and leaves long dead. Yet somehow the air remains unsettled. Like the clouds could darken, the rain could fall. Again and at any moment. Or maybe it's just the storm gathering inside me.

At Seaside Sweets, the OPEN sign is turned off, the door locked. But the lights are on, and I know Marianne's inside. She'd once told me she kept worse hours than Jack, awakening well before sunrise to prep the shop.

I steel myself at the entry, afraid of what I have to do. The hornets' nest I need to poke. And it begins with a solid knock on the door, my fist rapping against the seashell logo.

Distracted, Marianne emerges from the back in a flour-spotted apron. She wipes her hands on a dish towel before she looks up and sees me standing there. I give a little wave, a sad smile, to disarm her. But the shock registers on her face. She's afraid of me.

Still, she comes to the door and opens it. A crack.

"Ava. Um . . . I don't quite know what to say. You don't have patients, do you?"

She probably doesn't mean it as a jab, but it stings anyway. Because I'm not sure if she means today or ever again. And honestly, I can only answer the first. "No. Not on a Saturday. May I come in?"

Her eyes—the ones she gave to Cooper—flit to the kitchen and back to me. I wonder if she's doing what I'd done with Ricky. A version of it anyway. Searching out all the ways she can defend herself from the Valentine Vixen. Death by bread knife, rolling pin, or sugar coma. I could come up with worse ways to go. "I don't think Jack would like that. Me being alone with you in here."

I sigh under the weight of the woman she believes I am. Though the truth is not much better. "Do you really think I would hurt you?"

"Of course not. But it gives the appearance of impropriety, cavorting with someone accused of . . . well, you know."

Marianne can't even say the word.

"To who?" I ask, waving my hand toward the street. It's so quiet I can hear the roar of the ocean, a soft murmur from here. "The seagulls?"

She says nothing for a moment, and I curse myself. *Me and my smart mouth.* But then she steps aside and ushers me in. "Just a few minutes. I have a catering order to get started on, and Olivia will be here any minute."

I wonder if Olivia is a real employee or a made-up person. If that's the sort of thing I inspire now. Fabricating a cover story so you won't be stabbed to death in your sweetshop. "It won't take long. I really just wanted to ask about Luke. How is he?"

She frowns as she busies herself at the already-spotless counter, wiping it vigorously with the floured towel and leaving a white trail down the center. "Oh goodness. I'm making a mess."

When she looks up at me, her eyes glisten. And I can hardly believe she's about to cry. The only other time I'd witnessed her tears, Cooper had been to blame. Well, Cooper *and* Luke. They'd nearly come to blows at a Donovan family dinner, one of my first a few months back. Cooper had racked up another citizen complaint, this one for excessive force, and Luke hadn't backed up his story. "You don't snitch on another cop, much less your brother. Did she put you up to it?" That's what Cooper had shouted before he'd pushed Luke in the chest. Jack had wedged his way between them; Marianne had cried; and I'd sat there stunned, still feeling the burn of his accusation.

"You seem upset," I say, employing therapist mode.

She sniffles, nods. "My sons got along once, believe it or not. But they've always been competitive. Cooper, more so. Especially when it comes to impressing Jack."

"I can see why. They've got big shoes to fill with Mr. Excellence in Investigation five years running." Marianne's smile, however brief, is a comfort. "Did they have a fight?"

She wipes her cheeks, straightens her apron. "Last night. They both came over for dinner. And it went downhill fast."

"Why?" Of course, I can guess the answer.

"You, dear." *Valentine Vixen herself.*

"What happened?"

"Well, Cooper overheard Luke leaving you a message. He got mouthy and left with a black eye."

I grimace to hide my satisfaction. Maybe I am a back-row girl after all, the sort who would take pleasure in a man going to blows for her. "And Luke?"

"I haven't heard from him since he stormed out." She turns her back to me, glancing toward the kitchen. And the room feels cold. "You shouldn't have gotten him involved in this. He's different than you. His heart hasn't been broken yet."

"And I'm not trying to break it." *Not trying.* Such a cop-out.

"Oh, Ava." She spins around, blue eyes afire, and spits out my name, bitter as a lemon peel. "What do you think will happen when you go to prison for murder? How do imagine Luke's going to look? As a cop? As a man? It will destroy him. And his career."

"He didn't even want to be a police officer. He just gave in to make you and Jack happy. Do you know he still talks about law school? All. The. Time." I say it mostly to hurt her. To show her. See, I know him better than you. "Besides, I didn't kill Ian. And I think Cooper—"

I retract my poison arrow. I can't fire it, not that one. Not at her. But I keep it in the quiver, knowing who it's meant for. Remembering what Ian had written in the last paragraph of the letter I'd reread at least a hundred times:

I'm not sure who Kate got herself involved with, but he's well-connected. Maybe a lawyer or even a cop. Because she knows things I didn't tell her. Things from W.B.'s accident report. The investigation. Maybe it will all blow over. Maybe it already has. Or maybe it's come out already and you're rotting in a jail cell somewhere. I don't know what she's planning, but she could destroy me with what she knows. And Aves, I'm afraid. For both of us.

"I think Cooper knows something. He went to Cliffside and pretended to be Luke."

Marianne swallows hard and sets free her own arrow. "Jack told me that little girl, Madison, is talking again. She's given a statement." Aimed right at the heart, it's a fatal wound. Jack would've been proud. My father too. *Don't give them a chance to fire back—take them out with a single shot.* That was his advice. "You should go before I call him."

But she's the one to do it, straight through the swinging kitchen doors, leaving me standing alone and talking to the empty display case. "I didn't do anything wrong." I say it again, louder this time, knowing she'll hear me.

From behind, the door rattles. A young girl steps inside, pockets her key, and takes out her headphones, still playing. I can hear the tinny sound of the music.

"Is everything okay?" she asks me.

I nod as I brush past. Then, I see her nametag. *Olivia.*

I'm the only liar here.

****

You have three new messages. Message one. Thursday, February 23, 7 p.m.

"Uh, hi, Doctor Lawson, it's Claus. I'm not sure if you're . . . uh, well . . . free yet. But I think it's best if we cancel Fridays for the time being. I wish you the best of—"

Delete.

Next new message. Thursday, February 23, 7:05 p.m.

"Doctor Lawson, Joan McCorkle here. I'm afraid I won't be able to continue in therapy with you for obvious reasons. I'll expect a refund for—"

Delete.

Next new message. Friday, February 24, 5:59 p.m.

"Ava, it's Luke. I tried your cell, but I'm guessing you ditched it. And your house phone's been busy for hours. Probably took it off the hook. Anyway, I'm at Mom and Dad's for dinner. And I'll be on duty till six tomorrow morning. Don't know if you'll get this but if you do, I'll be at our spot around seven. I need—"

I hang up and check the clock. 6:45. I can still make it.

But first, I have to get what I came for.

Inside my purse, I find the tiny silver key that fits the lock to the cabinet where I keep my patient files. My fingers search the well-worn edges until I find it. *CLEO CAMPBELL.*

Tucking the folder under my arm, I open the door, ready to run to my car. To the man who defended my honor. The man who punched Cooper in the face. Because he believes me. That thought is an antidote to everything else, even Marianne's arrow with its little poison tip: Maddie.

"David." I stop short in the threshold. "I'm on my way out."

"*Please.* I have to talk to you." He sounds as ragged as I've ever heard him and looks worse. In a coffee-stained SimuLife T-shirt, baggy blue jeans, and the pièce de résistance—a pair of mud-colored Crocs. David is a butterfly turned caterpillar. "Tara kicked me out."

"How did you know I was here?"

He jerks his head toward the window, then looks away, embarrassed. "I slept in the McLaren last night. Well, *slept* might be overstating it. Let me tell you, that car may do zero to sixty in three seconds flat, but it's no Ritz. Anyway, I was up at four, so I drove by your house, but you weren't there. Just a helluva lot of reporters. So I thought I'd check your office. And I saw the light on."

My father's watch ticks at me from my wrist. 6:50. "Have you seen the news? I'm probably not the best person to talk to right now. I'm not even sure I'll be able to practice psychology after all this is over."

I have a flash of me and Marbles sitting face-to-face on cold metal benches at a table that's bolted to the floor. The kind they have in prison. Where they can't even trust you not to wield a piece of furniture as a weapon. "Tell me more," I'll say.

"I heard about all that. And yeah, it was pretty fucked up of you to lie to me. You *knew* Pep. This whole time. Man, I can't get over it."

He lowers his voice to a raspy whisper. "But I don't think you killed him."

"Who, then?"

"That's what I came to talk to you about."

6:53. "Okay. But it has to be quick."

I lock the outer door and sit in my own waiting room. Waiting for David to speak. For him to give me what I've always needed. What I can't give to myself. *Absolution.* Just like I'd told Ricky.

"So I confessed everything to Tara last night. About the gambling. About the money I owed to Ian. How we're up to our eyeballs in debt. And the one night . . . with that girl."

"Cleo."

His Croc-ed foot taps in time with the second hand, and I ache at the thought of Luke waiting, wondering if I'm coming at all. "Yeah. Cleo. Cleopatra. Whatever. Anyway, Tara had an epic meltdown like I knew she would. The whole I-should've-never-married-a-loser-like-you speech. No surprise there. But she said something bat-shit crazy."

I do the therapist nod, calm and reassuring. But inside, my heart slams against my chest. Like a prisoner who's spotted a chink in the bars. A key left unguarded. A way out.

"Get this. She said she already knew about Cleo. That she'd known since it happened. That she *arranged* for it to happen."

"Arranged for it? What do you mean?"

"I mean, she went online and hired a fucking escort to test me. She said some of her friends had done it too. And that got me thinking."

The Fidelity Five. It sits like a rock in my throat and I can't speak.

"What if Kate hired Cleo too?"

The empathic murmur is all I can manage.

"It would explain why Cleo freaked the night she saw me and Ian at The Pearl. It was a while after we'd hooked up. I went to get a drink and she was there, talking up Ian. So damn nervous, she spilled my drink. She probably thought I'd tell him. Ruin the whole setup."

"Wow." That's what squeaks out. Just *wow*.

"When I saw this story about Kate being knocked up by some other guy, it all made sense."

I try to find a thread to follow, but the tangle in my brain only knots tighter. My thoughts a jumbled mess, I stare down at my watch. 7:01. I'm already late. But I feel weighted here. To this chair. To the words he's about to say. Sink me or save me, I have to hear them.

"Tell me more," I say, a hysterical laugh spurting out after.

"Kate and Ian had a prenup like half of Carmel. If it had an infidelity clause, Kate would've been screwed. Literally and figuratively. But not if she got proof Ian cheated first, so—" He shrugs. "Now Kate's dead. Ian's dead. Cleo's in the wind. And the only one missing is . . . well, whoever he is. That's a heck of a coincidence."

David's still talking. But I only hear Ian's words as clear as if he'd spoken them to me himself: *I picked the wrong girl to get it right with.*

"And it turns out Tara didn't even care I screwed a call girl. It only matters now because she knows I'm broke. It's just one more thing she can hold over my head. I feel like a man without a country."

Through the window, I glimpse the sleek McLaren, parked at least two feet from the curb and safe from any nasty scrapes to its rims. An exile with a half-million dollar car. He'd survive.

"I'm sorry, David. I have to go." I stand up and head for the door with newfound purpose.

"Wait. What should I do? About Tara?" His voice trembles, his eyes tear, and it comes to me in an instant.

"Money, fame, and glory may bring you the woman you want. But the woman you want is not always the woman you need."

"Hey, that's good. Who said that?"

"Ian." I'd highlighted it, a bright-green mark of contempt, in *Love CPR*. But now, I wonder if he'd written the line from experience. And I marvel, not for the first time, at the irony. At the one lesson hard-learned in the years since graduate school. Therapists never can take their own advice. "Ian did."

****

As soon I start the car, I type Luke's number into the burner phone to tell him I'm on my way, but I stop myself from dialing. Erase the digits one by one. Marianne is right. I've already gotten him in enough trouble.

Still, I find myself heading up Ocean Avenue like a woman possessed. Toward First Murphy Park and The Valentine statue. It's only 7:17. Surely he hasn't given up yet.

I take the left on Lincoln and slow to a crawl, obeying the primitive prickle at the back of my neck.

Our spot is vacant. Just the stone couple fixed in love.

Near the front of the park, a stack of media vans. All the local channels. A group of reporters, mic'd and waiting. An electric buzz in the air. And here I am, a dead woman walking. Well, *driving*. The Valentine Vixen on her way to her own burning at the stake.

I make a sharp U-turn in the middle of the street. The need to flee, a power surge to my system. And everything accelerates. Heartbeat, breath, and foot on the gas pedal. It's full speed ahead. Clear for takeoff.

Mid-turn, I'm outed by a woman in a Channel Five News parka. "There she is!"

"Ava!"

I've got at least a ten-second head start, and I'm not about to lose it.

I make a hard left. And blow through the stop sign on Ocean, pushing forty.

When I look in the rearview, I see the stretch of a quiet tree-lined street. So I coast for a moment, high on relief and adrenaline. But a high like that isn't meant to last.

And I come down hard when the siren blares behind me. When the blue lights flash their urgent warning.

And harder still when I recognize the swagger of the approaching officer, hear the soft, inevitable thud of his footsteps.

I lower the window—*what choice do I have?*—and let the biting cold air inside. All hope rushes out on the wind and scatters wide, as unrecoverable as the seeds of a dandelion. "Good morning, Ava."

Cooper probably thinks I don't want to look at him. But I smile, eager to take him in. The bluish-purple mark under his right eye peeks out at me from under his sunglasses, the flesh there slightly swollen. And he's not in uniform. Which means he's off duty. Which means he's skirting the line of departmental policy by pulling me over.

"You were going pretty fast back there. Fifty in a fifteen. That's reckless driving. And you ran a stop sign."

"Don't forget the illegal U-turn."

He lifts his glasses, and I get a glimpse of the blood spot in his eye. A tiny red moon eclipsing a blue planet. "Oh, so this is funny to you. We'll see who's laughing when Judge Pardee revokes your bail. But hey, I'm sure Luke will visit you in prison. He'll still be your little bitch."

"Like you were Kate's?" The arrow is flung. And Cooper steps back. Not in retreat but preparation. Poised and ready to strike.

"You need help, Ava. My mom called me this morning, asking if I know something about Ian's death. She said you'd told her I went to Cliffside. And you've already poisoned my own brother against me. It makes me wonder what you've got to hide. What bodies you've got buried."

I tighten my grip on the steering wheel, suddenly aware of Cooper's gaze, fixed on Cleo's folder sticking out of my bag. Cooper's hand on his hip, his holster beneath it. Cooper's excited breathing. But shooting me would almost be merciful. Instead, he leans forward, coolly, his head half-inside the window, and lets his words do the dirty work of eviscerating me.

"I know about Wallace Bergman."

No one has spoken the name aloud to me in years. I've only heard it filtered through my own head, in my own voice. And I shudder when I hear it in his, as if he'd summoned a beast. Recited an ancient curse to loose the hounds of hell.

"Wallace who—?" I'm cut off by the roar of an engine. Several engines, in fact. And the glorious shouting of the reporters who've managed to suss me out yet again. Channel Five leads the pack of them, camera trained on Cooper, even as he warns them off with his hand.

"I think we're done here, Officer," I say, a little louder than necessary. "Unless you had some evidence you wanted to plant."

Cooper's expression is unreadable behind his shades. His eyes, two empty pits. But he keeps them trained on me as I drive away. And when I look back, a block down the road, he's still standing there, the reporters gathered behind him like the devil's brigade.

****

I drive to Cliffside. The only place I know the cameras—and Cooper—won't follow.

In the parking lot, I slide the burner phone from my pocket and check the home page again. News of the impromptu traffic stop hasn't gone viral yet. But there is a new headline. And it turns my stomach.

"Valentine Vixen to Issue Statement at Famed Carmel Statue: Will She Confess?"

According to *The Downtown Star* online, I'd emailed all the local networks this morning, with a titillating promise of a major announcement at The Valentine. I think of Luke and the last time I saw him—*I believe you.* But does he? Who would? Maybe it had all been a ploy.

I walk inside, head down, gait clipped, and hurriedly scrawl my name in the log book, careful to avoid everyone's eyes. And the whispers. I block them out, focus only on the sound of the wailing woman who's somehow awake and steering her wheelchair with her pink-slippered feet.

My mother is sleeping, her head lolled to one side, as if it's come unloosed. On her nightstand, I see a red foil wrapper. She's eaten one of Marianne's chocolates. The ones Cooper plied her with. And I ride a wave of panic until I see the slow rise and fall of her chest. The twitch of her hand.

I sit on the vinyl sofa and pull out Cleo's file, starting at the very beginning. The first day she'd arrived at my office with her red bicycle. I don't know what I'm looking for, only that it feels essential to look.

My notes are as sparse as scattered bones.

Name: Cleo Campbell
Session Date: 7/19/17

Client arrived on time for first session, oriented in all spheres. Reviewed limits of confidentiality and therapy agreement. Mood varied during the appointment. Initially, neutral. Then distraught, tearful. Discussed client's goals for treatment related to relationship and intimacy issues. Next session scheduled for 7/26.

But my memory is not. The vision of Cleo, cross-legged on the sofa, fidgeting with a strand of her hair, is as clear and shining as if I'd preserved it in amber.

"I'm sleeping with a married man," she'd said. And I'd nodded to cover my disgust, reeling inside. As if Kate had been sitting on my sofa. I'd briefly considered screaming at her, smothering her with a throw pillow. But then I'd realized what she was. A heaping dose of punishment. And I had to swallow it down like a big girl.

"How long have you been seeing him?"

"Not long, but it's more than what I was, uh . . . it's more than what I thought it would be. He's different." I'd wanted to say that different meant squat. That all cheaters are different. But exactly the same.

"Did he tell you he was married?"

"He didn't have to. I knew."

"How?"

"He was wearing a wedding ring."

A wedding ring. I nearly say it out loud. I'd taken her at her word. I couldn't have known then it wasn't true.

I shut the file and tuck it back into my purse, just as my mother calls out from bed. Her eyes open wide and fix on me with childlike terror. "Who are you? What are you doing in my room?"

I reach out to her from the sofa, but she pulls away, cowering. Hands shrinking to her chest like a bird's talons. "Mom," I say. And instantly regret it. I know better.

"You're not my daughter." She's so certain. So scornful. That I wonder if it comes from someplace real. Maybe I'm not the girl she once knew. The girl who'd tiptoed through the house, so careful not to crack the eggshells. The woman who'd compromised her soul for a man.

"Get away from me! No, no, no!" She's keening now, flailing her arms wildly. I try to latch onto the wrist nearest me, but she's surprisingly fast, and it smacks against the bed rail with a vicious crack.

Two nurses rush in and flank her, one armed with a needle. And I'm pushed to the side, powerless to do anything but watch. When it's over, my mother lies there, nodding off, like a spent shell. Her damage already done.

"I think she broke her wrist," I say.

"Okay, sweetie. We'll check it out when she wakes up. The Haldol kicks in fast." And when the nurse pats my shoulder, I've never felt more alone.

Or more afraid. Because David is right. And I have to find Cleo before it's too late.

THE FIRST CUT

****

Back in my car, I call the only number I have for Cleo. Seven times. And all seven reach the same dead end: *This number has been disconnected or is no longer in service.*

With no choice, I pull up the Spellbound Services website and scroll down until I find her. The red-haired girl on her knees.

I click "Make an Appointment," and another screen loads. I fill in my details—when and where and for how long—and take a breath.

I hope that, for once, I'm doing the right thing.

Reserve Cleopatra Now.

I push the button. And groan, defeated.

Cleopatra is not accepting appointments at this time. Please contact Spellbound Services directly at the number below, and we will be happy to assist you in finding your perfect match.

Before I can overthink it, I dial.

"Hello. This is Spellbound Services, where your fantasies are only a wish away. How can I help you?" *Yeah, a wish and a major credit card.*

"I need to speak to Cleo. Uh, I mean Cleopatra James."

"I'm sorry, ma'am. We don't encourage personal contact between our staff and their clients." I clear my throat with obvious disdain. Apparently, she has a loose definition of personal contact. "Well, I mean outside of your appointment time, of course."

"I'm not a client of hers. I just need to talk to her. And the number I have is disconnected. Could you possibly relay a message? It's urgent."

A heavy sigh breaks her silence. "To tell you the truth, Cleopatra is no longer employed by this agency. Could we find another girl who might be suitable for your needs?"

"I don't have any needs!" I shout at the phone, then laugh at my own ridiculousness. "I told you I'm not a client. You must have some way to reach her. Please."

"Alright, alright. I'll take the message, but I can't make any promises."

"Fine. Just tell her to call Ava at this number." I rattle off the digits I'd jotted from the screen of the burner phone. "And that I need to see her. It's about The Professor. She'll know what I mean." I wonder if I sound the way I do in my own head. Like an utter lunatic.

"I'm sure she will, ma'am." *That's a yes.* "Any other fantasies I can help you fulfill today?"

The magic of new love only lasts so long. Midnight comes, the spell is broken, and you'll be seen for the pumpkin you really are.
—Ian Culpepper, *Love CPR*

VALENTINE'S DAY
ONE YEAR EARLIER

AVA nodded blankly at her new 10 a.m., Joan McCorkle. The nod had become one of her go-to moves in LA—along with the empathic murmur and the curious, but the not-too-curious, *tell me more*—and she'd hoped to leave it there.

But the patients here in Carmel were just as pretentious. Maybe more so. They had the refinement that Los Angelians lacked. Mrs. McCorkle, for one, hid her expensive jewelry in a lockbox, in a safe room, behind the tall gates of her multimillion-dollar home. *Because you can never be too careful, dear.* In LA, she'd have shown up for a session wearing a ring on every finger.

"I think today is the day I've been waiting for." Undeterred by Ava's half-hearted nod, Mrs. McCorkle bounced in her seat.

"You seem excited."

"You have no idea. I didn't sleep a wink last night. Can you tell?" She widened her eyes at Ava, her lashes long and black as a spider's legs.

"Not at all."

"Well, I have been using a new caviar eye cream."

Empathic murmur. "So what has you so inspired today?"

"My daughter, Jacqueline—the one I told you about last week—is getting engaged. And her fiancé, Spencer, is a brain surgeon. Can you believe that? Who actually marries a brain surgeon?"

Ava gritted her teeth. *Since you said the exact same thing last week, I looked it up, and there are about 3,600 neurosurgeons in the US, so plenty of people. Actually.* "That's wonderful. Tell me more."

****

"I'm thinking Bora Bora for the honeymoon, but I'll fill you in on the details next week, dear." Mrs. McCorkle handed Ava a wad of cash as she stood from the sofa. "This should cover our next four sessions."

Ava counted the bills out on her desk. "I think you're one hundred dollars short. It's two hundred dollars per session."

Grumbling, Mrs. McCorkle pinched another crisp bill from her wallet. "Everybody tells me I should've been a therapist. Getting paid a small fortune just to listen. Now that's the life. But you know, I'd probably get bored."

"You probably would."

Forcing a smile, Ava opened the door. And for a moment, she forgot to breathe. Mrs. McCorkle, however, kept right on puffing.

"Oh my goodness—a celebrity! I loved your show, Doctor Culpepper. A real shame they canceled it."

Ian nodded but said nothing. He stared at Ava, fixing her to the spot. His eyes, the same impossible blue. The color of sea glass and just as sharp. She'd forgotten how it felt to be held in his gaze.

Mrs. McCorkle disappeared. At least that's how it seemed. Ava never saw her leave. But suddenly, they were alone.

"What are you doing here?" she asked.

He smiled faintly. "Here, as in this office? Or here, as in Carmel?"

"Uh, both, I guess."

"In Carmel, house hunting. Kate and I stayed at Casa Palmero in the fall, and she fell in love with this place. I don't need to tell you how enchanting it is. We're looking at a few spots near Pebble Beach. One spot, actually. On Cortez Road. We put in an offer."

Ava reeled, her legs heavy as tree trunks, her head light as a cloud. "You're moving to Carmel?"

She heard herself speak, as if from a great height. Like her head really had floated away, bobbing around in the sky like that heart-shaped balloon she'd freed years ago.

"You seem upset, Aves. I thought you'd be—"

"You thought I'd be *what*? Happy for you? This is my town. My home. How dare you. And don't call me Aves." He flinched at every word she spit at him. Then he sighed.

"I'm sorry. You're right. But Kate's got her heart set on it. And it's a great place to raise a family. I promise we'll stay out of your way."

"Is that why you came to my office? To warn me? To ask my permission?"

He shrugged, tugging at a loose thread on the hem of his Polo. And it reminded her of another Valentine's Day, their very first. When she'd still needed evidence of his imperfections. "I'm not exactly sure. I just wanted to see you. It's been a rough year."

"And you needed to come on Valentine's Day?"

"I don't celebrate Valentine's Day, remember? I guess you could say I'm *anti-Valentine's*." Though he said it with a straight face, the word practically winked at her.

"Yeah, well, I thought maybe Kate turned you into a believer."

He threw his head back and laughed, cheeks flushing. And God, the sound of it still made her shiver. "You look beautiful, Doctor Lawson. You've gained weight."

"You really know how to sell a compliment."

"You know what I mean. You got too skinny in LA." And before she could say it—*I was stressed, Ian*—he closed the distance between them and touched her hip. "You lost these."

That touch, those three fingers, maybe four, released her. She looked over her shoulder at the clock in her office. 11:13. Because

285

she needed to remember the exact time the flipping coin—love to hate to love to hate to love to hate—landed, and the remnants of Ian slipped from her soul like a demon spirit, leaving her absolutely unpossessed.

"So, is Kate here with you?" she asked, lobbing the question, easy peasy. She stepped away from him, immune, and his hand fell to his side. It had been a while, but she still knew how to play. How to draw him to the net. Some things you never forget.

"Not this trip," he volleyed back.

"When do you leave?"

"Tomorrow morning."

He left the ball bouncing on her side of the court. And she returned it with one swift stroke down the line.

"Want to meet up for a drink tonight at the worst bar in town?"

"As long as it's the worst."

"It's as anti-Valentine's as it gets," she said.

"Then count me in."

Ava beamed at him, victorious. *Game, set, match.*

****

Ava sat on a bar stool at The Mongoose Tavern, legs crossed. A black stiletto dangling from her tapping foot. She'd taken up her position hours ago, sipping club soda, popping peanuts, and fending off the occasional drunken grope. The time had nearly come. And she could barely stand the buildup. The wait. *This is better than sex*, she thought.

"Ava Lawson?"

Heart racing, she spun toward the voice and nailed the man in the knee with the point of her shoe. He stepped back, beer sloshing over the side of his glass.

"Oh my God. I'm so sorry. Are you okay?" *Breathe, Ava. It's not Ian.* "Luke, right?"

He grimaced. Or smiled. She wasn't sure which. But either way, she liked it more than she would've guessed.

"I will not be defeated by a mere high heel," he said. "But it was a good first effort."

"I'll keep that in mind."

Luke snagged the stool next to hers without asking, and she liked that too. "So, how long has it been?"

"High school, I think. I mean, I was in high school, and you were—" Ava chuckled as she held her hand out. Palm down, at the height of a small boy.

"I grew up."

She tried not to look at his arm—a man's arm—planted on the bar. The fingers that drummed against the counter. The muscled thigh a mere fingertip from her own.

"But actually, I think I saw you once a couple of years ago. Picking up your mom after work at The Seventeenth Mile. I waved at you."

Ava shrugged, noncommittal. Though she remembered it well.

"And I haven't seen you since. Which is crazy because Mom told me your office is right down the street from the shop. And I know your mom used to stop in sometimes before . . . I'm sorry. I shouldn't have brought it up."

"Was there a question there, Luke?" She eyed her father's watch, her stomach in knots. Ian would be arriving soon. Perhaps he'd even be early. Anxious to see her, to touch her again.

"Are you meeting someone?"

"Is that your question?" And right then, when he laughed—warm and goofy—she wished she'd been meeting him tonight.

"Do I only get one?"

Over Luke's shoulder, Ava peered through the panoramic window to the bar across the street. Under the neon glow of the Mickey's sign, she spotted Ian. A crisp, light-blue button-down, dark denim. Hair she could run her fingers through again. And lips that could be hers. He paused in front of the door and disappeared inside.

"I think one is generous. You are a cop, so you should be good at questions. Or at getting answers, anyway."

"You're absolutely right," he said. He sipped his beer, and Ava smiled, enjoying the banter between them. A lifetime had passed since she'd flirted—way back in the Age of Ian—and on any other night, it would've felt awkward. Or sad. But her plan had blown the dust off, cut the cord that tethered her to the past. And there she was, shiny and buoyant.

Ava's phone buzzed in her lap, and she tapped out a quick text in reply, shrugging at Luke apologetically.

He shook his head at her, with a chiding *tsk, tsk*. "Well, I could ask who you're texting but that would be too obvious. Or if you're single, but that sounds like a line. Plus, Mom already told me you are. Or if I can buy you a drink, but you're clearly not drinking. Or why you're here all alone on Valentine's Day. But I think I'll go with simple and straightforward."

"Simple and straightforward. I like it." Because what could be more unlike Ian?

"Do you want to go out on a date with me?"

Across the street, Ian pushed through Mickey's double doors, his face red with anger. He spun around on the sidewalk, searching in the dark. Until he stopped, stock still. Like he'd seen the ghost of Valentine's past.

Ava stood up. "Will you ask me again tomorrow?"

"Tomorrow?"

"Anything that starts today is doomed."

Luke started to laugh until he saw it in her eyes. That she meant it. "Tomorrow it is then."

"Forget you ever saw me."

"I will," he said, with a squeeze of his hand on her arm that promised otherwise.

Ava slunk out the back of The Mongoose and into the alley, where she'd left her car. She sat inside, letting the windows steam. And trying to imagine it. The moment Ian had walked into Mickey's and scanned the room for her long, dark hair. For the smile she'd always saved for him. The moment he'd texted *Where are you, Aves?*

And later, when he'd realized she didn't want him anymore. She wondered if he'd ever felt anything like it before, the searing burn of unrequited desire. The cold sweat of a *gotcha* gut punch. The moment he'd read her reply:

I'm with Wally's ghost. Julie's too. We're watching you. And laughing.

****

Ava lay in bed, studying a picture of Luke on the tiny screen of her cell phone—grinning, sitting on a small metal platform at the center of a dunking booth, a hand-painted sign above his head. DUNK A COP FOR A GOOD CAUSE.

My favorite picture, she'd decided, the moment she'd seen it on the Carmel Police Department (CPD) Facebook page. Until she'd found the *after*. Luke half-submerged in the tank, face dripping. The CPD T-shirt he wore clinging to his chest in a way that made Ava blush. Her new favorite.

The phone vibrated in her hand, and she jolted up, rigid and wide-eyed. Her heartbeat thudding like a hammer in her ears.

She'd expected a response, of course. Ian always had to have the last word. Even if it wasn't a word at all but a long scratch etched in the flesh of a Prius, a wicked swerve off the highway that left a track of black rubber, a fire that burned as bright as the LA sun.

Or a text with a link to her own website: www.askdoctorava.com.

She clicked it, and watched helplessly as the icon swirled. A wheel of fortune, rigged to land on bad luck.

When the page loaded, Ava gaped at it, numb with shock. At her defiled tagline, inviting prospective patients to *bang* Dr. Ava. At the girl posed seductively in the mirror, one hand covering her bare breasts, the other below her waist.

She'd sucked in a breath or two before she'd realized that girl was her. From eight years ago. The first night she'd spent in Ian's house.

"Give me something to dream about later," Ian had said, both of them fresh out of the shower and so in love it hurt.

She'd struck the sexiest pose she could manage, laughing as he snapped her photo in the mirror on his cell phone. Then he'd come up behind her and started kissing her neck—and they'd ended up back in bed where they'd began.

"Delete it," she'd told him later.

"Already taken care of," he'd said.

****

Rage could be useful. More than anything, it gave Ava purpose. It made her act.

And in the span of ten minutes, she'd created a strategy of war.

Opened a new email account: avengingangel@pacbell.com.

Located Ricky Sherman's contact information.

Composed a message and sent it.

> *To: Ricky Sherman <rsherm13@quickmail.net>*
> *From: Avenging Angel <avengingangel@pacbell.com>*
> *Date: February 14, 2017 11:58 PM PST*
> *Subject: Love Doctored*
>
> *Dear Ricky,*
> *You don't know me, and I prefer it that way. Consider me your avenging angel. An angel who's been sent to make things right, to even the score. Ian Culpepper is a fraud, a sham. A trickster. And I want the world to know it. If you're interested in revenge, I'll be here.*
> *Ready and waiting,*
> *AA*

But rage could fool you too. It could make you think you weren't afraid. That your wounds had scabbed over. It could make you feel alive, all the while killing you from within.

CHAPTER TWENTY-FOUR

SATURDAY AFTERNOON
FEBRUARY 25, 2018

THE Pearl Casino and Hotel rises up from the shore of Monterey Bay near Moss Landing. It's completely out of place there. A shimmering mirage. A gaudy jewel against the dark backdrop of the sea.

And inside, the illusion deepens. A world outside of time where the seasons never change. Glaringly bright, windowless, and teeming with the clamor of false hope. The jubilant ringing of bells. The hollow clink of coins against metal. The spin of the roulette wheel like the revolving chamber of a gun.

I understand how David was drawn here again and again, a moth to the flame. There's a rhythm to the place, a pulse pounding beneath it like a heartbeat. Make the bet, roll the dice, win or lose, and do it again.

A relentless throbbing pushes me forward toward the maze of tables and slots and into the Saturday afternoon crowd, until I'm immersed. Until the way out seems to disappear, like a magic door from a fairytale, swallowed by the wall as soon as I'd passed through it. And I imagine David under the spell of this place, tricked into believing what he had to gain added up to more than what he'd already lost. What he still had to lose.

I stand near a row of slots, watching for Cleo. And trying to quell my unease by counting the quarters Big Marge feeds into the machine. That's the name embroidered on the back of her silk jacket. She pulls the lever and leans in each time waiting to discern her luck, but so far her wooden face gives nothing away. She just moves to the rhythm. Insert quarter, pull lever, stare at screen. Repeat.

"Are you winning?" I ask, suddenly eager for a distraction.

She scowls at me, pulls the handle, and scrutinizes her fate. Three more times. Before she stands and faces me. "Not anymore. Now that you've gone and jinxed me."

I'd like to lecture Marge about probability and random-number generation. But on her feet, she *is* big, thick, and towering as redwood. So I stay quiet and make way for her as she stalks away toward the bar, muttering under her breath. I take the seat she left vacant and warm, checking the time on my father's watch.

Cleo is late. She may not show at all. But she'd sent a text to the burner a while ago, telling me to meet her here, Room 222, at 5 p.m. And I'd done what she'd asked, replied with a few desperate lines. Things only her therapist would know. So she could be certain it came from me. That I mean her no harm. Other than the harm I'd already done, of course.

I won't allow myself to consider the alternative. That Cleo is unable to get here. Or anywhere at all. That's she lying like Kate's twin on a dingy carpet somewhere, blood pooling beneath her from a gash on her neck. Draining from her until she's empty, soulless. Just skin and muscle and bone. Hair the color of fire. With my knife discarded at her side.

"Hey, lady, are you playing? You can't just sit here. People are waiting." Big Marge is back, and she's brought a friend. His bald head rises to her shoulder, shining under the bright lights. He stands slightly behind, puffing his chest, as she speaks for the both of them.

"Oh, sorry." I'm halfway up when I reconsider. "I'll play a round."

Marge scoffs. Like I'm a total pretender. And I'm glad I said it though I don't know why I did. Maybe I like the way it feels to nettle her, the way Ian would've done. Or maybe I'm not so different than David, succumbing to the lure, the titillating sorcery of easy money. But when I drop the quarter through the slot and wrap my hand around the level, I realize. I'm looking for a sign. Random-number generator or not.

One hard pull, and we're all captive, as the machine decides. *Lucky or unlucky?*

A bright electronic trill emits from the machine, the lights around its face flashing. And I sit, rapt, as the payout total climbs to $1,000.

"Are you kidding me?" Marge says, her legs, wide, like fence posts on either side of me. "I've been warming it up all night. And you stole my seat."

"Yeah. Technically, that money belongs to Marge."

Near the entrance, the magical doors appear again, offering a passing glimpse at the world beyond. The sky, a fading watercolor blue. And I watch as Cleo walks through them, her dark glasses fixed on the ground in front of her. As if every step must be carefully measured.

"Keep it," I say, tracking Cleo with my eyes. She approaches the front desk, speaks to the clerk, and retrieves the key. "Consider it your lucky day."

Marge's exaggerated whooping, like the cry of an exotic bird, carries over the din of the casino. I can still hear it, even as the elevator doors close behind me.

****

The door to 222 looms at the end of a long hallway, with its gilded numbers and its tiny peephole regarding me with suspicion. I conjure

Cleo on tiptoe behind it, peering through with one amber eye. Fear bubbling in her gut, just like in mine.

Before I raise my hand to knock, it opens slightly, confirming my premonition. And then a bit wider, enough to see half of her, the other half concealed behind the solid wood. I step into the room, a suite with a sitting area and a separate bedroom. The curtains are pulled back revealing a large window. And through it, the ocean, the waves near the shore catching the last of the afternoon sunlight.

On the table, a bottle of champagne chills on ice. And two tall glasses stand empty, guarding a plate of chocolate-covered strawberries. Though one has already been pilfered.

"It's my usual room," Cleo explains, sinking her teeth into its red flesh. "They always set it up the same. And I haven't told them yet."

"Told them?"

She sits on the edge of the bed, cross-legged like we're back in session, looking up at me. And I see what men must like about her. The way she appears innocent and guilty at the same time. "I got the axe. Pathetic, I know. Who gets fired from a job as an escort?"

She points a finger at herself, the beginnings of a sad smile twitching at the corners of her mouth. "This girl, apparently. I suppose it's for the best though."

"Why were you fired? The whole tabloid scandal?" *Because of me and the pictures I took.* Sister to my fear, the Hydra writhes in my stomach, in hearty approval of my self-reproach.

"That was the last straw. I was already on thin ice because of Kate. She'd told them everything."

I take the oversized chair opposite the bed, trying to assume my role. To give her the listening ear. The nonjudgmental gaze. I nod at her, a gentle prodding to go on.

"Kate hired me last June. She wanted me to seduce Ian. Or, I suppose, to try to test him. Some of the other Spellbound girls had done it before for other clients. They'd joked about it and called it the Fidelity Five. Like the thing on Ian's show. Of course, that was before

294

I'd met him. We agreed she'd pay when she had the proof. She wanted photos, but she offered more for a video."

"And you'd done it before too?" I ask. "This test?" I won't say those vile words, the ones that had been born from my own twisted mind.

Her shoulders droop, telling me the answer. "Yes. Once. With David Fairfax. And I didn't like it. It felt . . . I don't know . . . *slimy*. Even more so than usual. But the money Kate offered was too good to pass up."

How much? But I don't say a word. Because any therapist worth their salt knows when to shut up.

"So, when I met Ian at the casino that night, I was sure David would tell him we'd slept together. Or have me thrown out of the place. I didn't know if his wife had confronted him or not and what she'd told him. But Ian and I hit it off, and then I figured it would be a piece of cake."

"And?"

"You know the rest. I fell in love."

The rest, I think, with a pang of melancholy. Knowing all that comes after the falling. For me. For my mother. For Cleo.

"So you refused to give Kate the proof she wanted?"

"Right. But not just that. Ian decided he didn't want me doing it anymore . . . the whole escort thing. But I'd signed a contract with Spellbound through January, so he started booking all my appointments. And Kate figured it out. Spellbound frowns on that, you know. They don't want us having actual relationships with our clients. Certainly not our rich, married ones."

"I can see how that might be a problem."

"And that's when things started getting really weird. I keep thinking, if only I had ended things with Ian, maybe it would've made a difference. Maybe he wouldn't have . . . done what he did. Maybe he'd still be alive. But I couldn't let go. And neither could she. Not until she got her precious infidelity clause money."

"Did you know Kate was having an affair?"

"Not until the very end. Ian told me he'd figured out the guy was a cop, maybe from LA. Because he'd dug up all this dirt from back when the two of you were married. And Kate was trying to hold that over him too. It's like they'd reached a stalemate. An impasse."

"Or a breaking point."

"Exactly. We saw each other that afternoon like I told you, and he seemed more stressed than usual. Then he sent me that text about confronting her. I thought he'd just finally admit to the affair and forget about the money. But—"

"Ian was never good at losing," I say, like I'm any better. "It brings out the worst in him. So what do you think happened? To Ian?"

"Well . . ." A single dry laugh clunks from her throat. "I know you didn't kill him."

That makes one. And I cling to her belief in me, wondering what she'd say if I told her the truth. "How do you know?"

"The creepy phone calls. You were with me that night when I got one. That—and you're my therapist. C'mon."

"Cleo, I—" I start to confess. The pictures, the extortion. What I'd done that night. All of it. But I stop myself. *I need her.* "I think you should tell the police what you know. I understand you're afraid, but I'll go with you. I've been getting those calls too. And right now, the cops think I did it. And I'm pretty sure whoever's on the other end of the line has made sure I look guilty as hell."

I watch her face for signs of resistance. But in my job, you learn to expect the unexpected. To anticipate the revelatory. And still, I'm unprepared. "I already did. Before I came here. It's not like I had a choice. My dad's on the city council. He took me to the station himself. Neither of the homicide detectives were there, but Jack Donovan's son took my statement. He was really nice. He saw how nervous I was and said we could just go for a walk and talk."

"Which son?" Dread hollows my voice.

"Um, I'm not sure. I didn't know there was more than one. I got his card though." She searches her pocket for it. "It says Luke Donovan. Is that good or bad?"

"What did he look like?"

"Is this really—?"

"Yes. It's important."

She stares at me blankly, so I open the burner phone, pull up the browser, and type in a name. "Is this him?" I ask, showing her the screen.

"Yeah. That's him."

I curse under my breath, and hers quickens. She pulls her knees to her chest like a child, shivering like a small, terrified animal. "What's wrong?"

"You didn't talk to Luke. This is Cooper. And I think he's the one setting me up."

"That's really, really bad. Because I also told him I found something in Maddie's bedroom on Valentine's Day. When Kate nearly caught me and Ian, and I had to sneak away. He asked me to meet him there tonight. To show him."

"To show him what?" My fingers dig into the chair's plush arms, and I lean forward. Not unlike Marge. Wooden face, awaiting my fate.

"I can't be totally sure. I was in a rush to get out, but it looked like a secret cell phone."

"You didn't take it?"

"I'd planned to ask Ian about it when I saw him the next day, and then I'd just assumed the police would find it. But as far as I know it's still in Maddie's room."

Marriage is like a hurricane. Don't let anybody tell you differently. And no matter if it lasts five months or fifty years, it always ends the same. With only one of you left standing.
—Ian Culpepper, *Love CPR*

VALENTINE'S DAY
THIS YEAR

AVA rolled onto her side to get a better view of Luke. He stood at the dresser, his back to her, his lower half wrapped in a towel. The only light came from the cracked bathroom door, a thin spotlight splitting his shoulder blades.

"I'm watching you," she teased.

She couldn't see his face, but she could picture it breaking into a lazy grin. Luke smiled a lot. And she liked making him smile. *Could it really be that easy—that simple and straightforward, just as he'd promised her?*

"In that case, let me give you something to look at." The towel dropped to his feet, pooling without a sound.

Ava expected him to come back to bed with her, to press his still-damp body against hers, warm with sleep. But he didn't. Not right away.

Her eyes tracked his slow walk from the dresser to the chair in the corner, where he'd laid out his CPD T-shirt and jeans. He reached inside his duffel bag and turned toward her, grinning.

"Don't open it now," he said, tucking the red envelope between the lamp and the alarm clock. He'd carefully printed her name on the

298

front, and the thought of it, of him doing that, made her feel guilty somehow.

"I didn't intend to."

He laughed the way he always did when she goaded him. Like he couldn't tell exactly where he stood with her. Ava recognized the insecurity, as familiar as her own face in the mirror. "So, I've got the city council meeting tonight. Are you sure you don't want to go out after? To a proper Valentine's dinner?"

She didn't answer. Because she couldn't tell the truth. And she didn't want to lie. Not to Luke. Not if she didn't have to.

"Or I could cook for you at my house?" He wiggled his eyebrows at her, ever hopeful.

Someday, she'd say yes. When all this with Ian had blown over. Then, maybe.

"I'll get Chinese delivered." She reached for Luke's hand, tugging him back. Knowing he'd need no convincing.

"Happy Dragon it is," he said, sliding next to her beneath the covers. "But only if you get extra potstickers."

She found his mouth in the dark, knowing the way nearly by heart now. He tasted like her own toothpaste. And her guilt faded to a single, perfect thought: *Today, my Valentine's curse will be broken.*

****

Ava stared out her office window at Ocean Avenue, jealous of the tourists meandering the cobblestone street. She wanted to be a stranger in a strange place. Instead of herself, here. The buoyancy of the morning had deflated when she'd read Luke's card, replaced by her old friend. *Guilt.*

He'd bought the card from the gift shop at the end of the block. She knew because she'd seen it in the window and thought of him. And of her father and a card she'd given him once. Though she couldn't remember a Valentine's Day before he'd been too depressed for a *silly commercialized farce*—his words. No wonder she'd married a man who felt the same.

The card had an old-fashioned look to it, a cherub-faced boy peeking through the center of a ruby-red heart. Outfitted in the traditional blue uniform, he held a sign: "POLICE" BE MINE. Inside, the fancy type read, *I'm out to cop your heart.*

And Luke hadn't left it at that. Of course not. He'd written to her, the words as neat as her name on the envelope. Each demonstrative stroke a reminder of how much of herself she'd tried to hold back from him.

> *Dear Ava,*
> *I know you hate this sort of thing, so I'll be brief. Today is not your favorite day. It's cursed apparently, for good reason. But if you let me, I promise to change that. I'll make every day your favorite day. You'll be my favorite person, and I'll be yours (if you'll have me). I've told you a hundred times I love you, and I'd wait forever for you to say it back. Don't make me. Please say you feel the same.*
> *But tell me tomorrow, since anything that starts today is doomed.*
> *Yours,*
> *Luke*

Ava ran her finger across Luke's name, playing it out. If she told him she loved him—that she had for a while now—what would be next? Living together. Getting married. Having babies. The endless conveyer belt of expectation. And then what? How would it end? Because it would. Eventually. *End.* And she'd be right back here, the shell around her heart that much harder, reading some other schmuck's Valentine.

She slipped the card back into its envelope and tucked it inside her purse where it couldn't scrutinize her and issue its demands. She couldn't be soft. Not today. She had revenge to attend to.

Like a sign of approval from the universe, the bell in the waiting room dinged—her 10 a.m. neurotic, Georgina Wimberley—and she stood to answer it.

Mrs. Wimberley flashed a platinum smile. Her mask, they'd started calling it in their sessions. Because Ava had noticed the tightness around the mouth, the furrow between the eyebrows.

"Happy Valentine's Day, Doctor Lawson." And Ava smiled back, her own mask undetectable.

****

The day dragged. And the churn of unease in the pit of Ava's stomach ratcheted up with each passing hour. By five o'clock, a storm of epic proportions raged within her. A full on Category Five. And the sky outside matched, darkening like a bruise.

It had been one week since she'd given Ian the ultimatum. Since she'd waved him over in the parking lot of the Monterey Peninsula Country Club, shown him the *are-you-fucking-kidding-me* memory card, and told him what she wanted. Only what she deserved. Payment for the idea that launched his career. Not her fault he'd run it into the ground. And the money she'd paid a local computer guy to undo his *Bang Dr. Ava* handiwork, to make sure it wouldn't happen again.

There wouldn't be time for a run today, so she didn't bother changing. Just raced down Highway One to Monterey. She pulled off at the exit for Fisherman's Wharf, gently tapping her brakes and making the turn into the parking lot.

This is it.

She'd expected to feel different. Excited or emboldened, more alive. Instead, fear prickled at her skin, dried her mouth. And guilt—that too, *always* that—left her second-guessing. Maybe Ian had been right when he'd shaken his head at her threats, told her she'd never follow through with it. That she didn't have the stomach. And why couldn't she forgive him? He'd actually had the nerve to ask that.

"Watch me," she'd said. "Be there. Valentine's Day. Or else." Sounding like a lunatic who'd watched too many action flicks. He didn't know about Ricky, of course. Who Ava felt sorry for. Who'd managed, somehow, to be even more pathetic than her.

A part of her, a big part, expected him not to show. Typical Ian, to deprive her of the climax. But his sleek silver Mercedes stood out like a sore thumb in the lot, where most of the cars were cheap rentals or family sedans.

As she pulled alongside him, she caught her breath, horrified at the little girl waving at her from the car seat. Ava mustered the courage to wave back, hoping Maddie didn't recognize her, didn't tell Daddy—"That's the lady who took my picture." But Maddie had more pressing concerns. Like struggling to open the wrapper of her red-heart lollipop while maintaining a firm grip on her teddy bear.

Ava scowled at Ian. Now *this* was just like him. *Classic Ian.* He'd brought Maddie along to prove a point. To make her feel like scum. Which she did.

He rolled down his window, and she did the same, shouting expletives with her eyes since she couldn't speak them.

"Get out of the car," he said.

"Why? Can't you just hand it to me through the window?"

"So we can talk like civilized adults. That's why."

"As if you've ever been civilized."

Ava heard Maddie giggle, and for a moment, she thought of Kate and the manufactured twitter of a laugh she'd always made on *Love Doctored.* "Who's that, Daddy?"

"It's Daddy's friend. From a long time ago. Why don't you tell Mister Bear what you did in preschool today? Daddy will be right back."

Before Ava could protest, Ian had invaded her country. Right around the passenger side and into her car. He held a blue, canvas bank bag in his lap. And suddenly, the air seemed thinner. Toxic. With the cloying smell of chalk and sandalwood aftershave.

"You brought your daughter? I'll be sure to nominate you for parent of the year."

"Kate had a doctor's appointment and the sitter was busy, so I had to take Maddie. You know, I canceled a TV gig to be here. And those are a rarity these days."

"Oh no! Not one of your precious TV gigs. I'm surprised they still want you with all the blood on your hands."

She looked at his hands then. It had been a year since she'd felt them on her body. One of them on her hip, to be exact. "Trouble in paradise?" she asked, gesturing to his ringless finger.

Ian actually smiled at her, sheepish as the day they'd met. "I lost it last March at the country club. You know I was never really a ring guy."

"Must be convenient."

He sighed, sounding defeated. "We don't have to do this. This petty game." But she wanted him to fight back.

"Do you have it? All of it?"

"Part. It's all I can give you for now. I'll have the rest next month." He unzipped the bag, and turned its open mouth to Ava. She tried not to gape at the stacks of cash. The flat, perfect bills that she'd exacted from him. Her pound of flesh.

Ian tossed the bag at her, like he couldn't bear to touch her. And it landed heavy on her lap. "This isn't you, Ava. You're not like this."

She hated the way his face softened, the way his voice pleaded with her. "Like *what*?"

"Spiteful."

A strangled laugh croaked from her throat. "Really, Ian? That's *all* I am. That's what you made me. And you're no different. Spite is the glue that held us together."

He sat quiet, and she wanted to punch him. To shake him. To make him lash out so she could lash back. And she wielded her weapon. "Thank God we never had a child. I feel sorry for Maddie with the two of you as parents. Poor girl. She'll be in therapy before she can write her own name." Kept jabbing, poking, wounding, until he had no choice but to strike back.

"Kate's pregnant again." He cracked the door open and stepped out. Leaned down and leveled her the way no one else could. "She's more of a mother than you could ever hope to be. Enjoy your dirty money, Ava. Good luck getting the rest."

She braced herself, ready for it, but he didn't slam the door. He left it unfinished. And that was worse. Like he couldn't be bothered.

Ava's hands trembled with rage as she drove down the feeder road toward the freeway, Ian still chattering in her head. And the impatient sound of the low fuel light didn't help, fluttering her heart with its sudden ding. At the last minute, she swerved into the station and pulled her car to a stop.

She reached into the back and grabbed the bag of money, jerking it to her like the arm of a petulant child.

Started counted. *She's more of a mother . . .*

And started again. *Enjoy your dirty money . . .*

And again from the beginning. Until she finished, finally. The total, well short of what she'd asked for.

Desperate for release, she yanked the gear into reverse, intending to peel out, gas gauge be damned. But the blare of a horn stopped her cold. The bared teeth of a furious driver in her rearview.

The anger of twenty-one years gathered inside her. Like stagnant water, it seeped from her pores. Ran down her cheeks. It filled her, every bit. And it was no wonder there was no room for Luke. Or love. Anything good would be drowned by it, lost in the swampy muck.

When she finally opened her mouth to scream, she remembered her father's face—the raw anguish—the moment she'd said it. I hate you. I wish you'd just die. And nothing came out.

****

Ava drove away from Cliffside and sped for home, still barely keeping her head above the water line.

"Your mother had a bit of an outburst earlier. We had to sedate her." That's what Nurse Ellerby said when she'd arrived. And Ava felt relieved. And then awful. What kind of daughter would wish for that?

The kind with a bag of money she needed to stash.

So she kissed her mom on the forehead and headed for the closet safe, wincing as she turned the dial.

6/5/96

Some days are cursed, she thought as she pulled into her driveway.

And maybe curses can't be broken. Only endured.

She trudged inside, fully intent on grabbing a book, going for a run. Taking a hot shower. One of million things she'd counseled her patients to do. Healthy coping, she called it.

Well, fuck that.

She poured a glass of wine, whipped out her laptop, and went straight to her unhappy place. Kate's Facebook page. How long had it been since she'd checked it? She cursed herself for not being prepared. For not seeing whatever nauseatingly perfect *we're expecting* photo Kate had commissioned.

But, she didn't find it. Only this:

Kate Culpepper was tagged in a post.

Below, the trendy La Noche Restaurant had posted a picture of Kate and Ian at a window table. The caption read:

Love Doctors dining at La Noche on V-Day . . . love is in the air!

15 mins ago–Carmel, CA.

Ava studied the photo, opening it in full-screen view, paying attention to the particulars. Kate's flat stomach in her curve-hugging red dress. She couldn't be too far along. No alcohol for her, just water. Ian's glass of red, full. Far Niente, no doubt. His favorite. And she'd certainly given him a reason to drink.

The idea struck her—the way the worst ones do—as brilliant. She didn't have any Adderall, but she still had the Xanax Ian had prescribed her. And that was even better somehow. Fitting. Karma in the form of a little white bar.

Just a pill, she thought. *Or two.*
One last time.

**** ****

Ava parked on the street across from the restaurant. From here, with the Nikon, she had an unobstructed view of her target: the long, sleek, dark neck of the wine bottle, the gold foil peeled back, tipping toward Ian's glass. And she laughed out loud when she saw the waiter cart the bottle away. Probably to a serving station.

Child's play, she thought. Even easier than the first time. As long as she could be patient—which she could—and exact, holding out for the precise moment.

It came sooner than she could've hoped. But not before she made note of the absence of laughter between them. Only because she laughed so much and so often with Luke. Kate's face seemed dour. And Ian checked his cell phone twice. For a moment, Ava considered going home, victorious in the knowledge that she had Luke. That Luke would never do such a thing. That Kate and Ian were not the couple from the shiny Facebook photo but its negative, devoid of light.

When Ian rose from his chair, her heart quickened. And she felt she'd come too far. Too late to turn back now. But that wasn't true. Not really. She often told her patients it was just a line, an excuse, to do what you wanted to do. And what she wanted from Ian was always the same because it would never be enough. *Retribution.*

Ava barely breathed, trailing him with her lens as he emerged from the restaurant and headed across the parking lot. His mouth a straight, grim line.

Back to Kate, fingers pecking at her phone. She sipped her water, took another bite.

To Ian again. And . . . was that—David? They'd walked to the tall row of hedges in the shadows, talking animatedly. *Arguing,* she decided, when she saw David swipe at the air, dismissively.

Kate lay a finger across her cheek—a tear? an eyelash?—and returned to her phone, pressing it to her ear.

Now or never.

Ava could've been caught. Maybe a part of her hoped she would be. Ducking in through the side entrance, slipping down the hallway, sighting the serving station with its array of bottles. The Far Niente stood alone at the corner, as if it had been waiting for her. A willing conspirator.

She set her purse on the stand, pretending to search it. Looking for her dignity. Her moral compass.

Nope. Not there.

She already had what she needed concealed in her palm.

And then it was gone, sunk to the bottom of the bottle. And she was too.

In her car, she watched for a while. Until the waiter returned to fill Ian's glass.

"We're even." She said it out loud to him as he downed the first sip. But she meant it for herself. As a proclamation. *I got the last word.*

****

Ava remembered the extra potstickers. Pretty damn impressive, given the day she'd had. She set the table and started on the wine, allowing herself an extra generous pour. Luke wouldn't mind her starting without him. Not after she told him she loved him. Screw Valentine's Doom. She'd do it tonight. Like ripping off a Band-Aid.

She sat on the sofa, relieved to have made up her mind. And then she heard it. A single fat drop of rain on the window. Like the tap of a finger. The sky had been holding out all day, and it couldn't wait any longer.

Ava picked up her phone to text Luke. To tell him to be careful. To tell him the potstickers were getting cold. That she'd already eaten his fortune cookie. But as she typed, an incoming message appeared. And another.

From Ian. A drunk and medicated Ian.

hop ur happy this is what u wanted, rigth? me toend my pathetic excuse for a life

kate's gone

bye aves

Shit. Shit. Shit.

Ava hit dial, each unanswered ring firing a hit of panic through her veins. Until finally she hung up. She took a rattled breath.

Was he pranking her? Good one, Ian.

She reread the text, uncertain—*real or not real?*—and checked the clock.

9:39 p.m.

She could get to Ian's and back in under eight minutes. Nine, with the rain. Luke wouldn't be back till after ten.

She had time.

****

With no umbrella, Ava ran from her car toward the house on Cortez Road, making her way around the back, already soaked.

Blame it on the dark or the rain, but the house looked different than she remembered. Larger and hungrier. Like a beast sleeping on a hillside. One yellow eye lit at the center of its forehead.

From the glass pane in the kitchen door, she spotted Maddie sitting on the linoleum, knees tucked to her chest. And even through the rain, she heard her humming "Itsy Bitsy Spider."

Ava waved her arms until Maddie walked to the door on small bare feet.

And opened it.

****

Whatever happened is over.

That much Ava knew. Because the whole house held its breath.

"Where are Mommy and Daddy?" she whispered to Maddie, trying not to sound unhinged.

"Upstairs yelling. Daddy's mad." Maddie sniffled. "And I dropped my chocolates."

"It's okay. We'll get your candy later. I need to talk to your daddy."

Maddie clung to Ava's leg, her little hands like claws. "Can I go with you?"

"Not yet. I want you to wait here and watch the door like a big girl."

"For spiders?"

Ava nodded. And Maddie listened, her eyes wide and wary.

"Can you count to one hundred?"

"One. Two—"

"Good. If I'm not back here by the time you get to one hundred, is there somewhere you can hide?"

Maddie whimpered, pointing to the bookcase in the foyer, its shelves stocked with the Love Doctors' literary trophies: *Prescription for Love* and *Love CPR*. And Ava imagined Ian and Kate had penned their names on the cover pages—right below *"Love is Always the Best Medicine!"*—the same way they'd defaced the copies she'd requested through their publisher.

"It's a secret door," Maddie said. "Like in the movies. Mommy said I'd always be safe there."

And Ava turned from her, wondering if she should arm herself. The Wusthof set, her twisted little wedding gift, winked at her from its place by the sink. Any of those knives, sharp as the first cut of love, would do nicely. But she couldn't imagine it, stalking around with a knife. What was she afraid of?

The stairway beckoned to her with gauzy light from the bedroom.

It seemed to pulse. Like the twitching tail of the beast. So she moved toward it.

And crept up.

Step after step.

Certain her soft footfalls would awaken the dead. That, or Maddie's voice. She'd stopped counting at twenty-three, but her singing chased Ava, reminding her. *I'm here. I'm here.*

When she reached the landing, the smell, terrible and familiar, hit her first. Long after her father died, she'd read about the metallic scent of blood. And how early humans could track wounded prey by its scent. She felt primeval, moving animal-like, hair raised.

She passed the breadcrumb trail of Maddie's chocolates. And her knees weakened at the sight of her nightmare-come-to-life again. The bedroom door, ajar.

As she drew closer, the blood smell got stronger. Until she realized its source. The soaked carpet just beyond the threshold.

A broken lamp.

A foot. *Kate's?*

She stopped, not knowing why. *A presence? A sound?*

Then, a righteous clap of thunder, unheard of in Carmel, and she screamed.

Down the stairs she ran.

Into the kitchen.

Maddie was gone.

****

Ava made it home in five minutes. Five minutes that passed the way of an hour. She couldn't remember the drive. Only the sound of the wipers swishing, desperately clearing the rain from her windshield.

She took off her clothes.

Put them in the dryer.

Poured herself another glass of wine.

Arranged the food containers on the table and sat there, cold and empty, the Happy Dragon judging her from all sides.

She held her phone. Pressed the numbers—9-1-1—while *murder-suicide* ran on a continuous loop in her head.

Imagined what she would say. How she would explain herself.

But when Luke walked through the door, grinning and warm and safe, she dropped the phone in her purse.

She'd put on her mask—swallowed her guilt down along with those three words she'd intended for Luke.

And she left Wallace Bergman burning on the hillside. Again.

What was done was done.

CHAPTER TWENTY-FIVE

SATURDAY EVENING
FEBRUARY 25, 2018

IF the house at 151 Cortez Road could speak, what would it say about me?

I'm certain it would not call me friend.

Interloper.

Intruder.

Coward.

Wrongdoer.

Enemy, perhaps. Depending whose side it took.

It would not feel sorry for me. It would stand in judgment of my errors. My glaring omissions. My grievous miscalculations. My purposeful misdeeds.

I am the one to feel sorry. For this thing of grandeur, polluted now. Maddie will never pad barefoot down these halls. Kate's laugh will never echo here. Ian will never curse under his breath after spilling his coffee at the breakfast table. Forevermore, it will only be known as *that* house. Marked like the house of my childhood as a place where the unspeakable happened.

But it doesn't want my pity. It wears its infamy proudly as a new coat of paint.

In fact, standing here again at the kitchen door with Cleo beside me, I'm sure of all the things this house could say, it would tell me this: "Get out."

"Are you ready?" I ask Cleo, inserting the spare key into the lock without waiting for her answer. We'd found it in the backyard, stashed inside a hide-a-key rock, right where she'd said it would be.

The door relents—what choice does it have?—but the alarm wails, branding me for what I am. It's a blaring reminder I don't belong here.

"I can turn it off," Cleo whispers, in a voice steadier than I'd expected. "I watched Ian do it a few times. The passcode is Maddie's birthday."

Seconds later, the house is silent again, and I'm not sure if it's better or worse. Because in the quiet stillness, I feel it watching us. Watching me.

But we don't have long to get in and out before Cooper arrives, so I steel myself—it's just a house, after all—and start up the staircase, dreading this part the most. The slow, creeping climb and where it ends.

Eyes straight ahead.
Don't look in the bedroom.
Walk right past.

And yet it calls to me, like that half-opened door of long ago. It demands to be seen. So I oblige, jerking my head there and away again. As if I can look without seeing. See without looking. It feels dangerous and blinding. Like staring into the face of an eclipse.

Part of the carpet—*that* part—has been removed and carted away to an evidence room. And the blood smell is gone, swallowed by the bite of ammonia. Though I know it's unlikely, I imagine Sheila on her knees, scrubbing Ian's blood from the bathtub, smearing the remnants of my name across the mirror with a washcloth. Rubbing until she'd removed it entirely.

"Doctor Lawson?"

Cleo managed to get ahead of me somehow. And I hurry to catch up to her, wishing she hadn't spoken. Not so loudly. The house will take it personally. An affront. A show of disrespect. "Get out," it seems to say.

"Maddie's room," she tells me, quieter this time. I wonder if she can feel it too. How out of place we are here.

The hinges whimper with her gentle push on the door. Beyond it, moonlight streams in from the window, illuminating a pale-yellow bedspread. It's the color of the sun, of scrambled eggs and daisies, but knowing what's happened here turns it sour, jaundiced. Circus animals trapped in the wallpaper regard us with forced cheer, as if at any moment they'll go stark mad and trample us. The flat eyes of Maddie's dolls follow us, unblinking.

At the center of it all, a massive dollhouse, closed and shuttered, where Cleo crouches and slides her hand around the back.

"Can you believe the size of this thing? I stumbled over it trying to get downstairs after Kate came home."

From under one of the dark eaves, she produces the phone, Velcro affixed to one side. She powers it on, her pale skin shimmering like a ghost's in the artificial glow. Lingering in the doorway, I shudder.

"Let's go." My voice breaks the silence, a splintered crack in bone. And I'm already making bargains, promising the house I won't speak again. Not unless I have to.

"Don't you want to know what's on it?"

Desperately. But I shake my head.

"Get out," the house says again.

But my feet stay planted. And Cleo is transfixed by the screen. "Look," she says.

It may as well be an apple. Luscious, forbidden, and filled with the knowledge I'm powerless to resist. I step into the room and hold out my hand, preparing to take a bite. As I read the last outgoing message, I imagine the house roaring like an angry god.

Tuesday, February 14, 2018 9:33 P.M.

I tried to leave and he's scaring me. Threatening to hurt himself. Please come. No sirens. XO

"Who do you think—" A sound from downstairs, unmistakable and horrible, stops her mouth from moving.

The front door has been opened.

I look up and out the window, the one where Maddie had pressed her face so many times, her little nose bumping the glass, and see a police car unmoving on the street. Lights off and empty.

I meet Cleo's startled eyes in the window's reflection, my own terror reflected back to me, doubled. The house let someone in.

"Hide," I mouth, uncertain if I could speak out loud, even if I'd wanted to.

Cleo palms the phone and crawls under Maddie's bed, lying stiff as a mummy beneath it. And I scurry to her closet, wedging myself inside, sliding the door shut, and covering myself with clothes that smell faintly of bubble gum and baby powder.

I listen for the footsteps I know will come, but all I hear is the sound of my own breathing. Urgent as a freight train, impossible to stop. And I can't help but think of Maddie, how afraid she must've been hiding. The horrible things she must've dreamed. The awful reality that waited for her.

"Carmel Police, show yourself." Cooper's voice is a whip. It commands. Punishes. Twists your ear like a petulant child and makes you listen. "I saw you in the window. I know you're in here."

He thinks there's only one of us. And I'm grateful I'd left the car a few blocks away, insisting we make the rest of the trip on foot. I slide my cell phone from my pocket, the screen alight like a firefly in the dark. In its corner, two paralyzing words: *no signal*.

"Cleo, c'mon. Let's talk about this."

His voice moves like a whip too. Lashing from one end of the room to the other. I mash the buttons on my phone in a panic. Nothing happens.

"Did you talk to Ava? Whatever she told you, it's a lie. It's a part of her sick obsession with Ian. She's using you. She's already used you. Who do you think took those pictures? Now come out, and we'll find the phone together. Or did you already?"

His whip-voice trails off. And then it stops, leaving only unbearable silence. The kind of silence with a life of its own. A dark, pulsing life. Like the dry rot that had taken root in the home of my childhood the very moment *after* my father had pulled the trigger. The kind of silence that destroys. And that kind of silence can only end one way.

With a scream.

Cleo's.

I fling open the closet door and see her pinned to the ground, struggling with Cooper. Flailing, grabbing, clawing, both of them, for something at her side. The phone we came for has skittered from her hand, well out of reach. It cowers beneath the bed like it knows. And the house is laughing at us now.

Because I see it then, just as Cooper secures it in his gloved hand. My chef's knife, glinting in the moonglow.

He cackles bitterly at me, and it may be the worst sound I've ever heard. Worse than the desperate wail of my mother, my father's raging bellow. Or the times when he'd go quiet, walled off inside himself like the core of a nesting doll. Worse than Maddie's quivery singing. Worse, even, than Wallace's last-gasp moan.

"You're here," he says, like I've given him a gift.

His knee presses against Cleo's stomach, securing her like a mounted insect. She sucks in a desperate breath and gasps for another, pushing at him with her hands, as delicate and useless as a fly's wings. "Your timing is impeccable as always. The way you showed up on Valentine's Day. And tonight. It's like you want to be caught. You want to be punished."

316

"I called the police." I hold my phone out like a weapon. Not the useless hunk of aluminum it's proven to be. "The *real* police."

He doesn't even look at me. Or my phone. Only at the knife. "I know you don't have cell service. That's what signal jammers are for. I couldn't have Cleo dialing for help, could I? That would've ruined everything."

I start toward him, a tottering, off-balance step, but his eyes fix me to the spot. That and the knife—*my knife*—at Cleo's throat. Her body stiffens at the sight of it, balks under his weight, and he jams his knee in deeper.

"What is it about Doctor Ian Culpepper?" He's looking straight into her wild, bulging eyes. But he's talking to me. I can feel it. "You just couldn't get over him. And poor Cleo fucking him, the way you wanted to. *Still.* Even after he'd dumped you for Kate and you'd started duping my kid brother. Even after Ian's body started rotting six feet underground. So, what did you do? You followed Cleo here, and you stabbed her with the knife from your kitchen. And then, I had to shoot you."

It's matter-of-fact, his pronouncement, and a cold dread grips me. It's a poison pill on my tongue, ready to be swallowed: They will believe him.

I glance toward Maddie's door, closed now, and calculate the distance, the time it would take to get there. While the knife glints with intention, and Cooper's gun watches me from his holster.

"Why?" The impossible question I'd been taught to avoid. Ian had told me once that *why* is a wild goose chase—nobody really knows why they do what they do. They just do it.

And didn't I know that? As much as I'd railed against it, I felt driven by the past, a deep-churning current, a submarine river, steering my ship from port to port as surely as a sailor's wind.

Still, I need to keep him talking. Listening I can manage. Listening I'm good at. Listening will buy me time. Precious time.

"Why are you doing this to me?"

"To *you*? What about everything you've done? The things you've taken from me? My career, my family, my chance at happiness with Kate."

Beneath him, Cleo thrashes, a fish out of water now. In the last throes of effort, she reaches for his hand, for the knife just beyond her grasp. And my own chest seizes with the strain of her breathing. The way she heaves, then stills. Heaves, then stills.

"Cooper, I never meant to hurt you."

Another staccato burst of laughter chills like ice water down my back. "You think that makes it better? You didn't *mean to*. Is that how you sleep at night? Is that what you say to yourself about Wallace Bergman? Kate told me everything, you know. I saw the police reports. Did Ian drug him or was that your idea?"

Cleo stops moving, and I try to figure what to do, but my thoughts move like the undead. Dull and lead-footed. So I keep talking.

"I understand you're angry. You blame me for writing that evaluation. You think it hurt your chances of being promoted to detective. And you're right. I get that you're mad about Luke. You think I haven't been honest with him. And you're right about that too. But, until today, I had no clue about you and Kate. I couldn't have taken that away from—"

"You're the reason she's dead. Ian wasn't even supposed to be here that night. And Kate was going to leave with Maddie. I'd finally convinced her to make a clean break, to let the money go. And then, all of a sudden his plans changed, and he was collecting appearance fees from La Noche. With the mother of my child. And he's . . ."

His voice breaks like a wave, the words rushing from him. "He's stabbing . . . he's stabbing her. Because of your greed. By the time I got here, she was gone. And Ian was cutting on himself like a goddamned coward. He didn't have the guts to finish the job. Then you showed up trying to be some kind of fucking hero. When it was your fault all along."

My fault. His words feed the Hydra, and guilt cripples me. I can only watch as Cooper raises the knife to strike. And Cleo's face is Maddie is Wallace is my father.

With a primal yell, I lunge toward him, knock him off balance. And the knife goes awry, sinking part way into my outer thigh.

Merciful shock. I gape at it, feeling nothing but a white hot buzz in my brain.

And when I move, the knife does too. It's a part of me now. A dark-handled appendage.

I scramble across Maddie's bed to the other side, dragging my leg behind me. And down the hallway that seems to stretch on forever, unfurling like a lonely highway—*don't look back!*—with Cooper's grunting breaths just behind.

I fling the console table into his path, sending a picture of Ian and Kate and Maddie to the floor where it shatters. Broken pieces on the blood trail I'm leaving behind. Fresh stains on the carpet.

Cooper's hand claws at my shirt as I clumsily spin into the master bedroom, a drunken pirouette. I stumble over Kate, her body rigid and posed like a mannequin. The splaying wound on her neck draws me in—it's a sick red smile—and I can't move, can't look away. It's still bleeding. Still bleeding. After all this time.

Not real. Not real. Not real.

I do it then. Even though I shouldn't.

I look back.

Cooper's gun is raised and waiting for me. And a bullet whizzes by my shoulder, glances off the dresser, and lodges in the wall before I realize. He won't shoot me from behind. It doesn't fit his warped little story. The one he'll tell after I'm dead. Cleo too.

When I blink, Kate is gone again, only the half-there carpet where she'd lain. Where her heart had beat for the last time. Days ago.

It's one, two, three desperate steps to the bathroom. I barricade myself inside, slam the door behind me, and fumble with the lock in the dark, my fingers wet and trembling with each thwack of Cooper's boot. I stumble back as he fires another shot into the frame. And another. And another. And another.

I lean against the lip of the tub. Hands shaking. Breath sputtering. I catch my own pale face swimming in the dark mirror.

And stare down at my leg, my blood-soaked jeans, knowing what I have to do.

I touch the knife's handle and I feel it down to the bone. A radiating ache. I fold my fingers around it, suck in a gulp of air, and steel myself as the door lock splinters.

Cooper fires another shot. The lock blisters, then gives.

And with a guttural scream, I pull, stunned by the thing in my hand. No longer a part of me. I stare at the blade as the bathroom takes a sudden whirl around me. As a slice of moonlight cuts across the tile.

The door yawns open, surrendering slowly. And I steady myself behind it and wait. For Cooper's footsteps, his looming shadow.

I take a vicious swipe at his arm, surprised and satisfied with the sound it makes. The way it cuts through his flesh. The animal yelp it inspires. So different than firing a gun. And there's a sudden flash of Ian—teeth bared, mouth frothing with rage—punching the knife through Kate's soft skin as easily as holes in paper. Surely, he'd felt it too. A deranged gratification.

When the gun drops from Cooper's hand and slides across the tile, we both charge for it.

Cooper rams against me, my hip cracking against the side of the tub. I drop to my knees, still swinging wildly. Rip his shirt sleeve with another glancing strike.

With my free hand, I reach beneath the tub. Although it's too dark to see, the gun's cold flesh teases my fingers. But Cooper's gloved hands are there too, grabbing with the same desperation. And then, there's nothing between my fingers.

Nothing.

I stumble to my feet, backpedaling to the corner. Wave the knife at him, helplessly. I stare down the barrel, the way my father must have. Looking into its all-knowing eye.

"You don't have to do this," I say, cowering. My voice sounds impossibly far away. And ridiculous. As if I'm reading from a script. "Please . . ."

Cooper does what he's been trained to do since we were kids at the firing range staring down that paper bad guy. When we both still believed in the straight, hard line between good and bad. When we both knew which side of it we were on.

He aims for my chest and pulls the trigger.

****

"Wake up, Aves. Wake up," Ian whispers against my ear, his eyes impossibly blue. And I'm lost at sea just looking at him. He leans down to kiss me, and I wait to be taken in, swept away by the warmth of his mouth.

But his lips are cold. As cold as the mint chocolate chip ice cream I'd eaten every day the summer my father died and never again. As cold as death.

"Wake up."

Not Ian's lips after all. But white porcelain stained red. The bathtub cradles me like a lover, and I lie back against it.

It hurts to move. Hurts to breathe. Hurts to be. And the wound in my shoulder is pulsing blood. I press my hand against it.

My father's watch counts the seconds, but time doesn't exist here. Not in this house. Not for me.

I close my eyes and open them again. *Tick-tock*. And Cooper moves into my vision. Workman-like. The knife he'd taken from me secure in his belt and conveniently covered in my fingerprints.

As he starts to turn toward me, the room spins like a child's top. And it's my father there instead, sitting on the bed with his gun, sobs choking up from his throat, thick as vomit.

I hold tight to the tub's sill until it passes. Pinprick stars dot my vision. And I wonder if the house is on Cooper's side. If it wants to be rid of me just as badly.

Tick-tock.

Cooper's back again, dragging Cleo behind him. He arranges her at the foot of the bed and her head droops to her chest. Hair flung forward like a stage curtain.

Tick-tock.

And my father raises the gun to his head. He whispers to me—*I'm sorry*—and when the eyes we share meet, I say it back to him. But he's already disappeared. A wisp of smoke, a dream upon waking.

Instead, Cleo is there in his place. Her face slack as a rubber mask. And it's possible she's dead already. It's possible I am too.

Cooper kneels before her, reverent. Readies the knife, still slick with my blood.

I turn away, to the mirror, imagining the way it must have happened. How he'd taken Ian's lifeless hand in his own and written my name. Not a love letter. Not a warning. Not the last wish of a dying man.

But the perfect setup for the perfect suspect. Someone like me. Jilted. Obsessed. Sick with my own secrets. And so, so bitter.

I'm sorry. It's the drumbeat in my head as I run my fingers against the tub's sticky bottom. Inked in my own blood, I write.

THE MONTEREY COUNTY COURIER

"ARREST OF LOCAL POLICE OFFICER, SON OF HOMICIDE DETECTIVE, STUNS CARMEL COMMUNITY"

by Jackson Lamont

The Carmel Police Department (CPD) confirmed the shocking arrest of one of their own, Cooper Donovan, on multiple charges related to the slaying of Love Doctor Ian Culpepper, as well as the attempted murders of Ava Lawson and Cleo Campbell. Police now believe Donovan was involved in an extramarital affair with Kate Culpepper and had fathered her unborn child. Text messages found at the scene indicated Culpepper had contacted Donovan on Valentine's Day, expressing fear for her safety. Though CPD did not speculate on a motive in this case, the District Attorney issued a statement suggesting Donovan had likely discovered Kate's body upon his arrival at the scene and reacted in a fit of murderous rage. Later, it is alleged that Donovan staged the scene and planted evidence to implicate Lawson, Culpepper's ex-wife, and made harassing telephone calls to Lawson and Campbell using a state-of-the-art "call-bluffing" app, which enables users to disguise both their voice and the number from which the call originates.

Officers apprehended Donovan at the Culpepper home late Saturday evening, where Donovan's own brother, Luke, also an officer with CPD, convinced the suspect to surrender himself. Donovan remains in custody at the Monterey County Jail and has been denied bond. Both Lawson and Campbell were found to be suffering life-threatening injuries and were transported to the Monterey Peninsula Emergency Room for treatment. Campbell is listed in fair condition, while Lawson, who sustained multiple injuries, remains in critical condition.

CHAPTER TWENTY-SIX

I believe in karma. Because I'm nursing one hell of a stab wound. And a through-and-through shot to the shoulder the doctor called a lucky break. *Lucky.* Maybe those slots had pegged me right after all since Cooper's bullet missed the humerus and the brachial artery. Only soft tissue damage here. But mostly, I believe in karma because I'm not dead. Unless this is heaven, and the angel at the gate looks exactly like Detective Doreen Lennox.

"Good morning, sunshine." She half-smiles at me from the chair in the corner, a lipstick-stained coffee cup at her feet and a blanket draped on her lap like she's been waiting a while. The *Monterey County Courier* is unfurled on the table, the headline bittersweet.

"Is it . . . morning?" The last twenty-four hours are spotty at best, a spliced film reel of needles and nurses and prodding hands. Of white coats and scrubs and a stern mouth that called me lucky. *How long have I been sleeping?*

"It will be in about twelve hours. It's Tuesday night. Do you remember what happened?"

I take a quick survey of myself.

Body bruised beneath the thin hospital gown.

Massive bandage on leg—I wiggle my toes—that still moves.

Fire ants crawling up my shoulder, stinging. But better. Better than before. When the pain had raced up my arm and across my chest like fire up a dynamite fuse.

Tube snaking from my vein.

And a flash of the devil in Cooper's face as he'd raised the knife to Cleo. I shiver at the thought of it. Of what he'd intended. Of how close he'd come to pulling it off.

"Most of it." It hurts to talk, each word a razor scrape. "Is Cleo . . . okay?"

Doreen nods. "Collapsed lung but otherwise intact. Her father's here. And she's already given us a full statement about what happened at the house."

The house. The thought of it looms like a slumbering giant.

I shut my eyes and try to conjure the last moment before my mind went dark. My fingers, wet with my own blood, tracing Cooper's name on the mirror with a futile last-gasp. And I'd seen something there, someone, another face that slips back into the shadows just as I try to reach for it. As elusive as a sailfish.

"There is one thing." The question even the doctor couldn't answer when I'd mumbled it in a half-medicated haze. "Why am I alive?"

Doreen's laughter brightens her tired eyes. "The *why* you'll have to take up with the boss upstairs, but I can tell you the how. And the who."

"The who?"

"Yep. Ricky Sherman. Apparently, he'd followed you to the casino and back to Ian's house, thinking you'd stashed some money there.

Or knew where to find some. He watched Cooper go in and heard the gunshots."

A memory returns, then. As brief and stunning as a camera flash. The knife falling to the carpet from Cooper's raised hands. The way it lay there in surrender.

"So Ricky saved me?"

"Not exactly. That coward waited the whole thing out in the car. But we'd put a trace on Ricky's phone, and Luke pinged it. He got worried when your meet-up turned into a press junket and he couldn't find you anywhere. Ricky's signal showed up at Ian's house, and he figured he'd better check it out."

"Luke," I say, looking up at the empty window in the center of the door, aching with hope. Like I can summon him just by wishing it so. And Doreen gives me a sad smile I'm not sure how to take.

"He should be back any minute now. It was mission-critical to get my hands on some real coffee. A gal can't survive on this hospital sludge."

"And Jack? Is he here too?"

Another smile, sadder than the last. "I'll be taking over the investigation from here on out. As you can imagine, he's got bigger fish to fry."

I think of my father, then. The way he'd put a bullet in the center of my life without meaning to. Collateral damage. And I know how Jack must feel.

My shoulder throbs as I try to sit upright. To set free the words clamoring to get out. "I'm ready to talk."

I already know what I have to do, what I have to say. The three-word promise I'd made to myself in the house on Cortez Road where Ian and Kate had died. Where Cleo and I nearly did. All of it. Wallace and the pictures and the blackmail—and the Xanax dropped like a bomb in a bottle. I have to tell it all.

"You really should have a lawyer present, Ava. There are still some pretty serious allegations against you. I can call Ivy Mercer if you'd like."

"It's okay. I don't need an attorney. But I want Luke to be here."

And later, after it's all been spilled, the onion unwrapped right down to its ugly core, I know what I'll say then: "There's another murder I need to tell you about. DeAndre Mack's."

Because karma may be as slow moving as a freight train, but boy does she pack a wallop.

LA TIMES

"SEVEN LAPD OFFICERS CHARGED WITH CORRUPTION"

by W.J. Pierce

Seven decorated veterans of the Los Angeles Police Department (LAPD), including two Narcotics Division detectives, were relieved of their duties on Friday after a stunning investigation revealed a sordid trail of greed, corruption, and murder that began over twenty years ago. According to a departmental spokesman, the investigation began with a confidential source implicating deceased detective Jerry Lawson in a 1994 conspiracy to murder LA native DeAndre Mack—a small-time cocaine dealer who apparently had begun working with Lawson in the 80s, offering him a portion of the proceeds from narcotics sales in exchange for protection from prosecution and confidential information regarding planned drug busts. As Mack advanced through the ranks of his criminal enterprise, so too did Lawson, who was eventually promoted to Narcotics Division Detective in 1982.

In 1994, Lawson was hailed as a hero when he shot and killed an armed Mack inside an Artist District warehouse. The incident made national news as a record drug bust after five tons of cocaine were seized from the location, and Lawson later earned the prestigious Medal of Valor awarded to those officers who distinguish themselves through bravery or heroism above and beyond the call of duty. According to the confidential source, Lawson later admitted to his family he had planned Mack's death and staged the crime scene, planting a handgun on Mack, who had double-crossed Lawson. An investigation by Internal Affairs implicated numerous other officers as assisting in the cover-up of Mack's murder.

Lawson eventually retired from service, citing personal reasons, and died by suicide in 1996. He is survived by his wife, Frances, and his daughter, Ava, who is currently serving jail time in Monterey County relating to her actions leading up to and following the 2018 slayings of Love Doctors Kate and Ian

Culpepper. Though Lawson was cleared of the murder of her ex-husband, Culpepper, she pled guilty to charges of extortion, child endangerment, and food tampering. The Los Angeles District Attorney elected not to bring charges for any role Lawson may have had in the death of Wallace Bergman, the media mogul; however, she was forced to surrender her license to practice psychology in the state of California.

Citing his desire to spare his family further anguish, Former Carmel Police Department Officer, Cooper Donovan, pled guilty to Culpepper's murder, as well as the attempted murders of Lawson and Cleo Campbell, and was sentenced to twenty-five years to life in prison. Inspired by the grisly tale, BXA President of Programming Marty Emerson recently approved production on a television series, *Love Doomed*, which is scheduled to debut in the summer of 2019.

Since the officers' dismissal, Mack's family has announced their intention to file a wrongful death suit against the LAPD seeking monetary damages. Though Mack's mother, Carlotta, died of a heart attack in 2002, a spokesperson for the Mack family released the following statement: "DeAndre was a beloved son, brother, uncle, and father of four. He was no angel, but none of us are. Unfortunately, DeAndre paid the ultimate price for the mistakes he made, dying at the hands of a man who had been sworn to protect and serve. For years, DeAndre's murderer was regarded as a hero, while DeAndre was reduced to a faceless statistic. As a family and a community, we cannot turn a blind eye to injustice no matter when or where we find it. While justice should be swift, it never comes too late."

EPILOGUE

VALENTINE'S DAY
ONE YEAR LATER

AVA sits on a bar stool at The Mongoose Tavern, legs crossed. Just below the hem of her skirt, the waxy tail of a scar she's chosen not to hide. Because it's the mark of a survivor. Or as Marbles had told her: "It gives you street cred, girl."

She orders a glass of champagne, because why the hell not? After eleven months and three days in a concrete box, she's earned it. And the first dry, decadent sip is better than she remembers. A lot like her first sleep back in her old bed, ten nights ago. The first drive down Highway One, windows open and radio blaring. And the first bittersweet walk back down Wheelchair Row toward her mother. It tastes exactly like freedom.

She pops a handful of peanuts into her mouth, savoring the salty crunch—everything feels new again—and leans forward to the counter, reading the note she keeps tucked in her pocket now. The note she'd crafted with the help of Dr. Morris, her therapist in Monterey County Jail.

How to Kill a Hydra in Nine Steps:

Own your guilt.

Admit you did wrong.

Accept your punishment.

Learn to live with the consequences, dire though they may be.

Understand how you got here.

Help others.

Be okay with not being okay. Nobody's perfect.

Forgive yourself.

Ask for a second chance.

Ava had placed a check next to items one through eight. A check, not a strikethrough, because this sort of work—the lonely drudgery of change—was never really done. Only nine stands alone, unmarked. A single indestructible head whipping, gnashing its teeth inside her stomach. On her wrist, her father's watch ticks along, as predictable as always.

It's nearly time, and she can barely stand the buildup. The wait. The wondering if he'll show. *This is better than sex . . . with Ian. But with him? Not even a close second.* Though she's prepared to accept she lost the right to have it again long ago. And possibly forever.

"Ava Lawson?"

Her face breaks into a wide grin even before she spins toward the voice she's heard only in her head for the last eleven months. The voice she'd imagined with every unanswered letter she'd written.

"Luke, right?" she asks, playfully. Still nervous. "So how long has it been?"

Unsmiling, he takes the stool next to hers, and she's instantly drunk on the proximity of him. His arm on the counter, fingers drumming. His muscled thigh a mere fingertip from her own. The clean scent of his shampoo, at once familiar and new. "A while."

"Well, I grew up," she says. "Which is crazy because I'm actually eight years older than you. And I have a doctorate degree I can't even use anymore. And I made a lot of mistakes. Bad ones. And I'm sorry. So sorry."

"Was there a question there, Ava?"

"Do I only get one?"

Luke nods, suddenly distracted, tapping on his cell phone beneath the bar. "I think one is generous. You are a psychologist so you should be good at questions. Or at getting answers anyway."

"You're absolutely right."

She last saw him in another life, ancient and dust-covered. That's how it feels. And in this new one, she's a novice. A total rookie.

He's different too. He must be. The cracks are there even though she can't see them. His brother destined to rot in prison. His mother wracked with guilt, the way only a mother can be, by the endless refrain of *what did I do wrong?* And his father, a broken man—Ava had seen it herself in the newspaper photos, the hollows under Jack's eyes, the pitiful slump of his shoulders. The way his starched uniform hung loose, his shoulders thin and bony as wire hangers.

Luke is no longer unscathed. And no longer a hotshot cop. She'd heard through the Mercer and Mercer grapevine that he'd quit the force and enrolled in law school at UC Santa Cruz. Even as a defense attorney, he wouldn't be the biggest disappointment in the Donovan family. Not by a long shot.

And when she looks at him, a little awed by it all, she worries she'll seem awkward or sad. That there's too much darkness between them, a long stretch of uncharted highway neither can cross. But she does it anyway, holding his gaze.

"Well, I could ask who you're texting, but that would be too obvious. Or if you're single, but that sounds like a line. Or if I can buy you a drink, but you're clearly not drinking. Or why you're here all alone on Valentine's Day. But I think I'll go with simple and straightforward."

Finally—*finally!*—Luke smiles, and it already feels like a victory. "I like simple and straightforward."

She allows herself a small sigh of relief. "Will you give me a second chance?"

He starts to reach for her—and she can already feel the warmth of him—but stops midway, leaving her cold. "Wait. Am I supposed to tell you to ask me again tomorrow?"

"Now why would I want you to do that?"

Luke looks down, twitters a little. "Because today is . . ."

"My new favorite day," she finishes for him. And his laughter does it, swift as a blade.

The ninth head of the Hydra, not immortal after all, falls at her feet.

Now that you've finished *The First Cut*, please consider leaving a review. Reviews and star-ratings may not seem important, but to an author they are essential. They help readers like you discover my books! And they give an author a little "street cred" for those browsing for their next read.

So what's the best way to feed an author? Leave a review, of course. You can find all the links to review *The First Cut* on my website: ellerykane.com.

ACKNOWLEDGMENTS

Though an author writes alone, so many hands go into making a book successful.

The AnnCastro Studio team provided all editing services for *The First Cut*, including Ann Castro's developmental editing, line editing, and manuscript evaluation and Emily Dings's proofing. Their work has contributed immensely to my growth as a writer, and I am tremendously grateful.

Giovanni Auriemma and Mallory Rock never fail to impress me with their artistic talents. Giovanni produces one-of-a-kind, unforgettable covers, and Mallory makes the artwork on the inside just as stunning.

I also owe a debt of gratitude to my friends, family, and work colleagues—my cheerleaders—who are always there to sing my praises whether I deserve it or not.

And to you, dear readers, for devouring every sinful bite of the Doctors of Darkness series!

Finally, we all have a space inside us that we keep hidden from the world, a space we protect at all costs. So many people have allowed me a glimpse inside theirs—dark deeds, memories best unrecalled, pain that cracks from the inside out—without expectation of anything in return. I couldn't have written a single true word without them.

ALSO BY ELLERY A. KANE

The First Cut is the third in the Doctors of Darkness series of psychological thrillers by forensic psychologist and author Ellery A. Kane. Look for the next book, *Shadows Among Us*, coming soon. If you want to be the first to know when new books are released, sign up for Ellery's newsletter at ellerykane.com.

If you enjoyed *The First Cut*, look for these other great reads from Ellery A. Kane.

Doctors of Darkness Series
Daddy Darkest
The Hanging Tree
The First Cut
Shadows Among Us (coming soon!)

Legacy Series
Legacy
Prophecy
Revelation
AWOL

ABOUT THE AUTHOR

Forensic psychologist by day, novelist by night, Ellery A. Kane has been writing—professionally and creatively—for as long as she can remember. Just like many of her main characters, Ellery loves to ask why, which is the reason she became a psychologist in the first place. Real life really is stranger than fiction, and Ellery's writing is often inspired by her day job. Evaluating violent criminals and treating trauma victims, she has gained a unique perspective on the past and its indelible influence on the individual. And she's heard her fair share of real-life thrillers. An avid short story writer as a teenager, Ellery recently began writing for enjoyment again, and she hasn't stopped since.

Ellery's debut novel, *Legacy*, has received several awards, including winning the gold medal in the Independent Publisher Book Awards (young adult, e-book category) and the gold medal in the Wishing Shelf Independent Book Awards (teenage category). In 2016, Ellery was selected as one of ten semifinalists in the MasterClass James Patterson Co-Author Competition.